When Bones Whisper

REBECCA L. GARCIA

When Bones Whisper

ISBN: 978-1-912405-88-6

Editing: K. Morton Editing Services

Playlist

Never Forgot by Kendra Dantes
Make the Angels Cry by Chris Grey
Haunted by Isabel LaRosa
You Belong to Me by Cat Pierce
My Name by Reed Wonder, Aurora Olivas
Eyes Don't Lie by Isabel LaRosa
If u think I'm pretty by Artemas
Love me by Ex Habit
Mind Games by Sickick
Shameless by Camila Cabello
RUNRUNRUN by Dutch Melrose
Taste by Ari Abdul
Control by Halsey
Butterflies by Isabel LaRosa
Worship by Ari Abdul
Wires by The Neighborhood
3am by Boy Epic
I'm yours by Isabel LaRosa
WRONG by Chris Grey
On your knees by Ex Habit
Devil in Disguise by Marino
Stay by Ari Abdul
Sleepless by Dutch Melrose
Who Do You Want by Ex Habit
ALWAYS BEEN YOU by Chris Grey
Obsessed by zandros, Limi
Scream My Name by Thomas LaRosa

Author's Note

This is a dark, gothic romance. The content in this book is intended for adults.

While the book is set in Victorian England, the language has been written in American English and is not a historical fiction, therefore may not always be historically accurate.

The witchcraft practiced in this book is fictional and is not an accurate representation.

This novel contains subject matter that may be triggering for some readers, including:

Alcohol use
Anti-religious rhetoric
Attempted sexual assault (on-page)
Blood and gore
Blood play
Bleeding out
Chasing
Demonic possession
Decapitation
Drinking of blood
Emotional abuse
Explicit sexual content
Graphic violence
Grieving sibling and daughter
Graphic depictions of blood and death
Hallucinations
Human sacrifice
Murder
Misogyny
Multiple character deaths

Mentions of child and animal sacrifice (off-page, mentioned, not depicted—no children or animals are harmed in the book)

Murder of an adult child and spouse by a parent (mentioned, flashbacks)

Ritualistic murder

Suicidal ideation

Suicide (mentioned) and attempted suicide

Physical parental abuse (mentioned & flashbacks)

Physical assault from a family member (on-page)

Physical harm inflicted upon the main character

Unprotected sex

Prologue

1863, London England

Charlotte Lovett made certain her sister was dead before they put her in the ground. Ensuring Alice wouldn't be subjected to the horror of being buried alive was the least she could do after letting her die.

The other mourners faded from her periphery, a group of moths instead capturing her attention when they flew between the weathered headstones. She watched them flutter erratically as one, with a broken wing, broke away from the group and tumbled down into the six-foot-deep hole.

Its wings trembled when it tried to fly out so as not to be dragged into the earth with the corpse below but quickly gave up and landed on the muddy wall next to the casket, unaware that in its descent, it had narrowly escaped the beak of a wren circling overhead, which instead consumed its faster friends.

After a couple of minutes of the priest droning on, the moth crawled out, and the bird was gone. Much like the insect, Charlotte was also alone, broken, and surrounded by predators. Except, unlike the wren, those in good society hid their predacious natures behind finely embroidered frocks and insults disguised as compliments.

She watched them all from behind her black crepe veil as they avoided eye contact with what they perceived as the less accomplished sister. A beauty, yes, with her wild black curls and wide, green eyes, but her skin was kissed by the sun from the long days she spent barefoot in the garden, and she could never tame her hair into the fancy updos suitors preferred.

Charlotte closed her eyes, breathing in the heavy fragrance of damp earth and wilting lilies. She had grown to hate the flower that had once been her favorite. Her mother's burial, just a few days prior, lingered with the same musty odor. It clung to everything—her clothes, her hair, and no matter how much she bathed, she couldn't get rid of the smell.

Voices filtered through the inaudible whispers and sniffles surrounding her, but the loudest, not in sound but in accusation, came from the Baron Ellenwood and his wife, Victoria, who were standing beside her.

"I heard the father murdered three maids too, after he killed his wife and daughter," Victoria stated in a low voice, just loud enough for Charlotte to overhear their conversation.

Her husband replied with less of a hushed tone, a single lily pinned to his black suit. "Terribly tragic. Although I am not surprised after what their mother did to the Eringhorn family."

Victoria hushed him, but the tilt to her lips gave away how much she enjoyed her husband's salacious remarks. "It is true. She should never have allowed her daughter to fraternize with a chimney sweep." She hid her lips behind her gloved fingers and murmured, "Lord Eringhorn's son had no choice but to break the engagement after that scandal."

Baron Ellenwood shook his head, his fist tightening around the handle of his cane. "Quite right. It was not as if Alice could have done better than the second son of a baron."

"Yes, and shortly after the news spread, the Eringhorn's housekeeper fell ill and the family lost their wealth," Victoria stated.

He tsked under his breath. "Perhaps that is why the father killed them all. Their mother, at the very least, had the evil eye."

Charlotte pursed her lips, fighting the hot, angry tears that brimmed in her eyes. She instead tried to focus on the casket in the large hole in the ground, her stomach dipping at the thought of her sister's body inside, unmoving and cold, her throat covered in bruises that matched her own.

"I wonder if the youngest daughter will inherit Lovett Manor?" Victoria asked, and Charlotte clenched her jaw.

Did they have no sense of propriety? Discussing such rumors at a funeral, especially when they were false.

"Surely it will go to Mr. Lovett's brother," Baron Ellenwood responded, side-eyeing Charlotte's uncle. "If he has any sense, he will marry the girl off. That is if anyone will have her. Twenty-five years old and still unmarried."

With a loud cough, the priest cleared his throat, and the whispers faded into a dull murmur.

Her family didn't practice witchcraft, and Alice did not fraternize with anyone. The Eringhorn's lost their wealth because Baron Eringhorn gambled, and their housekeeper did not fall ill. She was pregnant, and according to scandal sheets, the reason she was sent away was because the father was Alice's fiancé, Baron Eringhorn's son.

The truth didn't matter, not when the lie better suited their delicate sensibilities. They wanted to demonize her family, and it would not have done for anyone to discover it was Alice who broke off the engagement.

They were an aristocratic family, and everyone knew the aristocracy could do no wrong.

God, she hated them all.

With a deep breath, she lifted her glassy stare to the somber, cloud-shrouded sky and grasped at the gold locket hanging around her throat, containing a lock of Alice's hair. She refused to think about the Baron and Baroness Ellenwood any longer. They were notorious gossips, and she wouldn't give them the satisfaction of showing that their words had any effect on her.

The priest's voice floated back into her awareness, closing the end of the service, but Charlotte wasn't ready to say goodbye. Alice had promised never to leave her. They only had each other, and now she was gone.

Pressing her lips tight, she looked at the casket, praying that this was all a dream and her sister—her frustrating, wonderful, charismatic sister—would be back home, in her room when she awoke, berating her for stealing the tonics from her dresser.

No matter how hard she pinched her wrist, nothing changed. The world continued moving despite Charlotte's being torn apart.

A single tear escaped, trickling down her freckled cheek. She heaved back a sob, holding her breath so she would not explode into fits of tears. Letting in even an ounce of grief meant drowning in it.

Curling her fingers into her palm, she dug her nails deeper into her skin until the pain temporarily distracted her from the agony blooming inside.

As the world shrank and dirt toppled onto Alice's grave, she turned away, the knot in her stomach tightening. She scanned the vast graveyard through hazy eyes, not yet ready to leave while at the same time, desperate to run out of there.

A wisp of gray and white caught her eye from between two crumbling graves. The fog took form as a semi-translucent figure, partially obscured by the morning mist. Squinting, Charlotte lifted the veil, her gasp frozen in her throat when she saw the ghost of her sister, with skin stretched taut over her lips, muffling her screams. Alice's white eyes wept blood as she fought against unseen bonds anchoring her to the cold earth.

Help me!

Her voice echoed in Charlotte's mind, a sound she never thought she would hear again.

"Alice," Charlotte whispered in a strangled breath, taking a hurried step forward, almost tripping on the dull, black fabric of her dress. Tears streamed down her face, her breath catching in her throat as she ran as Alice faded and she tripped over a wayward rock. Her uncle's hand tightened around her wrist, halting her fall to the damp earth. The pain radiating in her ankle didn't stop her steadying herself and trying to run forward again, but Alice was already gone.

"Are you mad?" her uncle Theodore asked.

She turned to face him, his pale blue eyes mirroring her father's, the anger in them almost as potent. "I saw Alice," Charlotte stammered, pointing at the graves. "She was right there."

He glanced at the space between the weathered headstones and turned his glare back to her, adjusting his wide-rimmed, black hat. "They already believe your mother was a witch. Do you intend to confirm their suspicions and have everyone think you inherited her *habits?*" he hissed, his voice a low, dangerous whisper, only forcing a smile when people turned to see what the ruckus was about.

With a sharp tug on her arm, Theodore pulled her back to face him when she didn't immediately answer. "Are you not listening girl? Do you not understand the precarious situation we are in?"

She did. It was all she had heard from him since he had arrived shortly after the massacre. The last thing she wanted was to evoke his anger further or give his revolting son a reason to tease her more.

"Yes, Uncle. I apologize. It must be the grief."

He nodded. "You have been tired."

"I have," she parroted, telling him what he wanted to hear. That was always the best way.

"They are gone," he told her, as if she needed a reminder. "You must accept that and move on. No more talk of seeing the dead," he whispered, looking around briefly as people paid their respects. "Hysteria can make you see things. That is all it is. Put it from your mind."

It wasn't hysteria, but he was right. She stared at the graves, her stomach dipping. Nothing but a layer of undisturbed fog coated the area. Thoughts of Alice had plagued her since that fateful night. Perhaps her nightmares were bleeding into reality.

It wouldn't be the first time.

"I will," she promised, letting out a tense sigh. Once satisfied, he smiled and greeted a wealthy merchant friend of her late father's, leaving her standing alone, wiping her tears with her veil. She had to remain composed.

Her family had a long history of accusations of witchcraft, but the massacre breathed new life into them. If she wasn't careful, she would be ostracized for a craft she didn't even practice. It was forbidden by her family, but that did not stop her from reading her great-grandmother's grimoires that were filled with sacrificial magic, every night since she was six. Neither her sister nor mother ever used dark magic, nor researched it. They said it was evil, but she had wondered ever since they died if the magic they feared above all could have saved them in the end?

She thanked those who attended the burial alongside her uncle and cousin, William, not even looking the guests in the face as she took their hands. One by one, they grasped her fingers, offering words of condolence. When a woman squeezed her fingers between her ringed, wrinkly palms, a powerful scent of rosewater brushed the air between them, before she left.

Finally, they were alone.

Her eyes glided over several tombs belonging to her ancestors, the Lysanmore Witches, as she followed her uncle from the graveyard. Upon reaching the gates, she turned back, swearing she could feel the eyes of the dead upon her, boring into her soul like daggers of ice.

Chapter One

One Month Later

She had barely fallen asleep when she was awakened by three loud bangs echoing through the quiet of her bedroom.

Loud, ragged breaths sounded from the corridor outside her bedroom door. She glanced around the shadowy corners of her room, trying to lift a finger or toe, but she was frozen under the heavy weight anchoring her to the bed. A deep, throbbing pain pulsed through her hip from where she'd discovered a bite mark after her sister's burial. She breathed through the acute pain, catching a whiff of rose mixed with sulfur, and wondered why the bite was suddenly acting up, or maybe she was more aware of her body now she couldn't move.

Another pounding hammered against her door, this time more frantic. The edges of her vision blurred when she looked at the door. Her lips remained closed despite the impulse to call out for reassurance. Surely, the staff would have announced themselves by now, and neither her uncle nor cousin would have bothered to knock at all.

Tears trickled down her freckled cheeks and into her long, dark curls.

Help me. Please.

The prayer was nothing but a comfort blanket, something done out of habit, for she was certain God could not reach her in the depths of Lovett Manor where death clung to the corridors like cobwebs.

She held her breath when the banging stopped, followed by a long creak of a floorboard. After several long seconds of silence, she wondered if whoever was out there had gone. With something akin to a gurgle, she tried to open her mouth, but her scream was stifled by an invisible grip over her mouth. The seconds stretched for an eternity as she remained trapped beneath the blanket, desperately trying to will feeling back into her body.

A slow, deliberate rattle of her doorknob shook the wooden frame, and her eyes clamped shut. The sound grew louder, and she tried to recall whether she had locked the door before going to bed. Normally, she would have checked, but she had been so exhausted earlier that night.

With a final abrupt clatter, the rattling stopped, replaced by an unnerving silence.

Charlotte cracked her eyes open just enough to see the shadow of the door. It remained closed, but her heart thundered as her mind raced with images of what might await her on the other side. She moved her gaze across the room. A sliver of moonlight peppered through the closed drapes, and the shadows of the furniture took on a life of their own as her eyes adjusted to the room.

A flicker of movement caught her eye in the corner. She held her breath, but let it out once she saw the brown, glossy body of a cockroach scuttling across the ground before vanishing through a crack in the floorboards.

She closed her eyes, concentrating on the subtle movements in her left hand, willing her finger to lift. Sweat beaded on her forehead as she visualized the movement, and a hot flush crept through her face. A flicker of sensation surged through her wrist, sparking into her fingers. The paralysis slowly receded as she twisted her hand, gasping when she could finally move. She sat upright, inhaling deeply and looked at the door.

Before she could fully catch her breath, a sudden weight landed at the end of her bed. A loud scream reverberated from her throat, and she kicked her way up the mattress until her back was pressed against the headboard.

Her cat's yellow eyes glistened in the dark. He blinked slowly, tilting his head and meowed.

A sigh of relief whooshed past her lips. "Duke!"

He nudged his damp nose against her fingers, gently nuzzling closer until he nestled himself onto her lap. "Where did you come from?" she whispered, running her fingers over Duke's silky, black coat. She glanced at the door again, but everything remained quiet, as if nothing out of the ordinary had happened.

She tugged him closer to her chest, holding him tighter as she buried her face in his soft fur. His purrs vibrated against her lips, and she smiled. "Did you sense something was wrong?"

Duke hardly ever came into the house, but she always left the window open for him anyway. Her uncle and cousin didn't want him in the house, even though it was *her* house, and even the servants would shoo him away no matter how much Charlotte protested.

"You can sleep here," she said, placing him on the blankets beside her. "Just leave when the sun comes up.

Duke twisted his body, playfully arching his back against the mattress and curling his paws toward the ceiling of her four-poster bed. She dragged her fingers over his belly. Most people believed black cats were dark omens and hated humans, a sentiment she could not understand because Duke loved people. It was just too bad they didn't like him back.

He fell asleep quickly, his light snores calming the anxiety still buzzing through her veins. He wouldn't have fallen asleep if there was still something nefarious lurking nearby, but she couldn't ignore the pit of dread building in her stomach. She tried to think of anything else, but the more she tried to suppress the thoughts of ghosts and death, the larger they grew. Images of her sister and mother's bones, crawling with insects, flashed through her head.

You are going to die. Just like them.

The thought intruded on her senses, and she jolted. "I am perfectly fine. Everything is fine. I am not going to die," she said, repeating the same words she'd told herself for the last month.

She pulled Duke closer to her side, turning her mind instead to the problem at hand. The dead could be frightening, but she was far more afraid of the living, and if she didn't do something soon, she would be forced to marry the most heinous of them all.

Practicing sacrificial magic was something she had never contemplated putting into practice until now, despite soaking in every spell in her great-grandmother's grimoire. Abstaining from magic had not done her family any good, and it was the only thing that might save her from a most wretched fate.

In just a few days, she would be forced to stand before a priest and commit herself to her cousin. If she didn't go ahead with the wedding, her uncle would make good on his threats to have her committed. Despite his claims, she was not insane, but that didn't matter. She was a woman in a man's world, and no one was going to believe that she wasn't a witch, especially since she'd accidentally left one of the grimoires out and he'd stumbled across it.

That was a horrific Tuesday. She could still smell the burned parchment in her nose.

Even though her father's estate now belonged to her, Theodore was the executor of her father's will, and in the eyes of society, the house may as well have belonged to him. Her uncle wanted it for himself, and the best way to do that was to marry her to his son. She assumed he was angry at his brother for willing the estate to his daughter instead of him as the last living male heir, even though he had no need for more wealth. Theodore had an entire fleet of merchant ships, a house in central London, and a large estate in the country where his third wife lived in seclusion.

His son, William, was just like him—boisterous, impertinent, and greedy. It had been her cousin's gloating yesterday that propelled Charlotte down the path toward witchcraft. He bragged how he would soon fill her with enough babies that they would be the envy of society.

The thought of visiting his bed sent bile rising in her throat.

An intrusive, sweetly sick voice spoke in her mind again.

Kill them. They deserve it.

She shook her head, and Duke stirred a little. Murder wasn't a word she wanted to entertain. Taking someone's life was an abhorrent thing to do, no matter how much she didn't want to continue living under her uncle's oppressive thumb. It wasn't her place to play judge and executioner, but there were other ways to get rid of them.

The mirror.

The voice echoed again. She'd first thought of it last night. The cursed mirror was hidden in her attic, behind a layer of cobwebs and trunks filled with ritual items. She'd promised never to go up there, but of course, that made her want to go even more.

It was the voice in her head, her inner voice, that reminded her of the cursed mirror. The voice appeared after the burial as if her consciousness had fractured from the grief. She had to lock her uncle and cousin away. For the mirror, from what she had read in the grimoires, was an ancient prison, cursed to house the very worst entities. While performing the spell to trap them in there forever was abhorrent, she was desperate.

Her gaze flicked over to the window as she mulled over what her life would be like if she didn't go ahead with the spell. She would likely be with child soon after the wedding. She wasn't even certain that her body could withstand that. The mysterious sickness that had plagued her for the past six years wasn't showing any signs of relenting. Her joints ached no matter how much rest she got, and while she had days or even weeks where she felt better, it was always followed by periods of sheer exhaustion.

Her uncle and cousin already looked down on her for being bedridden a week ago and announced they wouldn't put up with it anymore once she became William's wife. In fact, she was given a list of things that would be expected of her once she was married to him.

She grimaced, her stomach churning. The urge to use magic had swirled in her mind for years, but she repressed it. She'd gone back and forth so many times since the funeral, incapable of deciding on whether to use it, but as the night ticked into morning, she realized she had little choice.

It was almost two days until the wedding, and she had exhausted all other options. If she was going to have any chance at happiness, they needed to be gone.

She wasn't certain what time she had fallen back to sleep, but by the time she awoke to heavy footsteps echoing down the long corridor, Duke was gone, and sunlight arrowed through the window. Her heart hammered against her ribs as the pounding grew louder.

Damned and Hell. She must have missed tea with the Grantham family.

Charlotte scrambled to her feet as the door flung open with a loud bang, making her jump. She stepped back, pressing her back against one of the wood columns of her bed.

"You missed the tea," her cousin bellowed, his long face heated red. "Are you *trying* to embarrass me?"

Her lips parted, but the words were trapped halfway down her throat.

"Answer me, *wife*."

The word shot through her like an icy splash of water, but she knew better than to remark that they were not yet married. Instead, she lifted her eyes to meet his narrowing stare. "I apologize. I did not sleep well."

"That is no excuse. Do you know what pains I went through to secure an invitation after everything your family has done? Your maids said they could not wake you *again*!"

Tension carved through her jaw, and her fingers gripped the wood post of the bed. It was his family too and if he was referring to the murders, then it was only one man's fault.

"Speak!" he spat and she jumped.

Inhaling deeply, she uncurled her fingers and looked at him. In her gentlest voice, carefully crafted and perfected over the years, she whispered demurely, "I am so sorry, William. I know you have done a lot for us."

Lies. All of it lies.

His eyes traveled to her white chemise, and she instinctively covered her chest. He turned his stare to her bed, spotting the cat fur against her white blankets. "What did I tell you about letting that fleabag in the house?"

She looked at the floorboards, hoping her silence would quell his rage. If she said what she really thought of him, she would be in an asylum by the end of the day, or worse.

After a long sigh, his shoulders relaxed. He wasn't much taller than Charlotte's five-foot five stature, but when he closed the distance between them, she felt tiny, like a caged animal.

"Hmm." He brought his thumb to her bottom lip and dragged it down, pressing his fingerprint against the fleshy inside of her mouth before allowing it to flick back. "You are fortunate you know," he said and brushed his fingers over her cheek. "No one else wanted you."

Defiance laced her eyes, but she didn't dare let her mask of civility slip, no matter how much she wanted to shove him away. She didn't care if no one in society wanted to marry her. Not that she was averse to the idea of taking a husband, but she had always held out hoping to find love or friendship. It was ironic that now she would get neither.

He brought his fingers to her long curls, drawing closer, as if he might kiss her. His whiskey-laced hot breath lingered around her face, and she scrunched her nose.

"There are ways you may make it up to me, to show me how grateful you are," he said.

"Please," she whispered in a voice that swallowed itself. "We are not yet married."

"There is no need to be shy." He pressed his body against hers, and she could feel everything, including the small bulge in his pants. "You cannot deny the feelings between us," he said. "It is only two days until our wedding. No one will be any the wiser if you become with child now."

She wanted to crawl out of her skin. It wasn't because her virtue was at stake. God knew that had been taken by another long ago, when she was young and believed herself in love with someone who did not deserve it, but she couldn't reconcile herself to being intimate with William of all people.

Not that he knew that. Her purity was her only card to play.

"Please," she begged. "I want to wait until our wedding night."

"You need not play coy, my sweet, innocent girl," he said wheezily, with eyes that promised to take that from her. "Let me show you the ways a woman can be pleasured."

Her face blanched. "I said no." It was a word that felt heavy on her tongue, usually unspoken. As soon as she said it, she knew she'd made a mistake.

His eyes narrowed. "What did you say?"

"I...Please, don't do this." She looked at him with soft eyes, pressing her lips tight. Normally, her cousin liked it when she begged, and it was enough to avoid too much conflict with him. Except, this time, it wasn't working.

She glanced up and stared directly into his bright green eyes, which was her first mistake. He mistook her look for something more and pushed his lips to hers. His all-too wet tongue darted through her lips before she could stop him. He tasted of tobacco and liquor. She pushed against his chest, but he only groaned in response. Her muffled protests were lost in his lust as he pushed his long skinny fingers down the front of her chemise, grasping at her chest as if he was kneading dough.

"Stop!" she screamed into his mouth, but her actions only seemed to spur him to go harder. With a grunt, she lifted her knee and slammed it as hard as she could between his legs.

He stumbled back, hands clasped over his groin, eyes bulging.

All it took was one look, a glare that turned cold and empty as a void, and she knew she had to run.

It wasn't the first time she had seen murder in a man's eyes.

The world spun around her as he chased her, shouting her name with spittle that sprayed across the back of her shoulder. She grabbed the doorknob, twisting it in time to creak the door open an inch, but was wrenched back before she could escape.

Air whooshed from her lungs, her back thudding on the hard floor, her eyes dazed, unfocused on the ceiling above.

His sharp features twisted with something dangerous as he straddled her.

"Please stop!" she screamed, clamping her eyes shut in time to feel his fist connect with her cheek.

A high-pitched sound rang in her ears, and blood coated her tongue and teeth. The floorboards pounded the back of her head as he punched her a second time.

Tears slid into her hair, and she covered her face with her hands when he slammed his fist against her trembling fingers, prying them apart.

"Don't!" she screamed again, twisting her torso to the side, but his legs locked her in place. "William, please," she spluttered when he dove for her throat.

She blocked his hands with her forearms, forming a cross over her neck.

"You will not deny me what is mine!" he yelled, pressing her arms against her own throat, his strength easily overpowering hers. She turned her face in time to feel a spray of spit hit her cheek.

Repressed sobs quaked her chest as she tried desperately to bury them, her entire body shaking. "Y-yes," she stuttered. "I know. I am yours."

"You are lucky to have me!" he yelled, pushing her down harder.

"I know," she lied, her stomach knotting as she forced her expression to soften despite the pain throbbing through her cheek and eye. "It is only that I wish to remain pure before our wedding. I'm sorry, please. What will society think if they see me with bruises?" she added, and he sneered.

With a twitch of his sharp nose, he pushed down on her one last time before standing.

She turned onto her side, cradling her throat as she tried so hard not to cry. It would only anger him, but every breath was a struggle. She couldn't stop shivering, and the more she tried to control it, the worse it would get.

"Clean yourself up," he said, temporarily pausing over her with a solemn expression, as if he might have regretted hitting her.

She nodded, but once she heard the door slam shut, and his footsteps had faded to a safe distance, she let out a wail into her palms to muffle the sound. Tears flooded her eyes, snot poured from her nose, each sob wrenching her chest.

Slowly, she climbed onto her knees, barely able to catch her breath. She wretched hard, her throat dry and aching as vomit crept into her mouth. Fluids leaked over her closed lips, and she wiped them away with the back of her sleeve.

She ghosted her fingers over her throbbing cheek and swollen lip, a cry quaking her entire torso. William knew what had happened to her sister, how she had been strangled to death just two rooms down from where she lay.

With a grunt, she stood slowly, her legs wavering beneath her weight, forcing her to collapse against a wall. She stared at the floorboards now painted with a spray of her blood.

Everything around it faded from her vision. Her mind emptied, and all other sounds muted until she shook her head and blinked twice.

Her chest quaked when she spotted her black cat standing on the ledge of the window. He darted across the furniture, his paws pattering over the mahogany dresser, before jumping into her arms.

"You were right to leave early," she cried against his neck, her tears dropping onto his fur. Her eyes closed when Duke's paw landed on her cheek, his second meow rising an octave. "It is okay. I am okay."

He nuzzled into her neck, as if sensing the lie. Holding him close to her chest calmed her enough that her full-body shudders turned into infrequent shivers. She glanced at the door while running her thumb over Duke's head, tucking back his ear. "I'm going to do it tonight, Duke," she said. "I'm going to lock them both away and they can never hurt us again. We'll get our home back and it will just be us."

He purred against her chest. Murder was not something she ever wanted to consider, but she had no choice. Once they were imprisoned in that mirror, she could never let them out. A body could not survive long without a soul and if she ever tried to undo it and let them out, she'd have to release all the evil inside and God only knew what was in there.

After all, her mother's family had kept it hidden for centuries for a reason.

Chapter Two

Charlotte did not want to feel sorry for herself. There were far worse situations to be in. At least she was alive, unlike her mother and sister. Yet, as she walked into the gardens while the sun slowly set, she couldn't stop the tears that had been building for hours from spilling onto her cheeks.

Muffling her sobs with her palm, she squeezed her eyes shut and told herself not to cry. Not because of her uncle's demands, as he was at the gentleman's club for the evening, but because if she didn't suppress the anger and hurt, she feared it would swallow her whole.

"The hedgehog," she said aloud when she removed her hand. The thought helped. Focusing on anything outside of herself made her forget how much pain she was in.

She hurried to the corner of the garden and kneeled by a collection of horse-chestnut trees. The tips of her brown boots sunk into the earth, and her long, black skirt billowed out around her. While she continued to wear mourning dresses made of dull, black fabrics, Charlotte refused to wear the veil any longer. It only got in the way and she was certain Alice would forgive her for the slip in custom. Normally, she would be mindful that if she was seen outside of her home not dressed in the deep mourning attire, it would harm her family's standing. But she was the only one left, so she no longer cared, especially after the way her family had been treated.

With a slow exhale, Charlotte looked out over the gardens. They were beautiful in the light of the early evening. The pond reflected the darkening blue sky in ripples, and the flowers on the neatly trimmed beds shimmered, each in full bloom.

"Someone is out of hibernation early," Charlotte exclaimed upon spotting the hedgehog walking out from the familiar stack of logs under a collection of bushes and tree branches. It was silly, really, but she needed this. A small victory. Her little friend had made it through his hibernation.

The hedgehog's tiny nose twitched, sniffing the air. She kneeled on the damp, soft grass and slowly extended her hands, palms up. "Do you remember me? It was a long winter."

The creature's beady eyes met hers, and he took a brave step forward. She gently gathered him in her hands, the tiny quills prickling her skin slightly as her fingers caressed his round form.

She lifted the hedgehog to her nose, facing him directly, and smiled. "I checked on you every day," she announced. "You only moved a few times, but don't worry, I kept you safe."

Beyond the beds of flowers, neatly trimmed bushes, and stretches of luscious grass, were tall, iron fences that made it difficult for predators to dig under and long strings of garlic bulbs hung from the spires, to deter any that might try.

The gardener had set traps too, but Charlotte had quickly dismantled them, not wanting to hurt any animal if it could be helped. With a small smile, she placed the hedgehog on the ground. He dipped his nose into the tall grass, inhaling deeply before his slow, unsteady gait carried him away.

A wave of honeysuckle, lavender, and petrichor washed over her as she inhaled deeply, the chilly wind a welcome reprieve from the flush on her face. If she could get away with it, she would spend all day surrounded by the fragrant blooms.

With all the darkness of the past month, Charlotte had learned to enjoy the small moments, ones that had been seemingly unremarkable before the massacre.

"Duke," she exclaimed, spotting him at the edge of the garden, his paw batting a flower petal. It had only been an hour since he'd left her side, after she'd gone downstairs to join her cousin and uncle, but she missed him all the same.

In a flash, he darted across the steppingstones, his nose bumping her shins. She leaned over, carefully scooping him into her arms. As she straightened her spine, a sharp crack sounded in her back, making her wince.

"That didn't sound good," she murmured, a frown furrowing her brow as she pulled Duke close, his soft fur brushing her chin.

A deep, resonant purr vibrated through her face as she nuzzled into him. A soft wince escaped her lips when his mouth brushed against the purple bruise marring her left cheek.

None of the staff said anything when she came downstairs earlier. In fact, most of them refused to meet her eyes at all. She understood why they didn't speak up. They would be dismissed or beaten themselves if they tried, and it would do no one any good. But even before her uncle had come, none of her father's friends, nor any of the visitors who frequented their home and witnessed the bruises from her father in the months leading to the massacre, ever said a word. Charlotte learned long ago that the only person she could rely on was herself.

"Stay out of sight," she warned, placing Duke back onto the grass. "If William or Theodore returns from the club before I return and see you, I am afraid of what they will do." She took a step back and looked down at her black feline. "Do you understand me? You mustn't go near the house tonight. Not until I have completed the spell."

He tilted his head, yellow eyes shining with a slow blink.

"It's just a few more hours," she promised and kneeled, placing two fingers under his chin to pet him.

She brushed the dirt from her black pelisse and walked out of the gardens and down the small, winding dirt path to the graveyard.

The temperature dropped a few centigrade by the time Charlotte reached the iron gates. She nestled her chin into her mother's fur shawl, searching for pockets of warmth. More than once she had argued with her family about buying anything trimmed with the fur of innocent animals, but now that her mother was dead, she couldn't bring herself to throw the garment away. The faint scent of her mother's perfume—elderflower and jasmine—still lingered in the fibers. She breathed it in, closing her eyes in a soft blink before looking into the lamp-lit graveyard filled with crumbling headstones and gray crypts. Darkness had swept over London, dark clouds blotting out the last remnants of the sunset before the horizon swallowed it altogether.

She peeked into the distance, spotting a small child giggling and running through the rows of graves. Her translucent body faded through the obelisk and to the other side, and her moss-stained dress floated in white wisps.

Quickly, Charlotte averted her gaze, ignoring whatever was mimicking a child, because if she had learned one thing from the grimoires, it was that only evil remained behind in this world. Hell was not a destination. It was all around them, separated from the living by a thin veil.

She supposed it was quite a perfect punishment for the damned, to forever walk the Earth, unable to move on. Damned souls remained behind either as ghosts or twisted into something lacking any humanity, like demons. Everyone believed those entities wanted souls, but she knew better. According to the grimoires she'd read, demons needed bodies. Without them, they were aimless observers, mostly unable to interact with the world, and they hated the living for it. She wondered if her father was now one of them. In the end, he turned evil, but there was a time when he was not. When he was her *everything.*

Even after all he did, his laugh still haunted the halls of Lovett Manor. In moments of despair, Charlotte swore she could still feel the phantom tightness of his hugs, which offered little comfort when she knew how quickly his gentle caress could turn monstrous.

With a sigh, she walked down the long path, through rows of graves when a loud clang sounded from the entrance. She whipped her head around in time to spot the sexton walking inside, straining his neck to check the pathways for any lingering visitors. With a sharp inhale, she hid behind a crypt and waited for him to lock the gates and leave.

Once he was gone, she stood and looked at the ancient stones in front of her. The inscriptions engraved were barely visible beneath the carpet of moss and lichen.

One grave stood out to her.

An intrusive, honeyed voice ripped into her consciousness once again.

This one.

Charlotte halted before a grave, the name barely visible. Her inner voice had not led her astray yet.

Leaning down, she wiped away the moss but could still only just make out the letter D and the last name, Lysanmore.

A thrum of power echoed from it, her intuition pulling her closer.

"Forgive me," she whispered.

Moving the lid off the lawn crypt of her ancestor's grave took more effort than she anticipated. Her muscles screamed in protest as she heaved until she finally pried it off. She knew she would pay for her extraneous activities tomorrow, but for now, she pushed through the pain.

She peered inside at the bones, coughing when a musky odor pinched her nose. A rush of unintelligible whispers rushed into her ears when she touched the bones, as if they were sentient. Before she could change her mind, she pulled several of them into her arms.

A shiver traveled down her spine, and before it could finish running through her, an icy embrace stole her next breath. She gasped as a pulse of magic rippled from her body, beating audibly, as if her powers had a pulse. Wide-eyed, she turned, watching the veil between the living and dead fall around her in ribbons of gray light.

Wild-eyed, she peered into the swirling fog for any sign of movement.

One by one, the ancestors of the Lysanmore bloodline stepped out of the darkness, translucent and faded, as if they were barely holding onto the essence of this world.

A chorus of distorted voices floated between realms, sounding inside Charlotte's mind.

Leave now, the voice commanded.

She held the bones tighter and ran as fast as she could down the fog-soaked paths, ignoring the icy tendrils grazing her cheeks. When she reached the gates, she pushed the bones through the bars before climbing over them.

The skirt of her dress snagged on a spike, and she tumbled down the other side of the gate, crashing onto the ground with a loud thud. Her breath whooshed from her lungs, her ribs aching under the new bruises.

Their voices sounded collectively in her head again, the chatter growing clearer until it became one sound, the voice of one of her oldest ancestors.

Do not run.

Her ancestor's harsh tone bit through her mind, but unlike her inner voice, it ached her skull.

The faded figure of a woman, with no real distinct features, swept closer, her bare, pale feet floating a few inches off the ground. She stopped at the bars, as if there was an invisible barrier preventing her from going any further.

We have been waiting for you to return.

Rising to her feet, Charlotte faced her ancestor, trying to appear braver than the tremor in her hands betrayed. "You're a ghost."

One word echoed through her thoughts.

Yes.

"Are my family here?" she asked when her mind finally processed the idea that she was talking with a spirit.

They are.

She swallowed hard, but it did nothing to budge the lump in her throat.

"I want to talk to them," she said, picturing Alice and her mother, the thought of seeing them igniting the pain that had been long burrowed in her chest. "Please."

They cannot talk to you.

Her brows pinched together. "Why not?"

They have not earned the right.

"What does that mean?" she asked when the memory of seeing Alice's ghosts, the semi-translucent skin of her lips knitted together. "Did you do something to them?"

No, but my energy is stronger than theirs. Only I can talk to you.

She wasn't entirely convinced, but a niggling feeling told her not to question the ghost further. "What do you want? Why have you been waiting for me?"

Her ancestor's voice, a deep, raspy tone, carved through her skull in a splitting pain.

You are in danger. The Avery witches are coming for you.

"Who?"

They are a powerful family and an enemy of ours. They want you dead before the vampires discover our bloodline has not died out. Before the vampires discover the Avery family have been lying to them.

"Vampires?" Charlotte stated, eyes widening. She'd read snippets about them in the grimoires, how they were cursed by witches, but they seemed more myth than anything real. "Why does anyone want me dead?"

Only a witch from our bloodline can break the curse of vampirism and you are the last in ours.

Shock coursed through her, along with a hundred questions. "I know my great-grandmother was born in secret, and she took another name. You Lysanmore witches refused to acknowledge us.

For good reason! Your identity remained hidden for generations. Your mother, grandmother—they were never on any official family tree. However, the Avery family discovered our secret some months ago.

"This is insanity. I have lost my mind," Charlotte said, looking around at the barely visible ghosts standing amongst the graves. "It's the grief."

This is all real and soon, if you do not follow our instructions, you will die and your fate will be sealed with ours. We created the curse of vampirism and only one born of our blood can break it, but the vampires do not know this. They were fed a lie by the Avery witches and told they needed to eradicate our bloodline to become mortal again, so they would kill all of us who could help them.

The night was darker, the last wisps of mist dissolving into the cold air. Suddenly, she was aware how vulnerable and alone she was. "Why could we not tell the vampires the truth?"

They will not believe you. Those creatures do not use reason. They kill without mercy or listening to reason, which is why we are all dead. I made a mistake in cursing the first of them.

Charlotte's heartbeat thumped in her ears. Her jaw dropped as she tried to comprehend what the spirit was telling her. There was so many questions that she struggled to grasp the most important, but eventually landed on, "Why would the Avery witches condemn their own to die? What do they care about the vampires?"

They use our power, siphoning our energy from this graveyard that we are trapped in.

"Then... my family are being siphoned too," Charlotte said, wild-eyed, slowly backing away as her ancestor became more tangible.

Yes. Centuries ago, as punishment, the elder of the family, Gertrude Avery, placed a curse on our bloodline so we would be bound to this graveyard, she said into Charlotte's mind, whose eyes swept the expanse of the graveyard. Her ancestor continued, the rush of her voice aiding in the building headache forming in her skull. *She used the first vampire, Nathaniel Sallow, as an anchor for her spell on the graveyard so it could become a well of power, to imprison us. As he is immortal, the magic holding us here never faded. That is why we cannot move on. We are forced to remain here, at the mercy of the other witches who siphon our energy, to feel the pain of every victim killed by our creation.*

Her lips parted as she struggled to find the words in response to the revelation. Most witches practiced what they called folk magic, the power they were born with that was taken from the Earth and could not be used to harm other, but some enhanced that with sacrifices and the dead so they could break that rule. When a soul passed over, its energy was so strong it could be harnessed and used for the darkest of spells. Normally, it was fleeting, but if her entire bloodline was in fact trapped in one graveyard, that made it the perfect source of energy that could be consistently channeled.

Charlotte watched the spirit float over the ground, eyes darkening.

"How can I free my sister and mother from this purgatory of a fate?" she asked, recalling Alice's spirit the morning of her burial. It was not some hallucination. It was real.

You must sacrifice yourself in a blood ritual, her ancestor instructed.

She slowly walked backward until her heel hit the cold metal of a streetlamp. The realization washed through her, chilling her from the inside out. "You want me to die?"

Yes, your days are numbered. You have already been marked for death but commit yourself to this ritual before another ends your life, and you can free your family and yourself from this horrendous destiny.

"There has to be another way."

There is not. This is the only way. You can decide what your death will mean.

A strange, hollow feeling dipped her stomach as the first patters of rain landed on her shoulders. A familiar voice broke through the long pause, breaking her heart.

Don't listen to her. Run, Lottie. Run now!

Charlotte's lips parted, fresh tears blurring her eyes. Only one person ever called her that.

"Alice."

Run and don't come back. Leave your home, Lottie. Get as far away from here as you can.

The frantic voice in her mind twisted her ancestor's expression into something far more insidious.

"Sister," she choked out, but her ancestor's command boomed into her head, silencing all else.

Stop!

You are making a mistake by taking those bones, the spirit warned, the words fading as she ran, her calves burning with each step, each breath like a sharp, cold dagger in her chest.

Rain pelted her body, saturating her blouse and long skirt. Dark locks of hair slathered against her freckled cheeks as she raced down the foggy path until she reached the looming silhouette of the tall manor. She halted by the gate, panting deep breaths.

Thick, heavy tears welled in her eyes as she looked up at the inky night sky, blinking away raindrops. Her chest heaved with each sob as she wailed into the silent, unforgiving night. Her voice. She'd heard Alice and she hadn't imagined it.

Her sister was in pain.

With another controlled scream ripping through her dry, sore throat, she looked at the house. Alice had warned her to run, told her not to come back. She couldn't trust the spirit of her ancestor. There had to be another way to help free her family. She just had to find it. Because she could not die, not when she'd not even started living yet? For her entire life, she had waited for things to happen to her, for a future to bloom out of fantasies in her mind, but the massacre woke her to the truth: she could die tomorrow. Death had once been little but a rumor to her young ears; it was now a heavy force, constantly reminding her that tomorrow was not promised.

There was no waiting anymore. She had to survive, because she wasn't ready to go yet, but, ever since the night of the murders, death's icy touch had followed her, and she had a horrible feeling it was closer than she knew.

A prickling unease replaced the heavy raindrops that had abruptly stopped. Charlotte peered through the dark bars, her fingers clamping around the bones in her hands. A burning scent of sugar and decaying vegetation filled her nostrils. Her eyes flicked to the arched windows of the manor, the lights flickering erratically inside.

Something was wrong.

Heavy layers of mist shrouded the shadowy depths of the garden, and the once vibrant green lawns were now a dry, sunbaked brown. With a gasp, she spotted her carefully tended flowers, now drooping and brown, their petals withered and lifeless.

Everything was dead and something was standing behind her, casting a shadow over hers.

Chapter Three

Ragged breaths sounded behind her. Charlotte sucked in a deep breath, determined not to glance over her shoulder, instead focusing on the shadow smothering her own. A harsh scent of sulfur burned into her nose, making her grimace.

Slowly, she turned her head over her shoulder. As she did, the silhouette disappeared.

Wonderful. That was all she needed. More ghosts haunting her.

Her heart stumbled, and she wondered how long the organ would continue ticking after the string of frights she'd had recently. At least the surge of adrenaline numbed the agony of the searing pain in her legs and torso.

She sighed, glanced back at the gate. With one step forward, she jumped, almost dropping the bones when she spotted a cockroach in the path of her boots. Its antennas probed the air, the moonlight glinting off its mahogany exoskeleton. "Careful," she whispered and stepped out of its way. The insect scuttled under the iron bars, its wings flickering as it ran out of sight.

With a deep breath, Charlotte pushed open the gate with her hip and slipped inside.

Time seemed to stretch out for an eternity with each echoed step along the gray path to the front door. The closer she got to the manor, the further away it appeared. A cold sweat broke out across her forehead, prickling into her cheeks and neck in an icy caress.

She assumed that after coming face to face with a spirit, she'd feel a little braver around the paranormal. It wasn't the first time she'd been around a ghost. In fact, she'd gotten used to the dead haunting the halls of Lovett Manor since she was a child, but their presence was only made known with knocks on walls, footsteps at midnight and items falling from shelves. Never had she seen a full apparition until tonight.

She scanned her surroundings, walking stiffly ahead. Dead roses hung over the sides of the pots on either side of the large oak door. Even the lion's head knocker was now a warped, twisted metal gargoyle.

The door creaked open, and Charlotte walked inside, closing the door behind her. A wave of heat rushed over her. After a few seconds, she peered outside through the long window, surprised to discover the garden was as before.

A cold tingle skittered down her spine.

"Demons," she said with a drawn-out breath. Ghosts could not cause illusions like that. With a shiver, she turned her back to the door, refusing to give it another thought. If it was a demonic entity that had stalked her from the graveyard, she wasn't about to give it any attention to invite it in further.

A loud dong resonated from the grandfather clock, disrupting her wandering thoughts. Her uncle and cousin would be home soon.

She headed toward the attic, her legs as heavy as lead as she ran up the staircase, coming to a stop at the top. Hunched over, she leaned against a cool marble column, her breaths coming in shallow gasps. The dull ache that had been with her all evening transformed into a sharp, stabbing pain that spread through her joints. She crouched, a loud groan rumbling from her throat as her stiff knees cracked, sending a jolt of pain through her legs.

Muscles moved of their own accord in the tops of her hands, rippling under her skin. She tried to steady herself and stand upright, but her muscles protested her every movement. All she wanted to do was take her boots off her aching feet and climb into bed so she could sleep for an entire day, but her mind, unlike her body, was far from weary.

An anxious flurry of thoughts consumed her. She had to find out more about the curse on her family, the vampires, and Avery witches.

A determined sigh pushed from her lips as she struggled to rise, the stiffness in her muscles stretching making her eyes water.

"One problem at a time," she told herself. Breaking down was not going to help anything and putting off the spell even for one more day would bring her closer to a marriage with a man who saw her as nothing more than chattel, one who would beat her again when given the chance. When they were gone, she could focus on the next imminent danger.

Her lips trembled, a silent plea escaping when she reached the end of the long hallway, her legs unsteady, threatening to buckle beneath her. Leaning over, she bundled the bones in a makeshift carrier from her skirt, using the material to cocoon them. With her spare hand, she grabbed a candelabra and struck a match. The wicks came alive with flames.

Tilting her head back, she stared up at the attic door, a dark rectangle against the pale ceiling, and tiptoed to reach the hanging string. With a groan of the rusty hinges, the heavy door swung downward, revealing a sturdy wooden ladder that slid out halfway with a clatter.

The dusty air hit the back of her throat and a rattling cough escaped her lips before she heaved the ladder the rest of the way downwards, its legs finally settling with a thud against the carpet.

She glared up into the dark space above her, a cold draft snaking down to chill her to the bone. Her teeth chattered slightly behind her lips, and a dull ache pulsed in her neck as she strained to look up. She grabbed the candelabra she'd set down beside her and lifted the glow of the candles to meet the blackness of the attic.

Dark images of shadowy creatures and evil spirits that could be lurking up there spun in her mind. Her father had always said Charlotte had such a vivid imagination, which she was finding to be more of a curse than a blessing.

Her limbs seized, a shudder wracking her body from head to toe. A thick lump in her throat constricted her breathing as she stepped onto the first step of the ladder, the aged wood creaking under her weight. The overwhelming need to run seized her, causing her to quickly close her eyes.

"There is nothing up there that can hurt me," she whispered to herself in the smallest of voices, as if something might hear her.

A second, louder creak echoed as she ascended with the candelabra, her other hand holding her skirt bundled with the bones. Peeking inside, she winced, picturing a ghostly figure creeping towards her on all fours.

She shook her head. The attic was eerie enough without her imagination adding to it.

I'm fine. It's just an attic. It's just another room.

Fighting back the urge to close her eyes, she set down the candle and climbed inside, coming face to face with the musty wooden floor. The bones scattered over the boards, and she quickly gathered them. She couldn't afford to give up now, despite wanting to descend the ladder and go back to her room.

One spell and it'll be over, she said internally, urging herself forward. *I can do this.*

In the dim light of the dusty attic, Charlotte spotted the ornately carved ancient mirror leaning against the wall, its surface clouded by a net of cobwebs. In front of it were heavy chests. Approaching slowly, she paused a few feet from the massive frame, its intricate carvings of vines and roses catching the candlelight. It had been twenty years since she'd first found it, when she'd climbed up there during a game of hide and seek with Alice.

With a gulp, she bent down and placed the bones before the mirror. Kneeling on the dusty floorboards, she opened an old chest, the scent of rosemary reaching her nose as she rummaged through her great-grandmother's grimoires until she found a set of unused black candles and a ritual dagger at the bottom. Rustling through the pages, she found the spell she'd read years before, to unlock the mirror using blood magic. After all, it was her bloodline that cursed the mirror centuries ago, so she was the last who could open it. The bones shook against the boards, as if they could sense the evil trapped behind the murky glass. Every spell required an anchor, and she wasn't going to use herself, considering the darkness attached to the object. The bones of her ancestor, along with a few drops of her blood, would be perfect.

Her chest heaved as she stared back at herself, half expecting to see something pop up in the darkness behind her. With trembling fingers, Charlotte leaned forward, stretching out her spine, and brushed her ringed fingers against the surface.

She hated mirrors. It was no wonder that the prison made for whatever ancient evil lurked inside was created using one. They were the most powerful objects a witch could use. Not only did they reveal demonic entities, as they could not hide from their own reflection, but they were portals too, for spirits. It was why priests used them during exorcisms. Demons could not bear to see themselves and witness their once beautiful souls now twisted and ugly. It was ironic, Charlotte thought, how they embodied darkness and yet did not wish to perceive the evil they had become.

Which was why Charlotte was so afraid when she peered deeper and noticed the black of her pupils expanding until it stole every fleck of green from her irises. Her reflection vanished and the mirror contorted into a flurry of grotesque faces, their hands pressing up against the inside of the glass. She recoiled with a gasp, her heart pounding in her ears.

Using the candelabra, Charlotte passed the flame onto the wicks of four candles that were inside the chest and placed them around the neatly stacked ivory bones.

The ritual knife was heavier than she expected. Her fingers curled around the obsidian handle with a sapphire set in the middle, her lips parting when the flames on the four candles grew taller, as if the candles were greeting the dagger.

She hissed a breath between her teeth when she dragged the blade diagonally across the pad of her index finger. Bright red blood coated the sharp edge. Clamping her eyes shut, she let out a groan when she dug deeper, ensuring there was enough blood. Tipping the dagger down, she watched as drops of blood pooled at the end before falling onto the bones below. Something was working, because they sizzled the moment the blood came in contact with the femur.

"Ouch!" She glanced at her finger, the stabbing pain intensifying as the blood turned darker. It sprawled out like veins, covering the bones in a spiderweb of red. Panting, she clasped her wrist with her other hand, groaning as the last remnants of energy left her body.

The candles were brighter than ever, the flames so tall they fought off the cold draft circling the attic. The glass of the mirror rippled, and a rush of unintelligible whispers sounded from the bones.

With a thick swallow, Charlotte pulled out the hairs from the crease of her corset that she'd gathered that morning from her cousin's comb, along with a nail clipping she'd found from her uncle that she'd lodged into a small slit inside of her boot. Grimacing and wrinkling her nose, she placed them on the bones, glad to be rid of the essence of her uncle and cousin after carrying them around with her all day.

Careful with her intonation, and grateful for her Latin lessons as a child, she spoke the incantation from the grimoire aloud. "Haec ossa exhauri ut hoc incantamentum ancorare possis. Aperi portam ad hoc speculum sanguine sanguinis mei, et pone malum viris quibus haec pertinent adhaerens et eos in speculo include. Include eos in perpetuum et nihil aliud praeterire sinas."

She watched as the nails, hair, and blood vanished, absorbed into the cold, hard bones. A whoosh of wind blasted through the attic, sending her sprawling back from the mirror. The surface turned dark, reflecting the last bit of light before it stilled. Behind the glass, she glimpsed her uncle's face, warped with fear as he stared at her, with only the whites of his eyes. Her cousin was screaming, at least she assumed, by the way his mouth hung open, but only silence surrounded her.

It was done. They were gone, but something else had changed. A stench of sulfur pinched the dusty air, and the temperature dove into freezing.

With a shiver, she backed away from the mirror when a loud meow sounded from the hallway below. The light from the candelabra slowly dwindled, the last flame quickly flickering into smoke, plunging the attic into darkness.

She ran to the edge of the opening, peering down at the welcome brightness of the lamp-lit corridor, spotting Duke crouched low to the ground, ears pinned back as he hissed at an empty space to her left.

With a long, shaky exhale, she looked at the black cat. "Duke! Stay there. I just need to get the bones."

He hissed again, and her stomach dipped as a cold, long breath hit the side of her face. Her heart raced, and she grabbed the sides of the opening just in time to stop herself from falling out. A stronger whiff of sulfur assaulted her nostrils, an icy cold weight lingering around her neck like a noose.

A heavy weight slammed into her back, knocking the air from her lungs. With a strangled scream, the floor rushed up to meet her, and she landed on the carpet.

Coughing and spluttering, she climbed onto all fours and looked up, but there was nothing but darkness. Duke was still hissing, his ears tucked back as far as they could go, and the air held a new icy breath.

Something up there pushed her, and she had no interest in climbing back up to find out what.

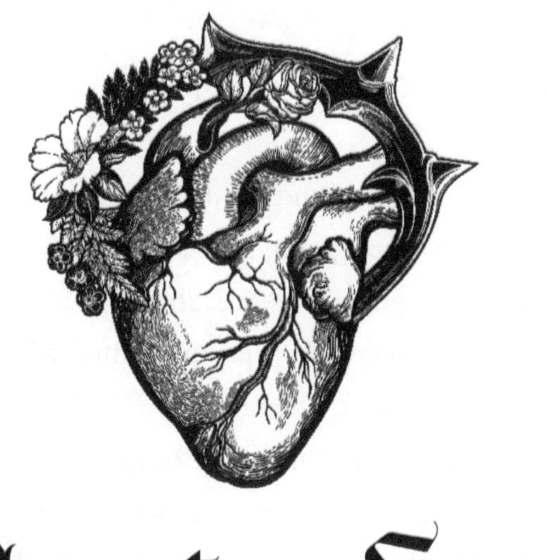

Chapter Four

Barely one hour after Charlotte had fallen asleep, the booming thunder jolted her awake. Purple flashes of lightning illuminated the sky outside her tall, arched window, and heavy rain lashed against the glass, rattling the frame.

While she normally loved storms, this one felt more like an omen. It had been eighteen hours since she had unlocked the mirror, and her uncle and cousin had been found dead. Their corpses were discovered in their chairs at the gentleman's club, so nobody suspected she was involved. Despite getting away with murder and getting her wish of having the house to herself again, she couldn't leave her room. Although she'd had her uncle and cousin's things placed in their bedrooms, their tobacco smoke and cologne still clung to the drapes and carpets. What was once her favorite place to be had become a graveyard of her family's possessions, reminding her of not only what she'd lost, but what she had done too.

Charlotte swung her legs over the side of the bed, her bare feet meeting the creaking, cold floorboards. With a heavy sigh, she curled her fingers into the fabric of her white nightdress and walked over to the window.

The wild storm battled behind the dark clouds blotting the night sky. Howling winds ripped through the gardens, swaying the chestnut trees stationed along the wrought-iron fence. She glanced at the patch of grass where daffodils used to flower each spring, smiling when she recalled last picking a bouquet of them for her mother. With a hard swallow, she turned and looked away from that patch of grass. If she allowed even a drop of pain in, she was afraid it would drown her entirely.

Lightning veined through the sky, lighting up the gardens, which appeared endless with their symmetrical flowerbeds, decorative statues, and pond. She stared at the shadowy corner hidden under long tree branches, unable to look away, as if the darkness was glaring back at her.

A shiver slid down her spine, along with a sudden urge to retreat.

Another flash cracked across the sky, revealing the ghost of her cousin, standing in the fog by the pond, his face contorted into a silent scream. Her heart stammered, and she gripped the windowsill. As quickly as he had appeared, he was gone.

With a gasp, she pulled the heavy drapes closed and backed away slowly. Picking at her cuticles, she glared at the drapes before grabbing a candlestick from her bedside table.

Regret ached deep in her chest, and she rocked back onto her knees. Even though they deserved it, she wasn't sure she could survive their haunting her. With a deep breath, she reminded herself of the awful things they had done. Her uncle was known for beating his last wife, and her cousin was no better, sending maids away after compromising their virtue.

Four loud knocks echoed through the empty halls, making her jump. She flicked her eyes to the door, every muscle in her body tensing. The sound had come from the front of the house. The rattling of the metal knocker was unmistakable.

Another three bangs resonated, and she slowly turned to face the door. Whoever had turned up was persistent, and if it wasn't for her ancestor's warning about witches and vampires, she wouldn't be so worried.

Quietly, Charlotte crept down the corridor, her aching, bare feet freezing against the cold ground. She listened intently from the hallway as the door opened and the housekeeper, Edith, conversed intelligible greetings to whomever had arrived. As she reached the top of the staircase, she peered down to see the visitor. A woman with eyes the color of oak removed the hood of her silver cloak. Her coiled amber curls fell to her shoulders, accentuating her distinctive diamond-shaped face and straight, long nose.

"I understand it is late," the woman said, her tone clipped. "But I am here on the matter of Theodore and William Lovett's deaths. I'm with the Pinkerman Detective Agency. May I speak with a Miss Charlotte Lovett?"

"Oh my. Yes, of course. Please come in," Edith said shakily, stepping aside, allowing the woman into the foyer. "I will see if my mistress is still awake. Would you like some tea while you wait?"

"Please, thank you."

Edith walked with the woman into the parlor room, and Charlotte ran her tongue across her parched lips. A detective was in her home. They couldn't have known she was behind it. Yet, she couldn't shake the anxiety building in her core. Her father had often lamented that she was a terrible liar. Her face told stories, he'd said.

Quickly, she hurried back to her room, clutching her chest as she walked inside. With a shaky exhale, she looked at the lone candle flickering on the bedside table, the shadows of the room darker than before.

With another step inside, the floorboard behind her creaked, and the door slammed shut.

Fingers clamped over her mouth, stifling her scream.

What the blazes...

Before she could process what was happening, a second hand gripped the back of her neck, spinning her around with surprising force, trapping her between a wall and a muscular body.

She wriggled against the intruder, testing her boundary, but it was as if she were pushing herself against stone. Slowly, she tipped her head back to meet the intruder's furnace-gray eyes. Her stomach clenched at the intensity of his stare and a flush of heat crept through her chest and neck as she held his gaze, and she was suddenly hyper-aware of every curve of his body pressed against hers.

"Don't scream," he ordered, his voice a low whisper as he bridged the gap between them.

She nodded once, and he tilted his head to the side, his rain-soaked dark locks curling over his forehead. As he got closer, she breathed in the scent of his cologne—musk, smoked wood, and cedar. Her pulse quickened, drawing his eyes to her neck.

Slowly, he released his fingers one by one, as if he was testing her to see if she would call for help. Once he'd removed his hand entirely, she heaved in a deep breath.

A surge of raw alertness charged through her nerves, and a tingle built at the base of her spine, creeping upward and into her shoulders.

"Charlotte Lovett?" he asked gravely, his full lips parting slightly.

"Yes," she answered, her breath hitching when he accidentally grazed his fingers against her forearm. "Who are you?"

"Nathaniel Sallow," he said with a tilt of his head. "I'm here to help you."

She'd heard that name before, in her ancestor's voice, all wrapped in warning.

"You're a vampire," she stated, noticing the subtle way his eyes flicked to her throat. "*The* first vampire."

He drank her in with his predator stare—pointed, magnetic, and endless. Looking into them felt like falling—dizzying, weightless, and deadly.

"You've heard of *me*, yet, until today, I had not heard of *you*." He pulled back just an inch when she didn't answer, barely enough room for her to breathe comfortably. "Are you afraid?"

She wasn't sure what she felt, but it wasn't fear. "No."

The subtle tremor around his lips betrayed the calmness of the rest of his face. "How intriguing. You do not fear death?"

Of course she did, but she wasn't going to give him the satisfaction of admitting that.

"Why? Are you going to kill me?" she asked pointedly, her breath stammering on the word.

"Not today," he said, leaning down. She breathed in the scent of the soap in his hair, a woodsy, citrus laced smell that made her heart race. Her stomach somersaulted when he licked his lips. Maybe it was because she hadn't been that close to a man, other than her repulsive cousin, in years since the man who broke her heart.

Clearing her throat, she asked, "Can you move back a little?"

An unsettling smile curved his mouth. "Are you uncomfortable?"

"Yes."

That wasn't entirely true, but the tingles she was feeling were entirely too inappropriate. Everything about him was designed to lure prey into a false sense of security, before tearing them apart, but goodness, did he have to be *that* handsome? Did all vampires look him?

After a few seconds, he relented, the tendons in his neck and arms roping when he inched back as if doing so was a strain on his body. His fingers gently swept against hers before he took a step back. Shockwaves pulsed through her clammy palms and into her chest.

Without breaking eye contact, he ran his hand over his short, dark stubble, then into his hair.

"Better?" he asked and pushed his sleeves up his forearms.

No.

"Yes," she said, and pressed her fingers to her chest, surprised at the way her body missed his closeness. "I have a visitor, actually."

"I know," he said. "She's a witch. Comes from a dangerous family."

"Let me guess," she said with a hard swallow. "An Avery?"

"You know them."

She peeled herself away from the wall and turned to face him, hyperaware of her state of undress. It didn't help when his eyes raked over her body, his fangs showing when he dragged his bottom lip between his teeth.

"I've heard of them. I was told they want me dead, just like you."

"Except I do not want you dead."

"You said, but that begs the question of why?" she asked, recalling the lie he'd been fed. Her ancestor had said he wouldn't listen to reason, that vampires were savage creatures, yet this one appeared entirely in control of himself.

"I don't want to become mortal yet," he explained. "Not when my enemies are plotting my downfall."

Yet. There it was. He was planning to murder her, just not right now. Well, not if she had anything to do with it.

"Killing me will not make you mortal," she stated simply, holding his stare.

"Is that so?" he asked, his resonant, baritone voice vibrating in her ears.

"Yes. Absentmindedly, she dragged her fingers through her hair, trying to tame the wild mess cascading over her chest, suddenly aware that she looked as if she had been dragged through a hedge backward.

"What makes you say that?"

"The witches lied to you, so you would hunt down and murder the only ones who could break your curse."

Her gaze dropped to his fingers flexing at his side. When she flicked her gaze back to his, his nostrils flared. "You prevaricate."

"I do not," she said, cheeks aching. "I am telling you the truth. I am last in my line so I am the *only* one left who can help you."

"Why would I believe you? You have every motivation to lie to me," he said, his eyes flicking to the door. "Do not move. Someone is coming."

Heavy shoes clomped against the floorboards in the corridor outside. After years of differentiating between footsteps, she knew those belonged to Edith. If her housekeeper walked in there, she had no doubt the vampire would kill her.

"It's my housekeeper," she whispered when he stepped forward, fangs protruding over his lips, nicking his skin with a kiss of blood. "Don't hurt her."

Her heart stammered when the sound stopped outside her door, followed by three loud knocks. "Miss Lovett, there is a detective here to see you."

The vampire watched her with a fixed stare, as if he was intrigued by what she would do next. Charlotte was certain he'd love nothing more than to be given an excuse to feast on her staff.

"Oh, I see," she called back, coughing out the croak in her voice. "I will be right down."

"Do you need help dressing?"

"No," she said, a little too quickly and adjusted her tone. "Please tell our guest that I shall be down in just a moment."

"Yes, Miss."

Once she was certain Edith had gone, she let out a heavy breath and pursed her lips.

"You did not ask for her help," the grave voice taunted from beside her. "Or try to use her to distract me so you might escape."

"That would not have worked *and* you would have killed her if I did."

He tilted his head, his mouth slightly open as he lightly ran his tongue over a pair of sharp, glinting fangs. "In my experience, most people would have tried and you did not."

"That cannot be true. No one wants to watch an innocent person get senselessly murdered."

"Oh, but they do, Miss Lovett. People often relish violence and death. You are just *kind*."

"Then your standards of kindness are extremely modest."

"Because I have seen the world," he added in a way that made her feel like a fool for believing otherwise. "Are you ready to go?" he asked, his expression shifting into a more formidable frown.

"Go where?"

"To my manor. I can protect you there."

Her jaw slacked. He was jesting, surely. "I can't just leave my home."

The muscles in his jaw feathered. "You have no choice, unless you want to die. In which case, I estimate you have maybe five minutes before Beatrice Avery's patience wears thin, and she comes looking for you herself."

"I can't leave." She looked around her bedroom, at her mother's perfume, Alice's jewelry box and the writing desk that was filled with bound letters. Everything in her bedroom was haunted, but it was hers nonetheless, and she wasn't about to leave the only home she ever knew. "There must be another way. All my belongings are here."

"Which will mean nothing if you are dead," he said.

She huffed out a sigh, knotting the fabric of her chemise in her fingers. Duke wasn't anywhere to be seen, and she wasn't even dressed.

"*Why* are you helping me?" she spluttered as the ticking from the clock grew louder. "You clearly don't believe me. What's stopping you from killing me when we arrive at your manor?"

"We share a common enemy," he said, and touched the back of his neck. "Besides, if you are telling the truth, then I'll need you alive."

She wetted her lips. "I can't go with you. If you want me alive to help you, then you'll need to stop the Avery family from killing me. Unless you're *not* strong enough to stop them."

His nostrils flared as he straightened his posture, jaw clenching. "They have power unlike I have ever seen. I can take on a few, but together they are too strong and here, in a place steeped with so much death, their magic is amplified."

Yes, because they were siphoning it from her dead ancestors.

"Someone else is coming," he warned. "I can hear their labored breaths. We must go. Now."

"But I only just got my home back," she whispered.

"The witches want you, not your estate. Unless you want to be sacrificed tonight, along with your staff, you will come with me."

Her stomach knotted into ribbons. *Damned and Hell.* What choice did she have?

"I need to find Duke first. He's my cat," she added when he shot her an incredulous look. "They *will* hurt him. *Please.*"

"We do not have time to search for your pet. Now, you can come willingly, or I will take you by force. The choice is yours, little lamb."

She shuddered at the nickname. A sacrificial lamb indeed.

His eyes darkened momentarily before glancing at her necklace. Instinctively, she pulled her long waves around her neck. "Promise you'll come back for him?"

"This is not a negotiation," he stated. There was no amusement in his expression, just an eerie stillness. "Hold on tight."

"Wait, what?"

Before she could grab her pelisse, he hooked his arm around her waist, pulling her up his body as if she weighed nothing. He slipped his other arm behind her knees, knocking her off balance before lifting her in his arms and careening them both through the window and onto the stone balcony just as her bedroom door swung open and the amber-haired woman and Edith walked inside.

"Close your eyes." His deep voice vibrated in her ears as she rested her head against his chest, her fingers crumpling the fabric of his shirt.

Chapter Five

The candlelit windows of her manor grew smaller, barely visible through the curtain of rain. Charlotte watched her manor fade from view as Nathaniel jumped over the iron fence of the garden. Her heart ached knowing she likely wouldn't see it again. Even if she, by some miracle, didn't die at the vampire's estate, her home might still be taken by the witches.

"I'm going to jump us onto the roof." Nathaniel's low warning resonated in her ears as he angled her body in his arms, so she could wrap her arms around his neck. Leaning her head on his shoulder, she breathed in his dizzying scent and peered behind him.

The air whooshed from her lungs when he climbed up the side of an abandoned textile factory. Raindrops hit Charlotte's bare ankles and arms like icy needles, her saturated chemise sticking against her skin. His arms tightened around her as he jumped from the factory onto the steeply pitched, slated roof of a terraced house. Below them, the city stretched out in a maze of gray cobblestone streets, the dim glow of gas lamps illuminating groups of people standing outside of bustling pubs.

Nathaniel's muscles tensed as he careened through the night at such speed that she could barely suck in a deep enough breath. After a few minutes, he slowed to a normal pace upon reaching a stone gable, the stars above them pinpricks against an impossibly rich, black canvas. She watched them twinkle on their way down the side of a theater. He landed them on a cobblestone street, his body absorbing all the shock of the landing.

The sounds of laughter and carriages grinding over dirt followed into the smoggy night. With a deep breath, she inhaled the mingling scents of coal smoke, horse dung, and the lingering waft of sewage that hung in the air from the River Thames. A baked potato seller shouted his wares, unaware of the predator with her in his arms, lurking in the shadows just feet away.

Charlotte closed her eyes to the blur of the side streets and alleys when he sped up again. After several minutes, Nathaniel came to a sudden stop on the uneven pavement. Slowly, Charlotte cracked open her eyelids. Beyond the towering, wrought-iron gates in front of them was a long path that wound through gray oak trees with leafless gnarled branches.

Gravel crunched under the vampire's feet as he walked them inside.

"You okay?" Nathaniel asked.

Craning her neck, she peered up at him, observing the stern look on his face and how his brows were set in a constant furrow, as if the world was always disappointing him.

"That wasn't terrible," she said, although the nausea building in her stomach begged otherwise.

Her fingers grazed the tips of his dark locks, and she had the sudden urge to delve her fingers into them.

What was she thinking?

It was that damned vampire charm. Much like other creatures she'd read about, vampires were predators with allure. Like the sirens in her fictions, who would entice sailors with a beautiful song before devouring them.

"Good," he said gruffly. "Welcome to Sallow Manor."

She craned her neck to look behind them, while keeping her arms around him. A stone manor emerged from the dissipating fog, the roofs a silhouette of tall spires and towers. Her eyes flicked up to the stained-glass windows inlaid in sweeping gables and the carved mouths of gargoyles trickling rainwater.

Nathaniel walked through the heavy layer of fog clinging to the steps leading up to the double doors, before walking inside and up the sweeping staircase. Shadowy halls adorned with portraits narrowed as he veered right. At this point, she felt silly for still being in his arms. She could walk from this point, but the break from any physical exertion was nice.

Without warning, he sped up and hurried them down a corridor and into a guest bedroom. He dropped her suddenly, and she flung her arms out, but was relieved to find a soft mattress to break her fall.

"G-good God," she stammered.

"Nathaniel," he corrected from the doorway.

With a tsk, she steadied herself by grabbing the edge of the mattress and sat upright. At least he had the decency to give her some space, if only several feet. Although a small part of her missed the closeness, which was insane. Something was definitely wrong with her. Or him. No, *definitely him.*

A faint scent of lavender and freshly washed linen surrounded her. She glanced around at the neatly tucked ivory sheets and blanket, and the intricately carved wooden posts of the bed. The smell was coming from a bouquet of lavender placed on top of a wooden dresser. She wasn't sure what she had expected at the home of a vampire, but that was not it.

"You did not vomit," he said, his voice strained.

Her piercing eyes flicked to his, and she asked, "Does that happen often to the people you abduct?"

"Yes," he stated, deadpan, "but I did *not* abduct you."

Her lashes flickered as she gripped the sheets in her fists. All she could think about was Duke, and the staff she'd left behind to fend for themselves. She squeezed her eyes shut and blew out a long exhale before opening them again. "No, but I also had no choice in coming."

"I got you out of there before the witches could murder you."

She tilted her head slightly to the left and pursed her lips. "How altruistic of you."

"I do not pretend to be a savior, Miss Lovett, but it does not matter. The fact remains you would be dead if it was not for me."

"Would you like me to thank you?" she asked, swallowing the frustration in her voice.

In truth, she was not really mad at him, but the situation she'd found herself in. Duke was gone. Her home was gone. Even though she'd crossed a terrible line to get her estate back. It was all for nothing. Anger bubbled through her core, searing each emotion in a cloud of resentment.

"No. I only require your compliance," he said, and she clenched the fabric of her nightdress in a fist. "You must remain here until I have taken care of the Avery witches."

"Will you allow me to return home after?" she asked, her arms shaking from the rage of losing everything.

"No."

"So I am to die?" she asked, her voice rising an octave, tears threatening to spill over. "You *do* want to become mortal, although like I said before, you are wrong about the method of getting there."

She studied his every move. The way he watched her, carefully, with ancient, hollow eyes, and the muscle feathering in his jaw when he met her stare.

No one wants to live forever," he said.

"Says the immortal vampire who does not feel pain."

"What do you know of my suffering?" he asked, the flare of his nostrils betraying the otherwise eerie stillness of the rest of his face and body.

"Nothing, but I know what I would choose given the choice."

It wasn't a lie. The first time she'd read about the curse of vampirism in a grimoire, she'd thought to herself that it did not seem to be much of a curse at all. Yes, living forever was not ideal, and the thought of drinking blood turned her stomach, but she would embrace it all if it meant living without constant pain. Most people only dreamed of holding that kind of power, the type where they could be strong enough, so they never had to fear another man again.

Her eyes drifted upward when Nathaniel ran his fingers over his neatly trimmed facial hair and stepped closer, a glint flashing in his pupils. "You wish to be like me?"

"Not like you, but a vampire, yes," she stated, clarifying the distinction. Because if she was cursed, she wouldn't kill an entire bloodline for her own gain.

"Why?"

She sucked her bottom lip between her teeth, and for the briefest moment, his eyes dropped to her mouth. "It would not be so awful to be invincible."

"You crave power."

"I want to be free of pain," she corrected, rolling her ankles against the bed, hearing the clicking of her bones as she did.

"What kind of pain?" he asked. When she didn't answer, he took another step forward. "Tell me, what is so terrible about being mortal?"

Her chest heaved. The better question was what she would miss about being mortal, other than the promise of an ending. After clearing her throat, she looked into his cold, unblinking eyes. "It depends. What is it you can't do that mortals can, other than eating regular food and dying?"

"Everything, Miss Lovett." Longing threaded his stare, making her stomach flip. "You get to experience everything with fresh eyes. Do you know what I would give to taste that novelty again? You get to watch the sunrise every day, unburdened by the shadows I am forced to hide myself in."

"You cannot go out in the sun?" she asked, surprised that part of the lore was true. "I thought nothing could kill a vampire?"

"It won't, but the sun weakens us, and I cannot afford to make myself vulnerable to my enemies. While I cannot die, as long as the Avery witches are in the world, they'll always find imaginative ways to make me suffer. Trust my word, Miss Lovett. You do not want this curse."

"No," she said, twisting her mouth. "I get to instead live a life that is pointless and die before it really begins. I would rather be a vampire than have the life I do."

His fingers flexed at his sides. "I've never met someone so eager to be cursed. Do you wish to watch all your loved one's die?"

She hated the judgmental tone in his voice and how quickly his emotions shifted.

"I already have. There is little left for me to lose," she said.

"Forgive me." He paused, his expression softening for a flicker of a moment. "I heard about the massacre, how you almost died at your father's hand."

Her stomach lurched at the shift in his tone.

"You read the papers," she said, her mouth twisting. Of course he knew what happened. Everyone did.

"I heard you attended your father's funeral."

Her heartbeat stuttered and she quickly averted her gaze. "Yes."

"Why?"

"I...don't know."

Because she was gullible and a fool? He likely thought so. No one understood why she did. How could she possibly explain that her father was not himself? They called her delusional, but she knew how far he was willing to go. At least, she thought she did. Coming to terms with that hurt.

"How did you find out about my existence?" she asked when he didn't say anything else.

"A witch inadvertently told me that your line had not died out."

"Inadvertently?" she repeated. "You mean you tortured them?"

"No," he replied but did not seem offended by the accusation. "I can taste memories, emotions too. I experience them through drinking blood. That's how I found out about you, the great-great-granddaughter of the secret child born to a Lysanmore noblewoman." He gestured to her. "The Avery family must have discovered the truth not long before me. It is why they were coming for you, although I cannot understand why they want you dead other than to punish me."

"Why *do* they want to punish you?"

His eyes darkened, but he did not answer.

"Keep your secrets," she said. "I do not care. All I want is for you to believe me about the curse. If you kill me, you will be damning yourself."

"Why should I believe you?"

"I have no way to prove it to you, but are you willing to take the chance that I'm lying and be wrong?"

He straightened his posture and shoved his hand into his pockets, glaring down at her. "No. I'm not. Tell me everything and spare *no* detail."

She mulled over her next words carefully and reined back the bite in her tongue. "I spoke with the spirit of one of my ancestors."

"What was her name?"

"I do not know, but she said she is the one who cursed you." His jaw clenched, so she hurried on and tried not to trip over her words. "The spirits of my family are trapped in that graveyard with her, and you are the one that anchors the curse preventing them from moving on in death."

A flicker of tension creased his lips. "How is that possible?"

"I do not know, but my ancestor told me that a woman called Gertrude cursed the Lysanmore bloodline centuries ago."

His eyes flashed, lips twitching to the side. The expression was so fast that she questioned what she'd even seen. "Gertrude Avery, I assume."

"Yes, and her descendants to this day continue to siphon the energy of the spirits in my bloodline, so they can grow in power, but holding so much energy in one place requires an anchor and Gertrude made you that anchor. You're immortal, invincible, and unbreakable. Perfect for ensuring a curse doesn't break. So, if you become human again, then my family will also be free."

"The Avery family will lose their source of power," he finished, rubbing his fingers over his chin.

"Yes. That's why they want me dead, because they know I'm the last one who can perform the ritual that can undo your curse."

Ignoring the rest of the information, his brows knitted together when he responded, "Fear not. I am going to murder them all before they can try."

Her nose scrunched at the thought of so much bloodshed. "Not the children I hope," she stated.

"No," he said, and her shoulders relaxed. "I don't hurt kids, but the rest will die. They will never stop hunting me, even after I am mortal."

"Why? They would have already lost. What would be the point?"

"We have a history. A blood one," he said in a controlled tone, but she could sense the untamed power behind his eyes, ready to snap at any moment. "So, you would perform the ritual willingly then?"

"Yes," she lied. "So, you believe me?"

"I want to, but you have every reason to lie to me."

"I don't know how else to prove it to you. I can take you to the graveyard and see if I can commune with my ancestors again."

"That will not work. Vampires cannot see the dead."

"That must be nice," she quipped.

"It is one of the few perks of my curse. It would be a nuisance to be relentlessly haunted by my victims."

Her stomach churned, and she tried not to look disgusted, but her expression told stories. *Victims.* She felt ashamed for feeling anything when she looked at him, even though it was just physical attraction, which cannot be helped. Nonetheless, his nature should have made him all the less appealing. So why didn't it?

He was a murderer.

So was she.

The harsh truth niggled in her core, like a maggot trying to eat its way free.

"I'm going to try something," Nathaniel intoned, his nostrils flaring when he glanced at her throat. Hesitantly, he took a step closer, and she winced.

"Try what?" she asked, her breath shaky.

"I'm going to drink from you, so I may access your memories and see for myself. I may not be able to see ghosts, but through your eyes, I can."

"Wait..." her breath stammered. He couldn't see the entire memory with her ancestor, at least not the part where she was told she'd need to sacrifice herself to complete the ritual to undo his curse. Else he would know she was lying about willingly performing the ritual and would lock her away. Any chance of escape would be gone. "I'm not comfortable with you going inside my head."

He stepped closer and ran his hand over the back of her neck, sliding her head to the side. "I need to trust you, and this is the only way."

"Have you never taken someone at their word?" she asked, leaning away from him.

"Yes, which is precisely why I don't anymore. I do not do this lightly," he said, grazing his finger over her freckled cheek. "We never allow our victims to live, but come what may of that, I must know for certain how to break my curse. Now, don't scream. I don't want to kill you, but if you act like prey, I might not be able to stop."

She flinched, leaning away from his touch, but his words echoed in her mind. *Do not act like prey.*

He sat beside her, drawing her near with one arm around her waist and with the other, brushed a stray strand of hair from her neck.

A shudder wracked her body as his fangs scraped her throat. Squeezing her eyes shut, she braced herself for the pain.

"Keep your eyes closed," he murmured against her, his fingers gliding over the crease of her waist.

Several loud pops sounded from his jaw, and the horrifying realization washed through her—his jaw was dislocating. The sharp edges of his fangs sunk into her throat with reckless abandon and she realized there were more than just two sets of fangs. No, there were several.

A whimper caressed the back of her throat, but she didn't dare let it out. Biting down on her lip, she suppressed the scream vibrating her chest, and only a small, guttural groan escaped her mouth.

His warning circled her mind repeatedly.

A sharp pain sliced through flesh and muscle, drawing deeper until a rush of heat enveloped her from head to toe. His fingers tightened in her hair as he pulled it back from her scalp, angling her better.

So this was how it felt to be food.

Her entire body stiffened, her vision vignetting with wave after wave of dizziness until the world was spinning. There was relief in surrendering. Her body collapsed into him, her senses dimming until all she could focus on was the dark behind her eyes.

The world seemed to tilt on its axis as she began to lose consciousness, and that's when she felt his presence inside her. It started with a spark blooming in her stomach, slowly pulsing outward until all she could feel was tingles all over her body.

A heavy weight crept into her mind, and she just knew it was him. It was as if his soul was inside of her, pressing against her mental barricades until they broke open and her memories flooded through.

The first memory Charlotte was plunged into washed over her like an icy splash of water. Mist surrounded her. She was back in the graveyard of her ancestors on the night she'd stolen the bones.

Watching from behind her eyes, she saw the conversation unfold between her and her ancestor about the curse. Nathaniel was there too, but not physically. He was a parasite in her head, observing with a sharpness that ached her skull. Yet, his harsh edges were softened inside her. She felt him squirm a little, a sense of unease surrounding his presence.

She was just glad she could make him feel a little uncomfortable too considering the violation. His tongue continued to glide over her wound, her blood pumping into his waiting mouth.

The words spilled from the ghost's mouth about the curse, the Avery family, and Gertude.

As soon as she'd decided he'd heard enough, she forced herself to feel the pain she normally numbed, allowing into to take her in waves of agony, forcing them out of the memory and into another.

His consciousness toppled with her, into scenes that spiraling when her emotions shifted along with the visuals. They were falling through darkness before landing at Lovett Manor on the eve of the massacre.

"Not this."

Her whisper echoed around her as she watched helplessly.

She pretended to be dead on the floor, her fingers twitching against the floorboards. She watched through cracked eyelids as her father's grip on her sister's throat tightened. The man she loved, the father who'd held her as a child and kissed her forehead every night before bed, was gone. His face was twisted into something demonic, and the blue of his eyes were rimmed with black, veining out from his pupils until darkness consumed his irises.

With a groan, she forced her way out of the memory, refusing to think about her father or that night again. Hope drowned out the dark thoughts Nathaniel was guiding her toward, and she reminded herself that the world was not that bad. While it was filled with suffering and bad people, there were also so many beautiful things.

Flashes of simpler days swept away the pain. In her mind's eye, she watched herself dancing with her sister, of Alice's hair cascading around like spun silk, golden under the candlelight. Another snippet of her holding Duke close at night, him purring against her, filled her up, then another, of the days where she dug her fingers deep into the soil of her garden, planting seeds and watching life grow around her.

Each dark memory was edged with a faint, ethereal light, and for a moment she wondered if she was dying. The creature was still feasting upon her like a wild animal. She could still feel him suckling on her throat, yet, now and then, she felt a hint of his emotion pulse through her, as if they were melding into one.

In the last memory, she felt a jolt of panic, and it was not her own.

Fortunately, the abyss snatched her away before she could feel anything else, but not before she heard a rush of whispers sound into her ears, welcoming her as the next victim to join the ghosts haunting Sallow Manor.

Chapter Six

"Death is coming."

Charlotte sat upright, panic surging through her as she awoke to darkness, her hair plastered to her forehead with sweat. She tried to recall the dream that had her spluttering those three words, but the more she tried, the faster it slipped away.

She gripped the sheets and glanced around at the shadows of the monochrome furniture across from the four-poster bed. While she couldn't remember what had happened in the dream to so violently jolt her awake, she couldn't shake the sense of doom building in the pit of her stomach.

The faint scent of lavender wafted into her lungs, and she grabbed the side of the mattress. For a moment, she'd forgotten where she was and who she was with. She looked around for any sign of the vampire, but there was no one else with her. Aside from the gentle patter of rain against the windows, everything was silent—too silent, as if the house had forgotten to breathe. Or perhaps she had gotten so used to the creaking floorboards and groaning walls of Lovett Manor.

Slowly, she brought her fingers to her throat, surprised to find nothing there. The pain was gone, along with any evidence that Nathaniel had bitten her and invaded her memories. The thought of him perusing her head and peering into the more vulnerable corners of her mind welled up a rage so potent in her core that she fisted the blankets and clenched her jaw.

Her eyes drifted to the drapes and the sliver of moonlight peeking through, just enough to illuminate a path to the dresser. Dust motes floated in the peppered, white light, and she watched them, thinking only of the vampire and his fangs on her throat.

She reached for the locket around her neck. It was the only thing she had left. The witches likely took everything in the manor after they found she'd escaped, or worse. Painted scenes appeared in her mind's eye of the bloodbath that likely awaited her back home.

Tears pricked her eyes. She didn't want any of this, but death seemed to follow her wherever she went.

Chills ran over her bare arms, as if the air was thick with something unseen and it was crawling all over her. Before she could dissolve into a panicked mess over the events of the night, the floorboard creaked beside her bed and her eyes widened. She didn't move and held her breath, listening intently to the sound of something dragging itself over the floorboards and over to her window.

A woman's soft voice spoke into her mind, the sound a familiar, sickly sweet whisper.

End it now, before they torture you.

She shook her head, squeezing her eyes shut. A full-body shudder ran through her back, arms, and legs.

Click.

Her eyes widened when the glass of the window rattled as the latch opened. Slowly, it swung open, and a gust of cold air swept into the room.

The voice floated in again, but the tone deepened, now disconnected and broken in places.

There is nothing to be afraid of. Death is freedom. The voice said all too sweetly. *You crave it, and it craves you. End your suffering.*

Her toes curled against the linen, fingers gripping the blankets. Charlotte glared at the door, suddenly desperate for the vampire to return.

The dream suddenly splashed into her mind like icy water. Her dead mother was reaching through the bars of the graveyard, desperately trying to get out. It was Alice who had warned her in the nightmare, telling her the witches were coming.

No, that they were already there. That she was already dying.

She threw the covers off her body but was too late. Cold, invisible palms pressed against her cheeks before releasing her. The stench of sulfur wafted through the room, forcing bile into her throat. The voice spoke again, the sound echoing in her head.

Just one jump and all of this will be over. You can be with your family again.

Her scream came out as a dry, raspy gurgle. No matter how hard she tried to yell for help, nothing was coming out. Trying to move was like wading through water. Every movement was slow, and her body was heavier than usual. Her limbs moved of their own accord, as if they were attached to invisible puppet strings.

With a tumble, she fell off the bed, her body crawling toward the open window.

She didn't want to die. No matter how painful life could be, she did not want it to end. A surge of fire spiked through her, the same one that she'd felt the night her father believed he'd killed her. She could have gotten up to help Alice, but she didn't. Instead, she played dead, frozen and weak, watching when her sister took her last breath. Because she wanted to survive, and by the look on her father's face, nothing could have stopped him. Not her. Not Alice. Nothing.

At least, that's what she told herself.

The voice spoke again, responding to her thoughts in a way that made Charlotte's stomach turn.

Do not feel guilty. You can be with her now. Alice is waiting for you. She misses you.

Her nails cut into the floorboards, splintering wood as she dragged them, bleeding, trying to fight against the invisible tether pulling her.

Help! The words formed in her mind, even danced on her tongue, but she could not form them into a sound.

"No!"

The plead came out in a choked cough. The weight in her chest turned to air, and she flopped onto the floor. A gas lamp flickered into her room, scaring away the creeping blackness around her.

"Help," she croaked in a half-cry.

She turned, expecting to see Nathaniel, but spotted a willowy man with refined facial features, high cheekbones, golden-blond hair and forest-green eyes.

"Why are you on the floor?" he asked, in a smooth, vibrant voice.

"Something was here. It was trying to get me to jump out the window." She placed several feet between the glass and her, her heart palpitating when she noticed it was closed.

Her brows deepened the line on the bridge of her nose. "It was open."

"Perhaps you were dreaming."

"I wasn't."

"Are you certain?"

She shook her head. "Yes. If I was, then why am I on the floor?"

"That was my question."

She didn't like the amused edge in his tone. "Are you human?"

His eyes flashed brighter. "Once upon a time."

She ran cold. There was more of them. "Oh, God."

"I'm afraid not, but it's an easy mistake to make. We are both beings intent on causing pain and suffering."

While she no longer knew where she stood with religion, she didn't appreciate his words. "You compare yourself to God?"

A boyish smile deepened his dimples. "No, no. I am far kinder."

She knew he was only teasing her, but she grimaced all the same. "I highly doubt that."

He smirked as if he was enjoying the interaction. These vampires were insane. "Who are you?"

"Alexander Young," he announced as if he was entertaining an audience. "I am Nathaniel's close friend. My aim is to make you feel comfortable here."

She scoffed. "An arduous task."

He took a step closer, his demeanor suggesting he enjoyed making her nervous despite stating otherwise. "One I am intent upon. We need you, so you need not be afraid. I am not going to hurt you."

"I am not scared," she lied, only to see his reaction, but there was not an ounce of anger etched into his soft features. Only curiosity.

"Then you have the heart of a hummingbird."

"I was just attacked," she said, surprised at how easily her remarks were spilling from her lips.

"By a nightmare," he taunted, the words rolling off his tongue.

She glanced over her shoulder, seeing nothing in the room. Whatever was haunting her had gone, but she couldn't escape the uneasiness in her stomach. There was no way she wanted to remain alone in the room.

A loud gurgle broke the brief silence, and Alexander's eyes dropped to her stomach. "Are you hungry?"

"Not really. My appetite disappeared when your *friend* sank his fangs into my neck earlier."

He tilted his head. "Your body does not lie, my dear. I will send for some food from the kitchen."

"I assumed you would only have blood stored there."

Yet again, he did not react to her comment and some of the tension in her jaw dissolved. "No. I prefer to drink from the source."

She tried not to make another face. Unsuccessfully.

"We have human staff here," he said when she didn't respond. "They require feeding. Let us find one of them so you do not pass away from starvation."

She followed Alexander out of her bedroom, hurrying her pace to catch up with him and the light he carried. They didn't talk on the way down the halls, but she used that time to observe him, from his elegant, arrogant stride to his manicured nails and silky blond hair that grazed his shoulders. He took pride in his appearance. That much was obvious from the tailored, embroidered knee-length frock coat complete with red and gold stripes, and gold silk bow tie.

With Nathaniel, she'd been certain the attraction and magnetic pull was all part of some vampire charm to lure her in. Yet, with Alexander, she didn't feel any of that. While he was conventionally good-looking and had a certain panache about him, his presence didn't make her skin tingle like Nathaniel's did.

Shaking her head to scatter those unwanted, dangerous thoughts, she focused ahead, the sharp pain searing through her legs making her wince. Alexander had obviously slowed his pace for her but was still too fast. Her body still hadn't recovered from yesterday. Every muscle in her calves were tight, and her knees felt as if they might buckle at any moment.

He veered into a narrowing, dimly lit corridor finished with baroque black wallpaper and large oil paintings, and she stopped, unable to keep up the pretense of being fine.

"Please. I need a moment," she said breathlessly when it became too much. Leaning against the black chair rail, she let out a long exhale.

"Mortals." He said the word like it was a bad thing and stopped in front of her, his lips curling inward. "Do you need me to carry you the rest of the way?"

She grimaced at the thought of being so close to one of them again. "No. Thank you. I just need a minute or two. There are a *lot* of corridors."

She sank to the floor, her back sliding down the bumps of the rectangular paneling.

"Let me help you, my dear," Alexander said in a tone and crouched to her level, placing the lamp next to them on the carpet. Lines creased around his eyes, and for a moment he looked kind, boyish even. "We can stop here. Can you make it to that door?" he asked, pointing a few steps away.

She nodded, taking his arm.

"Let me show you the library. There is an armchair and a fire."

"Why are you being nice to me?" she asked, grunting when she took a step.

"I am not *nice*," he said swiftly, lifting her. "The library is simply my favorite place, and you make an acceptable companion."

She wrapped her fingers around his forearm, eyeing him carefully, aware that behind his smile was a pair of fangs.

As he walked her into the library, he said, "I will ring the bell for the servants to bring you a light breakfast."

"Thank you," she relented, the pit in her torso hollowing with each passing minute.

The small doorway was deceiving of the labyrinth of black shelves and high, ribbed ceilings beyond it. Leather tomes filled each shelf, and sliding ladders beckoned Charlotte as she stared wide-eyed around the room. She breathed in the scent of wood smoke and parchment with a faint smell of roses. It smelled like home, from before the tragedy.

Slowly, she sat on the dark green, suede armchair. The crackling and hissing of the fire calmed her as flames consumed the logs and embers burned to ashes. She noticed the book Alexander was holding, his fingers stroking the worn spine.

"That's a heavy read," she mumbled.

He lifted the spine to his lips, eyes closing with a crease. "Indeed. I am often drawn to books that break me."

"Why?" she asked.

"So I may feel how it is to bleed."

Her heart pounded. She glanced at the shelves, grazing her fingers over where he had bitten her earlier. "Does Nathaniel like to read?"

"These are all his favorites," he said, waving his arms elaborately to the shelf behind the armchair.

She twisted her body, trying her best to ignore the aching in her bones. Charlotte could tell a lot about a person by what books they read, so she was surprised to discover that the stoic vampire who seemed to have no regard for humanity was a *romantic.* Or, at the very least, he once was. The books were covered in a thick layer of dust, yet the spines were deeply creased.

Her eyes swept over the titles: Wuthering Heights, The Scarlet Letter, Frankenstein, Hamlet, The Tempest, and several poetry collections. A slow smile curved her lips. Among the fictions, she spotted a small, leather pocketbook. It was the only book that had recently been disturbed. She plucked it out and ran her fingers over the blank cover.

"Which one is your favorite?" Alexander asked, each word flowing into the next.

She lowered her gaze, afraid if she looked him in the eyes for too long that she would invoke his hunger. "I quite enjoyed Wuthering Heights."

"Ah," Alexander said with a knowing smile. He leaned against the shelf, his weary gaze dragging over the aged spines. "So you choose forgiveness over retribution."

Her brows flicked down as she looked at the vampire with a gaze that glistened despite the dim firelight of the room, as if he was creating his own light. "I assume you think me foolish for it," she stated, threading the pages of the pocketbook under her index finger.

"Not at all," he stated, arching a light brow. "There comes a time, however, to choose one's sword over your heart. The witches who are hunting you will not be slain by kindness."

She inhaled sharply, her lashes flickering slightly. "Speaking of the witches," she said, treading carefully. "Has Nathaniel said anything about his plans for them?"

"Some, but they are not for me to share. All you need to know is that you are safe here," he said, giving nothing away. "We will not let them hurt you. You are too precious for that. With you gone, we will forever be without death."

"So you want to be mortal too?"

"Not particularly, but I also do not want to exist forever as an aimless body traversing space long after this world has burned."

She swallowed hard, imagining being trapped in nothingness forever. With a tense breath, she opened the pocketbook in the middle, her heart stumbling as she took in the rows of hand-scrawled names, many with the family name Lysanmore. "What is this?"

"Nathaniel's food diary."

She blanched. "These are all people."

"What did you expect?"

She grimaced. "This is revolting. Why does he write them down?"

"Immortalizing a name ensures they are not forgotten. Although he might just enjoy reliving the kill."

Wonderful. She was indeed living under the roof of two morally insane, homicidal monsters.

"Do you keep a record of your victims, too?" she asked, slowly closing the book between her palms, unable to stomach looking at the word Lysanmore over and again. It looked more like a sick list of trophies. As if he owned them.

"I do not concern myself with tracking my food."

She swallowed thickly. "I see."

"You are disgusted," he said, his smile dropping for the first time since he'd approached her. "We are conditioned to take lives. People die every day. It is no tragedy. Most deserve death."

Her jaw clenched. She thought about Alice and her mother, and a surge of heat flooded her body. "I don't believe that."

"Well, that is your prerogative. Although I am surprised you are squeamish of murder when Nathaniel relayed to me you were intrigued by the idea of becoming a vampire."

"I—yes I said that, but I would not want to cause others pain," she blurted. "Not innocent people, anyway."

Alexander sighed. "Eventually, you would become desensitized to the suffering of others."

"I hope not," she said, horrified at the thought of being without feeling or compassion. "Speaking of suffering, where is Nathaniel? Is he sleeping?"

"We are vampires, my dear. Our day is your night. He is somewhere in the manor."

"What is the time?"

"A little past three." A hint of a smile lifted his lips. "I shall leave you to read. I have somewhere I must be, but a maid will arrive shortly with food for you."

He sped out of the library in a blur, and once he was gone, she focused on the pain in her body, and the agony spreading over her hip. Slowly, she lifted her chemise and angled her torso.

A brownish-black mark was raised on her skin, with some kind of indentation in the center, with spreading redness around it. She'd assumed the small lump she'd found after the burial was just a bug bite, but it was growing larger. Perhaps it was infected. By the time she was done assessing the mark, she was surprised to find she was no longer alone. A woman with ash-blonde hair wearing a black wool dress and lace-trimmed apron, stood in the doorway holding a tray.

Charlotte let go of the fabric of her nightdress, allowing it to fall back down her body.

"My apologies," the young woman squeaked out in a thick, Irish accent, freezing in place with the tray. "I can come back later."

Charlotte's lips fell open. What did she think she was doing? "Oh, no need. I was just checking a...*nothing*."

"Do you require any assistance?" she asked and walked into the library, placing the tray on the table in front of the crackling fire.

"No, really, I am well."

The maid's eyes swept to her throat, before looking back at the tray. "I brought you some cucumber sandwiches, a bowl of stew, cheese slices, and biscuits. I wasn't sure what you would like."

"This is perfect. Thank you." Her stomach gurgled in response to the array of freshly made items and the glass of milk next to them. "I'm Charlotte. What is your name?"

The woman smiled, her round, pink cheeks balling. "Hartley, Miss. If you need anything, I am here night and day."

"Oh, you live here," she said.

"Yes." She turned back. "I've been here for three years. I'm hoping my time will come soon."

Her brows knitted. "Your time?"

"We all work here hoping Lord Sallow will make us like him. He chooses one of us every year."

"*Lord* Sallow?"

"His family has one of the oldest baronies. He served at Henry the Eighth's court, you know. He could have been promoted higher, but he's a recluse. He can't be too involved with society since he must disappear every decade."

"Because he doesn't age," Charlotte realized.

Hartley nodded. "Please excuse me, miss. I must attend to Lord Sallow's dinner guests."

"By guests you mean…" she said, trailing off.

"Everyone must eat. Even vampires," Hartley stated, but didn't seem anywhere near as horrified as she should. "Good evening."

She watched the maid leave and suddenly her appetite was gone. Guests, Hartley had said. Plural. He'd murdered more than one person that night. How much could he drink? He'd already taken enough of her blood.

She had planned on trying to find him after eating, to discover how much he had seen while inside her head, but the last thing she wanted was to see the creature covered in someone else's blood. She'd seen enough of that when her father had come for her, his shirt and trousers saturated in scarlet, the stench of copper clinging to him. He hadn't used the knife he'd killed the staff with on his family. No, his bare hands were the weapon of choice for the ones he loved the most.

Everyone knew that choking the life out of a person was far more intimate, almost as much as drinking their blood.

With a long sigh, she spent the rest of the night eating the food Hartley had brought and reading through Nathaniel's favorite books, wondering if there was anything in them that could help her understand him better, so she might survive him. Instead, she found herself enraptured by every page, her breath hitching as she became wrapped up in confessions of love and longing seeping through the pages, and forgot all about the haunting earlier, and the vampire that had bitten her.

Before she knew it, the sun had come up and peeked through a small gap in the thick drapes, and she was yawning. She tucked the book under her arm and stood. Her heart stammered when she reached the door, a strange tugging sensation pulling against the organ. When she left the library and headed back to her bedroom, she swore she spotted someone watching her from the shadows of the hallway, but when she looked back, there was nothing there, but dust motes caught in lamplight.

Chapter Seven

A putrid, thick stench clawed down her throat when Charlotte sucked in a deep breath.

Peeling back her eyelids, she dug her nails into the wood bottom of the coffin, her forearm brushing up against the soft fabric of the white dress Alice was buried in.

"No, God no," she spluttered, her eyes adjusting to the heavy darkness

This wasn't possible. She'd fallen asleep in her bed at Sallow Manor, unless, the witches had come for her in her sleep and somehow…

Slowly, she turned her head, her heart pounding violently against her ribcage when she saw her sister's corpse. Penny-shaped holes oozed sludgy liquids from her rotting skin as maggots burrowed deeper into Alice's flesh, feasting upon her glistening, decaying tissues.

The cloying, rotten odor was overwhelming, invading her nose and throat, making her gag until a fit of coughs wracked her chest. Wood splinters drove into her nail beds as she pushed against the coffin lid, but it wouldn't budge. Her throat constricted when she choked on her cries, banging her fists against the lids, forced still by the confines of the coffin walls.

Bugs crawled over her body, their bites sending tiny shockwaves all over her skin. "Stop it," she spluttered through coughs. "I'm alive. I'm still alive!"

Her throat was dry from screaming, the heavy silence punctuated only by the sound of the maggots and her own heartbeat. A loud scream rattled her chest when her sister's neck snapped to the side with a loud crack. The corpse's maggot-infested lips pulled back, and Alice screeched, "You did this to me."

With a jolt, Charlotte was wrenched from the nightmare and landed back in her bed. Sweat dripped from her forehead and into her dark eyebrows, her hands clammy when she gripped the sheets, getting her bearings. The soft moonlight filtered through the long, crimson drapes, and the sound of rain pattered gently against the window. She must have slept all day and was dreaming again. She did that a lot since they were gone, but this time it felt real. The smell of her sister's body still lingered in her mouth.

Her hand flew to her chest when an ache cracked through her core at the thought, her eyes brimming with fresh tears. It was bittersweet, to have been loved so deeply by her family. She was fortunate to have felt it, but it was all the worse now that it was gone, especially knowing she would never experience that kind of unconditional love again.

Her mother taught her so much, except for how to live without her.

A sharp pain shot through her hip, halting her thoughts. She angled her body to get a better look and hiked up the skirt of her nightgown. Her fingers brushed the dark veins spreading outward from the decaying core of the mark.

It was getting worse.

Tap, tap, tap.

The sound against her bedroom door sent her jumping to her feet and pulled her chemise over the decaying mark. She needed her clothes from home, or new ones. She couldn't remain in that nightgown much longer.

"Hello?"

"Good evening, miss," Hartley said shakily, walking inside with a tray before setting it down. "I didn't mean to wake you. I assumed you would be up. Everyone else in the manor is."

"I was already awake," she said, although it had only been for a few minutes.

Hartley placed the tray down and lit a second candle. "How was your sleep?"

"Fitful," she confessed. "Do you sleep during the day too?"

"We all do."

"Of course," Charlotte said with a shake of her head, feeling silly for asking the question.

"Is there anything else you need?"

"Yes. Some lavender, mint, and witch hazel, if you wouldn't mind."

It was a concoction her mother always used on bug bites, and she needed it before the one on her hip got any worse.

"I will bring that shortly after I attend to Mr. Young," she explained.

"Alexander?" she asked, trying to recall his name.

"Yes. He retrieved some of your things last night," she said before walking out the door. "You should check your wardrobe."

Her eyes widened. "He was in here while I slept?"

"He wouldn't hurt you, Miss," she said upon spotting the horrified look crossing Charlotte's face. "I will fetch you the herbs you require."

"Thank you."

She watched her leave, ensuring the door clicked shut, before turning to the wardrobe and pulling open the paneled, polished doors to reveal three shelves on one side, filled with drawers, stockings, petticoats, chemises, corsets, bonnets, gloves, silk hair ribbons, and a pair of unlaced brown boots. On the left, hanging from a rail, were all her dresses, including the ones Alice had made for her.

Sighing relief, she pulled the skirt of one to her nose, breathing in the faint scent of perfume. While she was happy to have her clothes returned, she would rather have had Duke.

Biting her lip, she picked out a dusty-blue tea gown. She was not yet out of deep mourning, but the entire charade of dressing in black was supposed to signal her respect for the deceased. Wearing Alice's dresses was more of a display of her grief than anything else could be and who was going to judge her? The vampires? Or a society that wouldn't see her?

Neither mattered.

With a long sigh, she decided to go and find Nathaniel. There was no more putting it off. She not only needed to know how much he saw while he was in her mind but persuade him, or Alexander, to retrieve Duke and her grimoires.

After dressing, she faced the window with a hard swallow. A brush of lavender painted the horizon, and the scattered stars faded into the indigo canvas above the most magnificent gardens that stretched on forever. She wished she could go outside, but before she could ask for a single thing, she needed to confront the vampire.

She looked at her outfit in the reflection of the window, as she'd quickly found out there were no looking glasses in any of the rooms, not even a hand-mirror. Her fingers traced the delicate, hand-stitched petals of the flowers tracing over the skirt. It was the last outfit Alice had made for her before she died. Of her sister's many skills, dressmaking was what she excelled at most, not that their father would have ever let her pursue such an occupation.

Despite all the horrible things about being trapped there, she found one small positive aspect to be away from the expectations of her uncle, staff, and society. She didn't have to worry about the remarks about her untamed curls and let them cascade down her chest and back. The vampires surely didn't care what she looked like, or that she was presentable. Hell, Nathaniel had carried her out in her chemise.

She grabbed a candlestick and walked into the corridor, turning left toward the sound of music. The oil-painted eyes followed her down the winding hallways. She turned into the candlelit darkness, following the sound of the piano into a large room with tall, vaulted ceilings all arching down toward a beautiful crystal chandelier.

If she didn't know him any better, she would have assumed he was heartbroken from the way he played. Except, he was a vampire who had no regard for human life and tracked them like food. By the way he acted, he didn't act as if he had a heart at all, much less one that could be broken.

Yet, while she hadn't heard the song before, it felt so familiar. She crossed over the threshold and slid down the side of the paneled wall, her eyes fixed on Nathaniel hunched over the mahogany piano, his fingers dancing effortlessly across the keys.

His shoulders tensed with each note, as if he were reaching into the deepest recesses of his soul. If he had much of one left.

The candlelight caught the angles of his face, highlighting the way he squeezed his eyes shut at certain notes. As the song faded into the stillness of the room, her breath hitched, and he whipped his head around to look at her.

Their gazes locked for a heartbeat, and in that fleeting moment, she saw the flicker of something unspoken—a glimmer of connection that shifted his expression into one of ruthless carnage.

"Leave," he commanded with a deepening frown, his eyebrows slanting downward. "Now."

"I just wanted to—"

"I do not have time to talk."

She wasn't sure what she expected, but that reception was not it. "I am not leaving until we speak."

He turned to face her, their eyes clashing across the room. "What is it you want?" he deadpanned, his lips pulling into a grimace.

Be nice. You need him, she reminded herself. She searched his eyes for a hint of humanity that she could appeal to, but there was nothing there.

She chewed on the inside of her lip, breathing heavily as she stared at him. "I have a few questions."

His eyes blazed to life when his gaze fell on her neck, lingering there for longer than she liked. After trailing his gaze over her body, he stated gruffly, "Find Alexander. He can answer any questions you have."

"I want to talk to you, not him."

"Why?"

Her chest heaved, shoulders tightening when she crossed her arms over her chest. "It must be because of your approachable demeanor," she said with a feigned smile, her stomach swirling when she caught the corner of his lip twitch upward. "I want to know if you got all the information you needed when you violated my mind?"

"Is that how you feel?" he asked, standing to face her. "Violated?"

"How could I not? You made me feel things I didn't want to."

His eyes blazed as if she'd lit a monochrome flame. "What did I make you feel, little lamb?"

There was that name again.

"Terrible things," she bit out far too quickly. "You made me revisit memories I would have rather left in the past."

"I was nothing but a spectator. Your mind went there on its own."

"Even if that is true," she spluttered, her fingers knotting into the fabric of her dress. "I didn't want *you* to see them. You could have stopped drinking from me, but you didn't. You stayed, you watched!"

"I took no pleasure from it," he assured, as if that helped.

"You drained me until I fell unconscious. You promised to stop."

"I did stop."

"I almost died."

He maneuvered himself onto the black piano stool. "Have you come in search of an apology? If so, I am afraid I must disappoint."

"No. I can't imagine you being capable of such humility. However, considering I am the key to breaking your curse, I thought you'd maybe check on me to make sure I was alive."

A wolfish grin shadowed his lips when he stood. "My, my. How quickly you have become outspoken in your short time here."

She snorted. "I don't see why I should continue the charade of civility when you refuse to be anything but discourteous."

"I didn't think you were capable of being anything *other* than civil."

Sucking in her bottom lip between her teeth, she chewed on the admonishment she wanted to throw his way. She still didn't know how much he had seen in her head, so reined in her anger and steadied her voice. "I want to know if you got what you needed."

He didn't answer.

"Do you believe me?" she intoned.

"I saw your conversation with your ancestor in the graveyard."

She swallowed thickly. "Then you know I can break your curse."

He paused, tilting his head and giving nothing away in his still expression. Everything about him was unmoving, still, except for his smoky, intense stare, which brimmed with untapped power, revealing the monster beneath.

"Yes. Your ancestor, the one you spoke with, her name was Elizabeth."

"You recognized her even as a spirit?"

"Mhmm," he said. "It was interesting, to see a ghost through your eyes. Sometimes, I wondered if they were real."

"Just because you can't see something doesn't mean it doesn't exist."

He chuckled darkly. "Spoken like a priest."

"So now you know the witches lied to you," she said, ignoring his quip.

His eyes and brows flickered on the intonation of her last word, his lips carving into his cheeks. "Indeed, I do."

She took one step closer, if only so she could examine the micro-movements of his face better.

"Good," she bluffed. "So, I will perform the ritual to break your curse. However, I need my great-grandmother's grimoires to do that. I am not a practiced witch."

The corner of his lip creased, and the flare of his nostrils sent a shudder through her body. "You cannot go back home."

She let out a long exhale. He didn't know the part where she had to die to complete it. It was a minor victory, but one nonetheless.

"I am not foolish," she blurted. "I know the witches will come for me if I try, but I want my grimoires from the attic, to know if my staff are okay, and most of all, my cat, Duke."

"Your staff are fine. Alexander heard them when he showed up to retrieve your belongings. Fear not. He spun a lie about your leaving, saying you had gone to visit your great aunt."

She scoffed. "And they believed him? That I left with no belongings in the middle of the night."

"We can be very persuasive."

"Then he, or you, can return and get Duke and my grimoires."

"I'll retrieve the grimoires, but the cat is not welcome here. They do not like me."

"Neither do I," she snapped, inhaling sharply. "Yet I am forced to live here. If you won't get him for me, then I will not help you."

"You will."

He turned back to face the piano, and she clenched her fists at her sides.

Her glare stabbed into the back of his head. "I will not."

"I have ways of making you."

She wasn't sure what had changed, but he seemed different before he bit her. He wasn't exactly a ray of sunshine then, but he seemed less grumpy, more forthcoming at least.

"Let me guess," she asked. "By torturing me? I won't give in."

He turned back to look at her, challenge threading his stare. "No?"

"I have lost everyone I love and have nothing left to lose, except for Duke. Keep him away from me and believe me when I tell you I will not perform the ritual no matter how much you hurt me. All magic must be done willingly, else it won't work."

He leaned forward, his smoky eyes narrowing as he pursed his lips. After a brief pause, he said, "You are stubborn."

She scoffed. "As are you. So, will you find my cat?"

"Fine," he said gruffly. "I will look for your pet tomorrow."

"Thank you." The words felt like poison on her tongue. She wanted to take them back, but she was used to placating monsters and swallowing her real thoughts.

"Your cat will be good leverage to ensure you uphold your end of our deal," he added.

She blinked twice, leaning back. "Deal?"

"Yes. I will bring you your grimoires and pet. In exchange, you will practice your magic every day with a witch I trust and prepare yourself to perform the ritual once I have vanquished our enemies."

"A witch you trust?" she asked, surprised he trusted anyone.

"She is highly motivated to help me," he explained.

"I don't need any witch helping me."

Her stomach dipped, flipping in circles as he closed the distance between us. "Do you think me foolish enough to allow you to be alone with your grimoires?"

Slowly, she rolled back her shoulders and jutted her chin. He was afraid of what she might learn, which meant there was magic that could help her escape and fight them. "Why? Are you afraid of my power?"

A bitter chuckle escaped his lips as he towered over her, so much so that she had to tip her head back to look at him. The fibers of his shirt strained against the muscles in his arms and chest. "I am not afraid of your using magic. The witch I am bringing here is for your benefit. You are unpracticed," he said, raking his eyes over her body, and lingering on her throat. "Who knows what kind of damage you might do trying to perform spells alone."

She didn't say anything but repressed the urge to swallow.

"You are precious cargo," he added, "and I will not have you accidentally killing yourself before you can help me."

Everyone treated her like that—cargo, chattel, anything but a person. She hated it and him for making her feel the same way William had.

"You are repulsive," she spat, forgetting herself in his presence. Rage boiled through her core, forcing power into every punctuated word. "You're no better than the witches you hunt."

His laugh was as dark and suffocating as smoke. "Then you are a fool. The Avery witches are far worse than any other creature you will ever encounter, including me."

She stepped closer, knowing that winning the argument could mean her death, but his arrogance made her want to scream. Heat flooded her face. She hated that he could see the blush creeping into her cheeks. "I doubt it. Do you know what, I think that while they may be cruel, you are another beast entirely. You hunt the innocent and toy with whomever you please, without a second thought. You wiped out my entire bloodline for your own selfish desire."

He strangled a laugh, one that was void of any amusement she'd heard from when he rescued her. "Do you know what I think of you, witch?"

"Enlighten me."

"I think you are nothing but an ingenuous woman with little substance."

Her lashes flickered, but she refused to look away from him. His lips tipped into a faint, enigmatic smile, as if he enjoyed watching the panic building in her eyes.

"At least I am not a monster."

His nostrils flared as he backed her into a corner of the room, his pupils forming into vertical slits. Veins began spreading out from his eyes, as if he was seconds away from shifting into the animalistic version of himself that would tear her limb from limb. "I may be a monster, but at least I am *interesting*."

A strange warmth pooled into the tips of her fingers, and when she looked down she was surprised to see her fingertips had darkened. "Really? Because I see *nothing* of interest."

His gaze flicked down to her hands, his tongue dragging over his lips as he leaned closer, pushing her into the wall. "Are you certain about that?

Your heart is racing and I can smell *everything.*" Her thighs clenched when he pressed himself against her harder. "Perhaps you are not as immune as you may think."

"Maybe you are right about me," she countered. "But at least I am not a coward. I know why you didn't return after you drank from me."

The slight flare of his nostrils was the only indicator that her words had any effect on him. "Why is that?"

"You were afraid."

He scoffed. "Of you?"

"Of my mind. You forget that while you were in my head, seeing my memories, I could feel glimmers of your emotions, too. Oh, how terrifying it must have been for you, a thing that hides in darkness, to suddenly find yourself standing in the light where hope lives."

His eyes darkened, fingers flexing at his side when he looked at her throat. With a tense exhale, he pushed himself back and said with a growl, "You should go. Now."

"Why? Are you feeling *violated?*" she asked, ignoring the voice in her head reminding her he could easily destroy her.

He ran his tongue over his sharp, gleaming fangs. She really was going to get herself killed. Power moved through her veins, pulsating through every pore of her body as she prepared to fight.

After a few seconds, he regained his composure, and her brows shot up her forehead. The veins around his eyes were gone, and his pupils were back to their circular, normal shape.

"Your magic is strong," he said in a strangely contained voice. "I can feel it pulsing through you."

She glanced at her fingers, which tingled with a thousand needle pricks, as if something was moving inside them. That had never happened before.

"It will come in useful when the witches come for you," he continued. "I've known many, and felt their power, but not like yours. You are strong, especially when you're angry."

"You want me to fight them, too?"

"Yes, I do," he said, tilting his head, the curve of his smile and deepening of his dimples making her heart stammer. "I am glad to see you have an instinct for self-preservation. All it took was a little push to get that magic to the surface. Alexander assumed kindness would pull it out of you, but I wagered it was rage. I can feel it in your soul, desperate to be unleashed."

"I'm not an angry person," she said and he chuckled darkly.

"Your power begs to differ."

"So, that was all intentional? No, no one can feign that amount of anger."

He pushed his index finger under her chin and closed her gaping mouth. "Don't look so shocked. I need you angry and ready to fight."

Her face flooded with heat. Never had she met anyone more infuriating. "No. Y—you were losing control!"

"I never lose control," he stated nonchalantly, and she was ready to throw something, anything at his head, just to see if that was true.

He continued rambling, as if he didn't notice the battle of confusion playing on her features. "While you may disdain mortality," he said, pacing in front of her, "I do not. I want the life back that was stolen from me, but I cannot get it while the Avery family are alive. They manipulated me into killing so many in your bloodline. I will not fall into their trap again. They will never stop their attacks on me, even with you dead."

"Why do they hate you so much?"

"There are many reasons," he said vaguely, and added, "but the most recent being I killed a couple of their own after their elders sent their daughters to spy on me. It was their fault for sending them here, but they will not see it that way."

Charlotte shook her head and scoffed. How wonderful it was to be immortal and never have to take accountability for anything. She watched him closely, his smirk curving his plump lips far too enticingly for her to look away.

"Like something you see, little lamb?" he asked, lifting his brows and making her stomach knot in ways she hadn't felt before. A surge of butterflies swarmed into her stomach when he moved closer, his scent utterly intoxicating her senses.

It was that vampire charm. It had to be.

"No," she stated too quickly. "I was just curious about your fangs."

He ran his tongue over his teeth, and her chest heaved. "What about them?"

"Does your whole mouth shift or..."

"Our jaws dislocate," he explained, but looked away from her. "We have three sets of fangs."

"I don't see them now."

He tapped the space above his upper lip. "They retract."

"What about your eyes? They changed just now."

His shoulders tensed. "Yes. The shape allows for sharper visuals, for more precise strikes."

Unconsciously, she bit down on her bottom lip, and with a brush of his thumb on her clavicle, he inhaled sharply, groaning when he pulled back. "If that is all, I will bid you a good evening, Miss Lovett," he said in a strained voice, his palm twitching.

With another grunt, he pulled back and walked out the room.

After a few deep breaths, she steadied herself and peeled herself away from the ancient stone. She could still smell his scent on her.

Closing her eyes in a soft blink, she breathed him in before walking to the piano. She had to think of something, anything else. On top of the wood, where music sheets sat dusty, she spotted a piece of stationery in the shape of a rectangle. On it, the word prey was written in red ink. At least, she hoped it was ink.

She turned it over in her palm and winced on seeing the blood splatter over the information printed on the back, detailing something called The Hunt. It was three days ago at midnight, one day exactly before he had come for her, and the location was the grand salon, the very room she was standing in.

Chapter Eight

A deep sluggishness eclipsed her every thought. She'd barely gotten a few hours of sleep, yet again, since arriving at Sallow Manor. Every time she tried to rest, the house would groan in protest. Floorboards creaked and the windows rattled. When she did eventually collapse from exhaustion in the early evening, the nightmares would plague her, sometimes bleeding into her wakefulness and paralyzing her body.

Despite the tiredness wearying her bones and the ache in her lower back that was slowly getting worse, she still refused to climb back into bed. Nathaniel left a note earlier that evening outside her door saying he was leaving to find her cat and grimoires. Ever since then, she'd waited by the window in her bedroom, watching the night darken into twilight.

She pressed her back against the stone arch surrounding the tall glass panes and stretched her legs out along the ledge, the rain hammering against the glass. Heavy droplets raced down the lead inlays, and she traced her fingertips over the intricate tracery, wondering if Duke was out in the storm. What if he didn't return to the manor after her absence? Her stomach dipped. Her poor baby probably thought she had abandoned him, just like his previous owners had.

Every muscle in her body tensed. What if Duke had gone looking for her in the manor, and then someone had done something to him? Without her there, he had no one to advocate for him.

Stop! She pressed her palms to the sides of her head. The thoughts spiraled with visuals of Duke hurt or worse.

No, she wouldn't think of it. Duke had to be okay, and Nathaniel would find him. He had to. Duke was the only family Charlotte had left, and if something had happened to him too, then she'd just give up. She pressed her forehead against the glass, trying to distract herself from the stream of panicked thoughts.

There was something about rainy nights that calmed her soul. Even from inside the manor, she could smell the deep, earthy fragrance of the rain hitting the ground through the cracks. At least the plants outside were well-watered, not that she'd been able to see the gardens yet except from her window. Much like the rest of the manor, everything was well tended.

A low growl resounded from her stomach. Her fingers flew to her stomach as a hollow ache deepened in her core. Suddenly, for the first time since her sister's passing, she was ravenous. She could almost taste her mother's mutton stew, followed by a large helping of layered sponge cake.

Another growl gurgled in her stomach, deeper this time.

She grabbed the candle from her bedside table by the gold-plated handle and walked out of her bedroom and into the narrow, quiet corridor. The kitchen had to be down from the foyer. She wished she'd asked Alexander for a map.

An icy chill enveloped her as she slowly made her way down the hallway, the plum-colored carpet muffling her footsteps. Shadows flickered against the large oil paintings hanging on the walls above the ornate paneling, all framed with antique gold.

She turned left, walking toward the dining room through the maze of interconnected corridors, each taking her deeper into the center of Sallow Manor. The last corridor was narrower than the others, the wall-sconces unlit. Her boot heels echoed against the ancient stone steps carrying her down into the cold, stone passage. This definitely was not the way to the dining room, although she'd sworn she'd gone in the right direction. Her breath fogged in front of her, the dwindling light of her single candle illuminating the dust motes hanging in the air.

Howling winds creaked beyond the walls, the whistles breaking through the eerie quiet along with the trail of her dress rustling as it dragged over cold stone.

Charlotte's breath caught, the candle almost tumbling from her weak grasp when she spotted a figure draped in tattered white, mostly obscured by the corridor, just beyond the reaches of candlelight. She glanced back toward the way she'd come, but the light at the end of the corridor was gone. Someone had extinguished the lamps in the upper hallways. From somewhere behind her, a drawn-out breath reverberated, and the temperature dropped, raising the hairs on her arms and neck.

With a roll of her shoulders, she suppressed a shiver, and swallowed thickly, her mouth dry. Her eyes focused on the darkness ahead, and the flickering of the candle that danced with every gust of air.

"Don't go out," Charlotte begged the candle, her hand shaking as she white-knuckled the handle and took a hesitant step forward, away from the ungodly sounds happening behind her. Determined not to look back, to acknowledge whatever was following her, she kept moving, her pace quickening despite her joints protesting against the sudden increase in speed.

With every step, the walls tightened around her. The rough stone brushed her forearms, her dry gasps echoing around her as the candlelight dwindled until it was nothing but a small, blue flame.

The scent of mildew and lilies hung in the air, the musky fragrance turning her stomach. The corridor twisted deeper into darkness, and as she descended the tiny, stone steps, her foot met the hard, icy edge, toppling her off balance.

She gripped the wall, her heart pounding in her chest as the ground beneath her feet disappeared for a moment. A spike of energy pushed through her body as she gasped in deep lungfuls of air and regained her balance.

The muscles in her legs tightened and twitched, a tremor flickering the muscles under her right eye. She needed to get back to her bedroom, or the library, anywhere but the creepy corridor that didn't even feel like it was a part of the house anymore.

Cold tendrils grazed her arm. She whipped her head back to look over her shoulder and screamed when she saw the semi-translucent figure of a young woman standing before her, with blacked-out eyes and long, dark hair hanging around her face like curtains. Dried blood crusted around the puncture marks on the woman's pale throat, her tattered, white dress stained with crimson.

The figure, its form barely visible in the dim, yellow light, hovered over her, arms outstretched. Charlotte spun, nearly losing her balance, and the candle toppled from her grip, clanking down several steps and plunging her into darkness.

In the unending darkness, Charlotte felt for the stone, her frantic climb up the stairs guided by her fingertips. Her heart pounded and each shallow breath scraped her throat.

As she raced out, ignoring the pain searing through her calves, the ghost's face, with its dark, empty eyes, burrowed deep into her mind.

Panting, she stumbled, her foot catching the edge of a step, and her knees met the ground with a thud. With a groan, she pushed herself up, crawling forward while the heavy, rhythmic pounding of footsteps grew louder behind her.

Robbed of her sight, she tried to focus on the feel of each step to navigate her way out, but the footsteps and ragged breaths were getting louder, faster, and while she moved as quickly as she could, the spirit was faster.

Meow.

Charlotte jumped, uncertain if she had imagined the sound, when a second, louder meow drifted down the hallway. A glimmer of light flickered ahead, illuminating the entrance to the corridor and Duke was sitting at the top, hissing as if warning her to hurry.

Icy fingers curled around her ankle, forcing another, louder scream from her throat. She was so close to the light of the upper corridor, and Duke, who was crouched close to the ground, had his yellow eyes fixated on the space behind her.

She fell out into the open space of the corridor, tears pricking her eyes as she sucked in a deep breath and kicked her way up the plush carpet, her back sliding against the floor.

Footsteps pounded from the staircase to where she was, and in seconds, Nathaniel was standing over her, worry etched into every line creasing around his eyes. "What happened?"

He turned his head when she pointed at the door to the passageway, but when she looked over, it was gone.

"There was a corridor," she spluttered.

Nathaniel pushed against the wall. He didn't say anything, but his brows deepened, wrinkles forming around his eyes.

She climbed to her feet, pointing at the wall. "It was right there. I'm telling you."

"It's been a long and tiring week."

"I'm not insane. I saw a ghost, a woman. She had—"

Meow.

Her heart leaped when she looked at Duke, forgetting for a moment about what had happened. He nudged against her ankles, his nose still wet from the rain. "Hello old friend." She leaned over and scooped him into her arms. Resting her cheek against his rain-stricken fur, she closed her eyes, breathing in his scent. "I've missed you."

Loud purrs vibrated against her chest, and she hugged him tighter. His claws curled into the fabric of her dress when she moved to put him down.

She looked at Nathaniel, who swept his fingers through his rain-soaked locks.

"You said there was a woman?"

"Yes." She ran her fingers over Duke's fur, his purrs calming the buzz pulsing through her body. "She had long dark hair and was wearing a white dress. She had bite marks on her throat. I think it was the ghost of one of your victims."

"What did she do?"

"She attacked me."

"Now, why would one of my victims do that?"

"I don't know, but clearly at least one of them is trapped in this house."

He glared at Duke, who tensed under Nathaniel's stare, then flicked his eyes to meet hers. "Likely more than one. Whoever it was, she probably attacked you to get to me. Ignore them."

"That's your advice? To ignore them?"

"What would you suggest?"

"I...don't know." She looked back at Duke. At least the monster had done one good deed by retrieving her cat, not that it was out of the goodness of his bitter heart. She was reminded that everything he did was for his own gain, believing she would break his curse. So, she refused to feel any kind of gratitude toward him. Not that he cared enough to want any.

The light around him moved in shadows when he reached her and Duke. Her lashes flicked up when she met his stare, everything around him vignetting into darkness.

"I had to chase him," he intoned, glancing between her and Duke, his eyes glinting with knowing. "He ran from me, and it took over an hour to find him."

"Don't feel bad," Charlotte quipped. "I would have run from you too."

His lips pulled into a hard line. "He shouldn't have been able to evade me like that."

She held Duke tighter, and his tail wrapped around her wrist. "He's quick. It's not the first time he's been chased."

"I am a vampire," he said, stating the obvious. "It was only when I said your name that he appeared."

"What are you trying to say?"

"That your pet is likely a familiar. *Your* familiar."

Her brows furrowed. She brushed her fingers over his fur, her arms aching from holding him. "I don't think so. He's not some demon shifter."

"They don't have to be." The corner of his lip twitched, and he leaned over her, his shadow consuming her entirely. "They can be spirits, like a guardian acting as a go-between for the spiritual realm and you."

"No, he's not," she spluttered, but the idea did cling to her. He'd come to her so many years ago, before she'd even considered using magic, and she'd never seen him shift or do anything out of the ordinary for a cat.

Yes, he was intelligent and appeared when she was in danger, but didn't all cats?

Nathaniel cleared his throat. "While you mull that over, I should tell you Katherine is waiting for you in the foyer. I gave her your grimoires."

"Who?"

"The witch whom I asked to instruct you."

A lump formed in her throat. The thought of being minded by another witch, especially one who kept company with vampires, made her shudder. "Will she be staying here?"

"Yes."

She couldn't hide her grimace as she placed Duke down when he finally let her. He stayed close to her feet, slinking between her legs.

"How many did you find?"

"Four." He tilted his head, a wolfish grin curving his lips. "I also found the cursed mirror you keep in your attic. I thought you didn't practice."

She swallowed thickly. Did he know? No, he couldn't see spirits. "I don't."

"Yet I found remnants of a spell."

"You sure know a lot about my craft for a vampire."

"I grew up with witches."

Her brows rose. Men couldn't be witches. It was passed through the female bloodline, but that didn't mean he didn't come from a family of them.

"My mother," he said when she was stunned into silence. "She was a witch, as were her sisters."

"What happened to them?"

He arched a brow. "It's been hundreds of years. They're all dead."

She shook her head, whistling out a breath. Of course they were. "Right."

"I discovered your uncle and cousin mysteriously died," he added.

There was barely a few inches between them now, his smile widening, sending shudders down her spine.

"Yes, they did," she whispered, but her voice was lost under his presence. His muscles tensed under his saturated shirt, the smell of rain, musk, and sandalwood lingering around them. She held his intrusive stare, deepening hers into the depths of his gray irises and dilating pupils. A shockwave traveled from her head to her feet and she looked away first.

"Hmm." He stepped back, looking pretty pleased with himself, which only made her hate him more. "Perhaps you are not as innocent as you pretend to be. What did you do to them?"

She held her breath, frozen in place. Goosebumps spread over her arms and neck, but she didn't answer.

He leaned down, his lips a whisper from hers. Her lips tingled from his hot breath. "Allow me to rephrase. What did they do to force someone like you into murdering them?"

She swallowed hard, but it did little to remove the lump in her throat. He knew. Somehow, he knew what she did and by the glimmer in his eyes and stretching of his lips, he was enjoying every second.

Two sinners trapped together. It was almost poetic.

"You don't need to tell me," he said with a sigh when she stayed quiet, and lifted his finger under her chin, gliding it all the way to the part of her throat where he'd bitten her. "Perhaps now you can come down off your high horse and not judge me for my actions."

That was enough. She stepped out of his shadow, which only made him chuckle darkly.

"What I did was out of necessity. William and Theodore were monsters. I did the world a favor."

"Yourself too. It seems you benefited most from their absence. Your staff were surprised to know you are alive. They assumed whoever killed your cousin, came back for his fiancée."

She breathed out a sigh of relief. Her staff were okay. She was too until she spotted Nathaniel's building smirk.

The words rattled in her chest. "We were not betrothed by my desire."

"I do not judge you, little lamb." He stepped closer again, backing her into the wall. "In fact, you just became far more interesting."

She slid out from between him and the wall, hating how her body responded to his closeness.

"We should not keep your guest waiting," she stated.

He tilted his head, his usual stoicism returning to his sharp features. "She is our guest, Miss Lovett. This is your home now too."

Sallow Manor would never be her home, but she'd argued enough with the vampire for one night and was too tired to think of a witty comment.

She followed him down the staircase, her knees popping as they descended. Even the smallest muscles in her ankles were tight. All she could think about was how she longed for a hot bath later to relieve at least some of the aches. The pressure was building in her bones, but she didn't dare tell Nathaniel. He would just use her pain against her, and she refused to show him any more weakness that he might take advantage of.

The woman standing in the foyer was beautiful. A dark blue ribbon hung from the back of the witch's golden-blonde hair, which was tied up into an elaborate updo, with coils poking out from under her navy hat. Silk covered the wide curving brim, and the headpiece was finished with a bow and three feathers at the front.

She was well-bred. No one but those she knew in high society wore such elaborate silk gowns or headwear.

The woman looked at Nathaniel first. Her smile widened when he approached her. Beside her on the half-moon table were the four grimoires, all aged with brittle pages and brown leather covers.

Katherine grinned when she looked at Charlotte, but the smile did not quite reach her eyes. "Nathaniel, you never told me your witch was so beautiful."

She didn't appreciate being called his anything.

"It's good to meet you," Charlotte said, offering her the kindest smile she could manage considering how she felt.

A slight inhale parted the woman's bow-shaped painted lips, and her fingers tightened around her vesicular bag until her knuckles were white. "I'm Katherine."

"Charlotte."

"I know who you are. You are infamous among the witches, and in society."

Nathaniel interjected, fortunately, because Charlotte had a bad feeling the conversation was edging toward her survival of the massacre. "Miss Ellenwood will stay until after the ball. She'll teach you everything you need to know."

"Ellenwood, as in *Baron* Ellenwood?"

"You know my brother."

Her jaw clenched. "In passing."

Duke darted between her legs and hissed at Katherine, who raised her brow in response.

"Well, Charlotte," Katherine said, somehow making her name sound dull. "You and I are going to have lots of fun together."

Wait, ball. Her brain caught up with her. "What ball? Nothing was mentioned to me."

A languid, sultry smile curved her lips. "Did you not tell her, Nathaniel?" She placed a hand on his biceps, and Charlotte's stomach knotted in response. She turned back to look at her, smiling. "He and Alexander are holding a party to lure the witches here. They're going to drug them, and you and I are going to ensure they cannot use magic while here. If we're lucky, we can get them all in one place and kill them before they kill you."

"What makes you think they will come?" Charlotte rebuked, her pointed stare landing on Katherine's well-manicured fingers, which were resting so casually on the vampire.

Nathaniel gently brushed her arm away and turned fully to face Charlotte, his eyes darkening. "Because they know we have you, and they're arrogant and desperate enough to knowingly walk into a trap. They know you are not practiced and are unaware of Katherine's involvement."

"When is the ball?"

"In five days."

Her eyes widened. "That's not enough time for me to learn."

"Katherine's an excellent teacher."

His muted expression remained unmoving, regardless of how much Katherine beamed at him.

"We can get started now," Katherine said, but Charlotte's eyes closed in response.

She rolled her shoulders, cracking her neck lightly and fought through the pain pulsing in her legs and feet.

"Tomorrow," Nathaniel announced, his tone clipped.

Charlotte opened her eyes in surprise. Did he sense her exhaustion or pain, or more likely, did he want Katherine to himself tonight?

Either way, she had time now to come up with a plan. In less than one week the witches would likely be dead, and that was far less time than she thought she had to get out of doing the ritual. If she didn't escape soon, she was going to die and everything she'd done to survive would have been for nothing.

Chapter Nine

The vampire is going to kill you.

The intrusive voice returned as a whisper, the words looping in her mind as she tiptoed barefoot down the cold corridor toward the library, the icy gusts raising goosebumps on her exposed neck. The candle's waning light dripped wax onto the bronze holder, casting a soft glow on her dark curls that spilled over her ruffled, ivory chemise.

With a hiss, the voice slithered back into her mind.

Run before he drains you. Flee through the gardens while they are distracted.

She wasn't sure if it was her own internal voice or something more nefarious, but it was becoming harder to shut out the noise.

"Stop!" She pleaded aloud, her voice swallowed by the silent corridors, which responded only with a ghostly echo. Slowly, she lifted her gaze to the shadowy end of the narrow corridor lined with locked doors and oil paintings.

The color faded from the maroon wallpaper, transforming it into the identical, charcoal-colored, baroque paper found at Lovett Manor. Above the paneling, cobwebs glistened over portraits as their expressions warped. Blood leaked from their dark sockets, trickling down into the bottom of the frames as their painted mouths opened in silent screams.

As she stumbled backward, the candle's flame flickered, turning an angry blue, before disappearing in a pillar of smoke.

You are losing your mind. Just like your father. You can end this now, before anyone gets hurt.

Footsteps dragged on the carpet behind her, sending an icy chill deep into the marrow of her bones. Holding her breath, she slowly turned her head at the touch of an icy hand on her shoulder and the whisper of a breath against her ear.

A scream ripped from her sore throat as she ran, feeling her way through the dark, her fingers tracing the cold chair rail. The library should have been this way, but the manor's layout was an endless maze of narrow corridors.

Footsteps pounded behind her, the sound of her father's harsh tone ripping through the air from the night of the massacre.

"Get back here you bastards!"

The sound of his voice froze the scream that was about to escape her lips. She jerked her head around, but there was nothing there. The scream of her sister yelling her name still rang in her ears, along with the unsettling memory of Alice grabbing her hand and ushering her into the bedroom, oblivious to the fact it would become her final resting place.

You should have died with her. You let her die. You wanted her dead, so you could take it all.

"No! That's not true."

With a deep breath, she shook her head, eyes clamped shut as tears fell down her cheeks. When she opened them again, everything was back to normal, and she hadn't moved an inch despite recalling running.

Wide-eyed, she glared at the doorway to the library, the scent of burning firewood and parchment carrying into the corridor as the flame of her candle danced shadows around her.

What the...

She was losing her mind.

The pain in her side throbbed deeper when she took a step forward, as if something was tugging her back. It was only when she finally reached the door and saw Nathaniel inside, sitting on the sofa facing the fire, his back to the door, that she understood why.

Something did not want her near him.

Breathless, Charlotte watched him flick a page of his book with his left hand, while swirling whiskey in a glass with his right.

"Don't linger in the doorway," he said, closing the book in the middle. "Come in."

When she got closer, she noticed the title—The Scarlet Letter.

"You didn't hear anything?" she asked, setting the candle down as the fire's flickering light wrapped him in shadows.

He glanced over his shoulder. "What is it I am supposed to have heard?"

"I mean, anything out of the ordinary."

"Only your heartbeat," he said, and her brows pinched together. Surely, he would have heard her scream, her pleading with the voice in her head to stop.

Unless none of it had happened.

"Why?" he asked and she bit her lip. If he knew what had just happened, then he'd think she was insane. While he wouldn't lock her away like most would, in some asylum somewhere, he would surely strip her of any freedoms she had left and contain her to her room, maybe place bars on her window.

Perhaps he would be right to do so.

With trembling fingers, she took the armchair to his left, and crossed her legs. The crackling of the fire hissing between the logs soothed her racing thoughts. "No reason. I thought I had heard something. It was likely from outside."

"Hmm," he said, clearly losing interest.

Rolling back her shoulders, she attempted to focus on anything besides what had just happened. Something was either happening to her mentally, or it was paranormal. She hoped it was the latter, but either way, she couldn't bring herself to trust him with the truth.

She had only left her bedroom intending to borrow a book from their library to entertain herself until she was ready for sleep, but now that she was in there with him, she didn't want to leave. In his presence, the voices faded away, and she felt some semblance of peace. It wasn't just him. Being around anyone helped. It was being alone, when everything was silent, that she hated.

"I assumed you would be with Katherine," she said, breaking the silence.

"Why would you think that?" he asked, taking a sip of whiskey, the firelight casting dancing shadows across his sharp features.

"She likes you. That much is evident."

Leaning forward with his elbows on his knees, he swirled the gold liquid and said, "Katherine only likes herself. Besides, she is here to help you, not me."

"Do you come in here often?" she asked when he let out a heavy sigh.

His pupils flared when he looked at her, reflecting the dim light of embers and fire. "Not for some time."

"I read that one the other night. It is surprising that you like that one," she said, pointing at the worn title.

"Why?"

"It is a book about redemption through suffering, and you are...."

"I am *what*? A monster who could never be redeemed?"

"Is that what you want? Redemption?" she asked, noticing the slight tremor in his throat as he swallowed.

"No, that is not something a vampire could ever ask for."

"Why not?"

"Because we are not deserving of such things."

She shook her head, leaning forward, brows curving. He truly believed that. She could see it in his face. "I don't believe that is true."

"Then you are naïve."

"And you are cynical," she said, with a deep breath.

"You would be too, if you had lived as long as I." His gaze traveled over her face, as if he was searching for something, before settling on her lips. "You've been reading my books. I noticed the dust disturbed."

She glanced at the long shelf beside the mantel. "Alexander said they were your favorites, and I wanted to get to know you better."

His lips pursed. "Why?"

"So I could know what I'm up against."

He pointed his glass at her, slowly nodding before leaning back against the sofa cushions. "You're not up against anyone, Miss Lovett. We are on the same side."

His dark shirt and pants strained against his muscles, his top buttons undone. The men she knew, who dressed in such fanciful clothes, never wore them so casually. Yet, he didn't seem to care.

"Stay and read, if you want," he said gruffly and returned to his book.

She grabbed the closest one and placed it on her lap but couldn't get past the first page. Every so often, he'd peer over the top of his, glance at her, then avert his eyes. She couldn't focus on a damned word. After several minutes of that, she closed the book and sighed. "I've noticed there are no mirrors anywhere. Not even in my room."

He lowered the book, staring at her, eyebrows pinched. "Aren't you inquisitive this evening?"

She leaned forward, picking at her cuticles. "I know they reveal the true evil in demons. I assume they do the same to vampires."

"That would be correct," he said nonchalantly.

"Hmm." She sat back, a slight smile curving her lips. "It must be a nightmare to groom yourself."

He laughed, actually laughed, the sound whooshing air from his nose. A smile almost curved his lips, a genuine one, not a smirk, when Alexander strode in and his face fell back into the same disappointed, stoic expression.

"What have I missed?" he asked, tilting his head when he saw Charlotte's grin.

"Nathaniel smiled."

"A trick of the light, I assure you," he grumbled.

Alexander tsked. "Ignore him. He forgot how to feel joy hundreds of years ago and punishes us for it." He winked, green eyes glistening. She was pretty sure he was exaggerating, but there was a chance he wasn't.

Nathaniel pointed a finger at me from the side of his glass. "Be careful with that tongue, lest I tear it from your mouth."

"You would miss my conversation too much," Alexander remarked.

"You jest. You are not interesting enough for me to feel your absence."

"Well, that all comes down to your dull taste," he stated with a boyish grin and turned to look at Charlotte. "Let me show you the rose garden and we can discuss the ball and how we plan on entrapping the witches."

"You mean, I can go outside?"

Nathaniel shook his head, shoulders tensing. "Absolutely not."

Alexander's lips quirked at the corners, hands in his pockets. "Don't listen to him. You need some fresh air."

"I am being serious," Nathaniel said, lowering his voice.

"Yes, well, that is your regressive state," Alexander quipped, earning a smirk from Charlotte who quickly tried to hide when she noticed Nathaniel glance at her.

"Once the Avery witches are taken care of, she can live in the gardens for all I care."

"Please," she asked, standing. "I fear I may go insane if I remain trapped in this manor. I want to look at the roses. I can see them from my bedroom window and they're in full bloom."

"It is too dangerous," he said and stood. "It is only one more week until you are free. Until we all are."

"So, that is it? What you say goes?"

"Yes."

"If I disobey and go anyway?" she questioned with a defiant stare.

He smirked, hooking a brow, his eyes threading with challenge. "I dare you to try."

"Fine. I shall return to prison then."

A heavy knock resounded on the door just as she was preparing herself to go to bed. Assuming it was Hartley, or Alexander, she called out, "come in," but it was Nathaniel who opened it, and took one step inside.

"I got you this."

Her brows pinched down when she looked at the freshly cut rose in his fingers.

"A rose from the garden," he said when she didn't speak, or move.

"Oh." With a thick swallow, she climbed off the bed and took the bright red rose in her fingers. She had always disliked receiving flowers as a gift. While it was a kind gesture on his part, they were a symbol of death. The moment they were snipped from their plant, they were dying and would soon wilt. "Thank you."

"You do not like it."

"They die once cut," she explained in a whisper, hating herself for saying that when he'd finally shown some measure of thoughtfulness. Why, however, she could not understand.

"I apologize. I should not have assumed."

He turned to leave, but she reached out and grabbed his arm. "Why did you bring me this?"

"You said you wanted to see them," he said, revealing nothing in his expression. "You were upset when you left."

"You just didn't want me trying to escape."

With a clenched jaw, he said, "No. I just wanted you to have something beautiful."

"Why?"

He didn't answer.

"Thank you," she said, if only to break the awkwardness.

"I am disturbing you," he said with a glance around her bedroom. "I will take my leave."

"You're not," she confessed. "Honestly, I hate being alone. Ever since my family died, I cannot cope with silence. My thoughts are loud," she admitted, unsure why. Anxiety spilled through her veins, and she added, "they're dark too and they're getting darker."

"When did they start?"

"After I buried my sister."

He pushed his hands into his pockets and said, "Our minds do that sometimes after a tragedy. They challenge us with the very worst parts of what happened, but you are not those thoughts. Let them pass, but don't linger on them. They're not you."

"I will try," she said, her anxiety easing.

His gaze drifted to her throat, before he quickly averted his eyes. "The sun is almost up."

"Yes, of course. I shouldn't have asked you to stay."

"I shouldn't." He took a hesitant step to the door, before turning, his mouth opening as if to say something, but instead, walked out.

"Good night," she called after him, staring at the door long after he was gone, her stomach in knots. Slowly, she brought the petals to her nose and breathed the scent in, before closing the door and turning to Duke who was sleeping in the chair by her bed.

Those dark thoughts were not her own. Those evil things that sometimes crept into her mind were not her. His words helped and she clung to them when she climbed into bed before blowing out the candlestick, feeling much better with Duke close by.

Chapter Ten

After sleeping the day away, Charlotte opened her eyes to the dimly lit room and glanced at the window. Through the crack in the curtains, she watched the horizon swallow the last of the sun's rays, leaving behind a dark purple sky.

She smiled when Duke snored from the bottom of the bed, his claws curling out against the soft sheets when he meowed in his sleep, his eyes restless from a dream. The scent of the single rose wafted over from the dresser, and she remembered she hadn't put it in any water.

"Sorry," she whispered to the flower after climbing out of bed and placing it in a vase with the bouquet that had been there since she arrived. Carefully, she pulled a petal between her fingers, rubbing the soft texture. She still wasn't sure the real reason he had brought her the flower last night, but she couldn't let one gesture get in the way of what needed to happen.

She would not feel guilty about betraying a man who would easily kill her if he knew the truth. She had two days left until the ball, enough time to sabotage their plans so the Avery family would live. While they were alive, Nathaniel would not perform the ritual out of fear of what they would do to him when he was mortal and weak. If she could postpone the ball, then she could find a way to escape, not that she had anywhere to go. Even if she somehow made it out of there, she couldn't go home. It would be the first place both the witches and vampires searched for her, and she didn't know or trust anyone else to take her in.

She was entirely alone, but she did have her magic.

There is another escape from all this suffering. One jump and it will all be over.

The voice rushed into her ears.

"I do not want to die," she whispered aloud, recalling Nathaniel's words. It was just a lingering effect from the trauma of the massacre, that was all.

No, you want to die. You crave it.

"I don't!" she said, a shiver running through her as the unseen thing brushed against her, raising the hairs on her neck. A full-body shudder ran through her. Just when she was ready to scream as the echo from the voice's words grew louder, a knock sounded at the door, slicing through the noise in her mind.

"C-come in," she spluttered, leaning forward against the dresser before brushing the creases in her nightdress and plastering on a feigned smile.

Duke jolted awake, his eyes scanning the room. When he saw Hartley walk through the door, holding a tray of food, a lit candle, and the supplies she'd requested, he let out a soft meow and fell back asleep.

"Good evening, Miss. Did you sleep well?"

Charlotte stretched out her limbs and rolled her aching ankles. "I wish I could have slept longer."

Hartley smiled and placed the tray on the small table in front of the unlit, black ornate fireplace. A gust of cold air howled down the chimney and fluttered the edges of a piece of parchment folded on the edge of the tray. "Lord Sallow has requested your presence this evening, in the ballroom. I have your dress here." She hurried to the door, and before Charlotte could question why he possibly wanted to see her there, Hartley returned with a dress on a hanger, folded over her arm.

Antique, black lace hung in tatters at the sleeve, and the silk fabric shone under the candlelight.

Charlotte leaned forward, clearing her throat. "Is that from Natha—I mean, Lord Sallow?"

"Yes." Her cheeks reddened, her eyes twinkling.

"He wants to dance with me?"

"Indeed, he does, Miss."

She was going to kill those butterflies that kept swarming at his gestures. "It's just in preparation," she said when Hartley suppressed a grin. "For the slaughter ball."

Hartley snorted. "Is that what we are calling it now?"

"What would you call it? It'll be filled with death."

"Yet another rich society party," she added. "You'd be surprised at how many people go missing at these events." She reached down to the tray and picked up the parcel of lavender, mint and a glass bottle of witch hazel. "I don't have much experience in creating potions, but I hope this will be enough."

"It's not a potion," Charlotte interrupted, wild-eyed. "I'm not doing witchcraft."

Hartley tilted her head, her ashy-blonde ringlets bouncing on her forehead from under her white cap. "Excuse me for being too forward, but you have nothing to feel ashamed if you were. I wish I was one sometimes."

"Well, you also want to be a vampire, so," Charlotte quipped without thinking and immediately regretted her statement.

"You make it sound like a bad thing."

She bit her lip and sat forward. "I apologize. That is not what I meant. I've considered it too you know—immortality that is. It would be a relief from the constant aches in my body, but I just cannot get past the idea of killing innocents and the idea of drinking blood."

Hartley nodded, her eyes lighting. "You don't have to murder good people, Miss. The world is filled with evil men, so tear their throats instead and as for the drinking of blood part, from what I have witnessed, it tastes better to them than food does to us."

"Is that why you want to become one?"

"I have a problem with my heart, you see. Doctors say I won't last long. My ma had a priest come and read last rites to me as a kid. I shouldn't have survived as long as I have. I can die any moment."

"I'm so sorry. I wish I could help."

"No one can. Nathaniel will turn me this year, though. I'm sure. I've worked harder than all the rest."

Her stomach knotted. Hartley had no idea what they were planning. "Do you know why I'm here?" she asked.

"To help Lord Sallow break his curse," she said. "At least, that's what I've picked up on. I only hope he will turn me before. If not, I suppose Alexander still can."

Charlotte chewed on her bottom lip. Breaking his curse meant breaking all the curses. Fortunately for Hartley, she had no plans of doing that. But she hated them a little more for using her like that and giving her false hope. "Do they at least pay you?"

"Better than the other households."

"With the promise of immortality."

"They never promised it," she said, chewing over her words. "He just lets us know there may be a chance."

"Does he know about your condition?"

"No. I rarely speak to him. He doesn't much like people."

Charlotte shrugged. "Well, I don't think they like him either."

She smiled, her cheeks balling. "Don't let him hear you saying that."

"He can't hurt me," Charlotte pointed out with a smirk, then asked, "You said Nathaniel chooses staff members to become vampires. Do you know anyone else he's turned?"

"Oh, yes!" Her smile widened as she recited their names. "Irene Long was the last. Bright woman. Smart. She was a maid. Before her, the last one I knew of was Zachariah. Handsome devil he is, but amusing."

Her heart stumbled a little. "Where are they now?"

"In London. Sometimes they come here, especially for The Hunt."

"I saw that somewhere," she said. "What exactly is it?"

Her face flushed, the redness fading the freckles on her balled cheeks. "It is like a game of hide and seek. Alexander started it actually, to appease the other vampires and ensure their loyalty. The predators wear masks as do the prey and after a head start, they chase them through the manor and grounds."

She thought back to the card she'd found reading prey. "Why would anyone choose to be prey?"

"Some like it, but mostly because the winner gets their request granted by Nathaniel. Most ask for money. Others—the smart ones—ask for immortality."

"He always grants them there wish then?"

"His word is his honor. He never breaks it."

"What do the vampires get from it?"

She held her breath for a moment before saying, "The thrill of the hunt."

"Let me guess, once they catch their prey, they kill them?"

She looked at her lap. "Sometimes. He likes when witches take part, especially when they make it difficult for him."

"How so?"

"Well, magic is forbidden to be used on the predators, but that doesn't mean they can't use it to cast illusions to get away."

"Why do you not take part?"

"I won't win," she said with a laugh. "I have no powers. I'd be found in an instant. Besides, I'd rather earn eternal life through servitude."

"I see."

Hartley stood and fiddled a little with the tray, before heading for the bathing room door. "I will prepare a bath for you before you dress to meet with Lord Sallow."

"Thank you," Charlotte replied, lost in thought.

That was it, her way out.

If she could somehow persuade them to let her take part in The Hunt, she could win and ask for her freedom, or at least allow her to live out her life before she sacrificed herself in old age. For the first time since arriving, her entire body charged with hope. First, she needed to gain his trust, to see if she could figure out what it is he wanted, other than mortality. After all, she needed something to bargain with.

She climbed off the bed and grabbed the note from the tray. It was from Nathaniel.

Meet me in the ballroom at midnight. I hope you like the dress.

Her eyes widened as she read and re-read it to make sure she hadn't hallucinated the words. He hoped she *liked* the dress? Since when did he care what she thought?

She ran her index finger along the torn edge of the parchment. With the ball just around the corner and the end of his curse in sight, it would make sense that he would want her to feel safe, so she would keep her end of their deal. Despite her already agreeing, why not butter her up to ensure her loyalty?

With a shake of her head, she walked into the bathroom in time to see Hartley finishing adding oatmeal and rose petals to the water.

"Enjoy your bath, Miss," she said and left the room.

Charlotte breathed in the evocative scent of honey and lavender, intermixed with the faint scent of wax from the candles flickering on every surface. She undressed before settling into the porcelain tub, her fingers gripping the edges. Pillars of steam swirled over the hot water as it enveloped her aching muscles, eliciting a soft sigh.

She sank deeper into the water until only her head was poking out. The water lapped around the sides of the tubs, almost overflowing when she shifted her torso.

Across from the bath, on the vanity stool, she eyed the note with a grimace. She wasn't going to rush her bath. It was the first time she'd felt any relief from the constant pain in her body. If he wanted to dance with her, then he was going to have to wait.

She grabbed the jasmine-scented soap and worked the lather into her dark curls, kneading her fingers into her scalp. She inhaled deeply, closing her eyes. The seconds stretched into minutes as she dipped her head back, her ears plunging into the water, as she rinsed the soap from her hair.

She sat upright and opened her eyes, the reflection in the darkened arched window catching her breath. The water splashed around when she jolted.

Her own horrified expression stared back at her, and beside her, a woman stood next to the tub, her black dress and long, dark hair saturated with water. A small pool formed at the ghost's bare feet, but there was nothing there. She took a second to glance away from the window and wiped the water from her eyes.

When she looked back at the reflection, the spirit turned to face the window, its all-white eyes latching onto Charlotte's, its gaunt mouth widening in an eerie, humorless smile.

The voice echoed around her skull, one that was not her own intrusive thoughts.

You can see me. I'm getting closer.

What the bloody hell did that mean?

The voice sounded excited, and it had come from the spirit judging by her unnaturally wide grin.

Duke let out a hiss from the next room, his paw batting under the closed bathroom door. Charlotte quickly jumped out of the bath, almost slipping on the water on the floor, and reached for her towel. She side-eyed the window, her heart palpitating when she saw the spirit follow her to the door. Flinging it open, she ran out. Duke darted ahead of her, his ears tucked back.

After a few minutes, and once Duke was calm, she tiptoed back to the bathroom door and peered inside. There was nothing there, nor in the reflection of the window.

"Did you scare her away?" she asked, picking Duke up and holding him against her towel. With a thick swallow, she stroked his head and looked at the bathtub. "The ghosts haunting this place are going to be the death of me." His pulse picked up under her fingers. "It's okay, Duke. They can't hurt the living."

She almost believed her own words, but this time it felt different. The spirit was excited, and she'd never felt such an absence of humanity from a person's aura before.

A throbbing sensation pulsed in her hip, distracting her from the flurry of dark thoughts. With a tense breath, she set Duke on the bed and lifted her towel. Angling her hips, she noticed the bite was worse than before. The necrotic center had darkened, and blue veins had spread outward, each one thicker and longer than yesterday.

Duke's yellow eyes widened, and he rushed to the edge of the mattress, nudging his nose against the mark repeatedly.

"I know, it's bad," Charlotte stated and bit the inside of her cheek. "I'm going to make an ointment to put on it."

Duke meowed, shooting her a concerned look.

"Honestly. It will be okay."

He meowed again.

Leaning over the tray, she ground the lavender and mint, slowly adding it to the half-filled bottle of witch hazel.

"See, I already feel it working," she said when she rubbed it over the mark. "Now, I need to go see Nathaniel, so I can hopefully find us a way out of this mess."

Duke dragged his paw over his ear and tilted his head.

Quickly lacing her corset and pulling the strings taut, she pulled on her dress, ready to face the next monster.

Chapter Eleven

As Charlotte descended the grand staircase into the ballroom, her eyes flicked to Nathaniel, who was standing in the center under an iron chandelier. His dark gaze followed her down each mahogany step, the smoke in his irises flickering under the candlelight.

With a deep breath, she lifted the heavy skirts of her midnight black dress, the lace rough against her fingertips. Lace trim adorned the sleeves, patterns reminiscent of spiderwebs and the velvet layers of her skirt bounced with each step.

Her heart was still pounding from the encounter with what she only hoped was a spirit and not something far more sinister. But the dead were the least of her problems. If she didn't find a way out of the ritual soon, she would join them.

With parted lips, he grumbled, "You came."

"You wrote," she said and walked to him, her gaze turning to the weeping, veiled stone statue behind him, surrounded by pillars and tall arched windows covered in black tracery and metal roses. Filagree molding sprawled over the baroque, velvet crimson wallpaper, which led up to an ivory, vaulted ceiling that reminded her of a ribcage.

When her eyes landed back on him, he extended his hand.

"May I have this dance?"

Hesitantly, she took his hand, her heart racing when his strong fingers enclosed around hers.

"Why do you want to dance now?" she asked breathily.

"Because you will be with me on my arm all night on the eve of the ball."

"So this *is* practice."

"Yes," he said in a low, grave tone, eyes fixed on her. "Come closer."

He placed his other hand on her waist, tugging her closer. His gaze dropped to the curve of her lips, which she had painted in a deep, velvet crimson. "The dress suits you."

The compliment only made her more nervous.

Music quickly filled the air. Charlotte whipped her head around to see a man in a dark suit over the instrument, his fingers dancing over the keys. Goosebumps bloomed over her arms and back as she closed her eyes, dragging her fingers over the back of his neck as he pulled her deeper into him.

I don't know what version of you is real," she confessed. "The predator or the gentleman."

"I can be both. Everyone has a devil in them, Miss Lovett. If they try to convince you otherwise, run," he teased, but it only sent goosebumps traveling all over her.

An uneasy, faint smile played on his lips, the corners creasing as if the gesture was foreign to him. She was certain the smile was meant to reassure her, but it did the very opposite. Was he trifling with her? Allowing her to feel a sliver of hope before leading her into slaughter?

He looked human, and handsome with his tousled black hair and that curl against his forehead that her fingers itched to smooth back. She wondered if it was as soft as it looked.

"You are flustered," he said when she didn't respond.

She steadied herself, allowing her body to move with his, a blush staining her cheeks. "I am acclimating myself."

With a deep inhale, her chest rose and fell. She could've sworn his eyes tracked the movement, but it was too quick to be sure. She'd had a lifetime of pandering to everyone else's wants. It should not trouble her to do it now, especially when her life depended on it. But dancing again, so soon after Alice, felt like a betrayal. "I'm also thinking about my sister."

"What about her?"

"It will sound ridiculous," she stated, her voice rising higher than she expected.

"Nothing is ridiculous."

He at least sounded as if he meant that.

They moved without structure. Not steps, just slow turns of two people unexpectedly holding each other while the piano notes surged. Despite being in the arms of a monster, she found his closeness oddly comforting.

"I haven't danced since she died," Charlotte whispered against his shoulder. "It was something we always did together. Unconventional, I know. We told our father it was a practice for upcoming balls, but in truth, we just enjoyed twirling around aimlessly. Doing that with someone else, it just feels like…" She paused, unsure of the right word to capture what she meant.

Nathaniel pulled her back to look at him, his brows deepening into the bridge of his nose. "Sacrilege."

"Exactly," she said breathlessly, trapped under his widening stare. "Although she stopped dancing long before her death."

"Why?"

"The Eringhorn family. She was engaged to one of them and he would cane her legs when she missed a step. Eventually, my mother made up a lie to get her out of the engagement after they found out he had gotten one of his maids pregnant, but that entire family made it their mission to destroy our lives."

"People are cruel."

Charlotte's lips tilted downward. "I wish I could blame them for my lack of humor."

"You are grieving," he said, tilting her chin so she would look at him, his thumb skimming her jaw. "It is okay to feel solemn."

"That is the problem. I don't feel sad all the time," she admitted for the first time since her sister's death. "I get moments where I don't feel like my entire world is crumbling, and I'm just me again. Then I feel guilty, because I shouldn't be happy while she's..."

"I understand," he said in a low grumble. "When we lose someone, it is not just them we mourn. So many things die along with them. If you're alive for long enough, and lose enough people, you will eventually stop enjoying anything."

Her heart rate picked up, thrumming in her ears so much that she could barely hear the piano. "Is that what happened to you?"

"For a time." He paused and inhaled sharply. "Take it from a master of suppressing happiness out of solidarity. It is not what anyone who loved you would have wanted."

There was something else in her chest that kept gnawing at her every time she came close to enjoying anything. With a slow exhale, she nodded and said, "Whenever I feel happy, I feel guilty. As if I'm living a life stolen from Alice. I just can't understand why I am here and not her," she admitted, unsure why she was suddenly confiding things she kept hidden to a vampire, but she also knew that if she had any chance of surviving she needed to nurture that shred of humanity.

"There is no answer to that," he said. "People die, and sometimes, it is a tragedy."

"Usually people try to give me some reason, like she died so I could discover some hidden strength or something," she replied, gritting her teeth at the sentiments she had received by the many neighbors who paid a visit since the massacre.

"That is an awful burden to place upon you," he stated, and the heaviness in her chest eased up. "I do not believe there is any grand plan where someone dies for the benefit of another. Your life is your own."

"Careful, you're showing your humanity," she said, latching her eyes onto his.

"That," he said, sliding his hand into hers with a gentleness she never expected from him, "Is a dangerous thing to believe."

"Perhaps, but I have this ability," she said, arching into his touch, and her breasts grazed his chest. "I can feel people, the things they're hiding under the surface."

He pressed his other hand firmly against her back, holding her in place. "What is it you feel from me?"

"That you want closeness and that is why you desire mortality, because you're afraid of hurting things you want."

"What about you?" he asked deeply, his gray, heavy-lidded stare boring into hers, pupils flaring. "Do *you* long for intimacy?"

Was he...*flirting* with her?

"Yes," she said, hating the way her body moved of its own accord, leaning into him, longing to devour the inches between them. No. Focus. She needed information. "Only with someone I trust."

His lips brushed the tip of her ear, his heavy exhale heating her lobe. "You can trust me. We want the same thing."

Her blinks slowed as she looked up, leaning into his firm touch. His lips pressed together, a low growl reverberating behind closed lips as he drank her in. With a gentle nudge, he removed what little distance remained between them. The scent of him was in her nose—a woody combination with cedar and musk.

Their faces were so close that if she lifted her chin, her lips would graze his.

"I found a card from your hide and seek game. The Hunt," she blurted to stop herself from doing something she might regret.

"What about it?" he asked softly.

"I want to play."

Her inhale stuttered when he stroked his thumb over her erratic pulse. "Why?"

"So I can win."

A dark chuckle tumbled from his lips. "You believe you can outrun a vampire?"

"Maybe."

"Then you are foolish."

With a step back, she stared into his widening eyes, something dark lurking within. "Perhaps, but I want you to let me try anyway."

"Why would I do that?"

"Because if you win, I will break your curse."

"You will break it anyway," he said, his dark brows knitting together. "Or did you forget we have an agreement?"

She couldn't admit the real reason without undoing all the rapport she'd built with him. She watched as his eyes darkened. The playfulness of minutes ago was now lost to centuries of paranoia.

"I did not forget," she said when his fingers flexed at his side.

He stepped forward but stopped when she flinched. With a glance at her throat, he let out a low groan and said, "That's enough dancing for one night."

"Where are you going?" she asked when he turned his back to her to leave.

With a glance over his shoulder, he mumbled, "To feed. You should find Katherine."

"Wait—" she called out, but he was already gone. With a deep breath, she headed back to her room, the mark on her side worse in his absence. Katherine would have to wait until tomorrow to practice. She needed a bath and cuddles with Duke while she tried to figure out what on earth she was going to do now that The Hunt was out of the question?

Chapter Twelve

It didn't take long that next evening for Charlotte to find Alexander in the library, leaning against the marble mantel with a glass of wine in one hand and a book in the other. Beyond him, faded spines lined the mahogany shelves beyond the long sofa, and carved gargoyles stood as bookends in between various collections.

She breathed in the burned wood, old parchment, and polish before walking to the sofa. "Good evening."

Alexander closed the book and placed it on the ledge. "Miss Lovett. How was your dance with Nathaniel yesterday?"

"It was short," she admitted and sat against the emerald-green pillows. "I asked him if I could take part in The Hunt and he refused me."

Alexander shot her an incredulous look. "How did you find out about that?"

"I found a card, and one of the maids told me the rest," she said, refusing to disclose it was Hartley in case she wasn't supposed to reveal anything to her about the event.

Alexander tipped his glass between his full lips, finishing what she only hoped was red wine. “He had good reason to deny you. Those who play usually end up dead.”

“Unless they’re predators,” she pointed out.

“Indeed.” A wolfish grin carved his face. “Is that what you want? To be a predator?”

“No. I just wanted to play,” she mumbled, and changed the subject before he could press her about her motivations further. “Where is Katherine?”

“I’ll take you to her.”

She nodded, forcing a small smile. “How are preparations for the ball coming along?”

“Invitations have already gone out. Now we must only hope the Avery family are arrogant enough to walk into our trap,” he said, green eyes flaring when he looked at her.

“You were able to reach them then?”

“Naturally. They have a small estate here in central London.”

“If they’re so close by, why haven’t you and Nathaniel gone to them?”

With a tilt of his head, Alexander grimaced. “It would be foolish to fight them on their territory. Witches like the Avery family often buy land in powerful locations where they can congregate. Undoubtedly, their estate is built around their devoted practice area where something terrible has happened with lots of violent energy for them to siphon.”

“So, why haven’t they come here?”

Alexander pointed at the dark window. “Because we have a lot of defenses. Death hounds patrol the perimeter of the grounds, which is one reason Nathaniel was paranoid letting you out. They may obey him, but they can be unpredictable.”

“What are death hounds?”

“Dogs turned into vampires.”

"What? How is that even possible?"

He shrugged. "They were not created by us, but another vampire that has since been exiled. He takes care of them here. They are loyal to him."

"That is so sad. The poor creatures."

"They are well taken care of," he assured.

"What will happen to them on the night of the ball?"

"Nathaniel will ensure they don't attack anyone who comes through these gates. It'll be the witches only chance to enter Sallow Manor without being torn apart by the creatures."

"Is that your only defense?"

"No. We have some protections in place from other witches, like Katherine, but the hounds are our best protection. Speaking of, let's go find her. I believe she is in the chapel."

"You have a chapel?"

He laughed. "Indeed."

"It's just from what you said when we met, you think so little of religion."

"You are correct, but we are not the only inhabitants of the manor. A few members of the staff visit the chapel. Nathaniel allows them their refuge with their God."

"He lets his staff practice their own religion without consequence?"

"Yes."

"That is surprising. It's just that it's a kindness I've not seen afforded in any other noble house. I must ask," she said tentatively, "How do you know Nathaniel? I mean, how did you meet?"

"He saved my life," he said without breaking stride.

"How?"

"By turning me."

Well, that much was obvious, but she got the sense not to keep pushing the subject.

By the time they arrived in the west wing of the manor, her knees were clicking, and ankles were ready to give way. "I'm sorry," she said, leaning over and placing her hands on her thighs.

"Does it hurt to walk?" he asked.

With her shoulders tense, she slowly lifted her gaze to meet his. "Sometimes, yes. Well, most of the time, actually. I don't know what it is, but several years ago I started getting tightness and pain in my body, and it's just gotten worse with time."

"You should have said. I can carry you if the long corridors are too trying."

"There is no need. I just need a moment before we continue."

"We are already here."

Alexander leaned over Charlotte's shoulder, candlestick in hand, and pushed open the heavy wooden door to the chapel. The musty scent mixed with dust, incense, and wax hit the back of her throat. Her eyes landed on Katherine, whose crimson dress was muted in the pale moonlight spilling through the arched, stained-glass panes. Fractured light cast on the stone floor around them, each window depicting angels in their winged forms. Raindrops spilled down their faces like tears from the storm brewing outside.

A Latin prayer left Katherine's lips in rushed whispers, her focus not breaking when the two of them entered.

Alexander's voice came out in a purr. "Praying, Darling?"

She made the cross sign with her fingers over her chest before looking at him and winking. "Not to whom you think." She climbed to her feet, and brushed the dust from the flowing, sheer fabric of her skirt. "If we're going to defeat the Avery family, we can use the aid of every deity. Especially the darkest ones."

She joined them, and linked her arm with Alexander's, while brushing his blond locks behind his ear. "You look a mess, dear."

Charlotte's brows furrowed. Were they together? She'd assumed Katherine was with Nathaniel.

Alexander let out a boyish laugh. "It's been a long day." He revealed his inked palms and tsked under his breath. "Nathaniel had me handwrite every invitation."

Katherine shook her head. "I don't know why you do everything he asks. That's a servant's task."

"I'm indebted to him."

She rolled her expressive brown eyes and looked at Charlotte and said, "Did you enjoy your dance with Lord Sallow?"

Every honeyed word fell from her lips like venom.

"It was adequate," she said carefully, watching Katherine's every shift in expression.

"Now that are you done with your diversions, we should attend to business."

"You mean magic?"

Katherine's lips curved into a wicked grin. "Of course. You need to be able to defend yourself against the Avery witches. We cannot always count on men to keep us safe and it would be a horrible shame if they got to you first and you ended up dead."

Chapter Thirteen

After waving off Alexander, Katherine sat in front of the fire in the library, her legs crossed. Her gloved fingers brushed the top of the stack of four grimoires. "Now that we are alone," she said, opening one to the middle, running her hand over the old, discolored parchment. "Tell me, what happened when you danced with Nathaniel."

"Is this an interrogation?" Charlotte asked, sitting on the other side of the stack of grimoires. "I thought we were practicing?"

"We are and it is not. I am merely curious. Did you kiss him?"

"No," Charlotte replied all too quickly. "Nothing untoward happened."

Yes, he had pulled her so close that she could feel every hard muscle of his torso, and he had given her that rose, but that didn't mean what Katherine thought it did.

"Good."

"You like him?" she asked, the heat of the fire burning her rosy cheeks.

"That is not why I ask," Katherine said, her brown eyes widening. "Alexander mentioned he fed on you."

With a hard swallow, she lifted her fingers to graze her throat. "Does that mean something?"

With a flick of her fingers, she pushed back Charlotte's hair to look at her blemish-free neck, and tsked. "Because, vampires do not feed on mortals and stop." She dropped Charlotte's strands, and the curls bounced around her chest. "Once they get a taste of a mortal's blood, they go into a frenzy and feed not only on their blood, but their emotions and memories too."

"Yes. I got to experience that firsthand."

"It creates a bond, an all-consuming bloodlust to finish what they started. The curse ensures they feel their victims' deaths, that they experience what they do. That bond only breaks at the point of death."

Goosebumps prickled on her chest and upper back, slowly spreading across her skin. "So, he wants to kill me?"

Her mouth quickly dried as she rocked back on her knees, pursing her lips tight. That was why he'd gotten so close to her throat earlier during the dance, why his lips danced around the top of her ear.

A strange swirling sensation sent tingles through her lower torso and thighs. With a shake of her head, she dismissed the memory.

"Yes, I've seen the way he looks at you and while I do not particularly care for you," she confessed without stopping, making Charlotte wince. "I do not wish to see a fellow witch torn apart, nor see Nathaniel and Alexander's only chance at mortality and happiness taken away, because he can't control his impulses. You must not find yourself alone with him again. Ensure Alexander is with you when you must be in the same room as him. Nathaniel has a lot more restraint than other vampires, but alone, in proximity to you, I fear he will snap and tear you apart." Her eyes hooded as she turned around, her back facing the lit fireplace. "Just, keep your distance, and I am certain he will keep his."

A flush crept through her chest, blooming heat in the area over her heart. A surge of energy shot through her veins, as her lips slowly parted, and a lump formed in her throat. Suddenly, she felt like prey. Not that she hadn't before, but it was worse now.

The bloodlust was likely the reason he lured her into the ballroom, and probably the reason he rushed out at the end to feed.

She recalled his fangs brushing her throat, his lips so close to her yesterday, and imagined him devouring every inch of her, and not in an unpleasant way.

"Don't," Katherine warned, and Charlotte jumped. "I recognize that look in your eyes. Don't think about him that way."

"I'm not," Charlotte snapped, her cheeks heating at the thought.

Maybe her mind had gone there for a few moments. He'd helped her with her grief and dark thoughts, and there were times she saw his humanity and wanted nothing more than to nurture it. So yes, for a moment, she thought she'd felt something like the tiniest twinge of a feeling flutter in her stomach. Nonetheless, she would never even consider being intimate with a creature who kept a log of people he ate.

"Good, because even *if* he was attracted to you," she said, with knowing eyes, "the desire to drink from you will always be stronger. Do not be pulled in by him. It will only leave you heartbroken."

"Is that what happened to you?" she asked, sensing the change in her tone.

She laughed, the corners of her eyes creasing. "No, he's a philanderer, a wolf without a heart. We have simply brushed in the past, but I knew what I was getting into. He has quite the stamina."

"You mean—"

"He is diligent in his activities."

Her teeth sank into her bottom lip, eyes squeezing shut for a second, and Charlotte wondered what memory she was reliving, and why she wanted to know more. It wasn't as if she hadn't done the act, although no one knew about the boy who used her for her body, romancing her into believing he loved her before leaving.

"It never meant anything more?" she asked. In the ballroom, she had felt his need for intimacy, that burning longing for wanting something more. Devotion was a key theme in most of the books he read. Charlotte cleared her throat and added, "Surely even a vampire can fall in love."

Katherine adjusted the hairpin in her golden waves and sniffed. "He cannot love like you and me. I don't believe that man has a romantic bone in his body. He is quite mechanical. Talented, with his body, but there is no feeling there. I do not mind it, especially when he fed me his blood after. The high is better than anything else."

Her jaw slacked. "He feeds you his blood?"

"He has before, but not for some time. We have not been intimate since last year. Although I am hoping to have some blood at the ball. It is part of his plan, to spike the drinks."

"Is that how you plan on drugging them?"

"Yes. Their blood is an aphrodisiac to mortals. It dilates our blood vessels, increases blood flow, and makes our hearts beat faster. It also amplifies something up here," she said, placing an index finger to her temple, "that inhibits our senses and makes us more open to suggestion. It is far better than any alcohol or opium." Katherine let out a long, shaky exhale. "Now, focus. Before we begin, we must siphon the dead," she added when Charlotte bit her lip. "Every single spell in this grimoire requires sacrificial magic or—"

"Strong power, siphoned from the dead."

"Yes."

Charlotte placed her hand on the grimoire. "I've read them all a dozen times."

Her eyes lit up. "I assumed you were unpracticed."

"I am, but I've always been curious."

"Good. Fortunately for us, Sallow Manor is haunted and steeped in a history of violent deaths. So, let us siphon one of those poor, lost souls." Katherine extended her lace-gloved fingers to Charlotte. "Now, give me your hand."

"Why?" she asked but took it anyway.

Katherine's green eyes sparkled when she said, "So the dead won't snatch you away once we enter their realm."

Chapter Fourteen

She may have only been teasing, but Charlotte knew what horrors awaited them on the other side. So when Latin incantations spilled from Katherine's lips, a shiver skittered down her spine.

Black, half-melted candles flickered to life from the windowsills, casting shadows over the moonlit glass.

Charlotte's words came out in a long breath. "This is a bad idea."

"We will be okay," Katherine replied, tightening her grip. "They can't hide from us when we're in their realm."

Charlotte's eyes flicked to the door. "Or we can't hide from them."

"They can always see us," she stated, as if that made it any better. "This way we can see them too. Now, help me recite these words. You must use the correct inflections. Follow my lead. You are my anchor for the spell."

"Isn't there another way? I'm not sure I'm comfortable siphoning the dead."

"No, unless you want to sacrifice a living person. Admittedly, that energy would be much stronger, but I am not in the mood to murder anyone tonight."

"You jest, but you don't understand." Charlotte glanced over her shoulder as goosebumps spread over her arms. "The ghosts here have been haunting me since I arrived. I am certain they will see this as an invitation to get even closer to me."

"Then stay close," Katherine warned. "Now, empty your mind and think only of the words on the page."

That was easy for her to say. Her mind was never calm. If it was, she'd be worried. At a minimum, there were at least three anxious thoughts swirling around in her head, along with some background noise that never stopped.

With a heavy breath, she tried to focus. The words all pulled together as they spoke them in unison.

"Permitte nos hunc mundum transire et in alterum ingredi. Velum quod nos separat solve, et spiritum nostrum a corpore separa donec cum mortuis simus."

The tension left her body as the familiar pulse of power, from when she had been in the graveyard, shot outward from her core and into the air. Tatters of gray fell around them like ribbons cut from a sheer curtain they couldn't see until now.

The library shifted into a decayed monochrome version of itself. The wallpaper, which had just been luxurious gold and black damask, was now a muddy maroon that was peeling from the rectangular panels.

A cold draft whistled through the empty fireplace, sending soot swirling across the stone hearth. Katherine squeezed her fingers, and Charlotte turned her head to look at her. Even in the realm of the dead, her green eyes still shone brightly, while the rest of her outfit had faded into a deep, earthy brown.

A layer of mist covered the marble ground, coiling around their crossed legs. Charlotte coughed as a faint scent of decay and rotted wood crept into her nostrils.

"What do we do now?" Charlotte asked, her whisper bouncing off the walls around them in an echo.

With wide eyes, Katherine lifted a finger to her lips. Her lips parted and she mouthed the words, *don't speak.*

They stood together, her knees cracking as she straightened her legs, and they stepped out of their bodies. Their breaths fogged the air, the icy chill creeping in from every side of the fog-soaked ground. The mahogany tables and cabinets were covered in dust and peeling varnish.

Katherine guided her toward the door and past the moth-eaten drapes that moved with no wind and worn shelves filled with the skeletal bindings of books. She glanced back before they walked through the door, staring at their still bodies, covered in an eerie, gray hue.

An icy gust bit at her fingertips, sinking deeper into her core, chilling her to the bone. Her body shook as she suppressed a shiver. With a deep, foggy breath, she followed Katherine into the endless, dark corridor.

Though the hallways were empty, except for the familiar oil portraits that adorned the walls, a feeling of being watched brushed against her senses. She glanced up at the painting depicting the man with a top hat. She'd walked past him several times, even stopping to stare once or twice, but this time was different. An awareness shone from his painted black pupils that made her skin crawl.

With a harsh tug, Katherine pulled Charlotte into an alcove just in time before a harsh, raspy breath sounded from the shadows of the corridor.

Footsteps echoed on the floorboards, the long shuffles growing closer with each step. Charlotte clapped a hand over her mouth, stifling the involuntary gasp threatening to escape.

Her stomach lurched, and her heart hammered frantically against her ribs.

The footsteps were closer now. Just feet away from where they were hiding.

Katherine's lips were pulled between her teeth, her fingernails biting into Charlotte's hand.

She hissed out a breath and yanked her hand away, rubbing her fingers over the crimson indents blooming on her skin.

As the spirit's breath rattled from inches away, Charlotte braced herself to face the ghost from the reflection in the window, and the same who had chased her through the corridor that appeared out of nowhere. Her bottom lip quivered when she envisioned the spirit, with its long dark hair hanging wet around its face, and that too-wide grin filled with rotten teeth.

As the figure rounded the corner, Charlotte noticed her ashen skin and the dark circles under her dull-brown eyes. That ghost was not the one haunting her.

It was a young woman in her mid to late twenties, dressed in maid's clothes with a white, frilly apron tied around her middle.

She couldn't have been much older than Charlotte when she died.

The woman's beauty was evident in her angular features, big eyes, and wavy dark hair. Yet, death had depleted all the radiance from her. Panic settled through Charlotte's ribs when the dead woman turned and faced them, her brown gaze pinning her to the wall. Her pale, split lips fell open, with only a ragged, dry rattle of a breath leaving them in what she assumed was a word.

She just couldn't hear her. The dead didn't talk. But this ghost wanted to. Desperately. She got closer, pointing her ringed finger at Charlotte. Shards of bone jutted out from her broken wrist, and blood seeped from her neck, wetting the ends of her dark hair.

Tears of blood rolled down her cheeks, a sadness creeping in through her bloodshot eyes.

Katherine positioned herself between Charlotte and the ghost, grabbing the woman's arm, muttering Latin under her breath that came out in a rush of unintelligible whispers.

The corridor twisted, spinning them back through the veil in a suction that stole the air from her lungs. Suddenly, she was sucked back into her body in the library. The fire was crackling with orange and red flames. The smell of wood smoke and parchment was heavy in the air. Leather spines adorned every polished shelf, and the grandfather clock let out two loud dongs.

Charlotte glared at Katherine. Her eyes were shut, incantations still spilling from her lips. Without looking at her, Katherine extended her hand in a motion for Charlotte to join her.

Hesitantly, she walked over and Katherine grabbed her fingers before she could protest. Shockwaves shot through her palm, her body absorbing every surge of bubbling energy. The tingles ran through her arms and into her neck in a shiver, before working their way down her spine.

It was *magic.* More than just energy, the power was also a feeling akin to a first kiss, to seeing a perfect starlit sky, and drinking champagne for the first time.

The horror of what had just happened slipped away. The power within her was alive.

It made her feel powerful. And once she'd gotten a taste of it, there was no way she was going back. This magic that sparked her soul to life was just a diluted form running through Katherine, just from one ghost.

She understood now why the Avery family siphoned an entire graveyard of dead witches. They sacrificed people and channeled the energy from an immediate violent death. It was a high unlike any other.

It was so good it was dangerous.

Katherine's green eyes flung open, the whites of them swirling with shadows. "Here," she uttered before pulling Charlotte toward the open grimoire. "This spell will disable the power of anyone in the Avery bloodline." She pointed at the sigils for each of the thirteen witch bloodlines and landed on theirs. "We will carve this symbol on the door they will enter through and infuse it with these spells."

"You are layering spells," Charlotte stated with admiration. "Sigils to hold the power, a spell to siphon the magic, and a spell to transfer it. It's clever. Do you do that often?"

"I've always experimented with magic," she deadpanned, her expression hardening.

"This power," she said, changing the subject, "it is unlike anything I've felt before. It's—"

"Terrifying?"

"Invigorating," Charlotte confessed, her heart racing. It was only when she imagined the weeping woman's soul that a twinge of guilt broke through the addicting high convulsing through her body. "What happened to the ghost? Did we hurt her?"

Katherine arched a blonde brow. "Hurt her? She doesn't have a body."

"She looked like she was in pain."

"It's all emotional. I assure you."

"What is it we did to her exactly? I mean, what will become of her?"

"We siphoned her pain and anguish, that's all. Her spirit will recover. What you're feeling is her emotions converted into energy through our magic. The more violent the pain, the more potent the power. It is only temporary, of course. However, it will suffice so we can cast the disruption spell." Katherine walked to the fireplace and held her fingers over the flames to chase away the leftover chill. "You did well. I've never gone into the Realm of the Dead before, but I suspected with you it would be easier."

Charlotte's brows knitted together. "What does that mean?"

"I was channeling you. Why do you think I needed to hold your hand? You've felt death. It lingers on you. I feel a darkness shrouding your aura. That's how I could cross through the veil. I'm just amazed it worked."

It seemed ridiculous to call what she'd done a violation, but it felt like it, nonetheless. "So my aura is damaged?"

Katherine glanced over her shoulder. "Tainted. You cannot break it. It's not a physical thing."

"I know that, and you know what I was insinuating," she quipped, tired of the condescension in her tone that made her feel like a small child when they were the same age.

With a heavy sigh, Katherine stepped away from the fire and walked back to the grimoire. "Your aura is fine," she stated dismissively. "We must prepare and see if this will work. We can only hope the Avery family will not notice their sigil on the doorway before they enter. Follow me."

Charlotte walked behind Katherine, surprised at how much the magic helped the pain in her joints. While the stiffness was not gone, the burning sensation was almost tolerable.

With a glance down the corridor where they'd met the ghost, Charlotte asked, "How long could we have stayed in the Realm of the Dead?"

"Not long and I warn you not to go there without me. When we travel between realms, our mortal bodies become the perfect empty vessels for demons who want to get a taste of being alive again."

She was certain that the woman haunting her was a darker entity than the ghost. The sentient, creepy smile and a nauseating energy were enough to turn her stomach.

"How can you tell for certain what is a ghost and a demon?" she asked, although she knew a lot from the journal, a practiced witch would know far more.

Katherine's voice echoed around the foyer as they descended the sweeping, dark staircase. "I suppose, the only way to truly know is if they show up in a reflection. Only demons can traverse the veil for long periods, and while in ghosts we see flickers of moments of full-body apparitions or orbs, in demons we can see them in mirrors or—"

"Windows."

"Sure. They can also, occasionally speak into our minds, even paralyze us, temporarily of course."

A lump formed in her throat. That was exactly what had been happening to her.

They reached the front door and Katherine got to work carving the Avery sigil—a wand with two knots—into the side of the wood doorframe where no one would think to look.

She took Charlotte's hand and pressed her other to the marking on the frame, whispering the spell that would disable their magic once they passed the threshold.

While she'd always wanted to use magic and wanted to soak in the moment, her mind was elsewhere. Because the entity had shown up in the reflection of the window and that meant only one thing. A demon was haunting her and that mark on her hip, which was growing with each passing day, couldn't have been a coincidence.

Chapter Fifteen

There were only just one day left until the ball and if she didn't act now, then the Avery witches would surely die.

Ticking from the grandfather clock followed her as she crept down the corridor and into the foyer that next afternoon, careful not to make a sound while everyone else was sleeping.

Sunlight sliced through the stained-glass windows either side of the arched, double doors. She'd almost forgotten how good it felt to bask in the warmth of the sun.

Duke darted ahead of her, stopping in front of the main doors. Fortunately, no staff members were there. She lifted the skirt of her favorite pale-green tea dress, trying to think of anything else but the tightness straining her muscles. The throbbing in her back and knees deepened, the cold of the marble seeping through her slippers. With every step, the relentless discomfort clinging to her every limb worsened.

She knew it was coming after all the physical exertion she had done recently. If she had paced herself, it wouldn't have been as bad, and she knew better. It was getting close to intolerable, but she only had to reach the sigil. Then she could rest.

A groan bubbled in her throat when she reached Duke, who tilted his head, his bright eyes blinking softly. "I'm okay," she whispered but scrunched up her nose.

She looked at the Avery family sigil carved into the wood frame. When she grazed her finger on the wood, a zap of energy shocked into her nail beds.

Laying her palms flat against the wood, she recited the Latin from the grimoire that she'd memorized yesterday. The hum of magic whispered against her fingers as she siphoned the magic from the spell Katherine had placed on it, her heart hammering as every pulse burrowed deeper into her soul.

If any of them discovered what she had done, they'd surely lock her away, maybe chain her up in the cellar, but she had no choice but to take the risk. If Nathaniel's plan succeeded, her own death would follow soon after. Even if she refused to perform the ritual after he discovered the truth, he wouldn't stop trying to make her, and she couldn't fathom thinking about the various torture methods he likely learned over the centuries.

She needed more time to figure a way out of this and unfortunately that meant keeping their enemies alive a little longer.

A wave of power washed through the room, making her gasp. The power ran through her like currents, spiking in her torso. She pulled away from the sigil, heart racing when the last of the magic pulsed into her fingertips. She waved her hand over the door, but nothing except an echo of a spell was left lingering in the splinters of the carved marking. She only hoped no one would notice before the ball.

The mark on her hip burned when the magic seared back into her body, sparking pain into the necrotic center. Despite applying the tonic daily, it had only gotten worse.

Now run, while you have the chance.

The voice rattled through her skull, making her jump.

Shaking her head, she stepped back, gazing through the window beside the door. Even if she did somehow make it past the death hounds, she had no coin to get out of London, or England for that matter. She couldn't return to her manor, and they would never stop hunting her.

No, the answer lay with magic. It had to. She just needed to get hands on her grimoires again without Katherine looking over her shoulder.

The answers lie in the Realm of the Dead. Return there.

The hiss of words ached in her forehead.

"No!" She stepped backward, Duke's eyes tracking her as she did. Was it her own thoughts urging her into those things, an inner monologue brought on from trauma like Nathaniel said, or something worse, like the demon that had been stalking her?

She wasn't even sure what was real anymore.

Turning quickly, she hurried back to the stairs before she gave into her baser urges and fled out the door without a plan.

The muscles in her legs spasmed when she climbed the stairs, despite placing all her weight on the polished banister. With labored breaths, she made it to the top before collapsing under her own weight, letting out a scream when her ankle rolled and knee let out a crack.

No matter how hard she tried to pull herself up, she couldn't.

After a couple of minutes of sitting there, she pulled herself into a crouching position and grunted. She couldn't keep going. It was too much for her body. Taking a quick nap on the floor was looking more appealing.

"What happened?" Nathaniel's voice sounded from somewhere behind her. He appeared in front of her in a flash, his hair a mess, dressed only in a white nightshirt.

Frenzied, smoky eyes inspected her entire body by the time she spluttered, "Nothing. Really. I simply tripped."

The shooting pains searing into her calves were threatening to buckle her legs again. Her expression crumpled as she whistled a breath through gritted teeth, her eyes squeezing shut.

"You are hurt. Is it the sickness that confines you to your bed?"

He knew, but only because he'd peered into her damned soul and memories the night he'd bitten her.

"Yes," she admitted in a hiss when the pain became too much to carry. "It happens sometimes, when I walk too much, or do any exercise. I was looking for Hartley," she lied, still feeling the remnants of the magic she had siphoned in her hands.

Heat rose through her chest and into her cheeks, reddening her skin. Thick tears slid over her freckles, and she quickly wiped them away, angry at herself for showing this to him. He would think she was being hysterical.

Yet, when she glanced up at him from her crouched position, he didn't wear the same weary look that everyone else had who'd witnessed her at her very worst. Lines creased the corners of his eyes as her jaw locked to hold back another sob.

"You should have told me," he grumbled and kneeled to place an arm around her.

"Oh no, you don't have to—"

He lifted her into his arms before she could protest.

"Where are you taking me?" she asked, tense in his hold.

"To your room."

He looked down at her as he walked at a mortal's pace, careful when turning the corners down the corridor. When they reached the doorway, he scraped his back so she wouldn't be anywhere near the frame and placed her on the bed with Duke in tow.

His wet nose bumped her chin after he jumped on her chest, his purrs vibrating through her ribcage and into her soul. It somehow helped take the edge off the ache.

Nathaniel took a step back, his breaths heavying. "Where does it hurt the most?"

"It's not localized," she said in a whisper. "It's all over, everywhere."

With a labored breath, she tangled her fingers in Duke's fur and closed her eyes. Even the act of stroking up hurt her wrist. Until now, she hadn't realized how bad it had gotten. The exhaustion went beyond physical tiredness. A deep-seated weariness settled over her, eclipsing her every thought.

"I will call a doctor," he said, watching flickers of discomfort crease her soft features.

"No, please don't. I've seen four doctors, and they all think it's a nervous disorder. Except for one who said the pain is a manifestation of my dissatisfaction from not yet being married. Another believed me to be malingering."

"How long have you had this?"

"Years," she confessed. "It comes and goes. "

In an effort to undo the tightness in her shoulders, she rolled them back, groaning as she turned onto her side.

She stretched her neck, letting out a soft moan, and quickly opened her eyes. *The bond.*

Katherine told her not to be alone with Nathaniel and there she was, elongating her neck in front of a vampire that craved her above all else.

Slowly, she sat upright when Nathaniel did.

"Let me help you," he offered in a deep tone. Before she could react, one set of his fangs elongated, the sharp points slicing into the skin of his wrist. With a swipe of his thumb, he collected a few drops and brought them to her lips. "Drink," he murmured, eyes darkening as he tipped her head back. "My blood suits you," he said silkily when he painted her mouth with it, leaning back to appreciate his art.Her mouth fell open and in a moment of madness and desperation, she licked the blood from her lips, surprised at how un-blood-like it tasted. His essence tingled on her tongue, sending sharp shocks into the roof of her mouth and throat. She dragged her fingers up her neck, her palm pressing over the area that tingled with desire.

"More," she begged when the tingling shot through her body, eclipsing the pain in her legs.

Wild-eyed, he pushed the wound on his wrist to the mouth. She closed her lips around it, swallowing as mouthfuls leaked into her mouth.

Katherine was right. It was unlike anything she'd experienced. She never would have thought she would enjoy drinking blood, but his was sweet, vibrant, and fizzled on her tongue like an explosion of bubbles. The wound quickly healed, and he pulled back, watching as crimson liquid dripped down her chin and onto her fingers.

Duke purred from the sheets beside her, as if he could feel the effects too.

Nathaniel's other hand ran up her back, sinking into her curls, his thumb stroking the back of her head.

"Good girl," he said in a deep purr as he stared down through hooded eyes, lips slightly parted, as if he was enjoying it as much as she was.

With her tongue, she licked the rest of the blood on her lips, before cleaning herself with the sleeve of her nightgown.

Lying back down, she shifted back onto herself, her back facing Nathaniel, and mumbled, "You taste good."

With a low hum, he pressed his lips against her hair. "It will help, but it won't heal you permanently."

"I've tried everything the doctors suggested," she whispered with her eyes closed. "Nothing has helped, but that does."

"There are so many more things we can try."

"We?"

"After you break my curse, I can help you. I have the means," he said, likely referencing his wealth and connections.

"Why would you do that?"

"Move onto your stomach," he ordered after seeing her wince again, and entirely ignoring her question. She did but instinctively pulled her hair around her throat.

Hands landed on her shoulders as the bed dipped behind her from Nathaniel's weight. He pressed his fingertips onto her shoulders, releasing the tension woven into her muscles. Every touch glided over the contours of her shoulders and neck, each stroke unraveling the knots. His strokes were firm, but gentle, the kneading moving up to the back of her neck.

She wanted to ask him why he did that, or to stop him so he wouldn't get too close to her throat, but his massage felt too good. A sigh whispered from her lips as tingles cascaded down her spine, pooling in her lower back.

Time fell away with each ebb and flow of her breaths, surrendering to his strong fingers. Somehow, he knew exactly where to press harder and when to go lighter, as if he could sense what she was feeling.

Duke watched them both, his paw on the top of her hand, claws softly extending out every so often as if to say he was there and wasn't going to let anything happen to her.

He ran his palms over her back and then worked his fingers up her neck, behind her ears and into her hair. A second, involuntary moan whimpered in her throat when he massaged her head, releasing the pressure from her building headache.

When he eventually stopped, she shifted back onto her side and looked at him. Sweat beaded her skin, sticking strands of her black hair to her forehead.

"Katherine told me about the bond," she said as the pain dissolved into the usual low thrum of agony—her normal. Slowly, a fire crept through her thighs, pooling between them and her blood-painted lips pouted when he didn't immediately answer. Duke jumped off the bed, spotting something in the hallway behind the open door and darted out.

She watched him leave and turned her attention back to Nathaniel.

"You're feverish," he said.

"Don't do that."

His brow creased. "What?"

"Ignore my questions."

"You didn't ask me one."

Her chest heaved, heart racing. Katherine also told her what vampire blood would do to her, and she wasn't lying. Her gaze drifted south, and a blush crept up into her cheeks as she caught sight of his length beneath his thin nightshirt. He was huge and he wasn't even erect.

"*Charlotte,* don't." Her name left his mouth in a plea and God had it had never sounded so good.

A twinge nestled into the crevices of her ribcage, making it harder to breathe. Heat throbbed in her lower stomach when he placed his palms on his knees, his fingers flexing. All she could think was how she wanted them between her legs, kneading the tension building between them. She arched herself against the sheets, a whimper leaving her lips.

"It's the blood," he said, his voice tight with restraint. "It will pass. I must return to my room."

"Wait," she said, not sure why she needed him to stay. Or why she wanted him to. It was the blood, but intermingled with the desire that already confused her, he was suddenly completely irresistible. Especially when his fangs slid out over his lips. Heat flushed her cheeks when she thought about all the places she wanted to feel them on her, sliding into her thighs, between her legs.

"Stay," she said breathily. "I know you feel it too," she said, her stomach dipping at her newfound courage. It was only lust, but it was undeniable and right then, it was all she could think about.

His nostrils flared. "Careful, little lamb."

"I'm tired of being careful," she confessed and licked her lips. "I want to taste you again. I want to—"

"What Katherine said was true," he interrupted her, his eyes darkening when she sat herself up and leaned toward him, looking at him in a way she hadn't before. "When I drank from you, it created a link between us, one that is usually broken by death. Your blood was in my veins, your emotions and memories mixing with my own. I never let anyone live before, and since I did, all I can think about day and night," he said in a deep, baritone voice stalking closer, slowly bringing his lips so close the bottom grazed over hers, "is tearing open your throat and devouring you until there is nothing left."

She dragged her fingers over her throat, breath hitching. "You wouldn't. You need me."

"I am trying," he growled. "But the thought of you consumes me. I crave you, Charlotte Lovett." His lips twitched. "I crave your death."

She swallowed thickly, her mouth drying. His words dimmed the effect of his blood, although heat still coursed through her.

They remained locked in eye contact until he grunted and turned away without looking back, stalking out of the room, leaving her behind in a puddle of hormones and embarrassment.

Chapter Sixteen

Later that evening, Charlotte awoke to Nathaniel's grave voice resonating through the dark of her bedroom. "You're awake."

The thought of him so close scorched a path to her thighs, a mixture of fear and lust dragging her breaths. "You shouldn't be here," she whispered into the darkness, hesitantly climbing out of the bed, dragging the sheet with her. "We can't be alone."

While he needed her alive to break his curse, he was going against his nature and if they were alone, he might not be able to stop himself.

I crave you.

His words from yesterday haunted her, the sound still purring in her ears.

I crave your death.

Their dynamic had been established since the moment he'd first pressed her against the wall in Lovett Manor. He was a wolf, and she was a lamb, meant to be sacrificed for the satisfaction of the predator. It was foolish of her to believe she could reason with the beast, when his true nature desired to slaughter her.

A pair of gray eyes pinned her from the doorway. She backed up to the bed, her calves hitting the iron frame. "Don't," she intoned, her thighs clenching when he walked over to her, one hand in his pocket, the thick veins of his arms showing from under his rolled-up sleeves.

The high from his blood carried her senses far from reason.

It was not Nathaniel who walked into the spray of moonlight in front of her, but the monstrous version of him. His pupils slit vertically against a charcoal black and saliva glistened on the three rows of razor-sharp fangs that sucked in labored breaths.

With a slow tilt of his head, not once breaking his intrusive hold on her gaze, Nathaniel pressed a clawed finger under her chin. A low growl rumbled in his chest when he removed the distance between them, tilting her chin with the curled knuckle of his index finger so she couldn't avert her eyes.

Not that she could even if she wanted to. Staring into the soul of a vampire was as captivating as it was terrifying. Sparks shot through her stomach and with one stuttered breath, she whispered, "I'm the only one who can break your curse."

"I only need a taste," he said in a deadly purr and pushed back her hair so he could lean down and run his tongue over her racing pulse.

Her knees buckled and she landed on the bed, kicking back against the sheets when they tangled around her legs and he climbed on top of her. She couldn't die. Not like this.

If she screamed, Alexander might hear her and maybe he would stop him. But she did not scream. All she could focus on was his body pressed against hers, his erection rubbing against her inner thigh with his every movement.

"I could smell your tempting blood from my bedroom," he said, dragging his lips on her throat, over her clavicle, creating a path all the way to her earlobe.

Every muscle in her body tensed, her stomach clenching when he pressed his hardness against her undergarments, directly over her throbbing clitoris, the thin veil of fabric, a woefully flimsy barrier between them. Her hips bucked salaciously, curious fingers running over his muscles, taut with definition under his shirt.

She had to stop.

Now.

He hiked her nightgown to her hip, one hand palming the curve of her ass, the other dragging into the thickness of her hair. Fisting several curls, he angled her head until her neck was fully revealed.

As they embraced, her nipples, already peaked and aching, pressed urgently against him. She had never known such a primal need, a wetness that throbbed, a desperate yearning for something more. He groaned and wrapped an arm around her back, crushing her against him. With buttons scattering, she ripped off his shirt, displaying his sculpted physique.

A sigh loosed from her lips when he sank his fangs into her throat, arching her back into him as her blood leaked down her neck and onto her chest.

His cock throbbed desperately against her, dripping desire over her nightgown, soaking it through as he sucked at her pulse, devouring every drop with unbidden, savage desire. Was he aroused at the thought of killing her?

Suddenly, the room twirled into darkness and her eyes flung open.

With a jolt, she jumped up in her bed and pressed her palm to her throat, relieved to find smooth, unbitten skin and that the bite had been a fabrication of her unconscious mind. But if that was true, why did her fingertips tingle as if in anticipation mere seconds before she tested the unblemished spot?

At the thought of his fangs, a tightness wound its way through her, aching to be undone. She slipped a hand between her legs, letting out a soft moan when she glided over her swollen, throbbing clit toward her opening, drenched in arousal. What the Hell was she doing?

Nathaniel had embedded himself in her subconscious and she allowed it to happen. The air stalled in her lungs, momentarily incapable of normal functionality.

In the dream, she didn't fight him. Instead, letting him bite her knowing it would lead to her death, all because she was turned on. *Desperately turned on.*

His blood was as addictive as it was dangerous and all she could think about was having more, the craving unrelentingly worrisome.

Begrudgingly, she removed her fingers despite wanting to continue, but remembering the fact of his inevitable plans for murdering her was too much for her brain to process.

She jerked backward, her body knocking into the headboard, pain radiating from the back of her skull to her shoulders. Wrestling with her contradictory thoughts, she allowed her eyes to run lazily over the length of the room, only stopping when something flashed in her peripheral vision.

With a whip of her head, she turned to look at the dark reflection in the window. There was nothing there. Yesterday's events flooded her mind. She bent at her waist, fingers crowning her tender head, and squeezed her eyes shut. Slowly, she climbed from her warm nest of quilts and pillows, her stomach still in knots. Trying to ignore the heavy ache in her groin, she walked to the bathing room.

Duke was nowhere to be seen, which should have been her first clue that something was wrong.

The room dropped several degrees and the sense of eyes burning a hole in her back brushed goosebumps over her neck. She wasn't alone.

In a slow turn, Charlotte braced herself as best she could for what was standing behind her.

The bloodshot, glassy eyes of the spirit they had siphoned met hers. Shadows encircled her drooping lids, her pale lips cracking when the ghost's lips fell open, a shiny liquid oozing from the split.

"It's you," Charlotte said with a whimper.

The apparition pointed at her hip, index finger trembling so hard the ring crowning the digit wavered slightly as Charlotte stared, but she could still discern the details. The black ring was carved with the letter A.

The words slid from her lips before she knew she'd spoken. "How did you die?"

With a lift of her palm, the spirit placed her hand over the puncture wounds now visible on her throat.

"Nathaniel killed you," Charlotte whispered, and the woman nodded, bloody tears leaking from her sockets.

Fading faster, flickers of her body moved beyond the veil so only pieces of her remained.

The ghost's eyes widened dramatically, and when she looked over Charlotte's shoulder, her mouth parted wider than should be natural in a silent scream.

Less than a second later, the ghost vanished, and Charlotte spun on her heel, spotting the demon staring at her in the reflection of the window, standing just inches from her with a sadistic, toothy grin.

The candle tumbled from her grasp as a scream tore from her throat and she ran into the bedroom. Closing the door, she lit every candle and closed the drapes.

A wave of nausea rose in her stomach, and the withdrawals from the magic and Nathaniel's blood drained the little energy she had left. At the least, the pain in her joints had gone back to its normal thrum of aching and tightness. For a moment, she wondered if she had hallucinated his hands kneading the tension from her muscles. Because why would a man, who wanted nothing more than to kill her, ease her suffering?

A sudden rush of voices flooded her mind along with a tightness clutching her chest, as if someone had wrapped their hands around her racing heart. The room twisted, its edges blurring until only fleeting glimpses of color remained. The veil between worlds flickered momentarily, immersing her in the stench of decay before pulling her back to her own world.

She screamed, her fingers throbbing against her temples as a blinding pain erupted through her skull.

Join us.

The word was spoken in several fractured voices. Ghosts flickered in and out of her view. The sound of the window unlatching on its own sent shooting pains into her chest.

No.

Not the window.

With a howl of the wind, the drapes swayed, revealing the tall arched window and the demon's reflection in it.

Stop!

She jumped up and pulled them closed, but the voices in her head only grew louder.

Jump. Before it's too late.

"Before what's too late?" Charlotte spluttered, tears pouring from the corners of her eyes as she fought against an unnatural wind.

"Ouch!" Something hot stabbed her in the hip. She jumped, wincing, and lifted the skirt of her nightgown to reveal the bite, which had covered her entire hip and waist in a purple and gray hue. Blisters surrounded the area, a couple of them oozing yellow pus. Grimacing, she pressed her fingers against the mushy skin and hissed out a breath.

The spirits consumed her thoughts until she couldn't grasp anything but threads of her fractured inner monologue.

Duke's yowl sliced through the air. His paws barely touched the ground as he sprinted across the room, stopping under the window. With pointed ears and a wagging tail, he crouched lower to the ground.

The wind stopped, the voices lifting and the heaviness of the room quickly dissolved, as if nothing untoward had happened.

With trembling lips, Charlotte peeked at the reflection in the glass, a loud exhale rattling from her mouth. The demon was gone.

"You really are my familiar, aren't you?" she asked, leaning forward so she could run her fingers over his sleek body. He turned, his yellow eyes closing softly when he looked at her. "Are you a spirit?" He climbed into her lap, paws batting her dark curls. She ran her finger over the glossy, black fur on his stomach and smiled. "You're definitely not a demon," she continued. "Or if you are, you are the cutest demon there has ever been."

His soft meow calmed her racing heart, and everything suddenly felt brighter. She brought him to her face, pressing her cheek against his comforting, warm body. "Don't leave me again."

Long, deep purrs vibrated through his chest and into her face.

Minutes passed in silence as she held Duke, her only friend in the entire world. Every so often, he would drag his paw over her stomach and hip. He wasn't the only one worried about the bite. If she told a doctor, they would use hot metal on the wound or bleed her out. Neither of which she wanted to do considering the last time she had an infection, the cure left her bedridden for weeks.

If only she could get her hands on her grimoires, which should have been easy considering they were *hers.* Nathaniel wouldn't let her practice from them on her own. Which was ridiculous, and if she wasn't so afraid of what he might do to her, she would find him and give him a piece of her mind.

I crave your death.

Those same words kept ensnaring her mind in an endless loop of thorny vines. Katherine was right. Being alone with him was a terrible idea. Especially when she couldn't get the thought of his hands on her body out of her head.

In a sudden leap, Duke darted across the floor, paws patting over something unseen by Charlotte. She jolted, torn from her dangerous thoughts of the vampire.

"What is it you have there?"

The points of his ears curled inward, his body crouching back and tail flicking. With a groan, she leaned forward to see under him, but his loud hiss stopped her from moving any closer. He'd never hissed at her like that, not with his fangs showing.

"What's wrong?"

Something wriggled under his paws. Charlotte glimpsed the large, glossy brown body of a cockroach and tsked under her breath. "Let him go."

With a flick of his head, he let out another violent hiss, but she wasn't going to let him kill a creature in front of her. What he did in his own time was none of her business, but to see an insect tormented like that was too much.

"Duke, I mean it! Enough."

With her hands around his body, she snatched him away. Duke writhed in her hold, his claws dragging over her wrist, but she didn't care. The poor, tiny cockroach scuttled away quickly, antennas twitching when he reached the edge of the floorboards as if the insect was thanking her. In a flash, he was gone and she let Duke go who jumped over to where the cockroach had disappeared.

She stood, crossing her arms over her chest when he whipped his head back and growled. "I'm sorry, Duke, but I won't allow that in front of me." With a huff, she added, "What you do in the gardens is none of my business."

It was hypocritical, but if she didn't have to witness it, then that was fine. He was an animal, and the primal urge, no, deep-seated drive to hunt was a part of him. Yet, if she could aid a helpless prey in its escape, knowing firsthand how it felt to be the target, she would.

Loud ticks sounded from the wall clock, pulling her focus. The gold pendulum swayed back and forth. Tapping echoed from the other side of the door, and Charlotte froze.

Hartley's voice sounded through the room, and she sighed in relief. "Miss, are you awake?"

"Yes, yes. Please, come in."

"How are you this evening?" she asked as Hartley placed a tea tray on her dresser.

Charlotte quickly combed her fingers through her curls, taming them back, and wiped the sheen of sweat from her forehead. "Do you ever see ghosts here?"

Hartley's face blanched. "Sometimes I hear things." She tucked back a blonde ringlet that had escaped under her white cap and looked around. "Knocking, footsteps, you know. The attic is the worst. I hate going up there."

"Why do you need to go into the attic?" she asked.

"Lord Sallow often takes his tea up there."

"He drinks tea?" she asked, surprised that was the first question that came to mind. "Although I have seen them drink whiskey and wine. I just assumed they'd only be able to tolerate blood."

"They can eat, but it tastes like ash to them. The alcohol gives them somewhat of a sensation, from what Mr Young has told me, but the tea is just habit." Lowering her voice to a whisper, she leaned forward and said, "I think Lord Sallow takes it to feel more human."

"Why does he go to the attic?"

Hartley fell silent, pursing her lips as if she wished she could take back the slip in statement.

Charlotte leaned forward, gripping the edge of the mattress. "Please, Hartley. Tell me."

"I should not have said anything, Miss. Please, put it from your mind."

"Of course, I will."

She would not.

With a tense breath, she nodded and rolled back against the headboard as Hartley poured her tea.

"I can do that," Charlotte offered, and Hartley shook her head.

"No need at all. Miss Ellenwood would like you to join her in preparing for the ball tomorrow night.
Would you like help dressing?" she asked, replacing the teapot in the center of the silver tray. "

Her stomach knotted at the thought of them already preparing for it.

"No, it is okay. Thank you," she said, picking at her cuticles. "You have been here for some time, correct?"

"Two years, Miss. Hopefully soon that will change."

She nodded. "I understand why you want to become a vampire, but do you not worry that would lose touch with your humanity?"

Hartley shook her head and handed Charlotte a small teacup. "I'd only kill those who deserve it. If you do not require anything else, I should go and serve Lord Sallow."

"In the attic?"

Hartley smiled but didn't say anything.

"Why is it only you serve me?" Charlotte asked before Hartley could leave. "I know there are more staff."

"Lord Sallow asked me to take care of you. He doesn't trust most of his staff, especially not the men. He wanted them all to stay away from you."

Her stomach clenched. "I didn't know that."

"How could you? You're in good hands here, Miss. You are his chance at a fresh start, at redemption."

Her heart palpitated. "Why does he need his curse to break to get that?"

"Because he believes himself to be a monster and by God is he right. He is adept at savagery, Miss. I've cleaned up enough after him to see how he leaves his victims. Alexander and the others who come don't come close. I think that's why he is so desperate to become mortal. Since you've arrived, he's fed three, sometimes four times a day. It used to be once or twice a week."

An icy slither wrapped around her, sinking through her pores. She brushed her fingers against her throat. She had a good idea why that was. The bond was driving him to madness, pushing him to destroy everyone else instead of her.

Chapter Seventeen

After searching for thirty minutes, she'd finally found a staff member to direct her to the attic.

She had gone completely mad. That, or her intrusive thoughts were correct, and she did have a death wish.

Slowly, Charlotte cracked open the small, black door at the end of the dim hallway from Nathaniel's bedroom, revealing an enclosed, spiraling staircase. With a deep breath, she took one stone step at a time, wondering what he would do when he saw her. The last time they'd been together replayed in her mind.

Cut yourself now. Feed the beast until he cannot stop. There is no better way to die.

The sudden voice in her mind jolted her, pausing her mid-step. She didn't want to die. At least, she didn't think she did.

Did she?

You are turning into your father.

She shook her head, repeating to herself in a whisper, "My thoughts are not who I am. I do not want to die," until the voice drowned into the rest of the noise in her head.

Her calves ached as she climbed the remaining stairs, the walls narrowing on either side, the darkness only relieved by gaslight when she walked out into the attic.

Exposed rafters covered the steeply pitched roof, and at the very back of the room, the moon shone through a circular window, casting shadows on the floorboards from the diamond-patterned tracery.

The hard muscles in Nathaniel's back tensed when the boards creaked as she hesitantly closed the distance between them, spotting the tall mirror in front of him, encased in a gold frame. His eyes latched onto her in the reflection, and the harsh line of his jaw clenched.

"You shouldn't be here."

She glanced at the gas lamp set upon a stack of old, leather suitcases covered in cobwebs, to the old, green armchair, and cabinet filled with an array of items.

"I needed to speak to you, after what happened," she said softly.

He rolled back his broad shoulders, straightening his posture. "There is nothing to discuss. You were intoxicated with my blood."

Her cheeks pinched with heat as she tipped her head back to look at him, heart pounding frantically against her ribcage. "Not that part."

His glare bore into her, the gray in them darkening like mortuary smoke. "You came to find me, on your *own*," he stated, disbelief caressing every word, "So you could talk to me about how I desire nothing more than to kill you?"

She nodded, recognizing how foolish that was, but she had to confront him. "I don't believe you will kill me."

His brows flicked up. "No?"

"You can control yourself."

"Is that a challenge?"

"What else would it be?" she asked. "The ball is tomorrow and if you cannot be around me, then your plan will not work."

It wouldn't work anyway, but he didn't know that.

"Why did you really come up here?" he asked and she swallowed hard, a lump forming in her throat.

What could she say that wouldn't make her sound pathetic? Certainly not the truth, that being around him made her feel better, how his advice grounded her, or that his touch made her feel alive.

Perhaps because she was worried she had no way out of this and hoped the flicker of humanity in him would spare her when the time came.

What a ridiculous thing to consider.

"I've been seeing the ghost of one of your victims," she said, deciding on that out of the many things that swarmed her mind. "The same one I told you about before, but she keeps haunting me. I don't know what she wants, but I feel as if I am going crazy."

He shoved his hands in his pockets, disappointment washing over his features. "That is something Katherine can help you with."

She frowned. "You're the one who killed whoever the spirit was. She looked sad, angry too."

"Well, yes," he said incredulously. "What ghost wouldn't be if they were murdered?"

"I think she wants something from me."

He took a step back, letting out a low groan, the sound rumbling in his chest. "Must you insist on helping every damned thing that crosses your path?"

Was he...*flustered?*

"You are upset with me."

"Frustrated," he corrected. After a sharp inhale, he closed his eyes, and let out a long, deep breath. "I apologize. I find it hard to be alone with you."

"I know," she whispered.

"Try hanging rue and rosemary over your bedroom door," he said after a brief pause. "I've heard it repels evil."

"What if the spirit is not evil?"

"I really consume little else, except for you," he confessed, leaning forward to drag a finger down her neck, rooting her to the spot. He quickly recoiled and offered her the armchair. "You are correct. I need to control myself. Soon, the bond will be broken, and things can be different."

His words ached with something she wanted to dissect but was scared to try.

"Speaking of, is everything ready for the ball?"

"Yes," he said, and relief flooded her. They must have still believed the spell on the entrance was intact.

"What if your plan doesn't work?" she asked tentatively. "I mean, if the Avery witches don't come or something else happens?"

"They will not pass on the opportunity to get close to you. I assure you, once they enter my manor tomorrow, they will not be leaving." Her eyes closed gently and he said, "do not worry, I won't let them hurt you," mistaking her fear for what the witches might do to her and not what would happen if they died.

"Mortality will not give you a fresh start," she stated, broaching the subject that had lingered since he'd said he was undeserving, since Katherine and Alexander made revelations to her about him.

"Do not say anything else," he warned, and faced the mirror.

"What is it you see?" she asked when he grimaced at his reflection.

"A rabid beast."

"You know," she said, stepping up beside him. "Sometimes, we need monsters to help us fight against the true devils in this world."

"I am the devil in this world."

She gave him a look. "I do not see that."

"No, but we have already established you see the best in anyone and anything, apparently."

"Does that frighten you?" she asked when he winced, and he averted his eyes from whatever image haunted him in his reflection.

"It makes it harder to keep you alive, when you're so easy to kill."

He almost smiled and she took it as a sign to relax, and took a seat in the dusty, green armchair to rest her throbbing feet. "Why do you come up here? To look in the mirror?"

"To remind myself of what I am," he stated. Also, as a child, I'd often sleep in the garret when I was afraid. Now, the loft is where I store everything I want to remember."

"Or everything you want to forget," she said, pulling back one of the oil paintings leaning against the chair, covered in dust. She let it go and looked at him, standing before the window, his hands in his pockets, his hair unruly as always.

"Is that a heart?" She asked upon looking closer at the small display cabinet. Slowly, she stood and walked to the glass panels. "A *human* heart?"

"Yes."

She examined it closer, wiping away a layer of dust on the mahogany cabinet with her index finger. The pristine jar was filled to the brim with a clear liquid, and the organ inside, pale and brown.

"That is…"

"Horrifying?"

"Yes," she admitted, "but only because it is the cleanest item in this cabinet. You polish the glass like a trophy."

"It belonged to the first good man I killed."

"An odd thing to commemorate."

"It was when I lost all hope and truly embraced what I am," he explained and she tsked, stepping back.

"What are you, Nathaniel? A vampire, yes, but that does not make you evil," she challenged, desperate to break his tie to wanting mortality, to desiring nothing more than to break his curse simply because he did not think he was deserving of anything with it.

"I should know what evil is, little lamb. I've consumed it. Embodied it. Created it."

"By turning other vampires?"

His face remained stoic as he let out a humorless laugh. "Yes, but my sins go back before then. Vampires are nothing compared to the witches I grew up with."

Her throat tightened as she swallowed hard. "You mean your family?"

"Yes." He leaned forward, hands clasped on his knees, staring at the ground before slowly lifting his gaze to meet hers. "I was betrothed to a powerful witch, you see, when I was still human."

"You were in love?" she asked, brows rising.

"No," he said with a scoff. "My mother arranged the entire affair. My betrothed was a witch from your bloodline."

Goosebumps pricked over her skin. Every so often, she forgot what he had done, and the reminder pierced her soul like an icy dagger.

He continued, turning to look at everything but her.

"She practiced sacrificial magic, the woman promised to me. She became obsessed with gaining more power. I'd known her since I was a child, but she was older. My mother's friend had when I became of age, she set her sights on me. The moment I became a vampire, I broke off the engagement, knowing there wasn't a damned thing anyone could do about it." With a sigh, he added, "It was a crueler world then. Women were killed constantly, accused of dealing with the devil, most of the accusations unfounded. Except for the ones against her. The witch bloodlines were obsessed with protecting themselves against persecution. I understood it, but their methods were not something I tolerated. They killed hundreds of innocents in their quest for more power, and my former fiancée became the most infamous child killer in all of London. So, I tore out her throat before she could become untouchable."

"Is that what you mean by your sins?" she asked, jaw slacking. "That is not your fault."

"She swore to me she was going to stop practicing sacrificial magic when she believed she would become my wife until I broke her heart."

"You didn't make her that way. People have their hearts broken every day and do not murder innocents as a result. She was already inclined toward darkness from what you said. It had taken root in her long before you."

"It bloomed in my abandonment of her."

Charlotte's heart ached when she looked at him, when he stood, shoulders back as if he had the weight of the world on them. "She did not become evil over losing you."

"You cannot know that," he barked and she clicked her tongue.

"No?"

"No." He faced her, and she crossed her arms.

"Don't be so conceited, Nathaniel."

"Excuse me?"

"You're excused," she said, jutting her chin. "You think you made her evil, but I say you didn't. You are not so special that a woman would abandon all her morals in your absence."

His pupils darted around her face, searching her expression, before the corners of his mouth curved with tension, and he laughed for the second time since they'd met. It was infectious, boyish, and she loved the deep, hearty sound.

Through hooded eyes, his smile settling back into a smirk, he said, "You might be right."

"I usually am," she teased, and his dimple deepened.

"I must leave. I have some final checks to go over for the guest list for tonight," he said silkily, her gaze following the path of his fingers when he pushed back a stray curl, tucking it behind her ear. Slowly, he brushed his thumb over her cheek, before pulling away. "Do you want me to carry you back to your room?"

Her chest heaved when his hand landed on her waist, eyes softening when he looked at her. "I'm okay," she promised, even though her muscles screamed at her in protest.

"Do you know your nose scrunches when you lie?"

He noticed that?

Her eyes widened.

"I'm not—"

"Don't be stubborn. Hold on to me," he commanded. "I'll take you back so you can get some rest. We're going to need all our strength for tonight."

As she wrapped her arms around his neck, his breaths hot against her throat, she glanced at the mirror and jolted when she saw a flicker of the demon's reflection, its humorless grin in contrast to the entities furious eyes when she glared at them before he whisked her out of the attic and to her room.

Chapter Eighteen

Charlotte pondered how many humans they had invited to the ball to make it appear legitimate, not that the Avery witches would ever be fooled into thinking it *wasn't* a trap. However, the clever caveat behind Nathaniel's plan relied on that reticence.

She only hoped that no innocents would get caught in the crossfire of their supernatural war. Though unfortunately, Alexander's words, spoken earlier that night when he collected her, did nothing to ease her nerves. What name had he used to address the arriving guests? That was it. *Collateral.*

Taking a sharp breath, she glanced at Alexander before descending the staircase and into the ballroom. Her painted fingernails ran over the intricate carvings of the balustrade as she looked down at the guests. There had to be at least four hundred people in attendance, most of them familiar faces from high society. It shouldn't have been surprising. Nathaniel was not just any vampire. He was a lord, and sometimes she forgot that.

The velvet skirts of her dress billowed around her in a dark storm cloud, the glitter shimmering against a velvet stream of midnight black. The lace on the sleeves ran up her arms like vines, meeting the tips of her long, raven curls that tumbled over chest and shoulders.

"They're all looking at me," Charlotte whispered to Alexander when they reached the half-way point, and eyes climbed the steps to land on her. "I thought the mask would obscure my identity."

He leaned in with a smirk and said, "That is not why they are looking, beauty."

"You flatter me."

He winked. "How are you feeling?"

"I am nervous," she admitted as he walked her down the remaining steps and into the heart of the ballroom. She spotted Katherine at the edge, deep in conversation with two women, her emerald dress in contrast with her tightly woven, blonde updo. Despite her painted, silver mask, there was no mistaking those golden ringlets or brown eyes.

She caught Charlotte's eyes, her pink lips tipping into a wicked smile.

"You are to stay with me for now," Alexander said, walking them through masked figures twirling around them, each couple a world unto themselves, "until Nathaniel identifies the Avery family. Then you will be on his arm while I join Katherine."

She nodded, looking around as they entered the throng. It was not only she who caught the attention of the nobles in attendance. Alexander moved with the grace of a swan, his golden hair loose around his shoulders, a silver mask over his face revealing those striking, green eyes.

Groups of people stood at the sides of the room, tipping back glasses of wine infused with vampire blood, some men dancing with other men, women kissing each other passionately, not caring who was watching. Others remained in alcoves obscured by sheer drapes, staring at dancers on raised platforms like glittering ornaments hired for the pleasure of those watching.

The vampire blood infused into the drinks had lowered all the guests' inhibitions. Even those she recognized in society who were normally straight-laced were libertine, their desires on show for all to see.

Turning away, she asked Alexander, "Why did you need to give everyone here your blood?"

"We need to be able to control them if anything happens, which is easier when they're already out of sorts. Don't feel bad. They're enjoying themselves, are they not?"

They certainly were. A stab of envy shot through her. She missed the way the blood made her feel.

A waiter, with a black mask approached them. He offered a platter of tall glasses filled with bubbling, light-colored liquid. Charlotte grabbed one, thanked the server who walked away, and brought it to her lips.

Alexander shot her a look before she could take a sip. "Careful."

"I need something to calm my nerves."

"Undoubtedly, but we need you focused."

"Please. As if I will be of much help with..." She lowered her voice to a whisper. "Magic. Besides, it helps with my pain."

After a brief pause, he let out a relenting sigh. "Who am I to say no? Not too much, though."

She drank, smiling when the bubbles hit the back of her throat. It wasn't just the high that captivated her, but the way it numbed the pain threading in her calves and back. The throbbing bite on her hip also dissolved when their blood reached her veins.

If she was going to get through the night, she couldn't be collapsing in agony. She promised herself that after tonight, she wouldn't touch it again. The last drops of champagne were sweet on her tongue, spreading warmth through her body, the tingling pooling in the apex of her groin.

She noticed him finishing a glass too and asked, "The blood does not affect you?" She clicked her tongue, feeling stupid once she heard the question aloud. "Of course it doesn't."

He laughed and took another large gulp. "As I'm filled with the stuff, Miss Lovett, no it does not."

Sweat beaded on her forehead as Charlotte awkwardly maneuvered around the dancers when Alexander broke contact for a long minute. She found his arm again and took it.

The music was loud, the air thick with the scent of cloying perfume and sweat. She searched for a familiar face behind the elaborate masks but couldn't see anyone she remotely recognized from society. *Yet.*

She moved deeper into the sea of people, the warmth of their bodies and swaths of fabric brushing against her. Heat rose in her cheeks as a couple whirled past, the man's fingers raising his partner's skirt to her thigh.

"I've never been to a ball like this. It is so scandalous."

Alexander laughed, the sound tinkling like the rising music. "Every good party should be."

She shuffled from one foot to the other, picking at the lace on her gloves. "Is the Avery family here yet?"

His forest-green gaze scanned the room. "I don't see them, but they very well could be. Do not worry," he said with a comforting glance. "We won't let them hurt you. Besides, they cannot practice thanks to your and Katherine's efforts."

Her stomach knotted. Alexander would not be so confident if he knew she had siphoned the magic from the sigil on the door, nullifying its usefulness.

Guilt shredded her insides, but she reminded herself that she had done it out of survival. If they destroyed their enemies tonight, then she would be forced to perform the ritual and she had no intention of dying for them.

She grabbed another glass, this time filled with wine and took a sip. The alcohol burned the back of her throat, but it did its only job—erasing the fevered anxiety spiking in her veins.

"Lord Sallow," a voice boomed from nearby, dragging Charlotte's attention to the helm of the ballroom.

Her breath hitched when she caught sight of him.

Nathaniel's fingers enveloped the hand of the man he was greeting in a tight grip. Her pulse raced as she eyed him leaning against the wall, so casual yet commanding. He was tall, towering over most of the others. With a flick of his fingers, he loosened the silk burgundy necktie around his throat and let it hang loosely over his black waistcoat.

Behind the matte black and crimson mask half covering his face, his furnace-gray eyes surveyed the room, his gaze unfocused, searching beyond the many faces as if intent on finding someone in particular. His fingers trailed through the unruly mass of dark hair, the soft strands contrasting with the shorter beard running over his chiseled jawline.

With another sip of the richly spiced wine, she watched him over the rim of her glass. Notes from the orchestra in the musician's gallery rose into a crescendo, matching the pounding of her heart. The dream, the bite, the massage, their talk in the attic—all came tumbling into her mind at once. A confusing wash of lust and fear sent butterflies swarming erratically in her stomach.

Nathaniel's eyes cut to hers and a trickle of wine dribbled down her chin.

Oh God. With a roll of her eyes, she shook her head and wiped the liquid from her beaded bodice. How damned humiliating.

Nathaniel's voice filtered through the music. "Excuse me," he said to the man next to him without looking away from Charlotte and walked toward her.

Wait. Was that the Baron Eringhorn and his wife standing behind them?

She recognized the triangular scar on the left side of his lip, and the slight upturn to his nose. An embroidered letter E shimmered against his orange and purple waistcoat, the colors of his family. He shook the hand of Baron Ellenwood, who stood beside his wife.

Her jaw slacked. "Who invited them?"

"Nathaniel," Alexander said nonchalantly.

"What?" Her jaw slacked. Nathaniel well knew what they had done to her family. She'd confided everything to him about how the Eringhorns destroyed her sister, how their son would cane Alice's legs and embarrassed her. They'd gone after Charlotte's mother too, spreading the rumors of their worshiping the devil and practicing the dark arts.

Rage roiled through her body. Hands clenched into fists at her side, and puffs of heated breath came out of her nose.

"Breathe," Alexander murmured. "Don't do anything rash."

She turned in time to see Nathaniel reach them, his eyes immediately dropping to her throat, then the rest of her.

"You bastard." Her jaw clenched, nostrils flaring when she noticed a smirk flirting over Nathaniel's lips.

He tilted his head, eyes wide. "Well, hello to you too, *sweetheart.*"

"Don't call me that."

He brushed a finger under her chin, which she pushed away. "Okay, *little lamb.* You look ravishing, by the way."

"Oh, you would ravish me, I am sure."

“I would take great pleasure in it,” he said with a purr, and her stomach clenched.

“Well, I would not.”

That was a colossal lie. God, there was something inherently wrong with her. When his eyes met hers, she wondered if he could see the pathetic longing that undoubtedly lingered in her gaze.

“You invited the Eringhorn family,” she stated before he could say anything else, her voice rising an octave.

The fire in her chest died when he didn’t immediately answer and instead raked his gaze leisurely over her figure, drinking in every curve.

“I did,” he said after a long pause.

“What exactly is wrong with you?” she asked, her tone settling into a breathy rasp.

His deep, baritone voice caressed her ears. “A multitude of things, I assure you.”

The bond hummed between them in a pulse of magic, like ropes tethering them together. It was infuriating and her anger toward him only seemed to blossom the primal need in her body, unconsciously drawing her closer until she had removed all the space between their bodies.

With her stare anchored into his, she said, “You’re despicable.”

A wolfish grin widened his full lips. “And you are beautiful.”

“Stop flirting with me,” she blurted, not meaning for it to come out that way. “I shouldn’t have come. I want to return to my room.”

His expression tightened, his dark-gray stare eclipsed by his black, intricate mask. “Wolves do not flee from sheep, Miss Lovett. Unless you wish to prove to the Eringhorn family how easily you scare.”

“I thought I was a lamb.”

“You are certainly acting like one,” he bit out, making her wince. “So prove me wrong.”

Challenge threaded his expression, and it was only when Alexander cleared his throat that she remembered anyone else was in the room at all. They were surrounded by people, many of whom were looking directly at them.

"Is there any sign of the Avery family?" Alexander asked in a hushed tone.

Nathaniel's glare flicked to Alexander, his lips hardening into a grimace. "No. Zachariah, Irene, and Katherine are stationed near the entrance and staircase."

A rush of adrenaline washed through her chest. Those were the names of the other vampires. She distinctly recalled Hartley telling her about them. Irene served Nathaniel for years before being turned. If only she could speak with them alone and tell them of the ritual, they might help her escape or convince Nathaniel not to go ahead with it. After all, why would they have worked so hard to become a vampire just to be okay with their immortality being ripped away from them?

"Can you introduce me to them?" she asked, still reeling from the fact that the Eringhorn family were in attendance, while also suddenly filled with the need to show that she wouldn't be run off by them. Nathaniel was right, not that she would ever, ever admit that to him. He was arrogant enough already.

Nathaniel lowered his mask to reveal his furrowed dark brows, his lips twitching into a straight line. "Why?"

She held his stare. "I want to see if the vampires you turned are as conceited as you are."

Alexander scoffed a laugh. "I assure you, no one could ever quite measure up."

"Says the dandy," Nathaniel quipped, and Charlotte noticed the sparkle in his eye and the way his dimple deepened when his lips curved.

It was surprising, if not refreshing, to see him enjoy himself. Even if only for a minute.

Alexander tucked an unruly wave of blond hair behind his ear. "I take that as a compliment."

Nathaniel actually smiled, one that reached his eyes, and she realized how deep their bond was for the first time.

Nathaniel's hand landed on Alexander's shoulder. "Will you give Miss Lovett and me a moment?"

Alexander's chest heaved and one brow arched high. He looked at Charlotte and asked, "Miss Lovett?"

She nodded, her knees feeling as if they might buckle at any moment. They were surrounded by people and he seemed in better spirits today, so she felt safe, for now.

With that, Alexander walked away and toward Katherine and her friend.

Once he was out of earshot, Nathaniel wrapped his hand around her waist and leaned closer. "I meant what I said earlier. You look beautiful."

She shrugged him away, despite wanting to do the very opposite. "You don't get to just do that."

"Do what?" he asked with hooded eyes.

"The *thing* that you do."

"*Oh,* what thing is it I do?" he asked, eyes dropping to her clavicle.

"Act as if everything is well after you invited them."

"Do not be angry," Nathaniel said.

"How can I not be?"

"I invited them for your benefit," he said and extended his hand, palm up, for her to take.

"What does that even mean?"

"You will see."

She inhaled deeply, holding the breath for a moment in her lungs before blowing it out. "You are infuriating."

"I know. Now, dance with me," he said in a voice that could seduce the devil into giving up his throne. "Or would you have me beg?"

"Would you?" she asked.

"I'd never lower myself to that. Not even for *you*."

His comment notwithstanding, she couldn't help but wonder how that would look. Fantasies blossomed in her mind, heightened by vampire blood pulsing through her veins, spreading warmth between her legs.

He could likely sense her arousal, smell it even. Heat crept through her body, embarrassment forcing her to avert her gaze.

When he erased the little distance remaining between their bodies, she ran her hand over the fabric of his shirt, closing her eyes as she explored the tight muscles of his chest. Damned, he felt good.

A familiar cackle of laughter sounded nearby, and she glanced over her shoulder, spotting Baron and Baroness Ellenwood embroiled in a dance. Unlike other balls, where dances were choreographed, this one had couples swaying to the music freely. It was quite scandalous, much like the host, and she secretly enjoyed it.

Nathaniel's fingers pressed into the sides of her chin, tilting her head back to meet him. "Eyes on me, *love*."

Tingles erupted in her heart. He lifted her into his arms until her feet barely grazed the floor. The barest touch of his lips against her earlobe sent a tingle searing to where he'd bitten her last. "You have been drinking blood."

Her heart skipped a beat. "I haven't."

She wasn't sure why she had lied.

"I can smell it on you." He leaned down, his lips ghosting over hers, her mouth parting.

"It helps my pain, and it makes me forget certain things."

"Forget what?"

"That you want to kill me."

He stopped dancing, his gray eyes gleaming when they dropped to her mouth. He gently tugged her bottom lip down, then released it to snap back into place. "It is not only your blood I crave, little lamb."

His confessions sent a shockwave through her body. "It is not?"

"It is your soul."

The confession swarmed butterflies into her stomach, all erratic and broken, pulling her somewhere between nausea and desire.

She could sense the carnal hunger burning behind his eyes. With a brush of his fingers along her clavicle, goosebumps blossomed over her skin, her body frozen under his riveting gaze.

All she could think about was surrendering to the desires of her body. To just give in before her next, panting breath.

"I need some air," she said, the oxygen in the room suddenly too thick for her to swallow. "Is there somewhere I can go? I cannot breathe properly."

Gently, his fingers landed around her waist. "Yes. Come with me."

Pulled through the crowd, Charlotte barely glimpsed Alexander amidst laughter with Katherine before reaching the locked double doors leading out to an enclosed courtyard.

While he retrieved his keys and unlocked the door, Charlotte found the yellow-green eyes of Charles Eringhorn, Alice's former betrothed, latching onto hers from the group of aristocrats gossiping at the side of the room.

Charles lowered his wine-red mask and hastened to her, his upper lip twitching. A sweep of blond hair was slicked back, his finger running along the length of his pronounced cheekbone. The smell of beeswax and tobacco smoke clung to his dark gray frock coat.

"Miss Lovett." His voice was as smooth as spider's silk. "How *intriguing* it is to see you here."

It was polite to courtesy, and expected for her to give him her hand, but she felt the cold sting of loss so deeply that the thought of letting him touch her made her want to claw back the layers of her skin where his lips might brush her knuckles. Besides, he did not even bow.

"*Mr.* Eringhorn," she spat, enunciating the Mr, knowing he hated his status as the untitled second son. "I too found myself disappointed when I was made aware of your presence here."

He laughed coldly and said, "I am surprised to see you are out of mourning already. Not even two months after your mother and sister's passing."

"I am not, nor will I ever be out of mourning. I just care little for social decorum," she said, fiddling with the lace of her dress.

"That much is obvious," he said with a snarl. "Your vanity and lack of respect for the dead is abhorrent."

"How dare you say that after everything *you* did?"

"You mean what *your* sister did."

Before she could lunge at him, and ruin any shred remaining of her social standing, Nathaniel's hand landed on her shoulder with a reassuring squeeze.

Charles's nose twitched, his lips curling as he held back the vicious remark he dearly wanted to impart to her. Instead, he bowed and said, "Lord Sallow."

"Mr. Eringhorn," he replied in the most disinterested tone. "Where is your new bride?"

"She is feeling under the weather and could not attend."

"Pity," Nathaniel said in a tone that sounded anything but. "If you will excuse us, I must accompany Miss Lovett to the courtyard."

"Of course. Have a good evening," he said, eyes fixed upon Charlotte's, jaw clenching. With a tense breath, he turned and returned to his friends.

Once he was gone, she spun on her heel and followed Nathaniel out into the empty, dark courtyard, sucking in a deep breath of smoggy air as he closed the doors behind them.

Her heart raced as the blood thirst moved through their bond, as if it was a living thing. Normally, she would fear being so close to him, but right then, all she could think about was punching him.

Chapter Nineteen

"How could you be *polite* to that vermin?" she admonished, a storm brewing in her stare, her lips quivering as she battled against a wave of hot, angry tears.

A shadow passed over his face from the tall, flickering gas lamps standing uniform beside eerie, gray statues, revealing the glint of silver in his irises. "He'll get what is coming to him."

She froze, unable to move as he stood under the stars, amongst statues covered in stone veils, obscuring their warped, angel faces. "Is that why you invited him here? To hurt him?"

"No. I invited him so *you* could."

"Have you lost your damned mind?" With a shake of her head, she started pacing the courtyard. It was getting harder to keep her emotions inside when he was being so infuriating, and the blood, his blood, was pulsing through her. "I cannot do that."

"Why not?"

"Because that would make me no better than him."

"I won't judge," he said in a deep tone that enveloped her. "We can kill him together if you'd like. Rats like him deserve it."

Her jaw slacked. Yes, while the thought of bludgeoning Charles Eringhorn to death filled her with a twisted sense of euphoria and justice, she knew she couldn't succumb to her baser desires. "Is that what you tell yourself to justify murder?"

"I do not need justification," he said smoothly, eyes darkening. "I can do it for you if you want, so you do not have to burden your soul."

"No! I don't want anyone to die because of me. Charles will meet his punishment one day, whether it is now or in death."

"No deity cares to punish the wicked, Miss Lovett."

"No? Did they tell you that?"

"In the three centuries I have been alive, evil has always triumphed. The strong and detached will always win."

"Fine, but hurting people *feels* wrong and I won't go against my instincts unless I am left with no other choice. Murdering Charles will not bring Alice back or undo any of the terrible things his family did to ours. It certainly won't make me feel any better. I've done things I am not proud of too and yes, I justified them, but all I can do now is try to redeem myself."

Something shifted between them and inside herself. She'd never spoken those words aloud before, but as she did, a newfound courage filled her up.

She looked at Nathaniel and sighed. His reason for inviting the Eringhorn family should not have appeased her, but it did. Even if they were wicked. It was also...touching.

By the way he stood still, hands in his pockets with a restrained tightness to his muscle, she just knew he was holding himself back. "Your kindness is terrifying."

She jolted. "Why?"

"Because in such a wicked world, it will be the death of you."

"Not if you have anything to do with it," she mumbled, feeling a little better after breathing in the fresh air and being away from that packed ballroom. "You need me alive, and you are the strongest creature to walk this Earth."

"For now," he said, and glanced at the moon.

A sharp pain coursed into her hip, the necrotic infection from the bite so tender under the scraps of fabric of her dress. Wincing, she hid her crumpling expression by briefly turning and focusing elsewhere to distract herself.

Everything in the courtyard had been designed beautifully, from the way the statue's hands were positioned perfectly over rose bushes, to capture the blooming flowers in a bouquet, to how they were positioned so their expressions appeared different depending on where she was standing.

Or they really were shifting, and she was descending into madness. The more she stared, she swore she could see their stone smiles stretching.

With a shake of her head, and a squeeze of her eyes, she looked back at them, relieved to see they were unmoving.

"Do you like them?" Nathaniel asked when she fell into a comfortable silence.

Charlotte gazed up at the sculpture of a man on his knees, a jagged hole in his chest, stone fragments of his ribs poking out. In his palms was his heart. The statue was eerily realistic, so much so that her brows creased when she looked at the man's eyes, clamped shut in pain.

"I see nothing but suffering," she said, her gaze passing over each one.

"They are a depiction of my life."

"I see none of your likeness, which is surprising considering how much you think of yourself," she quipped and he almost smiled.

"Perhaps I am not as vain as you'd like to believe."

Her lashes flickered in the icy breeze, heart softening. "Then you see your life through the eyes of others. Which is startling, as that would mean you have empathy."

"Why would that be startling?"

"How can someone who feels the pain of their victims so often be the cause of it? Unless you enjoy it?" Her brows knitted together. "Like some twisted form of punishment."

"You're very observant," he said in a deep, baritone voice. "I like that about you."

"You do?"

"I thought it was obvious. I enjoy your company."

It was, only because she'd felt like she was going crazy trying to decipher the spectrum of expressions, actions, and emotions she'd seen from him. "Yet, you want to kill me."

"Two things can be true at the same time."

Everything about him confused her. He was more than just morally ambiguous. There was nothing dichotomous about Nathaniel; he was good, bad, and everything in between.

"Don't think I don't see what you are doing," she said upon noticing how he steered the conversation with ease.

"Please, enlighten me."

"Every time I bring up anything intimate, like the statue's reflection of how you see yourself, you change the subject with a compliment."

"Well, the compliments *are* sincere."

"You are doing it again," she said.

"Lifetimes of habit, I'm afraid," he said, stroking a thumb over the dark shadows of his well-groomed beard.

"Why were you cursed?" she asked, surprised that this was the first time she'd asked. Everything about the courtyard was a story, each one unfolding its hidden truths, and the more she looked, the more she realized. He saw himself as a monster, maybe even more than she or anyone else did. But evil didn't paint themselves as so.

After a slow, tortuous pace around a leaf-covered bench in the center of the paved ground, he stopped next to the weathered, stone fountain and sighed. "It is an arduous and terribly depressing story."

"I cannot imagine it a happy tale," she said and stood in front of him, the cool breeze cooling the fever brought on by the blood high. "My ancestor didn't explain why this all happened, and I want to know why—"

She stopped herself. What else could she say? That she wanted nothing more than to know him better, to understand how he became the version of himself he was now? All so she could reconcile with her growing feelings.

"Do not try to pull me into your light," he warned, sensing the motive behind her words. "I do not seek to be redeemed, little lamb."

"Yet you consistently drag me into your darkness."

"You are tempted by it," he said brashly, making her breath hitch. "Don't feel bad. Most people are."

"Why do you think that is?" she asked, heart pounding.

He removed his jacket and rolled the sleeves of his shirt revealing the long, corded veins on his forearms. After throwing the blazer over one shoulder, he shoved his other hand in his pocket and glanced at the moon.

"People have long hidden evil desires behind their supposed good values, while disciplining anyone who has normal self-indulgent wants. You are tempted by the so-called darkness because there you don't have to hate yourself for embracing the most natural parts of who you are. It is beautifully human to be carried by a mess of emotions. True evil rarely hides in the darkness. It is often woven into the souls of those who come across as the most virtuous."

His explanation nestled deep somewhere in the crevices of her soul. Guilt had often chipped away at her will to live. It followed her now, still. With a deep breath, she added, "It *is* exhausting having to wrestle with every sinful thought."

His widening eyes flashed with silver. "Tell me them."

Heat flushed her upper body at his unexpected request, reddening her neck and cheeks. "I can't." She hoped he wouldn't press her, because they were mostly about him. "Besides," she added, "you have not yet told me the story of why you were cursed."

"You are not going to stop asking are you?"

She pursed her lips, lashes flickering in the wind. "No."

After a long sigh, he said, "It was over three centuries ago when my path to Hell began with a promotion to commander in Henry the Eighth's army. I was trusted to lead the campaign to cross into Scotland and lay waste to the southern towns and villages after Scotland's ruler refused to betroth the infant, Mary Queen of Scots and Prince Edward."

Her mind whirled. Hartley said she'd served in his court at some point, but to hear it made her realize just how old he truly was.

"I gave the orders to desecrate a town and burn its abbey to the ground," he continued. "We plundered and attacked without mercy, believing we were invincible with our numbers. We did not know how much our actions would strengthen the resolve of the Scots." With a shake of his head, he glanced at the stars, the black in his eyes absorbing their reflections. "I was so young and foolish then. I should have known that men who had nothing to lose were the most dangerous. They decimated my troops just days later, and when I came face to face with a sword, I saw an opportunity to escape. I stabbed the man in the foot and ran instead of dying with my men. I left behind my two closest friends."

Tears glossed his eyes in an unexpected display of emotion. Her fingers itched to comfort him. It was her deadliest instinct, to console those in pain, no matter the harm they caused.

"I'm sorry."

"Don't be," he said with a huff of breath. "I was a coward. We had grown up together. Our mothers were close friends," he continued, his gaze lost to memories she could not see. "They were brothers. Of course, Moor was their father's family name. Their mother's was Lysanmore."

Her stomach dipped.

"They were my ancestors?"

"Yes. Richard and Nicholas Moor."

"How old were you?" she asked, judging he was in his late twenties when he died based on his appearance.

"Thirty. Nicholas and I were the same age, but Richard was only twenty-three. That loss hurt his mother, Elizabeth, the most. It was, in fact, her sister, Delanie, who I was betrothed to. She tried to intervene, but Elizabeth was heartbroken, grieving, and angry. She stole the spell of immortality from the witches who trusted her and changed it, devoting and pouring the grief of losing her children into exacting vengeance against me. Three months later, she completed her curse and used it on me. It killed her to do it, but if I am being honest, I believe she wanted to die anyway."

"Christ," Charlotte blurted, slowly seating herself across from him with a long sigh. She wasn't sure what she expected to hear, but it was not that. "You didn't deserve that."

Slowly, he turned his head to meet hers, his brows knitting together. "I cost people their lives through my brutish arrogance and cowardice."

"Perhaps, but the punishment should fit the crime, if you can even call it that."

"Don't say that," he said in a pained voice.

"It's so easy to say we will meet our end with courage until the time comes," she replied, her own shame bubbling to the surface. "Yet, I did the same thing as you did, but to my sister. I never thought I could leave her to die, but after my father strangled me, all I could do was lie there, listening to her die, hoping he was distracted enough that he wouldn't notice I was still breathing."

"It's not the same," he said gruffly. "You could not have stopped your father, and you are—"

"Do not say a woman."

"I was going to say, you were younger than your sister," he added. "I was a commander. It was my duty to fight and die alongside my band of brothers. Instead, I panicked. My life flashed before my eyes and by the time I'd run and hid, I regretted my decision, but it was too late. They were all dead."

"So you couldn't have saved them?"

"We were outnumbered."

"Then, you are angry at yourself for surviving?" she asked incredulously. "If you had fought you would have died, and it wouldn't have helped them."

"It's not as simple as that."

"It is for me. I don't believe your friends would have wished for your death just because they met theirs. If they did, then they were not true friends."

"You speak of it as if there are no gray areas."

"I understand your sentiment, but I reject your self-loathing for simply choosing not to die."

"You are kind. I only hope you give yourself the same consideration."

"Except I could have helped her." She stood in front of him, placing her hand over her stomach as she wrestled with the stark truth that had haunted her since. "There were heavy ornaments I could have grabbed and if the roles were reversed, Alice would have tried everything to stop him from hurting me. I knew she was dying. I could hear her gurgling cries. When I cracked open my eyes, I watched her eyes fill with blood. All I could think was that I was glad it wasn't me."

He lifted his gaze to meet hers. "You were afraid."

"So were you."

"I was supposed to be strong."

"And I was not? I saved myself over the one person who always protected me. I should have died trying to help her and I didn't, so believe me when I tell you, I understand why you did what you did. Commander or not, we all stumble in the face of death. It's never too late to do things differently."

"It is too late for me. I am the creature better men die fighting trying to protect their loved ones from." He glanced at the fountain and sighed. "If you saw what I did, you would never think me capable of being saved."

"I think everyone is," she admitted and took a step closer. "It is my fatal flaw. You and I are similar, I think." Her tone rose an octave, her heart racing as the truth pierced her skull. "We both survived and hate ourselves for it. The only difference is you've had lifetimes of desensitization to death. Given the same chance, I might be just like you."

The corners of his eyes creased. "You could *never* be like me."

"Careful," she teased. "You almost sound *nice*."

His lips curved.

"Is that *another* smile?" she asked. "I'm beginning to think you do have a soul in there."

"Don't be ridiculous. I never smile," he said, *with a wide smile,* the kind that could break hearts.

A loud bang erupted from behind the double doors and for a moment she forgot where she was and what they were doing. Laughter tinkered after and rushed voices. Someone had fallen against the door, likely intoxicated.

Soon after, Alexander appeared behind the doors, his eyes landing on Charlotte in relief. Likely glad to see Nathaniel hadn't ripped out her throat. "They're here, Nathaniel, and there's something else."

"What is it?"

His face blanched, eyes widening. Charlotte had never seen Alexander afraid. He was always so well put together, but in that moment, he looked as if he might pass out. "Gertrude Avery has returned. I swear, I would have thought I was seeing things if it wasn't for her interacting with Katherine. She's alive. I don't know how, but the bitch has returned."

Charlotte's heart hammered. She'd heard that name before, but it couldn't be the same one who cursed her bloodline.

Nathaniel stood upright and quickly crossed the courtyard. "That is impossible."

"Yet, it is true."

"It must be a trick," Nathaniel said, shock carving into each of his words.

"Then it is a good one."

"How can she be alive?" Charlotte asked. "She lived over three hundred years ago, unless, she is a vampire."

With a squeeze of his eyelids, Nathaniel's fingers dove into his hair. "It might not be her," he said, with a desperation she'd never heard in his voice before.

"She's not a vampire," Alexander confirmed, only adding to their confusion.

Before she could press him further, Katherine hurried through the doors, followed by an incredibly handsome vampire who she guessed was

Zachariah. He flashed his fangs with the most charismatic, contagious smile.

"Nathaniel, the head of the Avery family is asking for you," Katherine said, standing beside a woman of bright red hair and blue eyes. Judging by the way she held herself, with the same fearlessness that only immortality afforded, Charlotte knew she was the other vampire.

"Zachariah," Nathaniel said lowly when the doors shut behind them, addressing the young man with dark-blond waves, wearing a deep red and black tuxedo. "How many are there?"

"Fourteen, well fifteen if you count the man they brought."

"He doesn't count," Nathaniel replied quickly, straightening his posture. Charlotte understood what he meant. Men couldn't be witches, only women. A man wouldn't have any magical ability and therefore, would not be a threat.

Katherine cleared her throat. "I introduced myself and from what I could tell, they didn't notice the spell when they walked in."

Charlotte pressed her lips tight together. They wouldn't have, considering it didn't exist.

"Very good," Nathaniel said, his eyes flickering to Charlotte's for a second with an approving smile. "Where are they now?"

Charlotte's stomach tumbled and she swallowed thickly, trying not to reveal anything in her expression. If it was true and a three-hundred-year-old witch was in fact with them, then she had made a huge mistake in disabling the spell.

"The reception hall," Zachariah answered. "Gertrude is asking for you."

"I will go," he said with a nod. "Before they disrupt the rest of the guests. Zachariah, you will come with me and Alexander, guard Miss Lovett."

Zachariah leaned against the doorframe, arms crossed over his crimson waistcoat, which was half-way undone. "Yes, my Lord," he drawled.

Charlotte stepped forward before they could leave, and placed her hand on Nathaniel's arm, the move not going unnoticed by Katherine, who glared at them. "How will you know it's really Gertrude and not an illusion?"

Alexander grimaced. "If anyone would know, it's Nathaniel. After all. She is his mother."

Charlotte's mouth fell open in disbelief, the revelation shooting shockwaves through her. The woman responsible for condemning the souls of her family to a purgatory, forever trapped within the bounds of a graveyard, was his mother!

"You failed to mention that," she said when her brain finally caught up with her mouth.

"It wasn't important," Nathaniel said simply.

She begged to differ, considering that had to be the reason Gertrude cursed her bloodline, out of vengeance for her ancestor cursing her son with vampirism.

"Why would she be aligned with your enemies?"

He didn't answer and instead turned to Alexander. "Keep her safe." Nathaniel's eyes locked onto hers, and he added, "Do not leave this courtyard. She's dangerous and will stop at nothing to get to you."

"Why?"

Again, not answering her question, he opened the ballroom doors. A flood of violin and piano chatter spilled into the courtyard when he, Zachariah, Katherine and Irene walked inside, leaving Charlotte and Alexander alone.

Chapter Twenty

Charlotte sat beside a statue of a woman weeping into her arms, lying over the side of a bed of roses. "Will you tell me?" she asked. "Nathaniel always evades my questions."

"Only because he does not wish to see your face when you discover the truth."

"What could be worse than the things I already know?"

Alexander huffed out a breath. "Nathaniel is the one who killed her."

"His mother?" she clarified, her lips falling open.

He nodded.

She placed her hand over her stomach, kneading the area under her ribs with her fist as bile crept into her throat. A shiver slid its way up her spine, raising goosebumps at the nape.

With a glance around the statues, all posed in grotesque statements of the people he'd murdered. They weren't just victims, but self-portraits of his bloodlust and staples of his existence. That's when she spotted the woman she assumed was Gertude. Scars covered her wrinkled face, her neck hanging at an unnatural angle, layers of necklaces around her neck.

"Why did he do it?" she asked, brows creasing. "There had to be a good reason."

With a head tilt and a scoff, his tongue ran over his bottom lip before dragging it between his teeth. "How quickly you jump to justify his actions."

Muscles flickered across her face. "I am not trying...I just think he wouldn't do something like that without a just cause."

"Yes, he would," Alexander said with an arched brow. "However, you are right on this account, but you of all people should know what he is capable of."

"What do you mean?"

"The *bond*," he intoned. "His obsession with you grows stronger each day. He yearns for you. I've heard him from my bedroom, muttering your name in his sleep."

"He *yearns* for me?" she asked, ignoring everything else he said.

"Your question confirms my suspicion. You are falling for him."

"I am not."

"Good," he said, drumming his fingers against the stone-pillared frame of the doors. "Because *that* would be a mistake."

With a tentative step forward, her next words came out in a whisper. "Why?"

I mean, she knew why. Yet, the question spilled unbidden from her lips anyway.

Alexander's expression hardened. "Obsession is not the same as true feeling. It's dangerous and I do not wish to see you end up dead after everything you have done to survive."

"You don't?" she asked softly.

"No," he said, brows creased. "We are friends and more than that, you and I are the same. We have both brushed against death more than once and felt the sting of being dealt an unfair hand. Like you, I too know the pain of broken family bonds and being the recipient of someone else's rage. What Nathaniel is exhibiting begins and ends with the blood bond created when he drank from you. Do not let your passions ruin your life."

Her heart stuttered. "My passions are also a result of the bond. It's just desire. Nothing more than a physical reaction."

His brows knitted together. "That's impossible."

She brushed her fingers against her throat. "It must be."

"Desire has no part in it. Think of it as a pull to finish what we started. We feed not just on a person's blood but on their soul too. Memories and emotions are devoured, shared, and we become a part of our victims for that short time. The tether breaks upon death, but when someone does not die, the need to consume what is left of them, to break that bond, becomes insatiable. That is what Nathaniel feels. He yearns for your death, to break the bond and it is wrapped in a desperate lust to drink from you and yes, maybe there is some attraction on his part," he added, wetting his lips, "but I have known him for centuries. Nathaniel does not want intimacy, and he certainly has never come close to falling in love. Any lust he might have for you is nothing compared to the bloodlust."

Disappointment slid into her stomach like a heavy weight. She couldn't assume she knew him better than his closest friend, but she swore she saw that desire in him, that he wanted something more.

She brushed her fingers over her throat, her mind turning to the bond instead of any dangerous, wishful thinking she had about his heart. "Have *you* left people alive?" she asked. "Nathaniel said he had not, but you speak of the bond with such familiarity."

He sat on the stone bench across from her, where shadows of stone fingers crept over his body as a stroke of moonlight passed through the statues.

"Yes. I drank from two of my lovers without killing them, at least, not immediately." He raked his long fingers through his blond waves. "I became tormented by their very existence. All I could think about was draining their blood and consuming their essence. Of course, there was feeling there once, but the bond dissolved it all. I was consumed with the need to kill them. Eventually," he said, eyes darkening as the stars were swallowed by dark clouds overhead. "Fantasy was not enough. I hunted them down and slaughtered them."

"I'm sorry."

"For what? My murdering people?" he asked with an incredulous smirk.

"For the supernatural pull to kill when it is clearly not in your nature."

"It *is* in my nature, Miss Lovett," he said.

"I mean your personality. Call me insane, but I don't feel as if you are a bad person."

"I'll try not to be, to you anyway," he promised and shifted his position.

"Nathaniel hasn't tried feeding from me since," she said, raking her fingers through her hair, recalling every lingering touch from the moments they found themselves alone.

"*Yet,*" Alexander intoned. "The desire will grow stronger, and he won't be able to stop himself. Even if he wants nothing more than to let you go."

Her mouth dried. "How can I stop it?"

"Just keep your distance until the ritual. Once he is mortal, the blood bond will break too."

"If the ritual doesn't work, for any reason, would I have time to run?"

"There is nowhere you can go that he won't find you, but do not concern yourself with that. It will work and until then, just don't be alone with him. He has incredible restraint, but we all have our limits. If you must be near him, I will be with you so I can try to stop him if he loses control."

"*Try?*" she emphasized.

"I am not as strong. He is the first vampire and therefore got the full breadth of the curse. For every vampire in his line, the abilities are diluted."

Charlotte's stomach churned. Even if she did ever escape, she would have the equivalent of an obsessed bloodhound on her trail for the rest of her life. Her thoughts turned to the witches inside, and Nathaniel's plan to kill them. Even with their powers, there were four vampires in attendance that night which she hadn't counted on. Surely it was enough to overpower the Avery family.

"Do the other two vampires know of your plan?" Charlotte asked. "Zachariah and Irene?"

The bridge of his nose creased. "They do, but they are unaware of the whole truth."

"Which is?"

"That the ritual will undo not only his curse, but all of ours. I would not open their eyes to that deception," he cautioned when she pressed her lips tight. "Your being alive is all that stands between our becoming mortal and staying vampires forever. If you tell them, they will snap your neck in a heartbeat. Many of us do not wish to return to the banes of mortality."

"Do you?" she asked, shuffling herself forward.

A rustle of leaves skittered between them, forming a line on the moon-brushed path leading to several more veiled statues.

"I did not ask to become a vampire, but I cannot pretend it does not come with its perks," he said, smoothing a thumb over his pointed chin. "There is an exhilaration that comes with being untouchable, with never having to fear another person, disease, or death. I enjoy life and all the beautiful things it offers. The only downside is I cannot choose to end things in centuries' time, when I grow tired of it all."

She pursed her lips. "When did you become a vampire?"

Blowing out a long breath, he dropped his hands in his lap. "Almost three centuries ago."

"You're almost as old as Nathaniel."

"We are but thirty years apart," he said.

"Why did he turn you? You said he saved you before, how?"

"It all started with my father, you see. He was the Earl of Derby and I was the youngest of nine. I hated the brute," he said, the bulb in his throat bobbing. "After my mother and brother died from the sweating sickness, I fled him and came across a troupe of performers. We went from town to city performing various plays. I took to the stage like a fish to water. I loved to entertain, to slip into a different skin each night and to feel the applause. After the pain of losing my family, I found another." His eyes gently shut. "It was exhilarating until the plague hit a small town we were performing in. The other players all died, and I too was on death's door." He glanced at the sky, the stars melding into the blue of his eyes. "That's when I met Gertrude. She was a noble's wife, so you can imagine my surprise when I saw her working in the hospital, tending to the sick. It was no place for a lady, but unlike many others, she was never afraid of coming close to the diseased."

Charlotte's heart skipped a beat, sending a wave of numbness washing through her limbs.

"In a way, I was ready to meet my end," he continued. "I didn't want to die, but everyone I loved was gone. Until, one night, when the man in the bed across from me passed in his sleep. It was common then, to witness so much death. Only he didn't stay dead. Later that night, he returned as a walking corpse. There was no intelligence or awareness in him. His eyes lacked any color and his skin was gray and gaunt. It was terrifying to see, but Gertrude was delighted. It was only later that I found out she was the one creating these monsters, after bringing them back from the brink of death to be her loyal soldiers. They were nothing but empty vessels manipulated by the strings of her power, loyal only to her, their master."

"She was using necromancy," she said, horrified. The practice was frowned upon, even among witches who used sacrificial magic. It rarely went right, and more often than not, souls did not want to return to this world once they passed on. Even if they did, it wasn't pretty.

"Yes," he said. "I was so close to death myself and knowing what my fate would become, I tried to flee but I was too weak. Then Nathaniel came," he said, a ghost of a smile forming over his thin lips. "He was so powerful, in everything from his stride to the way he commanded the witches there. He discovered what she was doing, how she had become possessed by the idea of growing an army, no matter the cost. See, witches were mercilessly persecuted then, so I understood her desire to protect her own. It was not her motives, but her method. To bring someone back from death, you must sacrifice an innocent. Someone pure of heart."

"No adult is innocent," Charlotte said.

"Exactly."

Her stomach churned. "Oh, God."

"She wanted to protect her family but also gain more power and she didn't care who she had to kill to get it. It wasn't just her. Nathaniel's ex-betrothed was helping her too. They both sought immortality without resorting to vampirism. Fortunately, Nathaniel killed them, including his mother. We have one rule: we do not feed upon children. For the longest time after, Nathaniel would meticulously track his prey, only feasting upon those he deemed deserving."

"Yet he hunted my bloodline," she pointed out, the only thing he'd done that she actually struggled to reconcile with.

"He became desperate to become mortal again. Believe me, he hated himself for it. Then, one day, something changed and whatever shred of morals were left in him was gone."

"What changed?"

"He thought he'd killed the last of your line and when the curse didn't break, he lost all hope. He traded his soul to murder hundreds of your ancestors to break it, and it was all for nothing. After that, he fell into darkness, and I walked into it with him. After all, he saved me and countless others. I looked up to him. I still do."

Her heart shattered as the scenes formed in her mind's eye from Alexander's words. "How is Gertrude alive?" Charlotte asked. "You said you believed Nathaniel killed her, but she might have found a way."

"She must have."

"Nathaniel said it could be a trick."

"I do not believe it is, but I can hope, because if not, then we are doomed. I have lived many lifetimes and have never come across evil like that since."

Charlotte jolted back when the doors opened. Alexander jumped to his feet, planting himself between her and the door, but it was only Zachariah.

"What happened?" Alexander asked, his voice rising an octave.

"We need you!" he stated, wild-eyed and pushed his fingers through his dark-blonde waves and out of his face. "Gertrude's threatening to kill everyone unless Lord Sallow brings the girl."

"What about the protections?"

Oh no.

"They didn't work," he replied.

"Where are they?"

"At the entrance still. Fortunately, the guests are distracted."

"Stay here," Alexander ordered.

"Wait–" she called out, but he was already at the doors, opening them before she could argue.

This was all her fault. If she'd know the woman who cursed her family would return, she would have taken her chances with Nathaniel. Judging from everything Alexander had said, Gertrude was far less merciful than her son.

The doors slammed shut behind them and Charlotte rushed forward, relieved to find they'd left them unlocked in their haste.

A thrum of magic ran through her when she splayed her fingers over the polished wood. There were innocent people inside. While Nathaniel and the vampires could withstand the Avery's powers, people like Hartley couldn't. Then there was Duke. She wouldn't leave without him either.

"Damned to Hell," she whispered, running her fingers down to the handle, her heart pounding in her ears.

Slowly, she opened the doors to the crowded ballroom, pushing her way into the fray. It was unlike any event she had ever been to. The beautiful dresses were torn, masks had been discarded and tossed to the ground, and drinks spilled over the marble floor.

Wisps of unruly curls flicked into her vision as she hurried toward the receiving hall. The deeper she moved into the room, the more debaucherous it became, with couples breathing kisses against each other's necks, hands gliding up inner thighs. Groups of threes engaged in salacious activities enough to force a blush into Charlotte's cheeks. One man dragged his tongue over the throat of a lord, while his wife hiked up the skirts of her dress and pressed her palm between her legs, eyes rolling back in ecstasy. Perfume, sweat and wine intermingled with the rising heat, making it difficult to breathe.

With labored breaths, she made it to the end of the room, her eyes fixed on the gilded doors. Her gloved fingers grazed over the ornate woodwork as she walked into the foyer, her breath catching when she spotted the Avery witches standing in the center of the foyer, mid-argument with Nathaniel, cloaked in deep purple, their velvet hoods embroidered with silver symbols.

Under the fabric, waves of auburn hair cascaded around their chests, their genes woven in each of their freckled diamond-shaped faces. Except for the man, who stood next to the tallest of them, and the elderly woman in the middle, with dark gray hair.

"You're not getting to her," Nathaniel warned, with Alexander, Irene and Zachariah blocking the entrance.

She spotted Katherine, standing to the left, while two servants stood frozen by the coats, terrified to move as they watched.

Charlotte hid behind a doorway, keeping to the shadows, her heart pounding as she watched the gray-haired woman take a step forward. Candlelight illuminated the dagger clasped in her bony fingers, and the scars marring her bulbous nose and cheeks. Chunky necklaces, strung with crystals and talismans, bounced around her chest when she walked.

"Do you want to feel the breadth of my power again, son?"

Son.

Were it not for the resemblance of her grave-gray eyes, she would never have guessed that she was Nathaniel's mother.

"You never said how you returned," he snapped.

"Like you, I found a way to slow the hands of time," she said, shrugging the comment off as if they were discussing something as trivial as the weather.

"Yet, you have remained a witch," Alexander said from behind him.

"Indeed," she said, removing her hood. "Now, enough chitchat.. Where is my sacrifice?"

The possessive tone set Charlotte's nerves on edge.

Nathaniel snarled, fangs pointing over his bottom lip. "She's not yours. She is *mine*."

Her heart fluttered unexpectedly.

Step aside, my son, and allow me to finish this," she said, her eyes cutting to Nathaniel's. "I do not want to use my power on you, but I will."

"I overpowered you once," he snapped. "I won't hesitate to do it again."

A woman stepped away from the throng, her fingers outstretched as she muttered an incantation under her breath. Nathaniel lunged at her before she could finish, his fangs sinking into her throat, ripping flesh from her like a savage beast. His fingers curled against the witch's chest, her scream lost in a gurgle.

Charlotte yelped when she saw Gertrude and another of them grabbed the two servants and dragged their daggers across their throats, spilling a waterfall of crimson onto the polished floor. A loud hum of power lifted through the room.

Her palm flew to her mouth as she muffled her scream, eyes widening while she watched them die.

Alexander launched his way across to help Nathaniel as one witch that Charlotte recognized, the one who came to her home that night and called herself Beatrice, tried to pry him off his victim.

"Enough," Gertrude shouted.

A predatory smile stretched her thin, wrinkled lips. She lifted her hand toward Alexander, who was about to bite one of them. He hunched over the floor before his fangs could reach her throat. On all fours, he let out a loud groan, and Nathaniel dropped the body of the dead witch with a thud, before wiping the blood from his mouth with the back of his hand.

Gertrude let out a weighty sigh, clicking her tongue. "How easily you resort to violence. It should come as no surprise. Your father was a brute too and you still bear his name. *Sallow.*" The word dripped like venom from her tongue.

"I would rather have his name than yours," Nathaniel spat blood on the ground, chin jutting out.

She walked to him, stopping just a foot from them both. "I miss when you were little. You had no time for your father, but you used to look at me as if I was your entire world. How so much has changed. Now, when I look at you, I see nothing of that little boy I loved so dearly."

"You do not know how to love," he snapped.

"Of course I do," she said with a scrunch of her nose and brows. "Everything I do is out of love."

"That's not true," he protested. "You knew how to break my curse, and you didn't!"

He lunged at her but was forced to his knees by another spell. Zachariah sped beside him alongside Irene, but both of them were quickly paralyzed with just a flick of Gertrude's fingers, unable to move, rooted to the spot.

A band of tension rippled through the room. She could sense the weight of their power. They were all channeling each other. It ran in a looped current through each of them, but the strongest waves of magic came from Gertrude. Charlotte had never felt anything like it. Her eyes dropped to the dead servants, their throats slit, and swallowed thickly.

They were using those murders to fuel their magic. The thought made her nauseous.

"The Lysanmore witches needed to be punished," Gertrude spat as he tried to stand, a sharp edge piercing into her voice. "Keeping you as a vampire was only meant to be temporary so I could siphon what power of theirs was left. Once they were almost extinguished, I would have sacrificed the last to make you mortal again, but you turned on me and destroyed everything I was building. You killed your own family—your aunts, my sisters."

Nathaniel tore through the spell before the others, standing with hunched shoulders and a rabid expression. "They were compliant in what you were doing."

"I was protecting us!" she boomed, making the Avery witches flinch. "I was gaining power to stop those who were hunting us, who sought to harm us. Sometimes, sacrifices must be made. Your immortality was one of them, a perfect anchor to bind my spell to keep their souls bound to that graveyard."

"I know what you did and I may have ruined your plans, but you broke me," he said in a strained tone, and Charlotte's heart broke. "You were my mother. You were supposed to put me above everything else."

"You say this, yet you are the one who snapped my neck," she said her voice rising an octave, her tone still contained.

"You were animating corpses and killing children to do it."

Gertrude inhaled sharply. "I was saving hundreds more by doing that. Do you know how many children of witches have been slaughtered because of an association to witchcraft?"

"You are *sick*."

"So are you," a young woman's voice called out from behind Gertrude. "You speak of our elders' sins when you killed my cousins without mercy. My aunt too," she pointed at the body on the floor.

Charlotte gazed at the girl who could not have been over nineteen years old, with auburn hair that cascaded down her back, adorned with purple wildflowers. Her features echoed the ghost Charlotte had witnessed in the manor. The spirit they siphoned looked just like her, save for the auburn hair.

In fact, the spirit bore an uncanny resemblance to each of the Avery women.

Her heart palpitated when she glimpsed the family ring on each of their long fingers. Each was engraved with the letter A. It was the same one the ghost wore, which meant the spirit she and Katherine had siphoned was an Avery witch.

Beatrice grabbed the girl's hand when she lifted it, stopping what Charlotte presumed was a spell in progress. "Not now, Josephine. He will get what is coming to him in time."

Charlotte's eyes widened as she remembered a snippet from her great-grandmother's journals. If they siphoned the energy from an Avery ghost, then their bloodline would have been able to sense that in the magic. Meaning, even if she hadn't broken that spell, they would have picked up on the power she and Katherine had infused into the sigil engraved on the door, anyway.

Nathaniel's voice came back into focus, pulling Charlotte's attention onto him. "What did you expect?" he asked the Avery girl. "One of your cousins was sent to spy on me and the other tried to paralyze me with a spell."

"We did what we had to do," Beatrice chimed in, her voice coarse with pain. "My daughters did not deserve that. You won't even tell us where their bodies are."

"So you can consecrate their remains and gain even more power? I don't think so."

Beatrice raised her hands as Zachariah almost broke through Gertrude's spell, paralyzing them, but was pushed back.

"Enough of this," Gertrude stated. Flickers of disgust ran over her face when she glared at her son. "We are taking the witch."

"To Hell you are," he said, planting himself in front of the entrance to the ballroom, the music inside growing louder.

"Then you will know true pain again, son," Gertrude spat. Intelligible whispers left her lips as a spell landed over Nathaniel, wrenching a scream from him as magic contorted his body with invisible threads, angling his bones until they snapped.

"Stop!" Charlotte yelled, stepping out from her hiding place.

"No!" Nathaniel screamed, grunting through moans, only gasping when she lifted her hands and the spell dissipated, dropping him to his knees.

Gertrude walked to Charlotte with an arrogance only invincibility afforded. "There you are. I'd recognize that Lysanmore frown anywhere," she told Charlotte. "How lonely you must feel, being the last in your line."

A pained groan sounded from Nathaniel.

"What have you done to him?"

Gertrude smirked. "He is incapacitated for now. I shall return him good as new once we are done here."

Charlotte held her breath, her gaze flitting to Nathaniel's bloodshot stare. Silent grunts stretched his lips, one set of his fangs sliding from his mouth. Thin fingers curled into fists as he tried to push himself out from under the spell she had cast, but it was too strong. She could feel the pulse of magic from there—suffocating, heavy and enveloping.

How on Earth could she incapacitate four vampires, nature's strongest creatures?

"How is that possible?" she asked. Even with sacrificial magic, that was too much.

"Why are you surprised, dear?" Gertrude asked. With another slow, purposeful step forward, she said, "We are nature's warriors. The manifestation of our desires moves in our bones. It is embedded in our souls. There is no person nor creature alive that is stronger than us. Look at them. See how quickly these predators bow to us when we embrace our power. Now, you will come with us."

The scent of rosewater wafted around her when she took another step closer.

With a loud growl, Nathaniel broke free of her spell again, while the rest struggled, and raced to Charlotte, stretching out his arm over Charlotte's chest. "Don't touch her!"

"Step aside," Gertrude warned.

"No! You could have eased my pain once and now you plan to take away the only one who can save me."

Save me.

Charlotte's stomach twisted.

Gertrude scanned her eyes over Charlotte, forcing a chill into her core. "You truly believe this woman is going to help you?"

His brows creased and he shot her a wary glance, something potent breaking in his darkening stare. "We have an agreement."

"My son the fool," she said, and looked at Charlotte. "It appears you have not mentioned what the cost is to break his curse."

Nathaniel glanced at her. "*Charlotte?*"

Oh God. The way he said her name sent a blade of pain through her chest.

She averted her gaze, swallowing hard when a lump formed in her throat. The truth was about to come out and she couldn't look at him when it did, in fear of him revealing the truth that hurt the most—that the cost didn't matter and he would sacrifice her life if it meant becoming mortal. As much as she wanted to believe he'd softened toward her, she knew what he was and what he could do.

Gertrude continued when Charlotte did not speak.

"She must sacrifice herself."

Charlotte's stomach hollowed, heart thrumming in her ears. Slowly, she opened her eyes and saw Nathaniel's gaze fixed upon her.

"Is this true?"

She chewed on her bottom lip before nodding gently.

His face crumpled, a long, heavy sigh whooshing past his lips.

Looking away, to anywhere but him, her gaze landed on Gertrude.

A flicker of movement drew Charlotte's attention to her arm. A cockroach crawled onto her shoulder, its antennas flicking when it looked at her. Either she truly was losing her mind, or she had seen that exact insect before.

Her hip pulsed with pain, throbbing deep into her muscles, eliciting a short groan. There had been a cockroach in her room the night she heard knocking on her door at Lovett Manor, again on her first night here, when she'd arrived back from the graveyard by her garden gates, and when Duke had tried to catch it. The insect ran into her gray hair, settling there after twisting its legs into the strands. She lifted her index finger to its exoskeletal back and smoothed it.

It was Gertrude's familiar.

The realization stunned her to spot.

Oh God.

"You hexed me," Charlotte said, lips parting in disbelief.

"You did not know?" Gertrude asked, gray eyebrows rising, deepening the wrinkles on her wide forehead. "I assumed you would have figured it out by now, but then, just like your mother and sister, you shy away from our craft."

"How do you know that about my family?"

"After Amelia Lysnamore killed herself," she said, glancing at Nathaniel before continuing, "I believed that was the end of your bloodline, but when my spell did not work, I knew there was more of you somewhere."

"What spell?" Charlotte asked, latching onto the statement.

"To discover if there were more of you."

Charlotte's brows knitted together. That didn't make any sense. She was hiding something.

Gertrude continued, cutting Charlotte off. "Dalton is a clerk." She pointed at the man standing beside Beatrice, his hand on her shoulder as they all glared at Nathaniel and her, murder in their eyes. "He searched the adoption records of several orphanages," Gertrude explained, "until we discovered your great-grandmother. It took some time to find out if she was the child given away by the Lysanmore witch, and when confirmed, it was easy to trace her descendants. You, your sister, and mother."

Focused, pale eyes watched her, sending a shudder running through Charlotte's torso.

"What did you do to them?" she asked through gritted teeth.

Gertrude took a step forward, but Nathaniel held out his arm, and she stopped.

"I hexed him, as I did you. It was easy. You didn't even notice me at your sister's burial."

Her heart pounded. That morning had been a blur, as so many offered their condolences, taking her hands in theirs.

Gertrude continued with a tilt of her head. "Your father bore the same mark, before he lost his mind."

"You evil cow!" Charlotte lunged forward and was abruptly stopped by Nathaniel's hand.

"Careful," Gertrude warned. "I am far stronger than you."

All the terrible things she had said about her father after his death came rushing back.

Nathaniel cleared his throat, his jaw clenched. "What did you do?"

Gertrude white-knuckled the dagger. "It is the hex of a demon, The Smiling Woman." She looked at Nathaniel knowingly before adding, "It will drive her to madness and heighten any rage inside of her, although, fortunately for you, she does not seem to have much anger."

"My father was possessed?"

"*Oppressed*, yes, and it will happen to you too. Unless you come with me now. I can take it away and make your end painless."

This was her leverage. The hex. Charlotte was already dead long before tonight. The words from her first night in the manor came back to haunt her: *Death is coming.* She had assumed it was a warning, but she never thought it could mean she was already marked to die. Charlotte's world spiraled.

"Why not kill me right here?" she asked, taking a gamble with the witch's intentions.

"The why is not important."

"Oh, I think it is, else you would have stabbed me already with that blade," Charlotte rebuked. "I would rather die than leave here with you."

Gertrude tsked, averting her stare. "The Smiling Woman will find you," she said, looking through milky, pale eyes. "It is a fate worse than death and if you refuse to come willingly, I will take you by force."

"You can try." Charlotte's fingers curled into fists and Nathaniel stood firm.

Gertrude was wrong about one thing. Charlotte held anger, so much in fact that it consumed her from the inside out until her hands were shaking. Her entire body trembled when she looked at the woman responsible for her parents and sister's death, and desecrating her father's name.

For the first time in Charlotte's life, she wanted to kill. Bloodlust spiked in her veins, magic pulsing from the ground as if it was seeping over from the Realm of the Dead.

There was not a hint of fear in her gray eyes. Charlotte intended to change that. "I'm going to kill you."

Gertrude laughed, the sound screeching through Charlotte's head. "I can sense your heart, dear. You are not capable of murder."

The girl, untouched by grief with a thousand tomorrows, was now a woman rewritten by pain, ready to tear everything apart in the name of justice. With a lift of her bony fingers, Gertrude touched her obsidian, star-shaped pendant and said, "If you want a fight, then so be it."

Before Charlotte could react, Nathaniel's fingers were already gripping the curve of her waist, pulling her from the path and pressing her against the wall as Alexander broke free and lunged at Beatrice, who ran toward the ballroom, but Josephine and the others had already made it inside.

Katherine grabbed Zachariah, pulling him as Gertrude stormed ahead.

"Stop them!" Nathaniel boomed as he held Charlotte. Her vision blurred as he pushed against her, feeling the hard muscles of his chest under his shirt tense under her palm as they watched Irene grab one of the Avery witches, and Zachariah another. Alexander lunged for Gertrude, but it was too late.

A flood of guttural screams echoed from the ballroom. Nathaniel, gripping Charlotte's wrist, pulled her toward the closed doors, but the Avery family must have spelled them not to open. He fought with the handle, before turning in time to see a witch walking toward them with her arms raised above her head.

"Run!" Nathaniel commanded, his voice edged with panic as he whirled around in time to grab the woman.

The icy touch of death pressed deep into her core, following her as she ran. She turned the corner, but stopped when she looked into the ballroom, her mouth falling open.

Sharp blades dragged across the throats of unexpecting guests, saturating their finest evening wear in crimson.

It was too late to help them by the time the guests realized what was happening.

With every murder, the Avery family siphoned the energy, their combined power growing stronger.

The blood hazed her instincts, and she tried to channel the magic that was slipping into her, but nothing happened. A wave of nausea surged through her as the screams rang out.

They were all going to die.

Chapter Twenty-One

Beatrice's ringed fingers grabbed a fistful of Charlotte's black curls, wrenching her back when she tried to dodge her attack.

"No!" Nathaniel hurtled towards them, a snarl contorting his face as he lunged at Beatrice, his pupils forming into slits. As his jaw unhinged, three rows of razor-sharp fangs emerged, plunging into Beatrice's neck with animalistic abandon, savagely tearing away chunks of flesh. Blood streamed down her body in a gush, forming a pool on the marble below. Her body went limp within seconds, and he dropped her with no care, leaving her to hit the ground at a contorted angle.

Charlotte exhaled shakily, the shock crawling through her, swirling the building nausea in her stomach. The remaining witches grabbed a fresh set of humans and plunged the daggers deeper into their necks, applying enough pressure to cut through vocal cords, each hack motion spattering blood over their faces and arms.

The sacrifice's energy pulsed in the air before being siphoned by the witches who killed them. Whispering incantations, they directed incapacitation spells toward Zachariah and Irene, while Katherine was flung against a wall with a loud thud.

With a smile that didn't reach her eyes, Gertrude navigated the chaos, sending a shiver down her spine as she moved closer.

A loud crack echoed through the room, followed by a heavy silence. Charlotte turned to look around, her jaw slacking when she saw Nathaniel and Alexander on their knees too, unable to move.

The few guests remaining, including Charles Eringhorn, stood at the edge of the ballroom, their backs pressed firmly against the wall.

Under the flickering candlelit chandeliers, a woman bled out slumped against the piano, her hand clutched around her throat, the sound of her foamy gurgles filling the silence. Bodies surrounded her, a mixture of limbs from where the vampires had killed the witches and the intact bodies of humans who'd had their throats cut open.

She met Nathaniel's bloodshot, strained eyes as he tried to wrestle against the suffocation of his mother's spell, moving his extremities more than others, but not enough to break free.

Broken stained-glass windows spilled moonlight onto the faces of those who had been enjoying themselves strewn across the marbled floor. Charlotte steadied herself after almost swooning from the lightheadedness prickling in her head. It wasn't the first time she had seen so much death in one place. After her father had tried to kill her and had murdered Alice and her mother, he slit his own throat.

She thought they were the only victims, but it was only when she finally peeled herself from the floorboards, with sobs wrenching her chest, after she cried over Alice's body, that she walked downstairs to get help only to discover the defiled corpses of all the staff that had been working that day, scattered across the parlor room, foyer, and kitchen.

They were all too far gone to be saved, just like the rest in the room who the Avery family had already siphoned. They were all sacrifices to give more power to Gertrude, who had left only Charlotte free to move.

With a thick swallow, she counted the remaining guests. There were just eleven, out of hundreds.

Bile bit up her throat. Baron Ellenwood and Baroness Victoria were cowering in the corner, their arms brushing, looking at Katherine, who Charlotte had briefly forgotten was his sister.

Charles glared at her through glassy eyes, suspended in the same stillness as the others. If they didn't know her to be a witch before, they damned well did now.

"Now, dear, are you quite done?" Gertrude asked.

Charlotte jutted her chin, looking around, her eyes on Nathaniel's for a moment longer than the others. She was sick and tired of always being afraid.

No more a sacrificial lamb. If she was to die, then she would not go willingly.

"Not even close," she answered with a flare of her nostrils.

The magic began with a pulse in her core, traveling through her body in surges of tingles. A buzz of magic crept over her hands, her focus only on the energy of those who had died.

Summoning them was easier than breathing. Fractures of gray spilled through the veil separating the dead from the living. Throughout the ballroom, the ghosts of slain humans and witches materialized, their faces twisted in fury. All, except for the ghosts of the Avery women who were killed, descended upon Gertrude, who was either oblivious to their presence, or simply did not care.

Glancing around, Charlotte noticed no one but her was reacting to the hundreds of spirits attacking the elder of the Avery family, who stepped over their bodies, unfazed.

The spirit's anguish and pain rattled deep in her heart as if their suffering belonged to her. They slowly turned their heads, hurtling toward her when they noticed she could see them. Their mouths opened, but no words spilled in the Realm of the Dead. They did not lunge at her as they did Gertrude, but stood around her in a protective circle, as if they could sense her intention.

"Help me," Charlotte said aloud, halting Gertrude who stopped a few feet in front of her.

The ghosts linked hands, their residual energy, enhanced by anger, flowing into her. Tendrils of magic uncoiled from Charlotte's core, snaking outward through her skin in a mist of smoky gray.

The power speared through her fingers. Everything magical in Sallow Manor, from the boundary spell that had been placed around the property, to the ghosts Gertrude was attempting to siphon, was malleable and for the taking.

For the first time, she felt strong, like a magnet for the power that thrummed in the vicinity.

On a sharp inhale, Charlotte took a step forward, the fury of all who Gertrude had slaughtered in her veins, enhancing every morsel of magic into something deadly.

Gertrude's eyes flashed, the black in her pupils swirling. "I am going to destroy you for what you did. You left me entirely alone in this world."

With a building smirk, she said, "I am done with this little talk," Gertrude spat. "You are coming with me." She grabbed Charlotte's wrist and quickly recoiled when the power shocked into her fingers, charring them black.

Gertrude's gray eyes grew wide, and she gasped as she stumbled backward.

Charlotte waved her hand through the air, snapping the paralysis spell on the room like an elastic band. Energy crackled, followed by the sound of heavy gasps that rushed into her ears.

Charlotte grabbed Gertrude's arm, recalling one of the few spells from the grimoire that she had memorized in case locking her uncle and cousin in the mirror didn't work. Latin left her in whispers. "Ut malum quod mihi optas, tibi cadat."

Gertrude dropped to her knees just as Nathaniel raced to Charlotte's side. Blood spilled from her lips as she choked on it, gasping for air, grasping the ground. A tug pulled in her chest and Charlotte realized Gertrude was trying to take back her power, but she couldn't.

She'd never felt such clarity of action in her life. The power lifted her so high that she got a taste of how it must feel to be invincible.

Overwhelmed by the energy from her victims and Charlotte's magic, Gertrude remained on the ground, glaring up at them both with eyes that promised torture.

In a heartbeat, Nathaniel sped behind her, both hands on either side of her head, and with a sickening crack, he snapped her neck, leaving her to drop the rest of the way to the ground. Her head hit marble, blood pooling in a rush.

Katherine lifted her dress, running over to them, panting. "Is she dead?"

"She could come back," Charlotte said.

Nathaniel's brows raised slightly when he looked at her, pupils flaring, holding Charlotte's gaze. "I'll take her to the cellar and chain her up. If she isn't dead, then we can use her to find out how to get rid of your hex."

Katherine nodded. "I'll perform a boundary spell."

"There is no need to keep her alive," Charlotte interrupted. "I'll find some other way to remove the hex."

"Don't go," Katherine stated, grabbing her wrist when she tried to leave.

She shrugged her away, scoffing. "Don't touch me."

"This power you have—it's temporary," Katherine explained, wild-eyed. Tearing off her silver mask, she wiped a sheen of sweat from her forehead. "It's sacrificial magic. You're siphoning all those who died tonight. It's immense and you're an incredible conduit, truly, I've never seen anything like what you just did, but the moment you leave this manor that will go away. You will be hunted," she intoned, pleading in her brown eyes.

"I will not stay behind so that I can be killed. Especially not when I finally have the power to leave."

A familiar voice sounded from the edge of the ballroom, by the doors leading to the courtyard. Charlotte spun to see Charles Eringhorn. For a moment, she'd forgotten all about the few other guests remaining from society who had witnessed her power.

"I knew your family were evil," Charles shouted, and the rest of the guests fell silent.

"That will be enough from you," Charlotte snapped, forcing him to his knees with a wave of her hand. The spell fell over him, and she looked at Alexander, who rushed to Charles's side, ready for her orders.

"Stop the rest of them from leaving," Katherine urged, pulling back Charlotte's focus. "If you let them go, they will run to the authorities. Do you wish to bring more innocent people to this manor?"

She swallowed thickly, looking around at the carnage and blood splatters up the walls. Her limbs jerked unexpectedly.

Katherine bit her lip. “You can’t hold this much power for long. Release it.”

“It’s mine.”

Nathaniel’s voice floated into her consciousness, but it wasn’t out loud. It was in her head.

It’s not yours. It’s the spirits.

Her jaw slacked. “How did you do that?”

It’s the bond. It’s stronger now.

She blinked twice, shuddering at how he felt in her mind, how his deep voice caressed her darkest thoughts, especially the ones where she imagined slicing open the throats of Charles Eringhorn and the rest of his family.

“Get out of my head.”

Katherine’s eyes darted from him to her. “Enough of this. Charlotte, hold the boundary spell and don’t leave. For all our sakes.”

“I’ll take her to the cellar with Alexander,” Nathaniel stated. “Zachariah, Irene, kill everyone else here, except for Baron and Baroness Ellenwood.”

They didn’t try to leave, like the rest, and she realized they already knew what Nathaniel and Alexander were. The others attempted to sink into the shadows.

Charlotte panted, flexing her fingers, holding steady. “Don’t hurt them.”

“Then what would you have us do?” Nathaniel asked. “Let them go so they can tell everyone what happened here, and that you’re a witch. Your manor will be burned to the ground.”

“Persuade them. Bribe them. Whatever it takes. No one else should die today,” Charlotte told Nathaniel, her chest heaving. So much murder had already happened. The heavy energy of the souls who lingered slowly suffocated the room. "You speak of wanting to be mortal, yet you act like a vampire. You rely on it. You cannot just kill every problem."

"Those problems," he said, jaw clenching, pointing at the guests, "will come back to haunt us. To haunt you, more specifically."

Katherine tilted her head, sighing. "I can make them forget what happened tonight. I agree with Charlotte. There has been enough slaughter."

She watched Katherine walk over to the guests, her voice faint as she spelled each of them, staring into their eyes with her hands on their shoulders. The power in the room slowly waned. A hazy look washed over their expressions and one by one, they left the room, as if nothing out of the ordinary had happened, not even looking at the body parts all over the floor.

A dark figure caught Charlotte's eye from across the room, just beyond the pile of bodies. Her heart palpitated when she spotted Duke, darting through the ballroom and toward them.

"Duke!"

Yowling, he pounced through the air, grabbing the cockroach with his paws. Getrude's familiar wrestled underneath his strong legs. With one crunch, he bit into the insect, tearing the body apart. Shadows released from its body, swirling into the air before seeping into the ground in a shimmer of black.

The last time he'd done that, she stopped him. With a shake of her head, she said, "I'll never doubt you again."

He looked at her with wide yellow eyes as he devoured what was left of the cockroach.

After releasing the power back into the Realm of the Dead, Charlotte could barely keep her eyes open. The entire thing felt wrong. She had siphoned the ghosts just like Gertrude had done to her ancestors and family, although, the spirits tonight had consented.

Katherine and Nathaniel reappeared after dragging Gertrude's body away, who unfortunately had returned from the dead, while the others disposed of the body parts.

Charlotte turned to face Nathaniel. "Are we going to talk about what happened earlier?"

His eyes darkened. "Not tonight."

With a thick swallow, she glanced at Alexander who shot her an apologetic look, then at Katherine who was a little gray in her face, the bags under her sunken eyes showing the depletion of her magic. In the corner, Zachariah and Irene stuffed body parts into bags.

"Are you still going to kill me?" she asked pointedly, tired of being shrugged aside, especially considering she had just taken down the most powerful witch of their time. Still, she was careful with what she revealed about the ritual, knowing the other two vampires would kill her if they knew she could be used to make them mortal again.

Nathaniel stood, running his eyes over the four of them. "Leave us."

"Are you certain?" Alexander asked hesitantly.

"Yes."

Alexander took Katherine's arm, lifting her gently. "Come on, let's get you a cup of tea."

Charlotte watched them leave, her heart pounding once they were alone.

"We can talk freely now," he said wearily.

"Good," she said shakily, her lips buzzing from the adrenaline. "Are you going to answer me this time?"

"You lied to me," he said instead.

"I will not apologize for that. I was protecting myself from you. I knew you would lock me away if you discovered I had no intentions of doing the ritual, which, in case you were wondering, I would do in a heartbeat if the cost were anything but my life."

"Why?"

With a deep breath, she confessed, "Because I care about you."

"You shouldn't."

"Is that all you have to say?" she asked, scoffing.

"I am a monster and your caring for me will only get you hurt."

His lips curled as she looked at the decapitated corpses around him. She saw the moment the hope left his eyes, when his expression hardened into something more formidable.

"Yes, but I wanted you to be my monster," she stated, feeling ridiculous once the words left her mouth.

"I—do you think I enjoy being in this predicament?" he asked, standing now, stumbling over his words.

He never stumbled.

He continued, her heart racing as he towered over her. "Despite what you may think, I do not relish murdering innocents."

She snorted, noting that he did not rebuke her, and looked at the surrounding bodies. "I am not innocent. Tonight I almost killed Charles Eringhorn. Despite everything I said to you earlier, I considered murdering the man with no remorse, just like I did my uncle and cousin, and do you want to know my most sinful thought?"

"Always," he said in a deep rumble.

"I wish I had. It is my only regret for tonight because I am glad the truth came out. At least now we both know where we stand and there doesn't have to be any confusion over feelings."

With a wince, she sucked in a deep breath. He didn't say a damned word, just stood there, frozen, watching as shaky, angry confessions slipped from her lips.

"So you know," she added. "I will not go down without a fight and as you saw tonight, I'm no longer some sacrificial lamb you can order around. There is nothing I won't do to save myself."

With a lump in her throat, she lifted her dress and walked away, avoiding the puddles of blood. Her heart broke with each body she saw, their pain melding with her own. The heaviness of their suffering followed her like a dark cloud, all the way to Katherine's room. She could sense them, pressed up against the veil amid a well of confusion and anger.

Tears slipped down her cheeks, a surge of emotions washing through her.

"No more crying," she said aloud with a sniffle, wiping her nose with the back of her sleeve. After a few seconds, she rolled her shoulders back and lifted her chin.

If she had to embrace the darkness to beat it, then that was exactly what she was going to do.

Chapter Twenty-Two

The hex wound its way through Charlotte's mind, eclipsing the fringes of her every thought as she walked toward Katherine's room.

The shadowy corridors closed in around her, the air thickening with each hurried step. Her breath fogged in front of her, her fingers turning to ice.

A waft of sulfur lingered when she turned left, expecting to find the corridor to Katherine's room, but instead found a steep stairway descending into darkness.

Wide-eyed, Charlotte stumbled back, shaking her head when she saw something moving in the black depths.

Join us. Death is easier. You will see.

She stepped back, squeezing her eyes shut for a moment before slowly peeling back her eyelids to discover the corridor was back to normal, gas lamps flickering light over portraits that watched her with sentience behind their eyes.

The demon was playing tricks on her, and she wondered if that's who she had been hearing in her mind that whole time. The one she'd mistaken for an inner monologue.

A chill passed deep into the marrow of her bones.

Swallowing hard to remove the lump that formed in her throat, she picked up her pace and ran to Katherine's door, pushing it open before tumbling into the heavily jasmine-fragranced bedroom.

With her hands on her knees, she bent over, catching her breath before glancing up at the window.

"Christ!"

Her palm slapped to her mouth when she saw the demon watching her in the reflections, its grin wide, but eyes darkening.

She quickly closed the drapes. Was that also what her father had ensured in his last days? Being stalked by the Smiling Woman in every reflective surface, taunting him in his mind until he went mad.

With shaky lips, she forced back the sob quaking her chest. Her father had never said that's what was happening, but no one could understand much of what was happening in the end.

He suffered greatly.

The demon's voice screeched in her mind, the words wrapped in a building headache.

"Get out of my head!"

You can always be with him. The demon responded. *You fight to survive, yet there is nothing left for you here. Everyone you love is dead.*

"Go away!" she hissed, trying to keep her voice low so not to alert anyone to her whereabouts.

She had to get rid of that hex once and for all.

If only she could focus.

Unclenching her jaw, she steadied her breathing until her heart rate slowed, ignoring the brush of cold whisking over her neck.

With a glance around, Charlotte noted how neat everything was. The bed was made, linens crisp, fresh flowers were in a glass vase on her dresser, and her herbs and tonics were lined up. Nothing was out of place. Which should have made it easier to find her grimoires, in theory.

After rummaging through the bedside tables and dressers and finding nothing, Charlotte looked under the four-post bed and in the writing desk where she found a hand mirror inside one drawer.

She knew better than to turn it over, aware of what she would see behind her in the reflection, so left it in its place and turned her attention to the wardrobe. Behind it, she spotted the leather-bound grimoires stuffed between the wooden back and the paneled wall. "There you are," she whispered and wrenched them from their hiding spot.

A gnawing sense of urgency stayed with Charlotte as she retreated with the oldest of her family's grimoires in her hands, the heavy books weighing desperately against her aching forearms.

She hurried back to her bedroom, ignoring the shadows that moved in her periphery vision on her way back, or the voice that desperately tried to crack back into her mind.

Once she'd returned, she shoved a wooden chair under the door handle. Not that it would stop a vampire from getting in, but it would give her enough warning to hide the grimoires.

Duke mewled softly from her bed.

"I found them, Duke, but the demon is closer. My father lost time in the end. He was incoherent and couldn't talk. I fear I am close to that fate and don't want to hurt anyone, especially you."

He meowed in response, nestling up next to her when she heaved the massive books onto the bed.

"Will you help me?"

He blinked softly and slowly, and her heart ballooned.

After she climbed onto the bed, he nudged his mouth to her chin.

Crossing her legs, she pushed back a black coil of hair that had fallen loose. She opened the front cover, the dust and sharp parchment smell hitting her nose. With watering eyes, she flicked through the brittle, yellowing pages filled with symbols, rituals, practices, family history, and spells.

Her fingertips dragged over inked comments in the margins. Every page was a labor of devotion to the craft, and there were at least a thousand of them. She stopped quarter of the way through when she spotted a hauntingly familiar sketch. A shiver ran through her body as she dragged her thumb over the charcoal drawing.

The mark on her hip pulsed with its own heartbeat as she devoured the text.

Among the demonic beings trapped on Earth, the Smiling Woman, is the most ruthless. Once a powerful witch who became a demon after her death, she was imprisoned for centuries in a cursed object.

"Oh my gosh. Duke, I think she was imprisoned in the mirror."

Her lips parted. Had she let her out?

Was this her fault?

No, her father was hexed before she even touched that mirror. She dragged her finger down the page until she found confirmation.

For those who bear her hex, she can temporarily leave and attach herself to the victim, slowly oppressing them until they are consumed with darkness, often manipulating their reality until they either die or abandon their bodies, so she may take over their flesh.

An icy dread ran through her, and she closed her eyes, temporarily muting the uncanny sketch of the demon that she had seen stalking her in Sallow Manor.

Hours passed, the clock ticking mercilessly as she hurried through the pages of blood magic, a branch of sacrificial power, when she found the familiar ritual she had spotted before. The spell to break generational curses, which would potentially help her family, except it required a sacrifice from the bloodline and the caster of the curse. Meaning, she would have to die along with Gertrude.

She wished she was selfless enough to perform it, but every nerve in her body screamed at her to live. As the night swallowed what was left of the sun, Charlotte devoured every incarnation that might help, and the instructions on the ritual to break the curse. There wasn't any information about breaking the hex, but there was one about trapping a demon.

Shifting her position on the bed, she turned on her side, stretching out her aching limbs.

With fatigued fingers, she aimlessly sifted through the remaining pages to ensure she hadn't missed anything, struggling to pay attention when Duke's paw stopped her from turning the page.

A second paw landed on the page, his yellow eyes bright when he looked at her.

"What is it?"

She stroked him under his chin and brushed her gaze over the family tree.

She pulled Duke closer, squeezing him gently. "You are brilliant. You know that," she said into his fur, punctuated with a kiss.

The thirteen witch bloodlines covered each page. A large amount of magic was infused into the family line, spreading evenly across every witch. When a witch in the family died, that magic passed onto their closest female relative.

Her eyes glazed over eerie portraits drawn on an expired family tree. The Serea family. Each of them had a cross marked over their faces, their eyes crossed out.

They were all murdered.

She'd heard the story of Penelope Serea, the witch who had killed everyone in her family to gain more power and then killed herself.

It was a myth, a story to warn against seeking power, according to Charlotte's mother, but it was true. Penelope's portrait was the last one at the bottom of her family tree, and while she was deceased now, there was a note at the bottom.

That much power was not meant for one person. For when she died, it was taken from her.

Which meant, if she was the last of her bloodline, then all the magic meant for the Lysanmore's was hers. No wonder she could overpower Gertrude that night.

Charlotte's stomach hollowed. Her mother had read those grimoires, and her grandmother had warned her too. They didn't practice magic because they believed it wicked, but because they were afraid. Every witch had to unlock her power through her first spell. By warning her and Alice away from magic, she could stop them from activating the magic within their veins. Their mother knew what would happen if they did. There was so few of them left in the bloodline, that she didn't want either of her daughters ending up like Penelope Serea.

Wait a minute.

She glanced back up at the words under her portrait.

It was taken from her.

Someone stole all the magic from the Serea bloodline, which meant someone could take hers too. She was, after all, the last in her line. Which was likely why Gertrude hadn't outright killed her and hexed her. She didn't want Charlotte's soul, but her body, so she could sacrifice her in a ritual to take it all from her, to make herself even more powerful.

A wave of nausea washed over her.

"Katherine channeled me," Charlotte told Duke, who jerked at her unexpected conversation. "When we entered the Realm of the Dead. She gave me a load of twaddle, saying it's because I had been close to death, but it's because I'm powerful, Duke."

Charlotte bet it was Gertrude who took the power from the last in the Serea family and that was why she didn't kill Charlotte there and then. She wanted to sacrifice her on her ancestral grounds, so she could take all the magic from the Lysanmore bloodline. She did it to the Sereas, which meant no witch family was safe.

With a gasp, Charlotte told Duke, "Of course. Gertrude slowed down her ageing process. It takes an inordinate amount of magic to pull off a spell so complex and ongoing. The Avery bloodline is vast, their power is diluted but I felt Gertrude's. It was potent."

Wiping her forehead, she said, "I think I know what to do." Charlotte told Duke, who rubbed his nose against her fingers, relief in his eyes. "You knew, didn't you?"

He purred.

"If only you could talk."

He meowed and she smiled.

"I was told familiars aid witches with their spells," she said slowly, a glint in her green eyes. "Will you stay with me while I try?"

He tilted his head, blinking slowly.

"Good. Because I'm going to face my demon, Duke. I'm going to stop her" With a shudder, she glanced at the gap in the curtains, the reflection of the demon in the window, closer than ever.

She just hoped she could make it back to my body before she took it from her.

After she gathered all the materials from the kitchen, she sat cross-legged in the middle of her floor with Duke in her lap, surrounded by a circle of black salt, and candles, the flames illuminating the symbols inscribed onto the parchment spell pages of the grimoire.

She breathed in a heady breath of beeswax, mugwort, thyme, and rosemary. The patchouli would hopefully ground her enough.

The air was thick with smoke, her heartbeat raging as she looked over the incantations on the page to commune with the dead. Careful of her intonation, she recited the Latin. "Eos qui trans velum sunt invito ut mecum communicent. Adiuvate me. Velum rumpite, sed hunc circulum ne transeatis."

Charlotte closed her eyes, summoning the shadows that clung to the corners of the room. She took a deep breath, allowing the energy to coil around her.

"Fluat per me potentia tua ut inimicis meis imperare possim."

Sacrificial magic was needed because the power witches had on their own was not enough, but she had enough on her own. She could feel the magic of her ancestors coursing through her when the candles flickered wildly.

Duke stirred slightly, his claws curling into the bare skin of her legs. A jolt of energy pulsed through her palms, a bubbling power searing into her veins, flushing heat through her limbs, erasing any tightness in her joints.

All she had to do was lure it into the circle and trap it there and get back to her body before it did.

The veil fell in tatters around her. Mist shrouded the floor, hiding the circle of salt and candles.

Swallowing thickly, Charlotte stepped out of her body, looking around at the empty room.

Where was the demon?

Slowly, she turned, knowing it wouldn't come in if she was in the circle. Hesitantly, she stepped outside of it, leaving her body alone.

The temperature dropped, sending goosebumps prickling her arms and neck. With a shudder, she slowly turned, sensing eyes on her from the doorway. The smell of sulfur burned the air around her nostrils.

Breaths quickened in her lungs when she saw the demon again, but this time she was in its realm, and it was waiting for her.

Between a curtain of dark, long hair was an unsettling, too-wide grin and hollow eyes. Shadows darted erratically around her when she moved, her bare feet floating an inch off the ground.

Charlotte held her nerve, watching as the demon's eyes focused on her physical body, still sat on the ground, cross-legged.

Finally.

Whispers of Latin snaked from the demon's black, long, pointed tongue that slithered from her mouth. The mark on Charlotte's side seared with pain, and she dropped to her knees.

Panting, she wretched on all fours, trying to pull herself up but the heat in her stomach was so strong, all she could do was scream dry, raspy wails as she looked down at the fog.

Magic prickled her fingers and Duke's meow pierced through the veil, reminding her she was not alone.

That she was anchored.

She couldn't let her take her body. That bloody thing had taken her family from her and had disgraced her father's name.

Magic flickered in her fingers as she turned herself onto her side, feeling the grains of salt under her elbow. When she looked up, the demon was already standing over her body. The demon's long, charred fingernails grazed the back of Charlotte's neck, excitement widening its eyes, the hissing increasing in volume from her smile that reached the corners of her eyes.

No!

Trying to crawl back to her body took every ounce of strength left in her. Reaching out, she grabbed her own leg, screaming dryly as the demon hooked its fingers into her shoulders, a cackle echoing around them.

It was too late. She'd lost. The demon was already forcing its way into her body at the same time as she was, her mind splitting with agony.

A whirl of an eerie grin and darkness stole her vision when she tumbled through realms, relieved when she grabbed her thighs, blinking rapidly.

The room was back to normal, her heart racing, mouth dry. When she looked up, she spotted the Smiling Woman in the reflection of the window, trapped inside the circle and standing over her. This time, however, she was frowning, eyes fully black.

Duke hissed as she stood and stepped out, careful not to break the ring of salt.

Her lungs ached with each deep breath. "I thought it got me." Duke tilted his head, and she added, "I felt you on the other side. You gave me the strength to move."

A sigh of relief whooshed past her lips. It couldn't get her if it was trapped. All she had to do was not disrupt the magic there.

She jumped when three loud bangs erupted from the other side of the door.

Duke's yellow eyes shone in the darkness, signaling that it was safe.

She was met with the darkness of the hallway when she pulled the door open. Glancing down at the floor, she spotted a wooden chest with gold banding and embellishments.

Lying on top of it was two small, rectangular envelopes.

Both had her name on them, written in the most beautiful penmanship.

Inside the first was a card she recognized from the grand salon. On the back was the word prey and on the front, Nathaniel had written:

You always have a way out.

The date was two days from now. He had agreed to her former request to participate in The Hunt, or as she thought of it, a deadly game of hide and go seek from what Alexander had described. He was going to let her try to win her freedom.

Carefully, she placed the thick envelope on the dresser and opened the second.

Inside, it read:

Please accept this as my apology.
Sincerely,
Your Monster.

Charlotte opened the lid of the chest, her eyes widening when she saw the severed head of Charles Eringhorn. With a loud scream, she dropped the chest, watching as his decapitated head bounced onto the carpet, his bloodshot eyes still mirroring the terror of his final breath.

Chapter Twenty-Three

On the edge of the rain-soaked rooftop, Charlotte gasped, steadying herself against the howling wind, bringing her closer to the precarious end of the parapet.

"What the—"

How did she get up there? She had no memory of climbing onto the roof.

Peering into the darkness, amidst the fog stretching out over manicured lawns and blooming roses gardens, she saw the swaying translucent figures of her family. For a moment, she wondered if she was dreaming, but when she pinched her hand, nothing happened.

They were really there.

Her eyes brimmed with tears, rain soaking her hair as she looked at them, her stomach hollowing.

Alice wore the purple gown she'd been buried in, her soft, blonde waves tied back. Her mother's smile softened, her father's arm wrapping around the two of them with a gentle squeeze. They were together again, and all the anger that had consumed her father before the massacre was gone.

His familiar, deep voice sounded in her mind, cracking an ache in her expanding chest.

Come home with us, darling. We're waiting for you.

Tears flooded her eyes, falling thick and fast down her cheeks, mixing with the icy raindrops pattering over her and saturating her nightdress. She didn't think she would ever hear his voice again. For months, she'd spent every day recalling the intone to their words, replaying every conversation she could think of so she would never forget how they sounded.

Alice's soft plea tinkered into her head next, the sound wrapping around her like a warm blanket.

I miss you. Come home, Lottie.

Her stomach knotted at the name only her sister called her.

Slowly, her mother extended her hand, giving her a long, reassuring nod.

With trembling lips, Charlotte glanced down at the gardens below, captured by a sudden urge to jump.

Everything looked tiny from up there—the fountain, the statues, and beautiful flowerbeds. She hadn't even got to explore the grounds of Sallow Manor yet, but she could think of no more beautiful place to die.

The roses below were a bright crimson, encased in well-tended rock beds. Sprawling ivy covered the low, gray-bricked walls and in the distance, rain splashed against the dark surface of a pond surrounded by tall grass and a bench.

Death hounds, whose shadows moved against the sea of oak trees surrounding the property, growled when they noticed her silhouette poised against the dusky, indigo sky. Obsidian fur covered their large, muscular bodies. Their sharp claws carved into the wet earth as they readied themselves to run, saliva dripping from their canines.

Swallowing thickly, she looked down again, her head spinning.

Her mother's honeyed tone swept into her mind like a summer breeze.

It will only hurt for a moment. Then you will be home with us.

Her father's voice filtered in after.

You always were the one who held us all together. We can't be a family without you.

Her bare toes curled over the edge, lips shivering under the icy drops sliding down her face.

"I've missed you," Charlotte cried, a sob wrenching her chest.

As she moved one foot out, balancing herself hundreds of feet from the ground, Duke's yowl echoed through the rooftop, causing her to topple slightly. Arms outstretched, she balanced herself, her breath catching in her throat.

What was she thinking?

The last thing she remembered was locking Charles's head in the bathroom and covering it with a blanket before crawling back into bed. Something had lured her out there, or she had finally lost her mind to the hex.

Her body suddenly jerked forward, as if someone had tugged an invisible string inside her chest. The image of her family twisted, revealing the spirits' true faces—the witches that haunted Sallow Manor. The demon must have gotten to them, or they hated Nathaniel so much for killing them, that or they were punishing him by trying to get her killed.

"No! Please!" The plea came out raspy, the wound on her side pricking with heat. Blinking rapidly, holding her arms out for balance, she let the scream soaring through her throat rattle into the night.

"No!" she yelled when a second tug pulled her body. Her vision hazed through the tears, the hallucination of her family and all the comfort it offered, gone. No matter how hard she tried to walk backward, something was stopping her.

Duke growled from behind her, his nose nudging at her cold, bare ankles, begging her to turn back.

"I can't move, Duke!" she cried, panting. "I'm going to fall. Help. Help me. Please. I don't want to die."

A gust of wind propelled her forward. Her heart skipped a beat the moment she toppled over the edge, the rush of wind sucking all the air from her lungs.

Flailing her legs, Charlotte grasped around her for anything to hold on to, only clamping her eyes shut when the ground rushed up to meet her and her last second was consumed by a primal screech.

She didn't feel the impact. The silence of the landing was met with darkness. A breath curled into her lungs, then another, and when she opened her eyes, she realized she hadn't hit the ground at all.

Nathaniel's face hovered over her, his arms tight around her. Nothing hurt. He had absorbed all the impact of her fall.

Thick raindrops ran down his horrified expression, his wild gray eyes scanning her face.

Heavy pants left her chest, her eyes trailing up to the rooftop. "You caught me."

A sound crossed between a sigh and a groan whooshed past Nathaniel's lips. "I heard your scream," he husked. After a few deep breaths, he pulled her close to his chest. In a pained voice, he asked, "Why did you jump?"

"I didn't. It's the hex and the ghosts. I'm losing my mind, just like my father did. I thought I'd stopped it, but I just woke up out here, on the ledge. Oh God." She looked up at the dizzying rooftop. "Where's Duke?"

"I can hear him coming," Nathaniel said, and she heard his meow from the back entrance of the manor. "He's okay. You *are* okay. I'm going to find Katherine. We're going to break this hex, tonight, before it damned well kills you."

Chapter Twenty-Four

Charlotte closed her eyes, doubling over the moment Nathaniel placed her on his mahogany four-post bed. She breathed in his scent as she wrapped herself in his plum sheets, wincing as heat soared through the mark. Peering around, she noticed the faded pictures hanging over baroque black wallpaper, each one of beautiful landscapes with sunsets. Flames crackled from the small, cast-iron fireplace, smoke pillaring from the burning logs.

"Get Katherine!" Nathaniel's voice bellowed from the doorway.

She glanced up in time to see Zachariah speed away in a blur, and Alexander walk inside. They shared a quick, heated discussion before he too, left.

After a long exhale, Nathaniel turned to face her, his fingers gripping the deep wood of his dresser.

Coughing, Charlotte doubled over in pain, a fever consuming her mind. "I'm dying."

She wasn't sure if she'd spoken the words aloud until she heard his response.

"You *will* survive this." His voice was so certain that she almost believed him.

"Agh!"

Pulled mercilessly from the comfort of his bed, Charlotte was plunged into a hallucination of a memory so potent she could smell her father's cigar burning from the tray on the table.

"Charlotte," her father said, smiling from the armchair. "Are you ready for your first ball?"

"I think so."

She ran her fingers over her cheeks, trying not to wipe away the coverage, but it was so damned itchy. She'd tried her best to coat enough of the powder on her cheeks and nose to counteract the dust of freckles smattered across the middle of her face, but the faint tan still shone through.

"What's wrong?" he asked.

"It's the powder Mother put on my cheeks and nose."

"Come, let's wash it off."

"I can't. I need to be pristine tonight. It's the only thing that covers my freckles."

His brows creased. "Heavens, sweetpea. Why would you want to cover them?"

"Everyone thinks they're ugly."

He took a drag from his cigar pipe and blew out a billow of smoke. "Ridiculous. There is no girl more beautiful than my daughter. Believe me, one day, the woman in society will paint freckles on their faces so they can look more like you."

A laugh bubbled from her mouth. She knew he truly meant it too. "I hope tonight goes well," she said, picking at her cuticles. "I don't want to be mocked."

"You tell me if anyone says anything untoward to you," he said with a lopsided smile and smoothed down the sides of his black hair. "I'll have them exiled."

She leaned forward and grinned. "You are silly."

He walked to her and pulled her to his side in a hug before kissing the top of her head. "You know I'd do anything for you, sweetpea. Now, off we pop."

Before she could hold on to him and give him another hug, she was forced out of her memory in a splash of icy cold water, meeting the sting of loss all over again.

Tears welled in her eyes when she sat upright to find Nathaniel holding her hand.

"What happened?" he asked, wide-eyed. "You were convulsing and muttering."

Blinking slowly, fresh tears slid down her cheeks. "I slipped into a memory of my father, one I'd forgotten until now." Heaving back a sob, she added, "I never mourned him. What they did to him tainted all the good memories," she said, groaning as a fresh wave of agony seared not only through her body, but her tender heart.

Katherine's sharp tone cut through the room just as Charlotte tipped her head back, her heavy lids closing to the dim light. She hadn't even noticed anyone had returned.

"It's the hex," Katherine told Nathaniel and sat on the bed, judging by the sudden dip beside her. "It's going to force her to relive her worst pain, heighten it until she wants to die. For her, it is grief."

"I trapped the demon," Charlotte spluttered. "In a salt circle."

"It does not matter," Katherine said. "She can still influence you from there. She wants her to end her life."

"I won't let that happen," Nathaniel said gruffly. "What can be done?"

"I spoke with Gertrude, but she won't tell us how to help. No matter what I tried." She let out a long sigh and said, "But I might have something. I just need her grimoires, which I noticed were gone," Katherine said, and Charlotte's stomach knotted. She still didn't trust her.

"They're in my room," Charlotte relented as the pain got worse.

"Do what you must and it better work," Nathaniel warned. "Don't forget our deal, Katherine. You know what I'm capable of."

A brief silence hung between them before Charlotte heard muffled footsteps leave the bedroom. She felt someone squeeze her hand, the sound of her name echoing in her ears before she fell into another memory, this time at Lovett Manor with her sister.

Charlotte stood in the doorway of Alice's room, pushing her slippered foot sliding across the threshold.

Alice's mellifluous tone sounded from her bed. "What is it?"

"I can't sleep," Charlotte replied.

"Call Edith for some chamomile tea."

Charlotte chewed on her lip and walked inside. "Can I sleep here?"

Alice's head tipped back with a heavy sigh, her blonde waves spreading across the silk pillowcase. Even in her nightgown, with no powder on her nose, she looked beautiful. Not that Charlotte would tell her that. She wouldn't believe her if she did.

"No. You snore," Alice countered with a slight smirk tilting her rosy lips.

"I do not."

"That must be why you're not yet married," she teased, dragging them back to a recent conversation.

Charlotte scowled in her direction until her smile cracked the tension, and they both laughed. "I don't want to marry."

"Liar," Alice said and continued embroidering her tulips onto a small, square pillow. "That's what Father says. I've seen all your poetry books. You're a romantic."

Charlotte rolled her eyes and sat in the armchair below the window. Beyond it, ribbons of navy-blue blended together, alight with pinpricks of a thousand stars. It really was a beautiful night. "I haven't found anyone I like yet. Besides, no one calls on me. They think I am odd."

"You *are* odd," Alice teased and placed her needle and thread down. "It is not a bad thing. They are simply envious, for they are far too normal. You will find a wonderful man to marry soon. You must, if you have any hope of leaving here."

"I don't want to leave."

Alice's light brows knitted together. In the lightest of whispers, she said, "Of course you do! I won't be here to protect you anymore and Mama is, well, she can't help you either."

"Father isn't himself. He will be okay soon. It is the stress from business."

"You make excuses for him," Alice said, lowering her voice to a whisper, her green gaze flitting to the door before she stared at Charlotte, who felt two inches tall under her sister's hardened stare.

Charlotte leaned forward, her fingers crowning her knees. "After the wedding, things will go back to normal. Of that, I am certain."

Her lips parted, eyes turning cold. "So you are saying I am the problem? That it is my being here why he can't control his damned temper?"

"No!" Charlotte spluttered quickly. "It's just, well, your marriage will bring us more wealth and opportunity."

She shook her head. "Why do you defend him?"

Goosebumps traveled over Charlotte's arms and legs. Her sister was right. He'd grown more aggressive as of late, but after she confronted him he promised her things were going to be different now. No matter how dysfunctional things could get, they were a family. They only had each other, and Charlotte desperately wanted them to be close again, like they used to be when they were children.

"He's our father."

A defeated smile passed through her pouted lips. "You know I love him, Lottie. I do. No matter what he's done, but I can't—" Her voice broke. "I can't leave you here with him. I'm scared for you. Something has changed inside him. He can turn on a penny and if he hurts you or worse."

"He would never go that far, Alice," she said pointedly, her brows raised. "You know he wouldn't! He loves us."

"You're just like Mother. You both try to rationalize his behavior. Just promise me one thing: that if you're ever in danger, you will leave. You will always have a home with me, no matter who I am married to."

Charlotte smiled the toothiest grin. "Is this your way of saying you will miss me?"

"Don't be ridiculous," Alice replied, and put the pillow on her bedside table. "Now, I am weary. You should get some rest too. Tomorrow is the Pennyworth ball."

"Okay. I will try." She stood and walked to the door. "Goodnight, Alice."

Alice called out to her before she could leave. "And keep that cat away from your new dress too. The last thing we need is for you to be covered in fur."

Charlotte tsked. "His *name* is Duke."

She could hear her exasperated sigh from inside. "Why you keep him is beyond me. He is a wild animal and is likely plagued with disease."

"Well, so is Charles Eringhorn and you still want him," Charlotte quipped, and stepped out the way just as a pillow came hurtling in her direction.

"Close the door behind you!" she shouted, but Charlotte purposely left it an inch open. If only to aggravate her for saying that about Duke.

"Love you, Sister," Charlotte sing-songed and walked back to her room.

Her breath halted in her lungs as she hurtled back to the present. Sitting up, she spluttered and coughed, regret drowning her.

Nathaniel's stormy gray eyes became the anchor in her sea of grief. "Katherine is bringing a potion," he stated when she managed to fix her stare on him without toppling to one side from the dizziness. "It won't be long now."

With a sniffle, she tried to hold it back, but tears flooded again. "I said so many stupid things to my sister. If I had known what would happen, I wouldn't have said them because she was right about what our father would do, but only because he was possessed."

"Don't reminisce about what could have been. It is a horrid torture." Nathaniel's thumb swept her cheek, wiping the drops away. "These memories only hurt because they are filled with love. You loved your family, and they loved you," he said deeply as she choked out another sob. "Hold on to that. That demon, my mother, and all the Avery witches left in London will try to turn your soft heart into a weapon. You cannot let them."

"But I miss my family," she spluttered, a long guttural scream vibrating behind closed lips when the permanence of them never coming back sunk in. "They're never coming back and I can't breathe sometimes. It hurts too much, and I just want this to all be a dream. I want to go back."

Panic settled in, setting her nerves on fire. Trying to suck in deep breaths, she gripped the covers, unable to fully inflate her lungs.

Nathaniel's hands landed on her shoulders, and with wild eyes, he pulled her tight in an unexpected hug that elicited a gasp from her lips. "I'm sorry," he mumbled into her ear, cradling her head to his chest. She breathed in his intoxicating blend of musk and smoked wood, intermixed with fresh sweat. Somewhere along the way, unbeknownst to her until that very second, it had become her favorite scent.

"I know this feels like you're going to die," he said. "It's the worst kind of pain imaginable, but you will survive it. *I promise.*"

He held her for the next several minutes, stroking her hair as she screamed into a void of pain heating her from the inside. Even from the other side of the manor she could feel the demon's pull, but being in Nathaniel's arms, listening to his heartbeat through his chest, grounded her.

She clutched the fabric of his white shirt and squeezed her eyes shut, knowing if anyone knew how she felt, it was the centuries old vampire who had outlived everyone he loved, who even had to kill his own mother to protect the slaughter of children.

Katherine cleared her throat and walked inside. "Am I interrupting?"

"Did you have it?" Nathaniel asked, warning lacing his tone.

Zachariah nodded, walking in behind her. "I watched her make it."

"I'm not your enemy," she stated.

Charlotte pulled back from Nathaniel, her brows creasing. They didn't trust her either.

Katherine sighed. "The potion won't work right away, but by morning, the hex should be gone. You can only hope the demon hasn't attached itself too much already, because there's no getting rid of that."

"It's not. The potion will work," Nathaniel intoned.

"You almost sound concerned, Nathaniel," she said, spite lacing each word.

He didn't respond. Instead, he grabbed the vial of golden, bubbling liquid from her hands and brought it to Charlotte's lips. "Trust me," he said when she flinched. "It's safe."

She winced, breathing in the strong, perfumed scent. "How do you know?"

Zachariah answered this time. "Because Katherine won't risk the lives of her family."

Wide-eyed, she gasped, looking at Nathaniel. "You threatened her family?"

"From the very beginning," he said unapologetically.

No wonder Katherine acted suspiciously. She didn't even want to be there.

Her next question was lost in a wave of anguish. Desperate, she grabbed the vial and tipped the contents down her throat, the cloying liquid burning her esophagus on the way down.

Katherine tilted her head, watching carefully. "I'll check on Gertrude again and strengthen the barrier spell."

Nathaniel nodded once, letting out a sigh when she left. He looked at Zachariah and said, "We will manage now. You can go home."

Zachariah nodded and left the room in a hurry, along with Katherine.

Once they were alone, Charlotte hunched over, wincing against ripples of pain tearing over her spine. "This potion is like liquid fire."

"I know," he said, brushing back a lock of her hair. "It's just one night you have to get through, and then it'll be over."

She bit her lip, exhaustion rippling through her. "I need to lie down. Will you stay with me?"

He brushed his thumb against her cheek as she slowly closed her eyes. "Yes."

"I still need to talk to you about your *gift,*" she added with a yawn, letting him know she hadn't forgotten that chest he left at her door. Although she *had* told him she regretted not killing Charles, so she couldn't truly be angry at him doing it.

"Charles disrespected you and your family," he drawled as she edged into a slumber. "He deserved it."

"I shouldn't have said anything."

"I would have killed him even if you didn't," he added with a brush of his fingers through her hair.

"Yes, but..." A yawn cut her off and she rolled onto her side.

"His death is on my hands, not on yours," he promised, whispering reassuring words into her ear as she slowly passed out.

A searing pain shot through her forehead, right between her eyes, making her groan and squeeze her eyes shut.

Nathaniel's fingers squeezed tighter around hers. "I'm not going anywhere. You can get through this. Just hold on for a few more hours."

Those words shouldn't have been reassuring. If the hex didn't kill her, he eventually would. Even if he didn't want to. Alexander had even said he ended up murdering the lovers he'd blood bonded with. Yet, she couldn't help but hope. He had offered her a way out, even though her chances of winning The Hunt were low.

"What about the ritual you want me to do?" she asked, voice cracking.

"Let us not think of that right now."

"Will you hold me?" she asked faintly when she felt the urge to lose herself in another memory came over her.

The bed dipped when he climbed into bed next to her, his body pressing hard against hers.

She wanted to believe that every time that night, as the hours bled together, when Nathaniel pulled her tighter against him, that it meant more to him. But he couldn't feel those things. Alexander had said as much. It was all in her imagination and since arriving at Sallow Manor, she had allowed herself to fall victim to the very thing she'd been warned against, even by Nathaniel himself. She had grown to like him, to desire him even, to think of him constantly.

When he pulled away and left her alone in the bed to greet Katherine, she ached to have him close again.

His voice resonated in her ears. "Is there anything that can ease her suffering?" While Charlotte couldn't see Katherine, she assumed the worst judging by Nathaniel's groan.

"There is not. I'm sorry. Is she asleep?" Katherine asked.

"I think so."

"I can take over, so you don't have to be alone with her."

"No." The sharp edge in his tone made her heart race. "I can watch her."

"What about the bond?" Katherine protested. "You have been alone with her for hours already."

"I've got it under control." His tone teetered on dangerous, and Charlotte wondered if he actually did.

God, she wished she could know the true extent of how he felt. If he even thought of her like that? At least focusing on her confusing flutter of feelings was distracting her from the nausea and pain sweeping through her body in slow, but relentless waves.

After a few minutes, the hex deepened, clawing into her very soul, and the agony became so much worse. She was used to pain. Even on her best days, it was there. In fact, she could barely remember a time when she wasn't in some level of pain, but the hex was another level of torture, stealing her words and breath with the jabs of sharpness that made her want to die just so she wouldn't have to feel this anymore.

Something warm jumped beside her on the bed. Duke snuggled against her stomach, his paws on her abdomen, and she burst into tears, drawing the attention of both Nathaniel and Katherine.

His soft meow was everything in that moment, pulling her back from the darkest fingers of her thoughts. Claws extended gently against her nightgown, his wet nose nudged her chin when she contemplated giving up.

The pain was lessening. Only a smidge, but enough that she no longer wanted to throw herself from the window just for some relief. Once Katherine left, Nathaniel returned to hold her, his head hitting the pillow as he wrapped his arms tightly around her. "It's not long left now."

"Can you give me some of your blood?" she asked when the hex mark burned with a fresh wave of heat.

"I don't know if it will help with this kind of pain."

"Please," she said faintly. "I need something. Anything."

"Okay. Hold on." With a heavy exhale, he brought his thumb to his fangs and pierced his skin. "Here."

He pressed his finger to her lips, painting them with crimson. She licked them away, sucking gently for more until she felt it coat her tongue.

She shifted her body until her head was resting against his chest until she could hear the steady thrum of his heart. Clinging to him weakly, with closed eyes, she murmured, “Thank you for staying with me.”

She swore she heard his heart skip a beat but was too tired to think too much into it.

Chapter Twenty-Five

After a few uninterrupted hours of sleep, Charlotte awoke to the sensation of Duke jumping off the bed. She listened as he left the room, likely hunting for some milk from one of the maids, who she was glad to discover treated him far better than the staff at Lovett Manor ever had.

Her eyes fluttered open to the dark, the lids gently shutting when she felt Nathaniel's arm tighten around her as she adjusted her position on the bed.

Flickers of touch ran between them when she turned to face him, his fingers diving into her black curls. His breaths grew longer and more pronounced as she inched closer to him, his touch whisking her waist.

A flurry of butterflies stormed through her abdomen, her heart racing. She bit her lip as a thought shoved into the forefront of her mind. *Damned to Hell, he could hear her pulse.*

She hated that she couldn't even hide her body's reaction from his keen sense, yet she had no idea what he was feeling.

With a sudden tug, his arm was around her waist. He pulled her close, biceps tensing.

"Are you cold?"

"Yes," she whispered with a shaky breath, even though it wasn't true. The shivers running through her had nothing to do with temperature. With a smooth shift of his hips, he entwined her legs with his and moaned softly into her hair. Sparks shot through her lower extremities, tingling her toes.

The restraint in his low sound of pleasure was enough to send her over the edge.

"How are you feeling?"

"Better. The pain is gone," she said, turning to face him. "Even the pain in my joints. I almost feel normal again."

He trailed his fingers over her hip, sighing relief. "Good."

Tipping her nose forward until it brushed the tip of his, she let out a stammered breath, then held it.

"Don't do that."

"Do what?" she asked in a soft voice, the facade of innocence obvious.

He looked at her with hooded eyes, as their breaths mixed, lips just an inch apart. "You know what you're doing."

She pressed up against him once more, a smile lifting the corners of her mouth.

"Stop," he murmured against her lips, but his tone begged the opposite. "Before I lose all control."

Her breath caught at the thought and further flutters sprang to life, but this time, between her thighs.

Tempting the monster was a terrible idea. Awful. Dangerous. Foolish.

But she was trapped, eyes closed, her body arching into his. Cautiously, she pressed her palm to his firm pectoral muscles, and he snarled when his heartbeat galloped against her hand.

She threaded her fingers through the soft tresses of his midnight hair, her fingertips purposely grazing the back of his neck. His scent was intoxicating. She breathed deeply, her mind fogging with the temptation of desire, wondering if he would taste as good as he smelled.

Slowly, she lifted her lips closer until they were almost touching. She tangled her fingers deeper, searching his face to see if there was anything that revealed he wanted this too.

As her lips grazed his, shadows cast into his eyes until the darkness in them swallowed the smoke of his irises. "You don't want this," he husked.

Her lashes fluttered as the confession fell from his mouth. She consumed his words, allowing them to fill her up, before saying, "I do."

His eyes squeezed shut, his dark brows pulling together in the middle, wrinkling the skin at the bridge of his nose as if her words were a kind of torture.

"It's the blood. You're not thinking properly," he said in a pained whisper, but his questing hands told a different story. His fingers trailed through her hair before sliding down her neck to her clavicle.

"Yet you are not pulling away," she whispered, her heart skipping a beat when their lips brushed lightly with every word. "Let us pretend, just for tonight, that you do not wish to kill me and there is no ritual or blood bond."

His forehead dipped to touch hers, his fingertips gently caressing her spine, a warmth spreading through her core as he suddenly tugged her closer. "I *don't* want to kill you."

His pupils dilated when he looked at her, the shock of his penetrating, heated gaze making her gasp.

"Then why are you letting me take part in The Hunt?" When he didn't answer, she pressed him. "Tell me."

With hooded eyes and a thickly graveled tone, he said, "I just want a reason to chase you."

The thought of him chasing her through the manor sent an unexpected warmth into her core. She cleared her throat, then licked her lips and rushed on before nerves could tangle her tongue.

"I would want you to catch me," she said, her breath hot against his lips.

The silence was heavy, their lips flickering touches, when he finally grunted, "Fuck it," on a sharp breath, and his mouth claimed hers.

Her body tensed for a second before she kissed him back, his passion igniting something hidden inside her. Time stilled, his tongue teasing against hers. Excitement bloomed over her skin, his touch eviscerating all her other senses.

He deepened the kiss, and when he pressed himself harder against her, her thighs fell open, a silent, desperate plea escaping her in a moan as her lungs begged for air, but she couldn't pull away.

She didn't want to.

All she could think about was him consuming every inch of her, of how all she wanted was for them to stay like that, in the dark room where things between them were not contractual, or doomed.

A whimper left her lips when he rocked his erection against her, the large bulge taut under the thin fabric of his underwear. Heat drove through his length, and she imagined reaching down and taking the shaft in her hands.

Slowly, she dragged her fingers over the thick ropes of muscle contracting under her hand when she trailed over his lower abdomen, tracing the dipped V-shape, inching lower.

With a flexed jaw, he pulled away and rested his forehead against hers, panting. "Forgive me."

Blinking twice, she leaned closer to his lips, but he turned his head, leaving a hollow ache in her chest.

"*Nathaniel,*" she whispered when he wouldn't look at her. Soft fingertips grazed the sharp edge of his jawline as she tried to get him to turn back. "My doing this has nothing to do with your blood," she protested, knowing why he'd pulled back, the cold distance between them too much to bear.

With a sweep of his thumb over her swollen lip, he said, "When I take you, I want you fully lucid."

Dragging her tongue over the warmth on her lips, she let out a long, shaky breath as she mulled over the word *when.* With a roll of his hips, the head of his thick cock twitching against her thigh, he moved back, and her heart stammered.

He was aroused by her. She hadn't imagined it or mistaken his kiss for the bond. His lips were pulled into their familiar, neutral hard line, a sheen of sweat covering his forehead, his jaw ticking when he looked at her lips. Nathaniel wanted more than just her blood.

God be damned, she wanted him too. Even if it was just for one night, tonight.

"Don't go," she said when he shifted his weight, her voice breathy but with a surety that surprised even her.

He clamped his eyes shut, then opened them again and wrapped his arm around her. "I'm not. Now turn around and sleep," he commanded, brushing her hair back behind her ear with a softness she didn't think those strong fingers could produce.

She rubbed her fingers over his arms, a gentleness she assumed he was not usually afforded from the way he jolted. Slowly, she entwined her fingers with his and closed her eyes.

Chapter Twenty-Six

In the throes of a dream, a heaviness lifted from Charlotte's soul. When she awoke, she noticed the wound on her hip had dissolved, along with the constant ache that accompanied it.

A sigh of relief passed through her lips, her mind sharper than ever, but all she could focus on was Nathaniel's muscular arms secured tightly around her, the tips of his fingers precariously close to caressing the underside of her breast, only meeting the skin on a deep inhale. The hardness of his erection pressed against the curve of her back. As he dove deeper, she froze, bringing her bottom lip between her thumb and finger. The sheer size pressing into her sent a warmth blossoming between her legs.

His hot breath ghosted her neck as he moaned in his sleep, his fingers tightening on her breast, thumb grazing her peaking nipple, pulling her tighter.

A knot formed in the back of her throat. Lying there, knowing the bloodlust he held for her, with her neck so close to his fangs, unconscious or not, sent goosebumps rising as a tingle crawling over her skin. A tingle heavy with carnal promise. There was just something so thrilling about being prey while an unconscious predator slept at her back.

She turned her body to face him, shifting in his arms, dragging her palm over her thigh, hiking the fabric of her nightdress up with it. Her gaze trickled over the pair of fangs glinting in the darkness, beneath them a thin trickle of blood kissing his swollen bottom lip from biting down as he slept.

He moaned again when she rolled her hips up against him, his eyes dancing restlessly behind his lids.

Every slight flicker of touch set her nerves alight. It had been years since she had been with a boy, but Nathaniel was all man and made her feel things that robbed her of all sense, filling her with sparks in place of the consistent, dull pain that throbbed in her joints.

Pushing back a stray lock of dark hair from his forehead, she admired the way the light cut a contour under his cheekbones, enhancing his already sharp features. Slowly, she brought her fingers down, pausing at his lips.

Pressing gently over his skin, she gasped when she felt the outline of his fangs, grazing her touch over the sharp point. Closing her eyes, she leaned forward, almost pressing her lips to his, but stopped at the last second when her skin feathered his. Long, dark lashes flickered, fanning a delicately detailed shadow under his eyes and all she could think was how she wanted his hands between her legs, kneading the tension tightening in her stomach.

Slowly, she dragged her hand up, exploring the space between her thighs, and struggled to swallow a moan as wetness greeted her.

What was she thinking? He was sleeping and she was taking advantage. Carefully, she swiveled her body away from him, twisting until she was on her side and climbing out of the covers.

Strong hands grabbed her, yanking her back onto the bed, facing her to a now very awake Nathaniel. His stare darkened when he looked at her. "Don't start something unless you're willing to finish it."

She gasped when she realized he was referring to the almost kiss. "You were asleep."

"You woke me," he said with a low rumble reverberating in his chest, eyes drifting southward to her pouty lips as she bit the bottom one.

"It drives me crazy when you do that."

"It does?" she asked, a victorious smirk curved her lips, and she increased the pressure, her teeth sinking deeper into the swollen flesh.

"You look better," he intoned, gripping her hip solidly, then gliding his thumb over her hip in tiny circles, which was free of the wound.

"I feel better. The effects from blood have worn off too," she added, so he knew that what was happening was real.

Nathaniel crossed his arms over his chest. "Do you still want to leave?"

Her brows knitted together, then realization dawned. He was referring to her trying to climb out of the bed moments ago.

"No."

His hand blurred to her wrist and her stomach somersaulted as his nostrils flared. Her mouth watered, disbelief forming her mouth into an O as he dragged her arousal coated fingers closer and inhaled deeply. "What a naughty little lamb. Were you touching yourself while I slept mere meters away?"

A blush crept up her throat. "I—oh God."

She hardly had time to register her embarrassment before he drew the glistening digits past his lips and tasted her. Nathaniel's tongue circled the sensitive tips, then darted to the V of taut skin between her index and middle fingers, flicking licks.

Her eyes widened, utterly enthralled as he sucked them, never ceasing the deft motions of his tongue. Charlotte had no hope of muting her moan when his fangs grazed the pads.

"Fuck, you taste good." A deep, cavernous groan resonated in his chest as he watched her through shuttered eyes, pupils wide in anticipation. "What were you thinking about?"

She rolled her bottom lip between her teeth, guiding his eyes to her mouth. "You," she admitted huskily, the confession blushing her cheeks. "I was thinking about how it would feel to have your lips on me."

"Where *exactly*?"

Her heart thundered against her ribcage like a bird barred behind an unforgiving cage, her breaths escaping in shaky bursts, but she met his seductive stare and held it. "Everywhere."

Reckless, desperate need swam in his eyes. "Show me."

Heat flooded her cheeks as she looked at him with wild, glossy eyes. "I can't do that. It's improper and..." she trailed off before finishing.

"To hell with improper," he said deeply, every word a purr in her ears. "Now, show me what you were doing with those fingers."

Hesitantly, she searched his face, searching for any spark of a jest, but nothing in his hardened expression showed any sign that he was toying with her.

His intrusive stare held hers when she slowly reached down, sliding her fingers into her soaking folds, swallowing a moan when she circled her swollen bud clumsily, stroking up and down.

Nathaniel licked his upper lip. "Let it out," he commanded. "I want to hear you."

Her clitoris throbbed sharply with his stern command, her pulse thudding within the bundle of nerves just as her carotid had when his fangs sank into her neck.

Slowly, he ran his hands over her stomach, gliding them over the thin fabric of her nightgown until he reached the swell of her breasts, exposing them to the cool night air. Warmth cascaded from his skin to hers as he cupped, his large hands enveloping them entirely, and moaned when her nipples pebbled against his palms. Every part of her wanted him to dominate her, not that she wanted to admit that.

Goosebumps pricked over her skin as he circled his thumb over her nipple, sending shockwaves down to her clitoris. Pinching his fingers around the delicate skin of her nipple, he held it there until she whimpered. Arching off the bed, she rocked against her fingers, desperate for a release.

Her chest heaved, a faint breath escaping when he leaned over, nipping and teasing her with his tongue, fangs gliding over the swell. Finally, he drew her swollen peaks into his mouth, moving between both, his fiery licks sending heat soaring to her core.

Pulling back just an inch, he hovered over her nipple, and with a hot exhale said, "You moan so prettily for me, little lamb."

Delicious tremors quivered her lips, and she moaned weakly, her breath cutting off midway when pulses of heat chased through her spine. His praise deepened her thrill, her eyes falling closed. She couldn't believe that she was doing this, but God did it feel good.

His husky voice rumbled into her. "Hmm, so responsive to even the slightest stimulation." He paused, the corner of his mouth tilting upward. "Do you like it when I touch you there?"

Charlotte ached to explore his body in return. *Yes, she wanted him desperately,* she thought. She nodded, unable to form the words, sweat beading her skin.

"Use your words," he said in a purr, sliding a hand under her knee and continuing dangerously higher. Her legs fell open in invitation, a moan passing through her lips.

"Yes, I do."

He chuckled. "What about here?"

She arched into his stroking hands, her eyes rolling to the back of her head as he palmed her. His tone deepened and his throbbing cock ground high against her inner thigh. "You're so wet." His pained, hungry voice toppled her into delirious, inescapable *need.*

Every touch was blissful, a desirous torture as he prodded her opening, teasing her entrance with one finger. She pushed herself down, moaning when he pushed inside, the pad of thumb still rubbing her clit side to side, bringing her closer to the edge. Her walls clenched around him and he groaned, then lifted his head. "You feel so damned good. I *ache* to taste you."

Her heart skipped a beat, and she looked at him with those fuck me eyes, biting hard on her bottom lip. She rocked against the glide of his finger pushing under the hood of skin, sending sparks traveling into her legs and toes.

"Not yet, *love,*" he said when she edged closer, tasting the pinnacle of release.

"Don't stop," she begged when he slowed his strokes, chasing the warmth of his touch. "Please. *Nathaniel.*"

He grunted in a half groan, half laugh. "Keep saying my name like that and this will be over before either of us are ready."

"I want you to take me now," she begged wantonly.

A storm brewed in the pools of his eyes, gray and depthless. Tunneling her fingers through his messy hair, another desperate moan escaped her.

He ignored her plea and purred, "You're doing so well." His fingers rubbed her clit in slow, steady strokes, slowing every time she came close, brushing a spot that sent her hips arching off the mattress. "Tell me you're mine, *Charlotte.*"

A gasp knotted in her throat. It wasn't the first time she had heard her name on his tongue, but this time it sounded different. Desperate even.

"Could I be yours?" she asked, the bond straining between them like a tight band, ready to snap at any moment.

With a grip on her thigh, he drew her closer, holding her in a hard embrace, his thumb pressing hard against her swollen clit. "Do you know what that would mean?" he questioned, his tone serious.

"That you might eventually kill me because of the bond?" she uttered through a gasp, pleasure cascading through her core, and eyed his thick, pouty lips, wishing she could kiss them again.

"It means I would never let you go. It is not only the bloodlust of the bond that draws me to you," he admitted, bringing her closer with each sweep of his torturous fingers. "It is your soul, your heart, your mind, and yes, *your blood.* It is all I can think about."

She ran her fingers over his chiseled jawline, grazing the tips of his fangs protruding over his lips, struggling to focus as he wound her tighter until she was rocking her hips, chasing his prolonged, expert touches.

A shiver rippled the muscles in his back as just a dribble of liquid heat soaked through his underwear and against her leg, as she pressed her fingers against his fangs.

"Then bite me," she said, losing herself in his caress, to the way he pushed his erection against her body in fervent strokes.

She had definitely lost her mind, but those thoughts kept coming. He was darkness in her light, tempting her to wander. She never thought she would want to go willingly.

"I won't be able to stop," he said, eyes trailing to her exposed breasts, nipples peaked and damp from his earlier administrations. "It's already too much being this close to you and hearing your blood rushing through your veins," he paused and inhaled sharply through his nose, "your intoxicating scent perfuming the air and arousal running down my wrist, soaking the sheets."

"I want you," she said, swallowing hard. "I want *all* of you, *even* if it's risky."

He sat up abruptly, simultaneously slipping his fingers from her in one smooth movement, leaving an aching, empty void in their place. *No, he can't stop now.* She shivered, a wash of cold air slithered over her as she chased his body up, rocking against air, when his fingers came down in a slap against her clit.

"Don't tempt your death like that," he said, tone so deep the sound resonated, tickling her eardrums. "Or I will spank your ass until it's all pretty and pink."

She grabbed his sharp jawline between two fingers, challenge threading her stare, her words biting. "Then control yourself."

While she wanted him to dominate her, she wasn't going to allow him to hide behind the bond. He took so much pride in his restraint, so he could damn well control himself when it came to her blood.

A moan vibrated her teeth when he moved down, peppering kisses in a trail over her breasts, stomach, to between her legs. She ran her fingers over taut muscles, feeling the dips and valleys of his toned back before he moved down, his fangs splitting as his jaw unhinged, revealing three sets of fangs.

He rolled his erection against the bed, his fangs nipping her silky folds, spearing his tongue inside. Pulling back for a second, he said, "Damn, I'm going to come just from the taste of you."

Liquid fire ran through her veins, her stomach tightening with each lick.

"You like this?" he asked, humming against her.

"Yes."

"What if I stopped playing so nice?"

God, she wished he would. When his fangs nicked her skin, she winced, but the pain quickly turned into pleasure.

"Oh!"

Turning his head, she moaned when three sets of fangs sunk into the crease of her thigh in a sharp, precise bite. His moans reverberated through her skin, his essence inside of her like a disease, consuming every part of her until she was feverish and couldn't breathe.

What an exquisite, reckless, foolish, wonderful way to die.

Her fingers curled into the sheets, every biting sting of his fangs jolting a thrum of pleasure into the glistening area to his right.

Nathaniel's hips rocking against the covers as he continued with a hot suction against her skin, the rush of blood leaving her swept tingles all over her body, raising goosebumps over her exposed breasts and limbs.

It was only when she pushed her fingers between her legs, desperate to finish, that he pulled away from the bite, stopping her with a tight grip around her wrist.

"Mine," he grunted, blood leaking down the sides of his unhinged jaw.

There he was, her monster, with those dark veins around his features, his pupils vertical slits, and crimson spilling from those pointed canines.

Closing his eyes briefly, he let out a masculine hum from the back of his throat before burying his head between her legs, his tongue working the tightness from her clit before spearing inside her.

With a loud moan, she ground herself up against his mouth, screaming his name with a frantic thrust. "*Nathaniel.*"

Her walls clenched when he pulled back, placing one finger inside her instead while curling the tip of his tongue against her swollen bud, humming vibration into her folds. Soft cries left her mouth as she lifted her hips, reaching down to grab a fistful of his hair, holding him in place, grinding against his fangs. Slowly, he pushed a second finger inside, stretching her.

"Oh God, Nathaniel," she choked out, and he moaned into her, fingers gripping her thigh hard enough to leave bruises.

Every swipe of his beautiful tongue lifted her higher, until she was feverish, holding back a scream behind closed lips until she remembered what he'd said.

He wanted to hear her.

Letting it out, she screamed as he closed his lips around her sensitive flesh, sucking gently, tipping her into oblivion. Her release shredded through her, from the tips of her toes, through her entire body. She clenched around his fingers, pulsing rhythmically.

"Oh, fuck, I'm going to—ahh," he groaned against her wetness.

Broken, raspy grunts left his mouth as he held her in place, his hips shunting, spilling his release onto the sheets, soaking them with each primal moan against her, pulling the last pulses of climax from her body.

Easing his fingers out of her, he lifted his shuttered eyes to meet hers, pupils dilating back to their normal shape.

She tipped her head back, panting, watching as he swirled his tongue over his fingers, eyes closed.

"You were perfect," he purred, his fangs retreating into his gums. "I've never finished just from doing that before."

Rubbing her legs, he climbed on all fours, layering himself over her. His lips were glistening with her desire, and he pressed them to hers, kissing her softly before rolling onto his side.

"Are we still going to play in The Hunt tomorrow?" she asked, turning onto her side as the weight of what had just happened settled over her.

"Are you able to participate?"

"What do you mean?"

"How is your pain?"

She grazed her fingers over her joints. Ever since embracing magic, she'd barely felt but wisps of it. "Mostly gone."

"Then why would we not?" he asked, raking fingers through messy, dark waves.

"Because, you're going to catch me in seconds," she said, pointing out his unfair advantage.

"What would be the fun in that?"

"So you're going to hold back?" she asked, hope charging in her voice.

"Not at all," he said in a low growl, bringing his mouth to the tip of her ear. "You're going to have to find a way to stop me."

"If I can't?"

"Then you'll lose, and I'll have to sacrifice your tender heart."

Her muscles stiffened, her chest heaving in a breathy gasp. "You told me you don't want me to die. That you just want to chase me."

"I *want* you to *win,* but if you do not I *will* hold you to our agreement."

"Are you quite serious? After everything that has happened between us?"

"Did you think you were going to fuck your way out of this?" he asked, grazing his fingers over her hips, dropping lower until she stiffened. "I'm disappointed."

"So am I," she spat, tears welling in her eyes, fingers flexing. "I thought you cared about me."

"I *do.*" He edged closer to her throbbing, messy folds, her hips begrudgingly rolling when he reached the pinnacle. "Find a way to win like your life depends on it." After pressing a kiss to her throat, he whispered a breath to her earlobe and added, "because it does."

"I should never have trusted you."

"I gave you what you asked for. A way out," he rebuked from the bed, lounging back against the pillows with his hands behind his head. "It's astounding how much you underestimate yourself when you took out the most powerful witch of all time."

"Using the energy I siphoned from hundreds of people she slaughtered," Charlotte added. "I don't have access to that kind of power now."

"Even if you did, incapacitating me would be against the rules."

"I can't use magic?"

"Not on me."

Tucking her bottom lip between her teeth, she held her breath before climbing out of bed. She opened her mouth to protest again but sighed instead. There was less than sixteen hours until The Hunt and she wasn't going to get anywhere by arguing with him.

She recalled what Hartley and said. Witches used magic to hide themselves during The Hunt, so she would do the same.

Grabbing her nightgown, she walked out of his bedroom without so much as a backward glance at him. Prickles of magic shot through her fingers, spurred on by the mixture of hurt and anger swirling in her stomach. Walking barefoot, she hurried back to her bedroom, blinking back tears.

She had been so foolish to think the kiss, the soft words they'd exchanged, the things she felt and thought he did, would change anything.

Once she reached her room, she slammed the door shut and looked at the salt circle, broken in one place.

"Who let you out?" she asked, eyes widening. Slowly, she kneeled, running her fingers over the scattered salt. She could only be contained for as long as the circle remained intact.

With a deep breath, she ran her hand over the curve of her hip, now free of the necrotic mark binding her to the entity. Although now and then, she swore she could still feel the phantom decay moving under her skin like worms.

Shuddering, she turned away. As long as she wasn't hexed, the demon posed no threat to her. They could not harm the living, and she was never stepping foot in the Realm of the Dead again.

The pressure of The Hunt and winning overrode her fear of the Smiling Woman. She had to focus on one thing at a time, but first, she needed to wash the embarrassment from her body. His scent clung to her skin, swarming butterflies when all she wanted to do was kill them.

As she walked into the bathing room, the decapitated head of Charles Eringhorn stared back at her from the washstand, a milky film over his unseeing eyes. Her scream died in her throat. She'd forgotten Nathaniel's gift was still in there, but she could swear she'd covered his remains with a sheet. Although she had lapsed time when the hex had taken over and she'd climbed out onto the roof. God only knew what she'd done in that period.

Chapter Twenty-Seven

With a clenched jaw, she grabbed the head and stomped into her room. Shimmying the window open, she inhaled the cold, lavender and rose-tinted air from the gardens, before throwing it out, watching as his shocked expression rolled over a patch of grass.

Meow.

"Duke!" She spun on her heels, a sense of calm washing over her for the first time since she'd woken in Nathaniel's arms. He darted to her feet, then pounced into her arms. She closed her eyes, pressed her cheek to his body and said, "I have had an awful morning."

Purrs vibrated against her throat.

"I'm okay," she lied, when a well of emotion rushed through her chest and into her eyes. Damned, she hated how easily she cried when the person she was feeling such pain over likely felt nothing. Nathaniel had said such beautiful things to her, words that she had foolishly clung to, and had meant none of them. He says he cared, but did he even know what it meant? How could he? He was still willing to hold her to their agreement if she lost. What he didn't know was that if that happened, she was going to fight until the very end. She had the magic of her entire bloodline and the knowledge learned from all her studying of the grimoires.

He was toying with her all along and like a foolish little lamb she had wandered into the wolf's den and lain down on the altar.

Well, no more. To Hell with him.

Petting Duke's head, running her thumb between his ears, she said, "I need your help again. You are the only one I can rely on."

He let out a soft meow, his paws kneading her arm.

"I need to find a spell to help me evade detection."

Duke looked up at her, yellow eyes closing in a soft blink.

A knock resonated on her door, and she froze, Duke's tail wrapping around her wrist.

"Hello."

"May I come in?" a honeyed voice asked before swinging it open without waiting for an answer. Standing in a full-length olive house dress with a thousand ruffles, wearing her hair in two golden braids hanging in loops over her ears, was Katherine.

She had hoped it was Hartley arriving with her breakfast.

"Hello, Katherine," she said wearily, trying to force a smile. She had helped her at the ball and brewed the potion that removed her hex.

"Don't sound too pleased to see me," she said, waltzing inside, her layered skirt twirling around her ankles. She lifted a small vial of purple, shimmering liquid clutched in her manicured fingers and smiled. "Especially when I have something that can help you."

"Did Nathaniel send you?"

"He doesn't know I'm here," she said, brown eyes darkening. "I want you to win tomorrow. For all our sakes."

"What do you mean by all our sakes?"

Katherine leaned over the bed, stretching her legs. "If you lose, Nathaniel will sacrifice you and he, along with Alexander, will become mortal again. I can't have that."

"Why do you care? He has been threatening your family," Charlotte stated, placing Duke on a chair in the corner. He coiled himself up, but kept his yellow eyes fixed on Katherine, who sat across from her on the bed.

"He is not the only one. The Avery family have my brother. They're going to kill him unless I stop the ritual from happening."

"Oh," she said, trying to feign sympathy for Baron Ellenwood. "I'm sorry to hear it."

"No, you're not," Katherine said with a shrug. "It's okay. He isn't a kind person, but he is *to me,* and he's the only family I have left."

Charlotte inhaled sharply, before huffing out a breath. She knew that hurt well. If it was Alice in his place, she'd do anything to help her. "I thought we killed most of the Avery family."

"There are hundreds, if not *thousands* of them. They're the largest witch bloodline of us all and they heard what happened at the ball. They don't want the curse broken, so they asked me to help you."

"Not kill me?"

"No. They don't want Nathaniel's wrath after what he did to his own mother."

"What *we* did, Katherine," she pointed out when she noticed her expression twist.

"Nonetheless, as long as you promise to leave London and go into hiding, they are happy for you to escape. Honestly," she added when

Charlotte arched a brow, disbelief written all over her soft features, "I am certain they will come after you eventually, but for right now, this is the deal they're willing to make."

"Is that what that is?" Charlotte pointed at the vial in her fingers. "A way to help me escape?"

She nodded. "It'll make your blood poisonous to vampires. It won't hurt you."

"I don't trust you."

"I know. I can see it in your eyes," she said, her stare sharpening. "I do not blame you either, but recall, I did not ask to be here. My hand was forced."

Shivering, Charlotte leaned forward. "What's stopping you then from handing me over? How do I know the potion won't kill me? I know about the spell on the entrance. You never intended to disable the Avery witches' magic. Your brother was safe that night."

"It didn't mean they hadn't threatened him, or me. Without him, I have nothing to live for. I did what I had to do ."

"I'm not taking it," Charlotte decided, recoiling from the potion.

With an extended sigh, Katherine lifted it to her lips, swigging just a small mouthful. Charlotte watched it pass through her lips and into her mouth, leaving behind three quarters of the contents. "See. It won't harm you. You may not trust me, but what other options do you have?"

"What will it do to Nathaniel?" Charlotte asked, hesitantly taking the vial in her hands, the purple liquid sparkling under the afternoon light spilling in through the window.

"It'll render him unconscious, only for a couple of hours but it will give you enough time to get away."

"How long does it take to work?"

"Not long, so you need to take it right before you are caught."

She turned it in her fingers, before sliding it between her breasts and out of view. "I'll only use it if I have no other choice. I plan on not getting caught."

"Of course," Katherine said, not looking convinced. "It should go without mentioning, you will need to ensure he bites you for it to work, but with the bond being so strong, that shouldn't be a problem. Don't worry," she said when the burning question sparkled in Charlotte's eyes. "It'll hit him almost immediately after biting you and then you can run. Alexander won't stop you. He, unlike Nathaniel, has a big heart."

"What about the death hounds patrolling the borders?"

"I've got them under control. Just make sure he bites you and escape through the back entrance to the patio. I will meet you there with enough money for you to get out of this city." She stood and glanced at Duke, before walking to the door. "I must go. Best of luck, tonight. Just remember, don't take that until he catches you."

She nodded and watched Katherine leave. Saving her brother was motive enough, but she still didn't trust her. The potion was a last resort. She was going to find a spell to help her win first.

As soon as Katherine's footsteps faded, Charlotte turned to her grimoires, placing herself down on the bed to sift through the brittle pages.

Hours passed with little disturbance, other than Hartley, who she was relieved to find was okay, who brought her some toast with various jams and marmalade.

By the time she'd found a spell that could help, the light behind the drapes had already faded. Midnight was just a couple of hours away.

"Duke!" Charlotte exclaimed from her place on the bed, legs crossed behind her, lying on her front with fingers guiding over symbols and incantations. "It's concealment magic that will mask my bodily sounds, breathing, footsteps, and anything other noise made by my body to anyone else's ears. If I can layer it with a cloaking spell for any scents, then I should be able to evade Nathaniel. He'll be counting on his inhuman hearing and sense of smell to find me."

Duke meowed and her shoulders slumped. "I cannot do it just yet. I need the element of surprise and it's only an incantation. I can perform it during the countdown."

His yowl shuddered through her. Duke was right. It was risky, but she had no choice. Grateful to Katherine, who she had learned about layering spells from watching, she flicked between the three pages and worked on her intonement of the words to ensure she got it right.

By the time she'd practiced it a few times, there was a knock at the door, this time from Alexander who entered holding a simple ivory dress with sheer sleeves made from voile, and a gold and ivory mask of a lamb.

"How theatrical," Charlotte said, and Alexander smiled.

"He had it made just for you."

"I'm certain he did."

"We usually wear masks of lions and deer," he explained, placing them on her bed. "How are you feeling?"

"Much better from the hex, but still a little discomposed."

"I am not surprised."

Slowly, she lifted her gaze to meet his, her heart pounding. "Do you truly think he will kill me?"

His lips fell into a hard line. "I cannot stop him."

"If you could?"

"I am content being a vampire, at least, for the rest of your lifetime." He pulled a bottle from his pocket filled with crimson, complete with a tiny stopper covered in red wax. "This is for you. It's my blood in case you are forced into performing the ritual."

Her lips fell open. "He will hurt you if he finds out you gave this to me."

"I do not care," he said and she leaned forward and hugged him.

Once she pulled back, she said, "Won't that affect the ritual's outcome?"

"I do not know. None of us do but if it does, I will not be upset. We are survivors, Miss Lovett. Take it only if you must."

"Thank you." She pushed it beside the other bottle, concealed from his view. "I truly believed he felt something for me."

"I think he does," Alexander confirmed, making her heart jolt.

"I thought you said it was a bond?"

"It's more than bloodlust," he confessed. "I've seen the difference in him, but it doesn't matter what he feels for you. He'll still kill you anyway."

"Why?" she asked breathily.

With an incredulous stare, he said, "Because, that is the price of being loved by death."

Her heartbeat tumbled over itself. *Loved*? He did not—could not. Love had no place in murder or ritualistic sacrifice.

With a strained smile, he added, "I shall meet you in the ballroom."

Her mouth dried. She barely managed a nod before he walked out, hesitating at the door before disappearing.

With a heavy heart, she pulled on the dress, the neckline so low it revealed her cleavage, and secured the mask to the top half of her face.

Chewing on her lip and running her fingers through her curls to tame them, she looked at her reflection in the window, her stomach dipping when the room behind her was empty. The demon was gone and she still didn't know who let it out, or if she accidentally had during her memory loss.

With a shake of her head, she dismissed those anxious thoughts. She had to focus. It was almost time to face Nathaniel. A spike of adrenaline washed through her, and she wetted her lips, contaminated with thoughts of being caught by the devil wearing the mask of a wolf, imagining pulling it down to kiss him, so he could devour her once more before she met her death.

Maybe she'd gotten it wrong. Perhaps she was the one who was in fact obsessed.

Chapter Twenty-Eight

Charlotte ran her fingertips over the intricate gold markings on the horns and small ears, before dragging them down the rest of the mask covering half her face.

With a deep breath, she walked into the ballroom, noting how ordinary it looked. There were no signs of the massacre. How Nathaniel had gotten away with so many missing people from his ball, she did not know, but she assumed that as wealthy and ancient as he was, he likely had an inspector and a few officers in his pocket.

Nathaniel stood at the helm the ballroom, his face half-covered with a mask of a wolf. The ears, nose, and brushed edges of the mask were painted gold, while the rest of it, engraved to appear as fur, was a shade of dark gray. His black shirt was rolled up at the sleeves, the top few buttons undone. The muscles in his forearms tensed when he flexed his fingers, curling them inward and outward as if he was practicing for later. A shiver of anticipation cascaded over her from head to toe.

She should be angry, afraid, hurt, after everything that had happened, yet all she could think about was how good she knew he smelled. That musky scent of smoked wood, cedar, and his own masculine sweat was imprinted in her memory. Sometimes, she could even detect it in her dreams.

With a hard swallow, she tilted her head, her gaze trailing the snug fabric over his toned thighs, to the obvious print of his length, impressive even in its docile state. Heat scored the column of her throat, and she scowled at herself, aggravated not only that she had glanced there, but that *he'd* seen her looking. She was just grateful for the mask to cover at least half of her unpredictable expressions, although, surely, both he and Alexander had heard the pickup in her heart rate.

His lips curved into a wicked smile, flashing fangs stark behind those full, perfect lips sending an aching throb directly down and between her legs.

Damn him.

A shiver ran up her arms to her throat when she saw he was already glaring at her, his eyes that of a predator who's sighted easy prey.

I want you to catch me.

Her words floated back in her mind, a stupid confession said in the throes of lust when she didn't know any better.

Wide-eyed, she jolted when his words spilled into her mind, just like they had done at the ball. Nathaniel's deep voice sounded in her head.

I hope you're prepared. Don't make me catch you, little lamb.

She'd read in her grimoire how one of the vampire abilities was to speak into the minds of their victims.

Shaking her head, she mentally blocked out the seductive caress of his voice and instead glanced down at the spill of dark waves hanging over her chest, in stark contrast to paleness of her ivory dress.

His jaw loosened as he slowly raked his eyes over her body, the pace scarcely quicker than that of spilled molasses. Her skin prickled when he lingered on the curve of her breasts.

Alexander cleared his throat. "The rules of the game are simple," he enunciated, but all Charlotte could focus on was Nathaniel, standing behind him, watching her as if she was his favorite food.

She fought against a shiver and steadied her breathing as Alexander stated the instructions for their twisted game.

"To win, you must go an entire hour without being found."

Adrenaline spiked through her veins and momentary dizziness lightened her head. "How long is the countdown?" Nathaniel crossed the room in a blur, his lips tipping into a dark, salacious grin when her breath hitched.

"You have thirty seconds, *love*. Starting now." A wildness flared in his eyes, a low animalistic growl rumbling his chest.

Charlotte's breath caught in her throat. "That's not enough time." She stepped out of his shadow, fingers trembling when a carnal, predatorial hunger sharpened his features. "You're not even giving me a chance."

"Twenty-nine."

Her heart hammered in her ears, shock coursing through her veins. She didn't have enough time to perform the spell.

"Twenty-eight."

Bending at her waist, she grabbed one shoe from each foot, flinging them to the side before taking off at the fastest sprint her body could manage. His voice echoed in her mind, taunting the edges of her sanity.

Run, run, my little lamb.

With burning calves, each pained breath screeching in her lungs, she raced into the foyer, unable to think of anything as the seconds counted down her death sentence. The staircase loomed on the other side of the room. There was no way she could climb that in time.

Clutching her chest, she veered left into the parlor, nausea swarming through her when she knew her time must be up. Shakily, she whispered the incantation, messing up the order of the words the first time.

"Hell and damnation!" she whispered, digging her nails into her palms. With a steady breath, her stomach in ribbons, she incanted the spells once more, this time correctly.

"Aufer odorem e corpore, cela sonum ab omnibus auribus praeter me. Tege me silentio, sine ut nihil penetret spatium meum."

Nathaniel's warning resounded in her mind, splitting through her consciousness until she yelped.

I'm coming for you.

Bile bit up her throat. She had no idea if the spell had worked and didn't have time to check. She had seconds, if that. Dropping to the floor, she crawled over the rug and under the cream sofa, the thin layers of her dress dragging over the carpet.

Beneath the small gap, her stomach was met with the gritty underside of her sofa, and she drew her feet close, adjusted the dress over her thighs, and pulled her hair around her neck, to hide any loose strands.

Her lungs were on fire, and she willed her muscles to remain as still as possible. The mask's sharp edges bit into the soft skin of her freckled cheeks. She huddled up small, listening intently as she stared up at the woven fabric over the wooden frame, and the nails that held it together.

How in the world was she supposed to remain hidden there for fifty-five more minutes? Cramps seized her calves, but she fought against the urge to stretch them out. Muscles feathered in her limbs and her nipples swiped against the tough fabric underbelly.

The image of him hunting her, those strong fingers flexing at his sides, those pointed fangs protruding over his lips as he stalked the shadows, sent a wild thrill crashing through her veins.

A slow creak snapped the silence of the parlor, his dark boots coming into view.

Slowly, she brought her hand to her mouth, covering her trembling lips. She didn't move a single muscle, not even when her hips itched from the soft tickles of the thick carpet poking through her gown. Curling her toes against the floor, she side-eyed his shoes, her heart bashing her ribs when a low, eerie growl reverberated in the room.

Oh, God.

Had she left any signs on the carpet of her shimmying underneath?

"I can taste your fear," he said aloud, in a taunting tone.

A tremor rolled through her spine, convulsing her body as she fought against it.

"Hearing your clumsy footsteps run to this room was far too easy. Where are you hiding, little lamb?"

The spell must have worked. If not, he'd have been able to hear her heart and smell the sweat covering her skin.

He paced in a low, tortuous circle. Did he know she was there, and was just drawing this out?

Flashes of images, of him suddenly grabbing her ankles and pulling her out, carouseled in her mind. She couldn't stay in that position. *Everything* hurt from the absolute stillness she was forced to maintain. If she moved slightly, she'd be discovered.

A tug in her soul widened her eyes, magic scattering in her fingers and toes. She had the power of her entire bloodline in her veins but didn't know how to channel it well enough to do any spells without an incantation.

But she had done it. When she was stressed and angry, the veil had lowered around her in brief moments, as if she were traversing it, moving between both realms.

She watched him walk to the room separator, peering behind it and chuckling darkly when he didn't see her there. "Come out, come out, wherever you are."

A slither of dread, and admittedly, desire, swept through her, but thankfully, the logical side of her brain was working today, silencing the moan begging to break free.

If she didn't make him think she'd run somewhere else, she was going to end up dead.

Closing her eyes, she focused on the Latin Katherine had uttered to walk them into the Realm of the Dead, thinking them over and again, manifesting them out into reality. She didn't have any intentions on returning there, but what choice did she have? This was life or death.

The room darkened, the colors leaching from each surface. Every sound of Nathaniel's heavy boots on the floor was muffled expertly. Her ears strained to hear the placement of each step, heel to toe. Tatters of wallpaper hung from the walls, the furniture in various stages of decay, and a heavy mildew and smoky scent lingered in the damp air.

Charlotte slunk from under the sofa, glancing back to see her still body remaining behind, curled up in a tiny spot.

Her dark hair fell around her face like a veil when she rolled onto her side and stood. The ghost of her watched Nathaniel moving with predatory grace as he ran his hands over the panels, sniffing the air. The candlelight caught the sharp angles of his jaw, glinting off the gold on his mask.

He could have used his vampire speed to search the large room, but he was purposely slowing his pace, either to make her more afraid, or because he wanted to take his time and savor every second.

A layer of mist covered the floor, coiling around her ankles. She needed to draw Nathaniel away from the parlor, but how?

With one last look back at the room, she fled into the foyer, fog leaving her mouth in puffs of icy breath. The fire in the foyer died in the mantel, the embers lost the icy drafts of the dead.

The power in her soul felt heavy, suffocating even, as she tried to summon it there.

Charlotte dipped behind an ajar door to the morning room when she heard long, drawn out raspy breaths from the grand staircase. She covered her mouth, stifling her scream when the Smiling Woman hovered down, bare, pale feet gliding inches over the ground. Long dark hair hung raggedly around her cheeks, and the too-wide grin filled with rotten teeth did not match her angry, black eyes. The ashen skin under them had lost all contact with the bone below, the darkness in them promising pain, in contrast to her curved lips.

Her heart stammered. While she was no longer bound by the hex, the demon must have remained behind, waiting for an opportunity to snatch her body from her. That, or the concern Katherine had voiced had come true and the demon was so attached to her, it didn't need magic to keep that bond.

An icy tendril of dread froze her to the spot.

If the demon took her body, it would not last long. They never did when they possessed a person. Mortal flesh was not built to house such evil, but there was a short time when those repellent things could feel how it was to be alive again. The Smiling Woman craved it. Charlotte felt it when she'd lured her into the salt circle, using her body as bait.

Her lips quivered against her palm as she watched the entity from her hiding spot. Charlotte hid when the demon suddenly snapped her eyes to where she stood. Holding her breath, she stared at the globe filled with liquors, her back against the door, praying the Smiling Woman didn't see her.

Never did she imagine she'd be hiding from two homicidal beings that night who *both* wanted her dead.

After a few minutes of silence, Charlotte carefully peered through the gap in the door, running her fingers over the hinge, but the foyer was empty. Goosebumps traveled over her arms and neck, an icy nip in the air biting at the exposed areas of her skin.

A loud crash sounded from the rooms upstairs, along with another. Another few minutes later, Duke darted down the stairs, his eyes pinning Charlotte's through the veil in unspoken knowing.

He disappeared out of sight when Nathaniel sped out of the parlor and up the stairs toward where Duke had knocked something over.

Once he was gone, Duke reappeared and let out a loud yowl.

Her body. She needed to get back to it.

She ran into the parlor, through the fog-soaked ground, the air permeating with the stench of sulfur. Her eyes snapped to the demon crouched on all fours, peering under the sofa.

Charlotte watched in horror as the entity reached toward her body, now an empty vessel. The demon's long fingers brushed her neck with a possessive need, the craving for her body palpable with each stroke.

"No!" her yell echoed the realm, snapping the attention of every spirit in the manor to where she was.

Lunging for her body, she rolled underneath, almost vomiting when the Smiling Woman's grin suddenly snapped into a frown, her face twisting into a sadistic, warped scowl that chilled Charlotte to the marrow of her bones.

The demon's fingers grasped hers, each movement slowed by the heaviness of the Realm of the Dead.

After what felt like an eternity, she rolled underneath, panicked when clawed fingers grasped her chest.

Feeling returned to her body as she opened her eyes to the underside of the sofa, and an icy tone speared into her mind.

You cannot escape me. Your body is promised to me.

What the Hell did that mean?

Even in the realm of the living, Charlotte could still feel the icy brush of the demon from the other side. She slowed her breaths, remaining hidden for as long as possible, but the longer she stayed, the more her body became slowly paralyzed from fear, or the demon—she wasn't sure.

With a full body shudder, she decided to get out and find a new hiding spot. Rotating out onto her stomach, she climbed onto all fours and looked around.

Nathaniel's voice boomed into her mind.

At last, I can smell you again. I can hear your delicious heartbeat. I'm coming for you.

The spell hummed over her skin before dissipating entirely. Being in the Realm of the Dead must have weakened it. She tried the incantation again, but it didn't work.

Stumbling over her words, she fled, wondering how the Hell she was going to outrun a vampire for—she glanced again at the grandfather clock and the huge pendulum ticking back and forth—twenty more minutes.

Taking off, she flew through the foyer. Her calves burned as she ran up the stairs, and her breaths came out in wheezy pants.

She ran as fast as she could, the echoes of her footsteps reverberating down the dark corridor. As she passed by, the painting's eyes bled crimson, their mouths twisting in silent screams as she traversed both realms.

I can hear you, little lamb.

Her steps pounded the maze of hallways, the gas lamps flickering light onto wispy figures watching her from the shadows of rooms where the doors had been left open, disappearing when she whipped her head around.

Each breath stabbed painfully into her lungs, her heartbeat in her ears as she ran down into the gardens, almost stumbled into a bed of fragrant, blooming roses.

Weathered paths, glossy from the recent rain, guided the way to enclosed, hedged areas, where metal furniture stood surrounded by arches overflowing with thorny roses.

She hurried past a large fountain, the gentle babbling of the water following her as she gazed upon statues watching her from the center of vibrantly blue, neatly trimmed flower beds, their stone limbs slowly moving.

The demon's voice echoed in her thoughts, haunting her with each step.

You are mine. He will kill you. He kills everything he loves.

She halted, eyes wild when the demon appeared at the edge of the garden, standing by an iron fence, death hounds growling around her. Katherine said they'd been taken care of.

It only took one warning bark for Charlotte to back away, its low growls sending shockwaves through her. She accidentally bit her cheek, tasting blood. A foolish mistake to make when being hunted by a vampire.

Nathaniel's voice taunted the fringes of her thoughts, his warning reverberating down the bond.

Not the grounds, little lamb. My dogs will tear you apart before I can.

Damned!

With the last bit of strength she had, she sprinted back inside, her feet slipping on the wet stone, the drizzle of rain cooling her face.

Once inside, she glanced around, taking a second to catch her breath. Wheezing, she squeezed her eyes shut when tiny stars sparked in them.

I'm coming for you.

Nathaniel's tone caressed her mind, just as the demon's cold voice greeted her ears.

As am I.

She ran through the kitchen, where copper pots hung from walls, and bulbs of garlic hung next to the door. There were no staff around, likely sent to their rooms for the duration of The Hunt.

After making it through the scullery, she found her way back to the grand staircase and climbed up to the hallways.

Footsteps pounded behind her. She turned right, her pulse quickening when she glanced at a passing clock in a blur.

I told you I would find you.

Damned and Hell.

She plucked the vial of purple liquid from between the curves of her breasts and pulled out the stopper, quickly tipping the honey and rosemary liquid down the throat before throwing the vial on the ground and fleeing in the opposite direction.

The cloying liquid clung to her tongue, coating her throat, tingling slowly through the roof of her mouth as she turned a corridor, hiding behind a wall, listening to his steady footsteps getting closer.

With one hand spread over a wall panel, the other hiking up the skirt of her dress, she inched closer to edge before peering around the corner, spotting him under the dim light of a gas lamp, his lips curving when he saw her, fangs protruding.

A panicked whimper left her lips, and she took off, the soft carpet pounding under her bare feet. She reached the balcony overlooking the foyer, grasping the balustrade as she looked down, panting.

Strong fingers wrapped around her neck from behind, gently pressing against the sides in a possessive hold, turning her to face him.

"You almost got away from me," he said when her back hit the polished rail.

"Would you even have let me go?" she asked, her voice raspy as she sucked in deep breaths.

"No," he admitted. "I told you before, I am *never* letting you go."

Chapter Twenty-Nine

She brought her fingers to her throat, moving her hair to the side. If she was going to have any chance of getting away, she had to get him to bite her.

His gaze followed the path of his fingers as he traced them over her lips, down her throat and to her waist. Slowly, he lowered her against the wood railing, his eyes burning as he pressed his lips to her neck, the rough edge of the mask scraping her delicate flesh.

His fangs grazed her skin, and she gasped. The demon's voice tried to break through, but was muted in his presence, her thoughts focused solely on him, the man who was going to sacrifice her.

Closing her eyes, she waited for pain, but his lips met her clavicle with a kiss, his moan resonating into her chest. Aware of the glass bottle of Alexander's blood pressed between her breasts, she guided his head from moving any lower.

"Bite me," she said, revealing her throat to him, not only because it would poison him, but because she craved it. "I want to feel you in my veins."

Surprise flashed in his dark eyes when he lifted them to meet hers, his lips falling open.

"Please," she pleaded, focused on the sharpness of his fangs pressing against the soft flesh of his bottom lip.

Burying his head in her neck, he whispered her name against her skin like a prayer. "*My Charlotte.*" His fingers sank into the dark, unruly curls as his fangs pierced her with careful precision. As he lost himself in her blood, a haze of pleasure erased the pain, heat coursing through her limbs. Shockwaves scattered through her body, tingling into a pool, soaking her undergarments.

Pulling back, he wiped the trickle of blood kissing his lips on the back of his sleeve, smearing it over his jaw. "You taste like Heaven."

She swallowed thickly as something within his carnal stare sharpened on her, like a predator setting his sights on helpless prey. Yet, the danger lurking just beneath his skin only spurred the lust consuming her higher.

"Then drink more," she offered when her blood didn't affect him. How long did it take to work? Her mouth dried at once, her papery tongue thick in her mouth.

Unless Katherine had tricked her, and it was some strange test. Did he know?

Her stomach clenched as the ridges of the balustrade dug into her back as he leaned her backward, dark eyes sparkling in the dim candlelight.

"Patience, little lamb. I want to devour other parts of your first," he said with a deep growl, laying himself over her.

In the haze of his recent, brief bite, confusion muddled her sharp mind. Blood trickled from her throat, down to the swell of her breasts, veining into the ivory neckline of her dress.

He wrenched her against him, the sudden movement making her gasp, and she instinctively locked her legs around his hips. His arms wrapped around her, drawing her close, before his lips met hers in a surprise, ferocious kiss, his fingers tangling demandingly in her hair.

After a few seconds, their lips separated and panted only a hairsbreadth away. "I never want to let you go."

Swallowing thickly, she replied with a croak in her voice, "But I lost the game."

His fingernails cut into the curve of her ass as his hands squeezed her tighter, holding her up as if she weighed nothing. With the nose of the wolfs mask pressed against hers, he asked, "Do you think I would let anything happen to you? I wasn't going to before this game and I'm sure as Hell not now."

His words nestled deeply in her battered heart, warming her, but then why did he make her do this at all? "You said if I didn't win you would hold me to our agreement."

"If I told you the truth, you wouldn't have tried," he said, nuzzling her cheek.

Her brows shot up in a high arch, mouth falling open in a breathy gasp. He was never going to hurt her? Buzzing hummed over her skin as she drank in his eyes, her abdomen clenching, a sudden dizziness swallowing her thoughts.

After a few seconds of processing his admission, she asked, "Then why bother with The Hunt at all?"

He laughed softly, then his deep tone vibrated in her throat when he brought his lips to meet her neck. "I told you before. I wanted a reason to chase you, to hunt you so I could claim you as mine. You were so damned clever that you almost got away. I'm proud of you. Maybe I should start calling you a fox instead of a lamb."

Stomach clenching, sparks darted up her core and into her head. "I thought becoming mortal was the most important thing to you?"

"It was until I met you." Bringing his fingers to her back of her neck, he squeezed gently, holding her gaze on his. "Don't you see? You've imprinted yourself so deep in my damned soul that no knife could ever be sharp enough to remove you. Your light has haunted me since our first meeting and every thought I have is embedded with your essence. I am utterly and completely consumed by you, so completely that if I ever die and the bugs feast upon my flesh, all they will taste is my love for you."

The air froze in her lungs, unable to be swept into a single breath. Wide eyed, she stared at him, the invisible tether binding their hearts pulled tighter.

He dragged his thumb across her cheek. "Breathe, love."

Nodding, she sucked in a deep breath, never breaking eye contact as warmth filled her up, spreading through her slowly. She wanted to believe him. His words were so beautiful, so intense, but were they genuine?

In a croaky, faint voice, she asked, "What if those feelings are because of the bond?"

"It's not your blood I crave. It's you. How many times must I voice it? I'm *obsessed* with *you.*"

Her stomach cartwheeled, vision blurring as he held her close. "I am, with you too," she stated shakily.

"Say that again. Tell me you're mine."

With a breathy whisper, she exclaimed, "I *am* yours."

His erection strained against the fabric of his trousers, pushing against her with earnest intent. Still hooked around him, legs hoisted up over his hips, she ran her fingers over his chest, exploring the valleys and dips of his muscles, slowly undoing buttons.

Somewhere in the back of her mind, she recalled the potion, but the details were lost to his feather touches. He was lucid, and it hadn't worked. That's all that mattered.

Running kisses over his neck, she tangled her fingers in his hair, fisting strands as she nipped his skin, desperate for every inch of closeness between them to be consumed entirely.

"Do you want this?" he asked, eyes raking over her.

"Desperately."

He bit down on the curve of her chest, not yet breaking skin, the seductive tension coiling in her core building to an unstoppable need. Slowly, he pushed her back, inch by inch, until she realized she was hanging over the edge.

Squealing, she grabbed his shoulders, digging her nails into the backs of the muscles. "Nathaniel! I'll fall."

"So don't let go," he said with a wolfish grin.

Her heart raced when she glanced down at the two stories of space between her and the floor.

"Look at you," he said huskily through a groan, eyes raking her over as he tipped her head back. "So breathless, so fucking perfect, just begging to be ruined."

Whimpering, she hooked her feet around his hips, keeping her arms around his neck. He was the only thing stopping her from falling to her death.

A libidinous demand sharpened his features as he looked at her through hooded eyes from behind his mask. Her thighs clenched, and she felt the scorching flames of desire consuming her from the inside out, scattering embers not only in her skin, but in her very essence.

Trembling shockwaves traveled through her legs, her arousal close to dripping down her thighs.

Something about being suspended like that, knowing she could die at any moment, was a sensation she wanted to repeat endlessly.

He hiked the layers of her dress over her thigh and unbuttoned his trousers. His enormous cock slapped against his taut lower belly. As he swiveled his hips into a more comfortable position, she glanced down at the gap between them and sharply inhaled at the sight of the glistening liquid covering the tip, with veins pulsating along his length.

Her eyes widened as she dragged her tongue over her lips, taking in his engorged, twitching shaft, the head so swollen it must be painful, wondering how she would accommodate all of him.

Nathaniel chuckled against her ear, his breath ghosting the shell. "Do you see how much I need you? How much I crave to be buried deep within you?"

She half gasped, half moaned, then nodded, unable to articulate the words that she could not stand it anymore, that she ached desperately for him.

Her back bowed as he slid a hand from beneath her, eliciting a scream as she slipped an inch toward the ground far below. He pinned her to the railing with his hips and a drop of his seed spilled from the head, coating her opening.

He palmed the back of her skull with his free hand and drew back to score her face with his unrelenting stare. "I do not think I can be gentle just now. Part of me is sorry for it," he paused, then moaned as he ground himself against her opening, easily gliding through the slickness coating her, every miniscule movement back and forward rubbing over her bundle of nerves, "but the other part craves your screams of fear and pleasure, wanting nothing more than to plunge as deeply into you as I can, making you shatter around my cock."

Her head swam, unquenchable heat flushing from her chest to her ears. God, she wanted him to do just that. She didn't give a damn if it hurt.

Nathaniel dropped his hand from the back of her head, gripped her backside hard enough to bruise in both palms, and slid into her with one punishing thrust, a guttural groan slipping past his parted lips.

"You fit me so well, my love," he said in a deep, baritone tone. He panted softly above her, tension tightening his jaw as he held himself back from moving within her, allowing her a moment to adjust, if only a little, to the vast stretch of accommodating him.

She swallowed audibly, then lifted her head to meet his gaze. "I'm fine. I need you—" Her words cut off as he did just that.

The sound she let out was one she'd never made before, somewhere between a moan and whimper. He felt so damned good, filling her up, her walls clenching around him.

The restraint in his eyes snapped. He rolled his hips, gliding all the way to the end of her.

He ran one palm over her ass, the other gripping her hip, his fingers digging into her flesh. She met his gaze as he took her deeper and harder, rutting her with a fevered pace against the edge of the balcony, thrusting his hips rhythmically.

A low moan escaped her throat, and a matching groan echoed from him. As she leaned back, almost losing her grip, she felt the blood pounding in her ears as it rushed to her head. Fear struck her heart, but it was immediately replaced by a wave of pleasure.

Footsteps echoed down the silent corridor. Someone was running toward them, yet he didn't stop. Instead, his pace increased, fevered with possession. He held her hips tighter, his grip firm. In sync with his forceful movements, she let out a loud moan, feeling a surge of indescribable bliss as she reached the pinnacle, stars obscuring her vision.

"That's it, let go, little lamb. I love how you clench around me. You are mine," he stated, voice breaking. "Only. *Mine*." With every thrust, he growled the words with severe obsession, intensifying the pleasure that was on the verge of overwhelming her, enveloping her in a delicious darkness.

The sounds of their bodies slapping together filled the air as he moaned, the footsteps closer now. His muscles tightened, but whoever it was had veered off in the other direction.

With a click from his jaw, he leaned down, pressing his fangs against her, not breaking skin, but the pressure alone sent her to new heights.

Heat radiated from his thick cock, sending tremors through her. A sudden, primal roar ripped from his mouth, his mouth wide open as he came undone, jetting his hot heat into her until her quivering body was dripping with his release, pouring down the sides of his rigid length and her thighs.

Her body convulsed with aftershocks, and the force of her scream vibrated through the vast, echoing room as it shredded through her.

Rocking the final dregs of pleasure from her, husky, short grunts left his mouth, his shuttered eyes tipped down to look at her beautiful, pink glistening clit covered in his essence.

Gradually, he withdrew from her, leaving a path of his shining fluid trickling into the crease of her ass.

In a sudden motion, he pulled her back, his stare softening when he removed his mask, tossing it aside.

She wanted to tell him then, how she truly felt. The truth danced on her tongue, her stomach cartwheeling as she tried to voice those three world-changing words. Removing the lamb's mask, she wiped away the sheen of sweat that had formed underneath, and said, "Nathaniel, I—"

Her words cut off midway. Sliding down his body, she stumbled back, but he caught her. A woozy feeling, accompanied by a slight buzzing in her ears, washed over her. What was happening?

Stars danced in her vision, and she crumpled to her knees.

"Charlotte!"

His fingers were on her face, and she could barely utter a cohesive sound.

"What is happeni—" He stumbled back, falling to his knees.

The potion had worked, and she had been right not to trust Katherine. It had poisoned her too. She reached for his fingers on the carpeted floor when a void of darkness stole her consciousness entirely.

Chapter Thirty

A bitter gust of wind swept through Charlotte's long hair as she arose from the dreamless dark, held up by a pair of clunky, enormous arms.

She strained her gaze to the side, staring at the corpse-sewn giant that must have been one of Gertrude's monsters. He lumbered forward, the vibrations from each of his thumped steps amplifying the aching in her joints. Blotchy, gray skin stretched taut over the monster's unnaturally muscular limbs, a patchwork of discolored skin and scar tissue.

His bright blue eyes were obscured by a milky film, washing the darkness of his pupils into an ashy-white. There was no glint of intelligence or emotion in the hazy depths, as if his soul had become lost amidst his decaying brain.

Her eyes flicked open to the starless sky and full, yellow moon suspended in inky blackness. She stretched her mouth to scream, but the sound remained frozen in the back of her throat, unable to surface through the haze of the potion. Katherine had taken it too, so to gain her trust. Unless, that was why she left so quickly to go to her bedroom, so she wouldn't see the effects.

Panic hurtled into her veins. Where was Nathaniel? The potion would only last for a couple of hours, if Katherine was to be believed, so if she was awake, then he would soon be too.

Latin chants echoed in her mind from nearby, an icy cold biting her arms through the sheer fabric.

Gertrude's voice filtered into her ears when thick teardrops slid down her temples and into her black hair. "Well done, Katherine. It all worked out just as you said. You broke me out of there and got me the girl. You will be rewarded."

"All I want is my brother," she answered, her voice cracking.

"If the ritual goes well, we shall return you to him."

"Where is he?"

"Somewhere safe, in the city."

That damned traitor. Darkness coiled in her soul, eroding all the kindness that once softened her to monsters like them.

Oh God. They were going to sacrifice her, just as they had done to the last witch in the Serea bloodline.

Charlotte tried to swallow, but her tongue felt too big for her mouth. Peering through cracked eyelids, she watched the monster grunt, his jaw hanging open revealing the chunks of mold hanging from his yellowed, crooked teeth.

Grimacing, she looked away, scrunching her nose when a horrifying thought clawed its way into her mind. What would happen to her body after the witches siphoned the energy from her death? Would they leave her body to the monster, for him to feast upon her flesh and bones?

Peering to her left, she just managed to see the familiar tall hedges bleeding into the path of her vision. They were almost at Lysanmore family graveyard.

She wanted to scream at Gertrude and demand to know what they had done to Nathaniel, but the words wouldn't form. After tonight, she would never see him again and could never tell him the truth, how when she was with him, it felt like home, a feeling she thought was lost forever. He deserved love and a chance to start over, but now he would never know she thought that.

The inevitability of what was to come hung in her heart as the monster walked clumsily. When they reached the wrought-iron gates of the graveyard, the familiar, extended creak of its opening screeched in her ears. Only minutes stood between her and death.

The metal groaned as bars scraped against the stone path. With every sluggish step, his arms around Charlotte's torso tightened, his gnarled fingers scratching her skin.

It was getting harder to breathe.

A sea of frosted, skeletal leaves carpeted the ground between crypts and jagged headstones. While it might have been spring, everything that touched the Lysanmore burial ground seemed to quickly die.

Keeping her gaze, which pricked with stars, as far to her left as possible, she spotted the candle-lined path to the altar, illuminating a group of cloaked Avery witches waiting for them, their hands linked.

Purple and black wax dripped a fragrant puddle from their iron holders and the name Lysanmore was barely visible beneath the frost and lichen on the weathered stone crosses and tombs.

Sweat covered her upper lip, her hands clammy despite the frosty night air. Shivers ran through her in waves, wracking her body against the corpse's arms. The sacrificial altar came into view, placed upon a single crypt mausoleum. Her body shook when she took in the slab of stone encased in a tangle of nettles. On it, iron hooks clutched the ends of woven, knotted cords of rope and blackthorn, meant for her.

A croaked plea spilled from her trembling lips, but exhaustion squashed the words. Adrenaline speared through her veins and into her heart, making it thump loudly against her ribcage. The seconds it took to walk to where the witches had congregated passed in silence.

The vial of vampire blood pushed against her ribs. It was the only thing that might bring her back. She tried to lift an arm against the paralysis, but not a single muscle reacted to her mind's cues.

The silver light of the moon cut over the altar as the monster stopped above it, slowly placing her against the rough, freezing stone.

Her dress billowed out around her, the neckline tight around her heaving chest still stained with her blood. Gertrude planted herself on a large stone step, gray eyes that matched her sons intruding her tear-stricken irises.

With a clenched jaw, Charlotte glared at her with an unspoken promise of vengeance.

"I will take this," Gertrude said, her bony, ringed fingers sliding between her cleavage and plucking out the glass of blood. "Do not look so hurt, little Lysanmore witch. You would not have come back anyway. Not when your body is promised to someone else." Gertrude's eyes lit like a monochrome flame, thin, wrinkled lips stretching. "Now I will have the power of the Lysanmore bloodline and the return of my dear, departed friend."

Wait. *No.* How had she missed it?

Bile bit up her throat, making her mouth salivate.

The Smiling Woman had taunted her, telling her that her body was promised to her.

Gertrude turned her attention to the other Avery witches and Katherine who slinked out of view. Loudly, she announced, "After tonight, we will never suffer at the hands of humans again. They will bow to us. Her magic will enrich our bloodline, and once she is dead, we will hunt the others."

Choking on a gasp, Charlotte mulled over Gertrude's words. Her plan was always to eradicate all thirteen bloodlines but her own, so they might have all the power meant to be spread across the original families blessed with magic. The Avery family was a scourge on the earth, one that had to be stopped.

Gertrude lifted the dagger higher, the pointed, sharp edge holding steady directly over Charlotte's heart. There had to be a way out of this. If she could only focus on her power enough to break out of the paralysis. She couldn't die. There was always a way out. Just like the night of the massacre. She'd come so close to death, but she never fell in.

Her life couldn't end so quickly. It just couldn't. While she always assumed she would meet her death with dignity, panic took over, every one of her senses cowering.

The Latin chants grew louder, the sound swirling in her ears. Magic hummed through the altar, in a rhythmic pulse. Her eyes widened, focused on the sharpness of the blade. Paralysis kept her in place, her heart pounding faster and stronger than ever before, as if the organ knew it had only a few beats left.

Her lips quivered under the suffocating reality of death. The reality of the permanence of what was about to happen shot adrenaline through her veins, heightening her senses.

She wanted to fight back but was helpless to move.

"No!"

The plea left her mouth when she finally broke through spell suffocating her, but only enough to speak.

With her last seconds, Charlotte whispered the incantation she had memorized the other night from the grimoire, the one which could break the curse keeping her family bound to this world. If she died without it, she could join them in eternal purgatory.

She spluttered out the spell under her breath, feeling its dark hum settle over her, ready to activate upon her sacrifice.

The dagger met her ribs and a fiery sting blossomed deep with each inch of metal sinking deeper into her chest. A wave of warmth spread across her torso, blood pooling over her chest, her limbs turning icy cold.

Alice's cry and her mother's scream caressed her mind from somewhere distant.

She turned her head, taking in the view that had been hidden from her periphery until now. Nathaniel's body was lying still on the ground, at the feet of a second of the monsters belonging to Gertrude.

A tear slid down her cheek and onto the altar as her blood rushed from her too thick and fast to stop, every gurgling plea bubbling from her mouth in foamy bursts.

The veil split around her, and a light erupted as she floated in and out of her body, flickering between the living and dead.

Ancestors appeared around her and beyond them, Alice, and her parents' faces became visible, screaming for her, but they were helpless to stop it.

The words formed in her mind, and she only hoped her family could hear them.

I love you all so much. Papa, I know now it wasn't your fault.

Flickers of her life passed in her mind, comforting her as too much blood left her body, soaking the white fabric of her dress with red.

Heartbeats slowed, growing fainter and more erratic. She gave one last look at her family's longing expressions before they were pulled into the light with the rest of her family, leaving her utterly alone.

A loud meow sounded from the gates, but Charlotte was beyond being saved, even by the vampire who lay unconscious on the ground, or her loyal familiar that whined for her as her eyes fluttered closed.

After so long of feeling the near touch of death's embrace, it finally caught up with her.

Charlotte Lovett was dead.

Chapter Thirty-One

The world shifted, the color bleeding into gray tones. While there was freedom in the absence of the intolerable agony that had shredded her body moments before, the feeling was temporary, lost to the melancholy that came from being entirely alone.

Charlotte looked at her body destroyed beyond repair. Reaching out to touch her pale skin, her chest wrenched with a sob. She was dead and there was no going back.

Duke caught her attention as he darted onto the altar, laying himself over her moonlit, blood-drenched remains, nudging his nose under her chin, his paws padding her still chest.

"Duke!" she ran to him, her fingers ghosting his fur, which stood on end at her touch. "I'm right here. Please, see me."

Yellow eyes pierced hers through the veil. He meowed loudly and a sigh rattled her body.

"Get out of here, Duke. Before they hurt you!" she begged. "Go. You can't help me anymore."

Glossy eyes stayed fixed on hers, a sadness creeping into every part of his face. They'd saved each other countless times, but this time it was too late. No one could help her.

He emitted a high-pitched yowl, hissing when Gertrude pushed him away from Charlotte's body.

"Run! Please, Duke. Go!"

His tail twitched, ears flattening as he landed on the ground next the crypt. With a final, drawn-out howl, he sped down the path, disappearing into the shadows.

Charlotte watched Gertrude, who stood dead and center in the circle of Avery witches, her eyes closed, a subtle smile playing on her lips as waves of magic pulsed into her body, stolen from her.

A heart-wrenching scream shattered through both realms, the kind that not only reached one's ears, but their heart too.

Nathaniel had awoken and crawled to the altar, his fingers over her bloody torso, pulling her close to his chest, cradling her head in his large hands. Turning his bloodshot eyes to Gertrude, he spluttered in a tone so broken, it didn't even sound like him, and asked, "What did you do?" He grew louder when she didn't immediately answer, and shouted, "What the Hell did you do?"

Nathaniel's blood-curdling scream shook the veil when he held her corpse close, listening to the hollow silence of her heart. He clamped his eyes shut, lowering his head as a howl erupted from the pit of his stomach. He choked on another visceral, agony tainted wail, fingers crumbling into the stone slab, turning it to dust.

Charlotte watched through blurred eyes as he turned, crimson painting his fingertips, and lunged at Gertrude, the grief so potent it sliced through their spells, magic no match for raw, visceral pain. Freezing for a moment under the spell of incapacitation, he growled loudly, breaking free of it in seconds.

Gertrude stumbled back, fear potent in her eyes as she grabbed another Avery witch's wrist, the corpse-sewn monsters blundering toward him, but he was too fast for them.

Blood painted the headstones, cracking echoing around them as he pounced on their backs, his arms locking around their necks before wrenching off their heads with unsettling speed, blood and saliva dripping from the three sets of his fangs, more beast than man.

His pupils slitted, darkening as he tore them apart, one by one, spitting their flesh on the ground, animalistic rage guiding his every movement.

Gasps and screams filled the air, cloaked figures scattering. Magic skittered through the ground as they incanted spells, but nothing worked.

"Enough!" Gertrude yelled, but he fought his way through every spell thrown his way, his grief so potent it hurt Charlotte's soul.

Snapping the neck of the last witch who hadn't yet run, he tilted his head, glaring at his mother. "I left you for last."

"She's going to come back. I fed her the blood," Gertrude said slowly, caution rimming her dark eyes.

Charlotte spotted the empty vial of vampire blood beside her body, the crimson liquid inside coating her icy lips. Gertrude *had* fed her Alexander's blood, but she hadn't come back.

The demon. Of course, it was for the Smiling Woman.

This couldn't be happening.

"She is too far gone!" he spat, his voice shattering the air between them. "And even if she wasn't, you should be."

"I am immortal," she warned, stepping back and almost stumbling on a discarded limb.

"Not like me," he said with a tilt of his head, blood soaking his shirt, covering his chin and lips. "You are *not* invincible. You may be able to survive a snap of your neck but let's see if you can come back if there's no body to return to."

"Don't do this, darling. My sweet boy. I made you into this, I know, but everything is going to be different now. We have more power than ever."

"I want nothing from you expect your death."

"Everything I did was for our family. We were persecuted and your curse was supposed to be temporary."

"What about now?" he asked, brows rising, fangs bared.

"Do not do this. I am your *mother.*"

"You stopped being my mother centuries ago," he spat, getting closer. "All I see now is the evil bitch who took away the person I cared about more than anything."

The revelation stilled her, as it did Gertrude.

"Please, think about this. She will return."

"Then why is she still dead?" he yelled, causing a murder of crows to take flight from a nearby tree.

Gertrude turned, lifting her hands as Nathaniel lunged at her.

The ancient spell crept through the ground, vines erupting through the earth, wrapping around his ankles until he was forced onto his knees.

Thorny vines bound his wrists and legs, and Charlotte was by his side, her fingers hovering over his face as he yelled, his pain now hers.

Come on. Get up.

While he could not hear her, something had changed. He forced himself up, snapping the vines, his lips curving into a sadistic grin when he watched his mother stumble backwards, before falling on the ground.

She shot another spell his way, but he just laughed, as if the pain she'd sent crawling over his body was nothing but a mere inconvenience.

Towering over her, he let out a humorless laugh and said, "I'm going to ensure you stay dead this time."

She grasped around her, carving her fingers into the soil, yelling incantations as she lay surrounded by the bodies of her fallen family who did not escape on time.

He kneeled, his fingers wrapped around the sides of her head.

"Please, my son!"

Her ringed fingers dove for his eyes, but he just laughed, holding her still as he slowly tore her head from her neck. With a loud pop, and a grunt, her head ripped from her body, but it wasn't enough.

Screaming, he ripped apart her limbs, lost in a rage she was worried no one could ever pull him back from. Her limbs tore from her body, her flesh peeling away from bone. Piece by piece, he ripped her apart, painting the ground with her blood.

It was a truly horrifying scene to watch, but Charlotte was transfixed on her monster as he destroyed what little was left. The night was silent when all was done, Nathaniel's tears falling thick and fast.

"No!" he screamed into the sky. "Katherine, I am going to destroy you!"

Charlotte glanced around at the bodies. Katherine was smart enough to run while she could, but he would track her down. Of that much, Charlotte was certain.

Her fingers twitched as a faint heartbeat thrummed from her body, guiding Nathaniel's eyes to the crypt.

"Charlotte."

Her name left his mouth in a desperate plea. He ran his fingers through his blood-soaked, messy hair and raced to her, grabbing her hands.

It was happening. She had to get to her body. Running on the other side was like trying to push her way through deep water.

Come on. Please.

She had to get back to him.

A bone-deep chill spread through her as shadows moved in her periphery, briefly fading the grief that ached her heart. A prickle of goosebumps ghosted her ankles. The ground trembled slightly, drawing her attention down.

She stumbled back when she saw wisps of light carving through the fog-soaked earth below, unsure of what they were. It was only when they got closer to her feet that she realized the spectral light was in the shape of fingers. Her mouth fell open in a silent scream as hundreds of hands reached for her, arms growing longer as the spirits came for her.

Fingers clasped around her ankles, iciness running bone-deep, touching flesh that no longer warmed. A hoarse, raspy breath left her mouth when she tried to scream again as they slid up her calves, pulling her deeper, the earth giving way beneath them.

Soil crumbled around her legs, hips, then abdomen as she tried to fight against the things trying to drag her away.

When she looked up, half-buried in the thick soil, she saw the Smiling Woman standing by her body, neck angled, her grin more sinister than ever.

The demon's voice filled her head as Charlotte was dragged slowly into the ground.

It's you!

Charlotte gasped, watching her.

Yes, the demon confirmed. *Your body has long been promised to me. Your father leaving you alive was no accident. We ensured that you remained alive. That why he removed his hands from your neck just before your last breath.*

Fingers hooked into her soul as they dragged her down, but every sensation was desensitized to the sheet of shock permeating her mind.

Why my body?"

Delanie stood a few inches off the ground when she spoke into her mind again, each sick reveal driving a harsher nausea into her stomach.

Gertrude needed your power and I wanted your body. She promised, for centuries, that she would break me out of that mirror our family imprisoned me in.

Charlotte's eyes widened.

Our family?

Yes, my name is Delanie Lysanmore.

Goosebumps pricked her soul. No, it couldn't be. She knew that name. He had mentioned it.

You were Nathaniel's betrothed; she realized.

Yes, I have been waiting patiently for centuries to make him suffer. He robbed me of a life where I would become the most powerful witch of all time. Now, I will take the body of the only woman he loved, and you will watch, helplessly, as I make him fall in love with me, and then break his heart as he did mine.

He won't believe you are me.

Yes, he will, the demon responded, her voice so certain it sent a tendril of dread through Charlotte.

Delanie's frown deepened, making her wince in pain. It was then she noticed the carved wounds on either side of her mouth. She touched her face, her humorless grin spreading outward.

Charlotte's heart pounded, the earth reaching her chin now. *You have been in my head this whole time. You pushed me from the attic that night. You persuaded me to dig up those bones...oh God.*

Yes. They were my bones. You were so susceptible and now all you have will be mine. I will know how it is to live again, while you will take my place in the mirror and rot with the men who you murdered.

No! This couldn't happen. Desperately, she tried to claw her way out of the earth, but the grips on her soul were too tight.

The last thing she saw, before she was dragged from the graveyard, was Delanie step into her body and awaken to Nathaniel, who held her tighter.

No. No. Please, no!

Mouth wide in silent screams, Charlotte clung to the ground while hands pulled her down the path and toward Lovett Manor.

With a sudden rush, she was back in those familiar halls and up into the attic.

The power of the mirror pulled her closer, and she glared at the reflectionless glass of her eternal prison and the souls behind it who were waiting for her.

Chapter Thirty-Two

The evil attached to Lovett Manor was a suffocating darkness, slowly devouring and eroding any light left in her soul. Days crawled by, and Charlotte discovered time still existed, even though she had believed death erased its passage.

Her uncle's and cousin's souls pushed up against hers in the prison behind the mirror, an endless void filled with demonic beings, many of whom appeared as shadow figures with glowing eyes, except for one, a tall man with a chalky appearance, black eyes, wearing a suit and top hat.

Her uncle eyed her, tilting his head, flaring his nostrils. He likely thought it was justice, that she ended up in there with them. In a way, it was poetic how things turned out. Supposedly, when dark magic is used to harm others, it always comes back worse on the caster, although if that were true, then why did a demon win?

Her cousin glared at her through darkening eyes. The only respite from his presence was that they could not speak to each other, not even in their minds. However, she didn't need that to know the horrid things they were thinking about her. Especially when they came too close, her family's souls pushing into hers—the only thing they could do to her to cause any discomfort.

Any guilt she'd held for them was long gone. While she couldn't hear them, she could sense their desire to devour anything innocent. The evil they held while alive followed them into death, and it was growing each day.

She had a lot of time to think on the other side, trapped in limbo with her uncle and cousin, whose hate rippled beyond the dark shadows of the endless void. Her life had ended while she was waiting for it to begin and the only thing that followed her into death was the bitter sting of regret.

There was so much she had wanted to do outside of the expectations that had been placed on her such as building an animal sanctuary to help the local, wounded wildlife. She'd often dreamed of traveling too. She hadn't seen much of England, let alone any part of the world outside of it. Now, she was confined to one place for the rest of eternity. After all the talk of mortality, none of it mattered. The soul never died and now, just like the vampires, she was forever bound, but without the ability to live a life.

After all the tragedy, she was so close to feeling happy again, but now it was all gone.

After curling herself into a ball, hiding in a shadow, haunted by the hollowness there, she decided to leave the mirror again.

Slowly, she rose to her feet, always cold now, and soul slowly withering under the oppressive energy surrounding her. She'd only left the mirror once, discovering they could leave for a mere hour or two, as long as they remained within the confines of the property, before the curse would drag them back.

She left the attic and ambled through the familiar dark corridors. The wood groaned in the settling walls, and the moth-eaten drapes swayed in her presence. The silhouette of one of the demons detached from darkness, taking shape in the corner of her eye.

All she could think about was Duke and Nathaniel and the desperation to see them again, if only for a moment. Her feet glided over the musty carpet, while a thick layer of mist clung to everything when she heard a familiar sound—her own voice.

She floated down the stairs and into the gray foyer. Thunder rumbled outside, rain hammering down as Nathaniel, Alexander and Delanie, in her immortal body, stood in the open doorway.

Nathaniel took her coat, his gaze softening when he looked into the demon's eyes.

No.

How could he think that was her?

Her long, dark curls were tied into a tight bun, and an orange dress wrapped around her body. While it still looked like her, the expressions were all wrong and her eyes were different. Those green irises she'd seen in every reflection for years brimmed with a void that needled her through the veil.

Her lips tipped into a smirk and Charlotte gasped.

Delanie could see her.

Nausea swirled in her stomach when she saw Katherine walk in behind them. How could she possibly have been forgiven? Unless, Delanie had, and persuaded Nathaniel to let her live.

Were they working together?

They walked inside, Alexander smiling and hung his coat and hat on the rack. "It's raining cats and dogs out there."

Delanie glanced at Charlotte, before quickly averting her eyes and looking at Nathaniel. "Shall we go to *our* bedroom?"

Nathaniel pressed a kiss to her temple, eliciting a silent scream from Charlotte's ghost who watched helplessly. His low voice grumbled into the demon's ear. "Later," he promised, and took a step back. "Why don't you rest? Alexander and I will find us dinner."

Charlotte ran to them, pushing her hands against his chest, but they went right through him.

Please open your eyes. See what's happening.

She watched, defeated, as Delanie grinned. "I don't mind hunting for our food."

Nathaniel's dark brows shot up his forehead, his hands diving into his pockets. "I assumed you would not enjoy that part."

Delanie inhaled sharply, her eyes tracking Charlotte in her periphery vision. "I should embrace what I have become, no?" When Nathaniel grimaced, she quickly cleared her throat and added, "Maybe I *do* need some rest. It has been a long day."

Katherine walked beside her and said, "You can show me around this big house while they hunt."

The mirror's pull dragged her back just as Nathaniel squeezed Delanie's arm. She was only glad he did not kiss her on the mouth. The thought was too much to handle.

Tearless cries wrenched her body as she was sucked through the manor and back into the darkness of the mirror.

A few hours later, a hollow tapping sounded in the mirror, making her jump.

The souls of her uncle and cousin pressed themselves up against the glass, but she pushed herself beside them when she heard her name.

"Charlotte?"

Nathaniel's solemn face appeared on the other side of the glass, his fingertips caressing the metal roses on the ornate, silver frame.

Hope swelled in her heart, a desperate cry lost to the soundless void of the Realm of the Dead.

"I know you're in there," he said. "I'm going to get you out. I promise. Just hold on for me a little longer. I won't give up on you."

She watched him bow his head, letting out a prolonged, heartbroken sigh. He knew! He realized it wasn't her soul in her body.

Despite knowing he couldn't see her, she brought her hand up to the other side of the glass, anyway.

I miss you. She repeated the words in her head, hoping they could cross through the bond, but that had broken the moment she was killed.

The demons were getting impatient. Every lost soul haunting the void behind the mirror waited for Nathaniel's return, including her uncle and cousin.

Charlotte watched with bated breath. If he opened the mirror, then they might all be able to climb out before she had a chance.

Desperate to get away from the sharp buzz of energy zapping through the evil, she crawled out between shadowy silhouettes and landed on the floorboards. Her energy drained quickly, but she didn't plan on going far. Just being out of that dark void was enough. The darkness inside of their crawled over her skin. She could sense their desires. Demons were twisted beings and the ones imprisoned in that mirror were the worst of them all. If they got out, then no one would be safe.

Duke's meow jolted through her. Feline yellow eyes spotted Charlotte through the veil. Duke meowed when she reached him, and ghosted her fingers over his fur, which stood on end at her touch.

Dust motes floated in the orange hue of the candlestick as Nathaniel climbed inside, his sharp jaw clenching when he looked around at the stacks of old books and fading portraits.

Nathaniel looked right through her, but her familiar's loud meow halted him before he could reach the mirror.

"Is she here?" he asked, kneeling to stroke Duke between his ears.

Duke meowed again, this time louder, his tail flicking in the air.

"Where?"

Nathaniel tracked his eyes to her ghost, and he stood, his expression crumpling. "I am *so* sorry, love. I am, but I'm here now and we have a plan. Katherine is going to help us. I found her brother, held captive by the Avery witches," he explained, as if sensing her protest from the other side. "She will do what we ask."

A loud creak sounded behind him. Katherine pulled her way up the ladder, and climbed onto the floor on all fours, before standing and brushing the dust from her dress.

The temperature immediately dropped several degrees as rage coursed through Charlotte's body. *That treacherous cow.*

She raked her fingers through her golden curls, catching her breath. "Is she here?"

"Yes."

Katherine eyed Duke. "I assume he led you here."

"Not the first time. I could feel her."

Her lashes flickered. "The bond is broken."

"I don't need any damned bond to feel her. I know she is here."

"Are you certain?" Katherine asked, her upper lip twitching.

"I could tell the moment I saw her beautiful green eyes, that it was not my Charlotte," he stated, and her heart swelled.

Charlotte's fingers whispered over the nape of his neck, and he shivered under the touch. "Is that you, love?" She touched him again, and his brows pinched together, his forehead wrinkling horizontal lines.

Katherine rolled her eyes and let out a weighty sigh, only turning her head when Alexander ascended the ladder behind her.

"I am disappointed in you the most, Alexander," she said, turning to face him. "I'm forced into being here, but you're willing to go to all this trouble for some girl he got his cock wet for."

In a blur, Nathaniel's hand was around her throat, pinning her to the wall, her head angled under the low, slanted ceiling. "One more word from your mouth, and I will tear out your wretched tongue. Understood?"

She nodded and he released her, her legs crumpling beneath her as she landed with a thud. Spluttering and coughing, she stood, brushing the dust from her purple gown. "Now get on with it, before that thing possessing my beloved's body wakes up and discovers us up here."

"It's not as easy as that," Katherine remarked.

"If you want to see your brother again, you will find a way."

Alexander subtly shook his head in Katherine's direction when she opened her mouth to protest, and Charlotte noticed the way Nathaniel's eyes darkened, untamed power shimmering behind them.

"That mirror," she said, pointing at the glass, "is locked with blood magic. Only a witch in her bloodline can unlock it, and the demon controlling her body isn't going to do it."

Alexander strode to the oval frame, running his fingers over the ornate metal. "What about an exorcism?"

Her brows rose. "You cannot be serious."

"Mirrors have been used for centuries to trap demons. This one should be no different. If anything, it would be more powerful."

"It will not help her escape," Nathaniel stated.

"Portals go both ways," Alexander pointed out. "If Katherine can find a spell to temporarily open it, as a portal to allow the demon through, then Charlotte can escape and come back to her body.

Katherine shook her head. "It's not just her in there. It's a prison for a reason. There are demons in here and if they get ou—"

"I don't care," Nathaniel stated harshly. "Unleash Hell on Earth if you must. Just do what you must. What do you need?"

"The name of the demon," Katherine stated.

It's Delanie! Delanie Lysanmore.

Charlotte yelled the name repeatedly in her mind, but it didn't reach them. Only Duke watched her, his tail flicking as she tried to get the name across to them.

"I'll also need candles, the Lysanmore grimoires from Sallow Manor, restraints infused with rosemary, and most importantly," Katherine said, her voice lowering to a whisper, "You're going to have to get that demon up into the attic and tie her up."

Chapter Thirty-Three

Over the years, Charlotte persevered through the pain, her body screaming as she pushed on despite the searing agony in her joints and the overwhelming fatigue. No matter how awful it became, that unyielding tenacity helped her as she anchored herself in front of the mirror, holding fast against the desperate entities preparing to escape.

She wouldn't relent and spread her arms over the inside of the glass, so she could come out first, if it worked, but they still didn't know her true name, nor was Charlotte sure how they were going to get her into the attic.

Candles flickered in silence as Katherine prepared for the ritual on the other side. It was her fault that she died. She could have confided in them, so they'd hide her brother, or have him escape, but she poisoned her and handed her over to the Avery witches.

She didn't trust her for a moment, but she trusted Nathaniel, and he believed Katherine wouldn't fail. Not with her brother's life on the line.

Alexander climbed inside, with Duke in tow, holding the grimoires he'd retrieved from Sallow Manor.

"Thank you," she whispered, barely looking at him as she kneeled to sift through them.

"You broke my heart, you know that," Alexander said, now they were alone, or he thought they were.

"It wasn't you I betrayed," she said simply. "I was protecting my brother."

"You could have come to me. We have been friends for a long time, but you trusted Gertrude Avery over us, the same woman whose family killed yours."

"I didn't enjoy it," she snapped, quickly reining in her tone. "I didn't mean to hurt you, Alexander, truly. As for Nathaniel and Charlotte, I could not care less."

"She's a good person," he stated, sitting on a large, wooden chest next to an old cot and rocking horse, both covered in a layer of dust.

Her nostrils flared, mouth pulling into a grimace. "So I keep being told. Where is Nathaniel? That demon is going to flee the moment she figures out what is happening. He is fortunate she was sleeping when he came up here, but that won't last, and he can't restrain her alone."

"Zachariah and Irene are in the foyer. I believe they've already confronted her. They're almost here. I can hear them." Alexander pointed at the opening as footsteps pounded from the corridor below, pleading erupting in Charlotte's voice.

"What are you doing? Nathaniel! It's me. It's Charlotte."

Charlotte's stomach dropped from inside the mirror as she listened intently, her uncle's soul slowly oppressing her from the side, but she did not budge, even though her energy was quickly waning.

The floorboards groaned under Nathaniel's weight as he appeared first, his fingers gripping the thrashing arms of the demon, pulling her up until Charlotte could see Zachariah and Irene, both of them holding one of her ankles each.

"Alexander!" Nathaniel barked and he raced to help them, forcing her down onto the ground. "Tie her legs to that ceiling joist."

Alexander grabbed the ropes Katherine had infused with rosemary and magic, not that it would hold her for long, but with the strength of the four vampires, the demon wasn't going anywhere.

"Don't hurt Charlotte's body," Nathaniel ordered as they tied her up, keeping their hands on her.

"What are you doing?" the demon pleaded in Charlotte's soft voice, the tone cracking halfway through.

Zachariah grimaced. "Are you certain it is not her?"

"Yes," Nathaniel said with a low growl, positioning himself behind her head as she lay on the ground, his hands tight around her head, glaring into her eyes. "What is your name?"

"Charlotte," the demon crooned. "Your Charlotte."

"No, what is your true name?"

"I've already told you," she cried, screaming when Nathaniel forced her to face the mirror.

"Then look at your reflection."

Charlotte gasped when she saw her body and the demon writhing inside of it, pupil-slitted eyes focused on the glass. She snarled, averting her eyes, her lips twisting into a sinister grimace.

Duke jumped beside her, his angry, yellow stare pinned on the demon, his fangs bared.

"I knew it. Now tell me your name!"

She spat in his face, tugging on the herb-infused ropes. "Never."

Nathaniel's eyes cut to Katherine's, who was flicking through a grimoire. "Anything?"

"There's one part," she stated, "about The Smiling Woman, but it doesn't say much, only that she has been trapped in there for centuries."

It's Delanie! Charlotte screamed in her mind, but it was no use.

"Tell us, or we'll make this hurt."

Her lips twisted into a grin, a low cackle erupting from her lips as she hissed, "I do not fear pain. Like you, I consume it. It strengthens me." Tilting her head, she added, "Your beloved is gone, *Nathaniel,* and she is never coming back."

"Now, Katherine," Alexander barked.

Charlotte watched as Katherine turned her attention back to the grimoire, before speaking the words in a slow, shaky voice. "Audite me, vires daemoniacae. Relinquite hoc corpus, spiritus impure. Sub potestate noni sanguinis, vobis impero ut corpus quod abstulistis relinquatis."

A growl erupted from the throat of the demon as the flames grew taller, flickering shadows over the narrow walls.

The demon twisted her head to the side, her neck cracking as her eyes rolled back to reveal the bloodshot whites.

Katherine repeated the words, the low hum of magic pulsing through the ground, until Delanie's eyes snapped back, her instructive stare boring into Nathaniel's as she darted her tongue between her teeth with a hiss.

"How does it feel to lose the one you love?" she asked, her voice a mimicry of Charlotte's. "I will never relent of her body."

"Fuck you!" he snarled.

Irene grunted as the demon thrashed, wrestling against their hold. "She's strong."

"For now," Nathaniel growled and looked at Katherine. "Keep going."

"I need her name."

Charlotte's fingers gripped the mirror, desperately repeating the name over and over, hoping it could somehow traverse the realms into his mind.

The demon's voice dipped into a low, hollow tone. "Charlotte is suffering because of you."

She looked at Katherine, cackling before she taunted, "You do their bidding, even though they will kill you after. I can feel their intentions, their desire to rip out your throat the moment she escapes that prison world."

"Don't listen to her!" Alexander warned when blood trickled out of the eyes of the portraits stacked against the wall, the demonic, low distorted laugh echoing around them.

Katherine's next incantation stumbled a little, but she continued on with a shake of her head.

Exhaustion spread through Charlotte's body as she watched Nathaniel hiss remarks into her ears, the entities at her back pushing to get close enough that they could come through when it opened.

Her fingers curled into the sides, her energy remaining steady despite the overwhelming desire to give in to their suffocating weight and collapse. Despite having no body, a demon's energy was unexplainably dense.

"You are so intent on letting the girl out," the demon said, taunting him as her body writhed. Bloodshot eyes latched onto him. "When you know your love will destroy her. Evil cannot nurture good. You do not deserve love after everything you have done."

"Enough," he said, nostrils flaring. "You speak to me with too much familiarity. Who are you?" he yelled, his voice making the rest of them flinch.

"Retribution," the demon hissed.

It wasn't true, and Charlotte wished she could tell him how much good he had done for her. In the moments when she felt herself drowning in grief, he was there, pulling her back with comforting words, bringing clarity to thoughts she didn't understand. He showed kindness too, in ways that were unexpected, to his staff, to Duke, to Alexander, even forsaking his own mother to stop her cruelty against the innocent.

"Enough!" Nathaniel yelled, squeezing her head tighter, when Alexander grabbed his arm.

"Don't," he warned. "That's not the demon you're hurting. Ignore her."

Delanie. It's Delanie. Delanie.

Charlotte's fingers began to slip as she watched Katherine, who continued spilling Latin from her trembling lips.

Her body convulsed as Katherine's words echoed louder, and the demon let out a loud growl, her neck twisting at a contorted angle as she peered at Katherine with slitted pupils. "You made a mistake in siding with them against me," she hissed. "Your potion didn't remove the hex. It transferred it."

Katherine swallowed hard, the spell dying as she lowered the grimoire, wild-eyed. "No. It removed it."

"Don't listen to her lies," Alexander said. "She'll say anything to stop this."

Fangs protruded over the demon's lips, vying for his wrist.

With a grunt, he pushed Delanie's head to the side, palm pressed to her cheek, forcing her to look at the mirror. "Look at what you truly are!" he shouted when she clamped her eyes shut. "You might have her body, but you will never be free. Look at what you have done to your soul. I might be evil, but I am alive, free to walk this world while you are nothing but a parasite, desperate to hold on to a body for a glimpse of what you lost."

Leaning down, he hissed into her ear as her eyelids cracked open. "Don't you see, there is nothing to redeem, no point in trying to become human again. You are too rotten for this world," he spat. "There is no climbing out of the darkness you created."

"I am what you made me! You robbed me of the life I deserved. You, the devourer of innocents, will get what is coming to you."

His muscles tensed, lips falling open as he blinked rapidly. "Delanie?"

The name left his mouth in a rasp, his jaw slacking.

Yes! Charlotte gripped the mirror, her eyes closing as exhaustion flitted through her core. She could feel herself fading. The mirror trembled, its surface distorting and swirling. Charlotte felt the magic surge, rattling the glass, the tremors humming through her fingers.

Her soul ached for the freedom that lay just beyond it, but the entities behind her were closer than ever.

Nathaniel growled as Katherine's words grew louder. "Finish this. Her name is Delanie Lysanmore."

"Delanie Lysanmore, The Smiling Woman," Katherine said, her face blanching, eyes dimming of color as the magic bled from her in waves.

"You will regret this, witch! They'll kill your brother and you."

She shook her head, continuing the incantation, the demon's body convulsing.

"It won't work," Delanie shouted when Nathaniel stopped looking at her. "The girl has taken my place."

Nathaniel tilted her head, stalking closer. "If that's true, then why do I sense fear in your voice?"

"I will come back," she promised, her voice deep and distorted.

"My mother said the same," he taunted, "but I found a way to ensure she could never return, and I will do the same to you. Once you are in that mirror, I will make sure you *never* get out."

"You tore your mother apart until there was nothing left," Delanie said with a wicked, creepy grin akin to the one she had in demon form. "But you cannot destroy this body and with time, I will find a way out. I always do. Charlotte is mine. I have claimed her."

"You claim no one!" he shouted, but Delanie merely laughed.

As Katherine invoked her true name again, Delanie screamed, her grip on Charlotte's body slowly faltering.

Her body convulsed violently, tears spilling from her eyes as she screamed vile taunts at Nathaniel and Katherine, wrestling against the vampire's holds.

The demon's eyes bled shadows, tendrils of darkness ribboning from her like vipers. Charlotte readied herself, holding on until the last possible moment.

The mirror opened in a pulse, her soul almost falling through, but her translucent fingers gripped the inside of the frame.

Delanie's screech rang around the attic as the mirror pulled Delanie's soul from Charlotte's body, inch by agonizing inch.

Zachariah grunted when she broke through her binds, while Irene and Alexander pushed Charlotte's body against the floor.

Delanie's last screams turned to gurgles as her soul detached from Charlotte's immortal body, spearing toward the mirror in a dark cloud of smoke. The stench of sulfur wafted around them, and Charlotte let go, closing her eyes as she fell through the gaping void, propelling herself forward despite the mirror pulling her back, refusing to give into its magnetic pull. She hurtled onto the ground, spotting two shadow-figures darting through the attic, escaping alongside her.

She raced to her body before they could reach her, landing back in her body just as the mirror turned still.

A startled cry left her throat when a wave of sensations swarmed through her. The press of Nathaniel's fingers on her cheek, the thudding of her heartbeat, the thick knot in the back of her throat, begging for her to swallow.

She was alive.

Her nail curled against the splintering boards below. She listened to the sound of the wind whistling through aged wood frames, the crackle of the candle wicks as the candles dwindled, leaving only the dim light of a gas lamp.

Rosemary, smoke, and beeswax assaulted her nostrils with such potency she could taste it.

Slowly, she blinked Nathaniel into focus. Her vision sharpened with predator acuteness, revealing everything in beautiful detail. Her gaze traced a path from the stray, dark lock of hair against his forehead, to the striking gray and silver in his eyes, framed by dark lashes and deep-set eyebrows. His pupils dilated when he looked at her, a whoosh of relief passing through his lips.

He removed his hands and pulled her into his arms, stroking her black curls. "It's her." Nathaniel's tentative tone caressed her ears.

The others let go and she stretched out her limbs.

"You came back for me," she whispered against his shoulder, a swell of emotion curling into her chest.

"I always will."

Duke's nose nuzzled against her cheek, and she turned her face into him, smiling against his fur. "Hello, old friend," she said, relieved to hear her voice again.

Irene cleared her throat and stood. "Well, that was a novel experience."

Zachariah shot her an amused glance. "I've never successfully completed an exorcism before."

"*Successfully?*" she intoned, and he laughed, glancing at Nathaniel. "We'll give you both a minute. Let's go."

Alexander was the last to leave. Before he did, he said, "I'm glad you're back."

"You knew it wasn't me too," she said, and he nodded. "You also came back for me."

"You are family now, Miss Lovett. We will always protect each other."

"Katherine's gone," she whispered.

"I will find her."

"Don't," she said. A part of her also wanted to go after her, but the vengeance from earlier evaporated, *for now*. She was alive and with Nathaniel, and that was all she could focus on. "Let her go. She's already lost most of her family and her brother is an arse. Leave her to her wretched fate away from us."

"For you, I will. " He cradled her head, planting a kiss against her temple. "I won't touch her."

"I heard what you said when I was in there. What Delanie said too," she whispered, tears glossing her eyes. "You deserve love, Nathaniel. You saved me so many times, not just from this but from giving up entirely. You're not evil," she whispered, running her fingers over the taut muscles under his shirt.

After a few moments of heavy breathing, she slowly rolled her tongue over the sharp outline of her fangs, a deep ache throbbing in the roots.

He groaned into her hair, one hand running down her side, caressing a stroke over her hip, then her thigh. She closed her eyes and rolled herself against his touch, every flicker of touch between them spreading sensations so strong it felt as if the tingles were going to devour her alive.

"What do we do now?" Charlotte asked, smiling against him.

"What do you want to do, my love?"

"Apart from having you explore my new immortal body?" she asked with a teasing bite against his lips. "After everything that has happened, I just want to get away from here for a while," she said, craving more of the novelty that flooded her body.

"I'll take you anywhere you want to go," he vowed, fingers sliding up her thigh, head bowed against hers. "But first," he said, running his fangs over her neck, leaving a path of tingles scorching down her throat. "I'm taking you home. To *our* home."

"To Sallow Manor?"

"Everything I have is yours, my love."

She ran her tongue over the fangs receding in her gums, her stomach lurching when she realized how much he had lost. "I'm sorry I couldn't break your curse," she said, hooking her arms around his neck. "But there is always a way out and we'll find it, so you can be mortal again."

With a sudden movement, he lifted her up, so she had to wrap her legs around his hips. Holding her up by the curves of her ass, he pressed his forehead against hers and said, "I realize now it was never mortality I was searching for. It was redemption; it was *love.* Being a vampire no longer feels like a punishment with you by my side, not when I get to wake up every day without fear of a death that might separate us."

"I love you, Nathaniel," she whispered. "In case you did not know."

"I do now." He brushed his nose to hers, eyes closing softly. "And I love you too. I am yours. I have been from the moment I tasted your soul when I fed on you that first night and I will be, forever."

Epilogue

There was nothing worse than a happy ending.

Darkness pulsed through every fractured reflection in Lovett Manor as Delanie pressed her fingers to the window, watching through the reflection as the pair finally returned after months of traveling.

Charlotte and Nathaniel had no idea what was coming for them.

Soon, the Lovett men would be just like her. Their desire for revenge intensified daily, and their combined darkness infused into the bones of the house, and the two demons that had escaped lingered close by, awaiting her instruction.

Delanie glared at them as Nathaniel and Charlotte strode outside, hand-in-hand, to watch the sunset, his smile far too wide for her liking. He was just as evil as a demon. Their only difference was Delanie accepted who she was, whereas Nathaniel ran from the shadows of his desires, like a coward.

Together, with Delanie as the most powerful witch, and him as the first vampire, they could have had it all. No matter. One day soon, she was going to remind him just how similar they were.

Snorting, Delanie bared her teeth as she watched the relief washing over him as he watched the sunset for the first time in centuries, bathing in the rays that would weaken his abilities. He had become foolish in his infatuation with the girl, his arms wrapped around her, watching the sun with unearned confidence. They really believed they were safe, that their enemies were all vanquished.

Didn't he know his sacrificial lamb was still bound for the slaughter? Such a soft-hearted creature could never survive him. Kindness was a trait found in the losing side and that girl was making him weak. She'd even persuaded him to turn that dull servant of his into a vampire. He used to choose only the strongest to be blessed with such power, and now he was letting any old thing become one of them.

Anticipation throbbed through her, excitement widening her grin as Delanie sensed the familiar, burning pull of her sigil pulling her toward the next person who had been hexed with the sigil of the Smiling Woman.

She left Lovett Manor, following the path of the hex to an old butcher's shop in central London to find her victim, fingers diving into her golden curls, tears streaming from her brown eyes as she cried over the corpse of her brother, murdered by Nathaniel Sallow in retaliation of her betraying them.

Charlotte stupidly believed he allowed the witch to leave with no punishment, but Delanie knew his nature better. Nathaniel would never allow a traitor to leave unscathed and now she was primed for revenge.

Finally. Katherine Ellenwood. They were going to have so much fun together.

Also by the Author

CORRUPT SHADOWS DUET:

Corrupt Shadows

Broken Shadows

GODS OF DAHRYST DUET:

Night of Death and Flowers

SHADOW KISSED SERIES:

Shadow Kissed

Midnight Crown

Darkest Heart

Ruthless Royals

STANDALONES:

Night of the Witch

Spellbound

About the Author

Rebecca writes gothic and dark fantasy romance with morally gray characters.

Originally from England, she lives in Texas with her husband and two sons. She loves anything with enemies to lovers, slow burn, and lots of angst.

A book collector at heart, Rebecca loves creating something beautiful for her readers' shelves. You can find her special edition box sets on Kickstarter.

Find out more about Rebecca and check out her books here:

Website: www.rebeccagarciabooks.com

Kickstarter: https://www.kickstarter.com/profile/rebeccagarciabooks

Instagram: www.instagram.com/rebeccalgarciabooks

www.ingramcontent.com/pod-product-compliance
Lightning Source LLC
Chambersburg PA
CBHW020456310726
48979CB00016B/2677/J

9781912405886